HIGHLINERS

HIGHLINERS

WILLIAM McCLOSKEY

LYONS & BURFORD, PUBLISHERS

ACKNOWLEDGMENTS

THE thanks to every one of the people who helped form and encourage this book would make a chapter by itself. Where to start? In Kodiak, perhaps with Tom Casey, former manager of the United Fishermen's Marketing Association and activist for the rights of fishermen, whose vigorous mind showered me with information and perspective, and whose house always had a place for my sleeping bag. Other perspectives, along with hospitality and friendship, were provided in Kodiak by Don and Rusty Thomson; Norman and Dorothy Holm, Norm a longtime Kodiak fishermen and now marine surveyor for western Alaska; Hank Pennington, Kodiak Marine Advisory Agent for the University of Alaska's Sea Grant Program; and Bart Eaton, highline crab skipper and fighter along with Casey for adequate two-hundred-mile legislation.

On the boats, humble thanks to the skippers who hired me for a crew share and then tolerated my inexperience as I struggled to pull a semblance of my weight: Thorvold Olsen of the salmon seiner-crabber *Polar Star*, Merle Knapp of the shrimp trawler *Pacific Pride,* and Monte Riley of the seiner *Norman J.* Also to my crewmates, who refrained from throwing me overboard and chose to teach me instead, notably John Van Sant, "Oley" Olsen, and Andy Kuljis. Among those who took me aboard to let me learn the gear, thanks especially to Leiv Loklingholm and his hard-driving crew on the Bering Sea crabber *American Beauty*—Dale Dorsey, Frank Tegdal, Steve Dundas, and Terry Mason. And to Dick Ryser, skipper next to God of his open siwash seiner.

Of cannery managers who hired me on their lines, permitted me to trail them and ask questions, found me boats, even bunked me out in remote areas, let me thank: Glen Behymer and John Pugh of Alaska Pacific Seafood; Bob Erickson of B&B; Chuck Jensen, Willy Sutterlin, and Ben Bullinger of Pacific Pearl; Blake Kinnear and Carl Wyberg of Pan Alaska; Bill Hingston of Kodiak King Crab; and Ivan Fox of New England Fish Company.

Within the Coast Guard, my former service and longtime love: many, many pilots of helicopters and planes flying out on fishing patrols in the wretched Kodiak weather; administrators and support people at the Kodiak Base, District Headquarters in Juneau, and National Headquarters in Washington, D.C.; and the officers and crews of the cutters *Boutwell, Confidence, Gallatin,* and *Tamaroa* (the latter two from the East Coast). With apologies for all those not named, I must single out both the commanding officer (1976–1978) of the Kodiak-based *Confidence,* Commander Terry Montonye, and Leo Loftus at Washington headquarters.

In the National Marine Fisheries Service, again, there were more able agents and administrators who helped me in Kodiak, Juneau, and Washington, D.C., than I have space to name. They include, but certainly do not stop with, Harry Rietze, Alaska Regional Director in Juneau, and Jerry Hill at Washington headquarters. The fisheries agents with whom I had the privilege of visiting foreign fishing ships were dedicated and rugged men, as were the Coast Guard men who manned the power boats in sloppy weather and climbed the Jacob's ladders with them.

Among many helpful members of the Alaska Department of Fish & Game, I must thank especially Ed Huizer, deputy director in Juneau, and Jack Lechner, westward regional supervisor in Kodiak.

At the Kodiak *Daily Mirror,* I am indebted to publisher Jack Clark for his hospitality in letting me occupy a desk during long perusals of back issues. Thanks very much to Jerry Martini for the dust-jacket photo he took of me fresh from ten days king-crabbing.

I am extremely grateful to Bob Browning, author of the comprehensive *Fisheries of the North Pacific,* both for his encouragement and for specific comments on the fishing sections of the manuscript. Others who commented on parts of the manuscript included Norm Holm, Bart Eaton, and Ivan Fox, all mentioned above, as well as Jack Knutsen,

Acknowledgments

skipper of the halibut schooner *Grant*, Guy Powell and Jerry McCreary of Alaska Fish & Game in Kodiak, Richard Myhre, Assistant Director of the International Pacific Halibut Commission, and Ned Everett of the House Merchant Marine Committee.

At the Applied Physics Laboratory of Johns Hopkins University, I am indebted to Albert Stone, who recognized on several occasions that a restless writer needed leaves of absence, and to my supervisor Bill Buchanan and my secretary Alice Knox for their patience over three years as I worked both job and book under pressure.

In New York, without the imagination and enthusiasm of three sea-struck individuals, *Highliners* might never have left the notepad. They are: Tom Lowry, my agent; editor Steve Frimmer of Reader's Digest Press; and Bruce Lee, my editor at McGraw-Hill.

And in 1995, to Lilly Golden, my editor at Lyons & Burford, whose support and enthusiasm resulted in this present edition.

The book is dedicated to my wife Ann for good reason. Then there is my son Wynn, who shared fish boat and cannery experiences with me in Kodiak, and my daughter Karin, who was enthusiastic and supportive, both of whom have bolstered me with pride at their non-fishing accomplishments. And, not in Kodiak except often in spirit, my father Bill and my mother Evelyn.

Bill McCloskey, Jr.

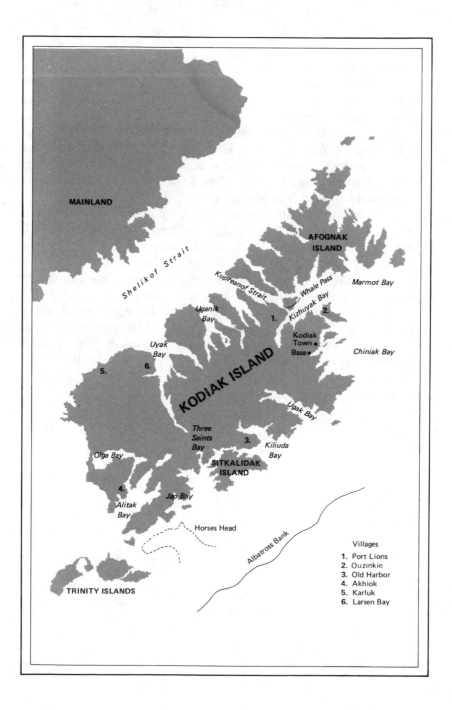

MAINLAND

Shelikof Strait

Kupreanof Strait

AFOGNAK
ISLAND

Marmot Bay

Whale Pass

*Uganik
Bay*

1.

Kizhuyak Bay

2.

*Uyak
Bay*

Kodiak
Town •
Base •

Chiniak Bay

5.

6.

KODIAK ISLAND

Ugak Bay

*Three
Saints
Bay*

3.

*Kiliuda
Bay*

Olga Bay

SITKALIDAK
ISLAND

4.

Jap Bay

*Alitak
Bay*

Horses Head

Albatross Bank

TRINITY ISLANDS

Villages
1. Port Lions
2. Ouzinkie
3. Old Harbor
4. Akhiok
5. Karluk
6. Larsen Bay

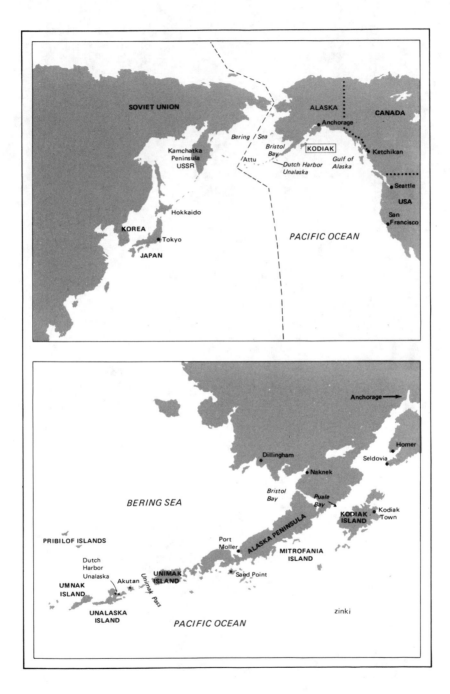

Contents

INTRODUCTION

FISHING is one of man's basic, hardest, most honorable occupations. It shares with farming a reliance on nature, despite the aids of technology in providing machinery to perform some of the heaviest work. The occupation has changed little over the centuries. Man still catches his seafood in any quantity by one of three methods—pots, hooks, or nets. The sea remains a force of primal brutality, and the experience of fishing in it for a livelihood remains universal the world over for the whole range of fishermen, from those who row out in little boats open directly to the weather to those who buck into open seas with the relative security of a warm cabin and a high-powered engine. This book focuses on a segment of that worldwide picture, the area of fishing communities in western Alaska from Kodiak waters to the Bering Sea.

The land mass of Alaska combines with water in a dual arrangement of watercourses and continental shelves that produces one of the great fishing grounds of the world. Ranges of mountains throughout the state accumulate snow, then yield it off in thousands of rivers and streams that serve as spawning areas for salmon. Extending underwater from shore are vast seafood-breeding continental shelves, those areas of relatively shallow water down to about one hundred fathoms which occur before the ocean floor plunges to several thousand fathoms.

Most of the seafood of the world is generated on continental shelves. The motion of wind and currents circulates the relatively shallow shelf waters all the way up from the seafloor, thus moving even the deepest water to the surface to mix bottom nutrients with sunlight and oxygen. The result is a stimulated growth of the organisms that fish and

1

crustaceans feed on, and a consequent abundance of sea creatures. To give some idea of the Alaskan potential, the shelves off Alaska cover 550,000 square miles, including a huge crescent of shelf around the Gulf of Alaska and the single 340,000-square-mile swath of shelf in the eastern Bering Sea. This compares to 300,000 square miles of shelf off the entire remaining United States, or, to take other major fishing grounds, to the 70,000 square miles of the Grand Banks off Newfoundland and the 12,000 of Georges Bank off New England.

The fishing scene in Alaska is varied and volatile. The people it includes have differing interests, and the communities range in size from large towns to seasonal settlements. Ketchikan, the leading city of the southeastern inland waterways (which also includes Sitka, Juneau, and Petersburg), once called itself accurately "The Salmon Capital of the World." In the 1960s, whether through Japanese and Soviet interception of salmon on the high seas, simple American excess by both sport and commercial fishermen, careless logging practices which destroyed spawning streams, destructive freezes at crucial biological times, or a probable combination, the great southeastern runs of salmon dwindled. The major salmon packs today come from a wide area around Kodiak Island at the western end of the Gulf of Alaska and from Bristol Bay, east of the Bering Sea.

Kodiak waters teem with salmon, halibut, cod, herring, and pollock; with five varieties of small pandalid shrimp; with dungeness, tanner, and king crab. It was natural that fishermen would discover the place. The town of Kodiak, which because of its remoteness had been for decades merely the base for local salmon boats and stopoff point for the halibut fleets of Seattle and Prince Rupert, became in the late 1950s the home of men who were developing entire new fisheries first in king crab and then in shrimp. (A fishery is a combination of elements, the essentials being the harvestable sea creatures, the boats, the fishermen, and the processors.) The Alaskan earthquake of 1964 generated a tsunami that washed out the lower town, boat harbor, and canneries. In retrospect, the disaster and its attendant demands for reconstruction vitalized the town. New boats were commissioned with the demands of crabbing and shrimping in mind, as was the case with new canneries. Kodiak today is one of the major salmon ports, the largest U.S. halibut port, and the center of both a ten-month shrimp fishery and a seven-month king and

2

tanner-crab fishery. Fishermen and processors out of Kodiak and Dutch Harbor are now engaged in developing from scratch an industry for pollock and other bottomfish which may evolve into the largest Alaskan fishery of them all in terms of volume. In terms of value landed, Kodiak is consistently the number-two port in the U.S., second only to the California tuna port of San Pedro.

However, just as the dominance in salmon shifted from Ketchikan to Kodiak, the dominance in crab shifted in the early 1970s from Kodiak to Dutch Harbor. Dutch is still barely a settlement, adjacent to the small Aleut village of Unalaska on an island in the Aleutian chain, but it is the closest large harbor for the American boats which fish with increasing concentration in the rich grounds of the Bering Sea. A difference in the shift is that the Kodiak crab men participated, financing expensive new boats to meet the Bering Sea demands, then driving them the 600 miles to Dutch Harbor to compete with Seattle-based crabbers and Japanese factory fleets. Dutch Harbor now runs Kodiak a race for position as second-in-value fishing port of the U.S.

Within the rough-and-tumble context of coastal Alaskan towns, where wilderness is always in sight and destruction at sea a constant possibility, Ketchikan has turned mellow, Kodiak bursts at the seams, and Dutch Harbor—still a raw outpost—perches on the edge of a frontier boom.

Alaskan fishermen come from several backgrounds and interests. Traditionally, Alaska has attracted a seasonal population of friendly, hard-working carpetbaggers—fishermen, loggers, construction and pipeline workers, and the like—who make their money and then return south with it to enjoy the comforts of more urbanized areas. The pattern has begun to change despite the wretched Alaskan winters. Most men fishing from Ketchikan and about half those of Kodiak are now residents, having been attracted to the open life of Alaska from all parts of the U.S. and from that traditional land of northern seafarers, Scandinavia. Dutch Harbor, on the other hand, is called home by few except native villagers. The American halibut fleet (there is also a Canadian one which fishes the same Alaskan waters) is crewed largely by first- and second-generation Norwegians who live in Seattle, and this group also dominates a large share of the Bering Sea crab fleet. (In Dutch Harbor, it sometimes seems as if no other food is served from boat galleys but lamb, fish balls,

3

and goat's-milk cheese.) Then there are the natives, who lived by fishing for centuries before the white man came. Boats from all the native villages have indigenous crews, especially in the far-north Eskimo country where whites are few. In the Tlingit country of the southeast around Ketchikan, voluntary segregation is sometimes strong, with certain areas of the same grounds fished tacitly by native boats and others by whites. The boats of Kodiak have an easier racial mixture, with Aleut-Koniag and American-Norwegian often combined in the same man.

Fishermen in Alaska, then, are a generally compatible mixture of whites and natives, Americans and Scandinavians, residents and non-residents. There is, however, another force of fishermen, most of whom never come ashore, that has for years thrown doubt and unbalance into the picture. These man the factory fleets of Japan and Russia.

For a decade before Pearl Harbor, Japanese ships had fished crab and bottomfish in the waters off the Aleutians, which are closer to Tokyo than to Seattle. In 1952, with self-government restored to Japan, the U.S. allowed the Japanese to come fishing again off Alaska. Soviet ships entered the scene off both coasts in 1959, followed on the East Coast by ships from Poland, Spain, and a dozen other nations and in Alaska by ships from South Korea. The foreign fishing effort increased steadily, often destructively to certain species, until 1976 and the passage by Congress of the Fishery Conservation and Management Act. To cite a typical year, the fishing grounds off Alaska were worked in 1972 by 907 different Japanese ships and 544 Soviet ships. The Japanese effort included eighteen factory fleets. The total 1972 foreign catch off Alaska was over five billion pounds, compared to half a billion pounds caught in the same waters by U.S. boats.

The American fisherman, both in Alaska and on the other coasts, is a different creature than the man on the Japanese and Russian fishing ships, despite what they might share of the fishing experience. The American owns his own boat or works for a crew share directly under the man who does; the Japanese is a salaried employee for a huge conglomerate, the Russian an employee of the state. The American works on a boat ranging in size from a 30-odd-foot purse seiner to a 110-foot crabber, as part of a deck crew that seldom exceeds five. The smallest Japanese vessel is a 90-foot salmon gillnetter with a crew of a dozen, the largest a 650-foot factory ship with a work force of more than 500.

4

Both the American and the foreign vessels often fish around the clock, but the foreign crews with their greater numbers do it in shifts. The Americans work gear as individuals and as seamen, while the foreign crewmen are often as specialized in their duties as a standard millhand.

Thus the concept of an American fishing "industry" is loose at best, comprising the freelance interests of many boatmen and processors. A fishery of this sort has no collective resource beyond the biological research of government agencies, and no coordinated battle plan. Compare this to Japan, where the government supports two colleges and more than sixty high schools of fishing, and where large conglomerates like Taiyo, Nippon Suison, and Marubeni control and operate in a single package their boats, seafood plants, research teams, and marketing facilities. These fishing conglomerates work so closely with the cabinet-level Japan Fisheries Agency that the one seems an extension of the other. With such an interlock of Japanese capital and administration, support is always available to develop the most modern fishing ships and equipment, and the risks inherent in a single fishery are buffered by options on a corporate scale.

The Soviet fishing fleets, as might be imagined, are financed and controlled entirely by the government. The Soviet Ministry of Fisheries runs the show by regions, allotting budgets and projecting requirements. The ships (many more modern even than those of the Japanese) have been built under five-year and seven-year plans, with a conscious goal of achieving a strong Soviet fishing fleet. As soon as Soviet ships entered the fisheries off the U.S. coasts, they began to abuse the tacit fishing privilege by equipping "trawlers" with electronic surveillance equipment, and they still do. The Soviet multiyear plans for fishing ships began before the Cuban Missile Crisis of October 1962 had revealed a Soviet weakness in seapower. The plans locked after this event into the larger strategic goal of building the Soviet Union into the maritime power that it is today of military, merchant, and fishing ships.

In the United States, the men who fish the sea are still of a type other callings have rendered tame and dependent. Even with all the power winches and hydraulic gurdies a fishing boat now can carry, the work is heavier and longer than most men can bear. It also requires wit and intelligence along with sea-sense, since as seafood stocks diminish,

5

more skill is required to seek them out. American fishing boats remain small, both against the foreign fishing operations and against the sea itself. In New England, the fleet is old and demoralized by the massive foreign overfishing of Georges Bank and adjacent grounds. The abundant fisheries for shrimp in the Gulf of Mexico, tuna off California, and the menhadden off the Carolinas and Virginia are vital each in its way, but they fish only a single species, in relatively placid water.

This leaves the newly aggressive and varied fishery that centers in Kodiak and extends via Dutch Harbor into the Bering Sea. The men who work it lead lives closer to death than most Americans. As with fishermen in all northern waters, they endure as a matter of course the drench and wind and cold. On violently unstable decks which require enormous energy merely to keep balance, they handle machinery that by a slip can eat relentlessly an arm or leg, with nets that can sweep them over the side into water too cold for survival, using hooks and knives that can slice to the bone through layers of clothing. They harvest more major species than all the other mainline American fisheries combined, in waters more treacherous than even the North Atlantic. Unique among American fishermen, they see the present as a springboard rather than a roadblock.

You who mourn the lost self-confidence and self-sufficiency of the American frontier, look here.

PART I:
1963, SUMMER

1

FISHING

FROM Dutch Harbor we bucked into a forty-knot northwester for fourteen hours to reach the grounds. One of my new crewmates offered me some thick rubber bands cut from an inner tube. I watched him adjust his own to squeeze the legs of his rain pants against his boots, but I was too seasick to follow suit.

Outside it was black night. Shadowy waves swelled higher than our heads, hail slashed under the mast lights, the wind roared and whined, and seawater foamed across the deck. The other men lit cigarettes and went into it. I followed. I had traveled on many ships and knew well that the sea was vast and brutal, but I had never worked on a deck this close to the waves. The awe I felt was unexpected, at the smallness of the fishing boat and at the hugeness of the water around us. Soon I was bending over a tub with knees pressed into it for balance as I stuffed chunks of herring into perforated plastic jars and retched helplessly from the smell.

Up came the first of our thousand-pound-plus steel pots, swaying with all its wicked weight. Frank and Dale grabbed the sides as it banged against the boat and guided it crashing into place on the deck rack. The pot held about sixty big purple king crabs and twice as many undersized ones and females. They crawled against each other sluggishly and stuck together as we leaned in and flung them out two to a hand.

A wave swept the side and drenched us. It hit my knees with such force that I had to grab the rail for support and cold water filled my boots where I had neglected to fasten the rubber bands. Leiv, the skipper, thrust his bearded face from the wheelhouse as his Norwegian "Har har" roared against the wind. "Hey, dot'll vake you bastards, eh?" The others cursed back cheerfully.

Everything in the operation was based on speed and economy, with no time accounted for rest. In five minutes the first pot was emptied, rebaited, and sent plunging back to the seafloor, and the line of the next was being payed in through the hydraulic crab block to be coiled on deck. The simple effort of maintaining balance was work in itself. The block might pull the ton-weights, yet the remaining bull work was tremendous. We pushed for what I judged to be at least three hours. The clock showed we had only been working for forty minutes. The distance back to the warm room ashore of nautical daydreams was infinite beyond imagining. When you've committed yourself out there, you're stuck.

During the next week in the Bering Sea the wind sometimes subsided, sometimes gusted to eighty knots, while the sea ranged from crashing to glassy. Since we were fishing for the largest possible share of the king crab quota, we took only what rest we needed desperately: sometimes only two hours a night. "I know just how far to drive my men," says one successful crab skipper from Kodiak who started his career on deck. "Farther than they think they can go. Just to that point where they'll let the gear start smashing them. Sometimes we haul gear for forty hours without a break." Said a halibut skipper when I asked if it was true that his crew slept only four hours a night for the twenty days running of a trip: "I tried three, but after a while it slowed us down."

During the first week of my initiation into king-crabbing, a man on one boat lost a finger and a man on another lost the bridge of his nose when a heavy hook flew out of control. The seas smashed in the windows of two pilothouses. On my boat, a vacancy had been created the trip before when two hydraulic bars converged at the wrong moment to crush a man's thigh.

The life of a fisherman is rougher and more dangerous than that of any other seafarer. Compared to them, the sailors on modern tankers and freighters, and the Navy salts of the great electronic warships, are clock-punchers who live in luxury. (Less so the small-boatmen of the Coast Guard when the time comes for a rescue.)

Do men go fishing for any reason besides money? In many parts of the world it remains a subsistence profession. An answer for would-be Ishmaels like myself: "It is a way I have of driving off the spleen, and regulating the circulation." Actually, most fishermen are locked in by tradition and geography. Fathers take their sons to sea and teach them the skills and survival reflexes, and the life's pattern is set. Even American fishermen—those in the environs of Gloucester, Crisfield, Pascagoula, San Pedro, and Anacortes, for example—show a strong pattern of repeated generations. It is almost uniquely in Alaska that the fisheries are so new that their history is counted in decades rather than generations, and the fishermen—many with college educations—have no excuse but their own free choice.

But why then, even in Alaska, given the alternatives available to Americans, would a man settle in a place of storm and cold like Kodiak, commit himself to a decade of hock for the price of a boat and gear, and thus consciously condemn himself to a lifetime of hardship to feed his family? Some go broke. The men who make it have a varied income depending on luck, tenacity, and skill. Some highliners (those who bring in the biggest catches) may have a spectacular income as a direct result of their driving labor. Each category returns to Alaska season after season to take its chances instead of finding some way to stay ashore dry and safe in an office or a welding shop.

Not to be coy about it any longer, seafaring enters the blood, and no form of it more than fishing. Stick a seasoned fisherman ashore and watch his restlessness when the boats gear up at the start of the season. Watch a crippled old fisherman caress the boats with his eyes. Does a retired machinist or accountant ever long after his lathe or ledgers in the same way, or fill the air with such reminiscences of shop and office?

Here I stand on the Bering Sea crab boat, green-faced and wretched, my hands deep in stinking bait that I can't smell without growing sick, my feet encased in cold water, a hundred miles from shore and at least sixteen toil-filled hours from my next brief sleep. I'm hardly joyous, and I would welcome a respite, but I wouldn't trade places with you. I stare at the surging water and I feel the wind. But for the little boat I would be extinguished. If a wave swept me overboard, the cold water would suck away my life in four or five minutes. I am living on a brink, tasting real salt as it stings into my face, alive each second as seldom on shore. Do you think this is nothing? More likely you wish you were out there also. Life back by the time clocks may be more comfortable, but how often in your day do you associate face to face with the primal forces? A fisherman with water in his boots yearns to be dry, daydreams of a warm hearth or barroom. But, after he has sniffed the clean and destructive infinity of the ocean, dry land becomes ever after a place of interim passage.

I first felt the essence of fishing in a mosquito-filled bay of Kodiak Island. I had ridden out from Kodiak town as a passenger on a salmon tender (which has since hit the rocks and sunk in the manner of fishing boats in northern waters, mercifully with no loss of life). A tender buys fish on the scene and carries them to the cannery, so our job was to await deliveries from the local seine boats. It was a day of rain and smoky mists. The Stonehengelike rocks of Kalsin Bay were dimmed to the substance of cardboard cutouts, as were the green forested mountains beyond the shore. We waited, nursing mug after mug of coffee, listening to the cry of birds and smelling an occasional whiff of spruce generated by the wet air.

My notion of a seiner had been formed among the forty- to fifty-eight-foot boats with bridges and masts moored to the Kodiak harbor floats, whose fantails held big skiffs resting on high stacks of cork and web. Instead, all I had seen was an open dory with a mere dinghy astern, which had been plying along the shore since daybreak. Eventually the dory headed for the tender. Two crewmen sat hunched against the rain. The third, apparently the skipper, stood holding a tiller attached to an inside-mounted outboard motor, a concentrated scowl of command on his face. Water rested like cobwebs in his thick, curly hair. His oilskin pants hung by a single suspender, and a soggy cigarette dangled from his lips. The bottom of the dory was a jumble of salmon, buckets, bags, and other gear. The skipper brought his boat alongside and stepped grandly aboard the tender for a mug-up, while his two crewmen grabbed the salmon by their tails and tossed them into a bucket for the tender's scale.

The captain of the tender introduced me to the dory's skipper, Dick, and, before I had a chance to back out, suggested I ride with him to see a siwash operation, the most primitive kind of all. The rocking dory had barely a place for my feet. Dick took us toward shore, then grunted that they might as well eat. Each of the three took a damp bag from a plastic bucket and settled by himself, while I sat grousing over my luck as a proper fine white seiner entered the bay and headed for the tender.

Suddenly Dick rose. His eyes narrowed toward a patch of water, while his hands started the motor and the lunch bag flopped unheeded. In a second, the other two also crouched at attention, Dave astern by the heap of nets and corks, Ron in the skiff, where he started a few-horsepower motor. The boat headed slowly toward the spot Dick watched. The water was calm, broken only by patterns of rain. As we came closer to shore, the water turned dark from reflections of the trees, and mosquitos settled over us. I was the only one who slapped; the others were too engrossed.

A salmon leapt, wriggled suspended for an instant in silver silhouette, splashed back. Down came Dick's hand. Instantly, Dave threw off the tow line, and Ron in the skiff headed out, pulling the net in a circle around the spot where the fish had jumped. For the next several minutes, with snap and precision, the three performed a continuous chain of work that encircled a school of salmon with the net, then drew the net into a smaller and smaller circle by pulling it back into the boat until the fish had been pursed into a bag alongside. On a large seiner a powered winch and a hydraulic block would have pulled a longer and deeper seine. In Dick's little open boat, but for the small collective horsepower of two outboards and a net of synthetic fibers, the three men fished as they might have fished two thousand years ago.

I entered the cycle to help "pull web." It was heavy, wet work, and all of us were soon drenched and panting. As the seine came in, Dave piled the corks on one side, Ron the leads on the other. The web, handled by Dick and me, fell between. As the circle narrowed, we began to see dark moving shapes. Each grip of web became heavier. It was the weight of fish. The frenzy of their swimming transmitted itself in vibrations. The surface within the purse began to boil with tails and heads. Whenever part of a salmon flipped above water its body glinted silver. We pulled and grunted, straining arms and backs. Slowly a whole bag of big silver fish rose to the gunwale, so heavy it tilted the boat. As we eased them aboard, they spilled over our legs, leaping and flapping with such collective strength that it felt like a tide pulling us off balance. There they lay around us. Their tails thumped the deck boards, their bright skins glistened.

The abundance and vitality of it blew my mind. I was hooked. For hours and hours I watched the water as intensely as the rest, my blood rising at the sight of each flash that might betray unseen schools of fish, eagerly gripping up the web even though I was soon dizzy with fatigue. I had stumbled into good company and had touched the gut way on the reason why, besides for money and necessity, men go on the seas to fish.

2

KODIAK

THE island of Kodiak combines with adjacent islands to form a 170-by-40-mile mass of mountains separated by waterways and surrounded by foggy storms. The island series faces the Pacific Ocean with its western side parallel to the Alaskan mainland within sight of distant snow mountains. Kodiak lies in a latitude which also cuts through northern Scotland and Labrador. Within Alaska, it is located approximately halfway along the 2000-mile coastal arc that stretches from Ketchikan in the southeastern tip to Attu in the far-western Aleutians.

The Kodiak mountains, lower than those of the mainland, average 2500 feet with a few (which remain snow-capped) reaching 4300 feet. Streams that originate in the higher country have eroded so far into the land that at places only a mountain or two separate the bays of the western from the eastern side. The differences between parts of the island are tremendous. Mean annual rainfall in Kodiak town is sixty inches (compared to thirty-nine inches in rainy Seattle), with ninety inches in some of the eastern bays and as little as twenty-four inches on parts of the western side. Although the axis of the island covers only two degrees of latitude—the distance between Baltimore and New York or between Topeka and Omaha—the north is covered with spruce while the south is bare of all but scrub. Each of the bays has a nature of its own. Huge brown bear feed along the flat streambeds of one, hilly spruce forests hide all else in another, and around a third the treeless land ends at the water in hundred-foot hardrock bluffs. The surrounding waters hold not only salmon, halibut, cod, rockfish, herring, crab, and shrimp but also their predators the whale, the seal, sea lions, and otters.

The island is far off and lonely, yielding only a bit of shoreland here and there for settlements. The nontransient late-1970s population is some 9000 (but growing) of whom about 5000 live in the area of Kodiak town, 3000 at the nearby Coast Guard Base, and a thousand in the six native villages of Karluk, Larsen Bay, Port Lions, Ouzinkie, Old Harbor, and Akhiok. In the early 1960s the population of Kodiak town was 2800 and that of the then-Navy Base about the same.

After the probable Bering landbridge migration from Asia, Koniag Indians lived for hundreds of generations in the coves and bays of the island, drawing their food from the abundant salmon and other sea creatures. Two centuries ago, in 1784, Russian fur traders established the first white settlements, first in Three Saints Bay, then in the wide natural harbor that now serves the town of Kodiak. The Russian influence remains principally in the Orthodox faith practiced by most of the natives; each village has a church, heavy inside with icons and the odor of incense, whose onion domes or boxlike approximations dominate the other buildings.

Within living memory, two catastrophies have altered life on the island. In 1912, Mount Katmai erupted on the mainland sixty miles away and covered the island with two feet of volcanic ash. The terrible black air of the fallout buried houses and made people suffocate. Layers of the ash remain today in the soil and beneath the lichens of old spruce trees. In 1964, the earthquake that uprooted Anchorage streets not far to the north generated a tsunami that swept away the boats and harbor buildings of Kodiak town and destroyed two villages (no longer inhabited). The aftermath in Kodiak town was a new layout of stores, canneries, and piers unrecognizable to a prequake visitor.

It rains and blows in Kodiak most of the time. The lower mountains are covered by thick scrub, which grows high and mossy green in the summer, then dries to brown under the winter snow. Fogs cling to the mountains, often erasing them from sight.

The names of the island, mostly Indian and Russian with an occasional blunt title in English, are as wild and beautiful as some of the places they represent. To fishermen, the words roll off the tongue like those of boats and wives: the major fishing bays of Uganik, Uyak, Olga, Alitak, Sitkalidak, Kiliuda, Ugak, Chiniak, Marmot, and Kizhuyak; such waterways as the wide Shelikof Strait which separates the island from the mainland and often forms a wind tunnel of terrible velocity, and Kupreanoff Strait, with its treacherous Whale Passage; such suggestive locations of the seafaring condition as Terror Bay, Tombstone Rocks, and Deadman Bay; the uninhabited Afognak Island to the north, with its huge virgin forest; the low and barren Tugidak and Sitinak islands to the south.

It was in the straits at Whale Pass, in the waterway that separates Afognak Island from Kodiak Island, that Hank Crawford first got his taste—he thought at the time it was his fill—of the local fishing condition.

This was August 1963, but by then he was an Alaskan of nearly three months standing. Hank had finished his exams at Johns Hopkins University and flown west all in the same thrust, en route to a western bay of Kodiak Island to take a cannery job arranged through a family friend. He made smooth connections from Baltimore to Chicago to Seattle to Anchorage, but there the thrust ended. The sun might have been shining in a blue sky on the purple Chugach Mountains surrounding Anchorage, but in Kodiak 250 miles south the fogs and winds were reported too severe for a landing. The weather lasted three days.

Fellow passengers relaxed in Anchorage with drinks and long conversations. Hank waited with little patience, his machinery geared for motion and his wallet almost empty. He ate sparsely, slept on an airport bench, and hitchhiked into town. The town failed to satisfy his image of Alaska despite a few rugged-looking people on the streets. The wide streets and nondescript square buildings could have been Kansas. And they all faced away from the water: he had never seen a seaport less oriented toward its waterfront. In one of the many Fourth Avenue bars he nursed a beer and watched a poker game, but failed to start more than a desultory talk with any of the bearded sourdough types. They appeared willing to talk only among themselves.

Everyone cheered when the plane bounced down on the Kodiak runway. The pilot had announced they might have to turn back, and the fog opening he found left small margin for error. Only the bases of mountains showed. The rest disappeared into fog. The growth on the slopes was thick and green. Hank checked at once with the charter service to reach his cannery on the other side of the island. Not until the ceiling lifted, since it was no emergency. The Kodiak airport was as bare as a bus stop, so he checked his bags and thumbed into town.

Kodiak was bleak and wet. People strode along the few paved streets in boots caked with mud from other roads. The main street, its wooden fronts weathered by rain, began and petered out before reaching any vestige of urban climax. There was a store with rope coils and raincoats in the window, another with guns, a grocery, a couple of eateries, several dark and noisy bars. Beyond Main, where the mud began, small wooden houses ranged up over a hill, dominated by an old white frame church with peeling blue onion domes.

The harbor was close to it all, with a wharf from which a ramp led down to floats. Several fishermen in oilskins mended nets on the wharf despite the weather. Masts rose close against each other, and men moved over the cramped decks shouting jokes and instructions. Hank stood a long time watching, hands in his pockets. Several fishermen passed him. The memory of his two previous summers crossed his mind like smoke—the ocean beaches back in Maryland, short-ordering hamburgers by day, attending beer parties on the sand at night. He thought of the bright leafy campus where he had stretched in the sun just a week ago. It all seemed vapid, compared to the nets and activity in front of him.

After two nights on benches, washing with paper towels and liquid soap in the airport restroom, he felt both unrested and sticky. His remaining cash for expenses: six dollars. Probably could wire home for more. But they had predicted disaster too heartily from the start. He glanced at the boats once more, then found a beanery.

On the griddle were slabs of salmon and steak, but he studied the menu to find the cheapest filler. "Okay, pea soup, please," he said to the waitress, and smiled at her warmly to show that this was his preference above steak.

Her hair was grabbed in a knot in back and her expression was grim despite an interesting wide mouth. She didn't increase her attractiveness by staring through him, or by banging the bowl hard enough to slop some of the soup onto the counter.

"Well, you squared away?" It was a red-haired guy who had also waited out the plane in Anchorage. He still wore dungarees as before (it surprised Hank that anyone would travel so informally) but the watch cap, slicker jacket, and boots indicated he had already gone home somewhere to change. He was wiry and short: probably if he had been more a conventional burly type Hank would have sought him out in hopes of meeting an Alaskan his own age headed for the same kind of work. Now he turned to him gratefully, and said he was waiting for a flight to the other side of the island.

"Hey, you got a boat over there?"

An hour earlier he would have said with more enthusiasm: "Job in a cannery."

"Uh." The guy turned to the steak on his plate, spearing big dripping chunks of it into his mouth. He appeared to pay Hank no more attention as he said to the waitress through his food: "Beef sauce, Jody." She turned from a coffee urn several seats away and sailed a bottle of catsup along the counter toward him. He sailed it back. "*Beefsteak* sauce, not catsup." She sent the correct bottle so hard it smacked his hand as he caught it. "Thanks, Jody. You're sweet." He turned to Hank and winked.

Hank cleared his throat. "I hear canneries work lots of overtime. I came up here to make the bucks."

"Yeh, you'll work some hours for Swede Scorden."

"He's the man I wrote to. You know him?"

"Just by reputation. Jody! Cup of coffee."

"You see where it is," she snapped in passing. The guy drew mugs of it for both himself and Hank.

Hank thought of the extra cost and tried to reject it with a stammered excuse. The cup remained midway between them. He needed more food to satisfy a hunger that had become ravenous from the odors of meat. "Could I have another soup, please?" She gave no indication she heard. He eased a basket of crackers close and ate them one by one, pretending to be absent-minded about it.

The red-haired guy turned to him again. "Well, I did that cannery gig here last summer. Never again. Going for the humpies."

"Is humpie a fish?" asked Hank, and regretted it at once.

The guy's laugh included the waitress, who stood with arms folded waiting for the cook to fill a plate. "Is it a *fish?* Oh, man, you'll be living ass deep in humpies. They're pinks. It's another name for pink

salmon. Then you've got sockeyes, dogs, silvers, and chinooks, all different kinds of salmon you'd better learn to keep straight." He picked a last
French fry from his plate and chewed it slowly.

"I guess you've grown up with all that, living around here."

"Me? I'm from Spokane. Never saw Kodiak before last summer."

The waitress, in passing, left another bowl of soup. Hank started
to eat it at once.

The red-haired guy rose. "Wish me luck, buddy."

"Sure. What for?"

"Going down to find my berth."

"You're on a boat!"

A toothpick moved lazily in his mouth. "I will be, once I've asked
around. *You* slit the fish bellies. This year I'll do the catching."

Hank hunched over his soup. Two in the afternoon. "Excuse me,
do you have a phone?"

"Use your eyes," said the waitress.

A phone hung on the wall by the window. With an act of busy
concern he called the bush airline, to learn he'd be lucky if the present
weather lifted day after tomorrow. Through the window, which had a
DISHWASHER WANTED sign, he watched the encounter of two men dressed
like fishermen. They were his own age, but both were weathered and
confident far beyond him. Another man joined the two, and they sauntered across the street to a bar. He watched them wistfully, then returned
to the counter.

Not that Hank felt sorry for himself. Just that the experience of
being nearly broke in a strange place was new. He was nineteen, a
sophomore, not bad-looking—heavy brown hair that tumbled into place,
athletic body with a square well-drawn face to match, playful blue eyes
and ready grin that he sometimes used to advantage with girls—aspirant
to varsity lacrosse, content in B grades and a social life of long weekend
parties and agreeable friends, his own person within a secure context.
By fall he would have to decide on a major in political science or eco-
nomics. Neither repelled him. Sometimes, when he read a book like *On
the Road* or joined a rally for civil rights, he felt calls that stirred him,
but to work the summer in an Alaskan cannery might be his biggest adventure before settling down. His parents, to whom he felt no need to
answer even though they still paid most of his expenses as a matter of

course, had thought a summer in Europe might have been better for his development, since such opportunities only come when you're young and footloose. The secret he nursed would surprise them: to make enough money to go on his own. As he sat nursing the remains of the bowl of pea soup, it seemed a distant hope for the gamble of all that airfare.

"You drinking this coffee or not?"

He looked up into her detached face. It would be at least twenty cents more, and an extra nickel tip, even though he wanted it. "I don't . . . The other guy got it, I don't drink the stuff." They stared at each other. "I don't mind paying for it, I guess, since . . ."

"Your friend already paid." She scooped up the cup and emptied it.

Outside, a chilly wind blew droplets in his face. His oxfords had absorbed enough water to wet his socks. Total cash besides airfare was now four seventy-five and some pennies. He returned to the harbor. No sign of the red-haired guy. He walked casually to a man mending net on the wharf. The thick white needle laced cord into torn sections, and under the man's sure tugs and twists new meshes were formed. Hank watched and watched. When the man glanced up, they exchanged nods. His face was young but full of creases around the eyes.

"You sure know how to work that needle."

"Ja? Vell, it's the vay she's done."

Suddenly Hank asked, with an intensity that surprised him, "You know any boat that needs somebody?"

"Ohhh." Pause, then "Nooo," as if it were out of the question. Just as Hank started to leave with hands dug in his pockets, the man said, "Maybe they let you sleep in jailhouse if you broke."

Hank wanted to rush and shake his hand. "Thanks!"

All at once he felt lighthearted, liberated. Within an hour the sergeant at the police building had told him to leave his gear, and he had been hired at the beanery to wash dishes until his plane could fly. He thumbed back to the airport, unchecked his knapsack and changed to work clothes, and returned to town. By evening he wore a smudged apron and rubber gloves, hot suds clung to his elbows, and the flavor of a steak lingered in his mouth. A half-drained can of beer stood beside him on the sink. He whistled one exuberant tune after another, as high on good feeling as if he had been given his choice of fishing berths.

21

Jody the waitress had begun to tolerate him. Mike the cook, who owned the place, motioned him over occasionally to try something new, like octopus or halibut cheeks. From the sink he could watch the passage of customers. Already he saw faces he recognized, including the Norwegian net-mender, with whom he exchanged grave nods.

It was eight-thirty, with closing time near, when he saw the red-haired guy slowly spooning a bowl of soup and filling it out with crackers. Hank caught his eye and motioned him back. After the preliminary joke about his new career Hank asked the important question.

"Salmon boats are on strike, and for king crab, never seen so many goddam full crews. You need a helper?"

Hank laughed in his turn as he lifted a stack of thick beanery plates from the rinse. "When my plane goes, take the whole empire." He felt relieved, even superior, and disappointed.

The guy's name was Pete Nicholson. Hank bummed something for him to eat. They swept down the place together as Jody straightened the tables. Jody remained aloof without being snappish as before. A tap came on the window and a heavy-lidded, bearded man motioned with his head, then walked into the bar across the street. Jody smiled for the first time. A few minutes later, with her coat on, she said to Hank, "Come back in the morning at six if you want to work." She was about to leave when she turned, "You need your money tonight?"

"No," said Hank. "Thanks anyhow."

After Hank and Pete finished cleaning and turned off the front lights, they sat in back with their feet on a table, eating crab legs that Mike had left them and drinking the last cans from the six-pack that Hank had bought himself. The crab legs were unbelievably big. Hank had never seen anything like them before. The meat came out in tubes. A single leg yielded all he needed, but the creamy taste of the meat and warm juice made him crave more. "Our crab on the Chesapeake Bay are dwarfs compared to these," he declared. "I don't know which I like better, but with Bay crabs you have to eat a half dozen just to start filling your stomach."

Pete was glad to share some of his Kodiak wisdom. "Take Jody, for instance," he said. "Think she'd give you the time of day if you weren't a fisherman? In this town you're on a boat, or forget it, man."

Hank in his turn described his previous summer and the lazy

beach life. "At night, I don't know which was thicker, mosquitoes or girls. I'd sometimes slap a chick and kiss a mosquito by mistake. Take your pick."

"Jesus, you got in every night!"

Hank offered no contradiction, although his one nervous seduction on the blankets had been a mighty occasion. He looked at his watch. The jailer had told him to get in by eleven. When he told of his sleeping arrangements, Pete gave a hoot. He'd probably see the lockup without an appointment if he stayed around Kodiak long enough, Pete declared. Come on to the barracks instead. It seems there was a house that the owner had converted to sleeping quarters, nothing else. Some kids had cots, some spread sleeping bags on the floor. Depended on what you paid and what was available. Pete had paid twenty dollars for two weeks on a couch and the use of the kitchen and a locked closet. It was the place to flop while you looked for a boat, or if you worked in one of the canneries.

"Well, look . . . I don't have a sleeping bag, and I left my knapsack . . ." The idea of spending his first night in jail appealed greatly.

But as he left Pete on the darkening street and bent alone into a cold drizzle, he began to doubt his decision. At the jail, the desk cop opened the barred door. There were several cells in a block. One was locked, and a man inside stood calmly at the bars, smoking. "What you want to do," said the cop, "is take any one that's open. Okay?" And the barred door clanged shut behind him.

"You're locking me in?" asked Hank, suddenly disturbed.

"No point in a jailhouse that don't get locked."

"I'm supposed to go to work at six tomorrow morning. I thought I'd just be able to wake up and . . ."

"Oh, we'll get you out." The man started to stroll away, then came back. "Nobody says you got to stay. Just don't change your mind after I'm sacked in."

Hank looked around him dubiously. A voice crackled on the police radio around the corner, and the man looked impatiently toward it. "I guess I'll stay. Thanks." The man was already on his way. "You're sure I can get out by six?" No answer.

Hank went to the far cell, avoiding the gaze of the single prisoner, which he was sure followed him. The cell had a toilet bowl without a seat, a washbasin, and tiered steel cots that lowered from the wall. No mattress or bedding, no chair. There were smells of both urine and disinfectant. He glanced at the prisoner, who was indeed watching him. A big, rough-looking fellow. "Hi," said Hank cautiously.

"Yep."

Hank laid coat, sweaters, long underwear along the steel cot as padding. No way to block out the bare bulb lights except with a sleeve over his eyes. As he lay back waiting for sleep, the smells became stronger. He placed a loose leg of underwear across his nose.

"Guess you didn't bring no bottle?"

"No, sorry."

"What are you, broke?"

"Yes, until I get paid."

"*Shit* but I need a drink. You sure you don't have some in that bag?"

"I'd sure give it to you if I had."

"Then get over here and let me beat your ass at two-hand."

"I ought to sleep. And I don't have any money."

"You afraid to play with matchsticks?"

What the hell. Soon Hank sat crosslegged on the low bunk of the adjacent cell, passing cards back and forth through the bars. The big man's name was Steve Kariguk. He was doing three days for disorderly, and he had enough cuts and bruises around his face to prove the fight had been a good one, although he couldn't remember the reason any more. Hank watched Steve's pawlike hands with bright scabs on the knuckles, dealing the cards. Hard to believe how recently he had spent the night in his parents' house four thousand miles away.

And harder to believe as the night progressed. The desk man and another cop brought in a pair with lumps and blood-streaming noses. Steve addressed them all by first name, including the desk cop, and directed that his buddy Ivan be placed with him, and Chip be put in number three cell "since Hank here's got number four, and we got a game in two." The cops were willing enough. Their main interest was how badly Steve was taking Hank at cards. The two new prisoners roared insults at each other, accompanied by exuberant goading from Steve. When Chip started to vomit, his face pressed against the bars, Hank found himself serving as mop and bucket man.

24

The game and noise subsided around three in the morning. At five, the desk cop shook Hank awake. Chip sprawled snoring on the floor in the adjacent cell, and Steve and Ivan lay in their bunks with arms and legs dangling. "What you want to do before you go is, grab your mop again and give this whole place a good soogie. Be sure the water's hot, and put in plenty ammonia. Yell when you're through." And the barred door clanged shut again.

Hank cursed to himself as he worked, but it lacked venom. Kodiak was okay. Did he really want to fly off to some deserted cannery for the summer?

3
WHALE
PASS

Two days later, Hank almost made it across the island. The little plane flew over a wilderness of green mountains out by blue finger-like bays. The valleys they passed were filled higher and higher with fog, until fog covered all but snatches of bare rocks on the high mountaintops. "Not going to land in this," declared the pilot, and returned to Kodiak. Hank shouldered his gear with no great distress and walked whistling to the barracks, where he had joined Pete after the night in jail. Danny was the only one in the main room, sitting on the floor amid jumbled clothes and sleeping bags as he plunked a guitar.

"Didn't make it? Pull a brew off the porch and bring me one too."

Hank complied. "Did Pete take my job?"

Danny strummed a few notes. "May be. Said he'd do anything to more cannery."

At the beanery, Jody raised an eyebrow. "Couldn't stay away?" She was becoming actually tolerable, considering this along with "Take care of yourself" when he'd thought he was saying goodbye the night before.

There was Pete by the tubs. His red hair stuck wetly to his forehead. "Man, this is no way to make money."

"Want to give the job back?"

"I only need the dough and free chow. If you only need the work and give me the rest we've got a deal."

Hank wandered to the harbor and found the *Rondelay* among the other salmon boats waiting out the strike. On deck, in the rain, Ivan

26

sat splicing. Sven and Jack were off buying groceries. Inside, Steve and Jones Henry the skipper squatted cursing over the disassembled engine. Since jail, Hank had spent parts of the last two evenings aboard, listening to boat talk and learning cribbage before trailing them to the bars. But in the working daylight they barely grunted in his direction. With the engine torn down, the cabin was completely cluttered. Boards blocked the bunks, and parts lay over the stove and sink. He sorted through a box of greasy tools to find a punch they needed, then braced a wrench while they put their collective weights against another to break a bind, but realized that they absorbed him if he stood around and managed just as easily alone.

Ivan called him on deck and pointed to a compact white boat gliding in through the rain-pocked water. "Old *Lincoln*, riding low, full of halibut. Go to that cannery where she's going to dock. Tell Buck I said you was a good boy to put to work."

Hank arrived on the run, just ahead of the *Lincoln*, which eased with a gentle thump against the pilings. A leather-faced man in a stocking cap threw him a coil of line. Hank slipped the loop over a cleat and watched with relief as the man accepted his action and pulled the line taut. The new experience made his blood pump. He looked down at the scrubbed wooden tables and bins built into the decking. Everything had the appearance to it of sea-work. Two of the men lifted a heavy hatch and lowered themselves out of sight. He could see their arms prying loose large white fish and moving them.

The skipper climbed a rusty ladder from his boat to the pier. Hank stepped back instinctively, but the man paid him no attention. About fifty, thick-waisted, he walked with heavy authority through one of the doors, the rolled-down tops of his hip boots slapping against each other.

Buck the foreman said: "I've got my crew for the day," barely stopping to hear Hank's introduction. That would have ended the conversation, except that Hank mentioned Ivan's name. "Oh, you know that wild bastard? Well, stick around. *Lincoln*'s going on the board. If we get his halibut I'll use you. Worked in a cannery before?" Hank explained he was on his way to the western cannery if the weather ever lifted. "Haven't you talked to Swede Scorden? Hell, with the salmon strike he's half shut down. We're part of the same company, you know. Follow me."

In a radio room, Buck grabbed a microphone. He snapped some

call words and then was talking to the famous Swede. Hank could gather nothing from the voice except that it was low, curt, and confident. "No, I don't need him until the strike's settled. Put him to work if you can."

An hour later Hank was hired, issued rain gear, and set to work on the halibut sliming line. He stood by a metal table with a brush and a hose, along with two girls and a guy he knew from the barracks. As the halibut slid down from the loading dock in a mess of ice and gurry, Tim positioned it by a guillotine that severed its head, Linda scooped a chunk of bloody impacted ice from a hole cut near the head, Hank brushed and hosed away the gore, and Jen eased the carcass onto a conveyor that passed it through jets of water.

He had never seen such fish. Most weighed at least sixty pounds, while some were declared to be over two hundred. If they stuck to the metal, it was a hard tug to budge them. Some were so wide that he had to lean across the table to swab their far sides. His elbows would rest on their firm meat as he brushed slimy blood and ice from the thick porous skin, and it felt as if he were embracing big leather cushions. What kind of arms did it take to pull such fish into a boat?

The cannery crew traded positions as they worked through the afternoon and into the night. The only limitation came for the girls, who stayed with the lighter tasks. At the end of the sliming line, the fish emerged from their washing to be weighed and placed in various carts by size. The weigher jabbed a color-coded tag into each tail. Each cart was then pushed—hundreds of pounds on grainy metal wheels over a concrete floor—onto a scale and then to the freeze lockers. The freezer gang wore extra hoods and sweaters. Hank, with no extra clothing, found himself nearly desperate with the cold. It froze the hair in his nostrils at the first breath and dried his throat to a cold scratch. The steam of their breaths dimmed the air. His rain gear froze stiff and crackled as he moved. They hefted the fish from the carts to tiers of frosty shelves, forty- to sixty-pounders overhead, two-hundred-plus-pounders at ground level. It was a strange, fettered place, akin to working undersea. Hank volunteered in short shifts as often as he could stand it.

Each job had its tricks. When he first lifted the biggest halibut carcasses they slipped from his grasp, sometimes sliding to the floor. Tim showed him. "Place your fist in the hole where they cut out his guts, then twist your other arm so the hand faces out and grab the tail. Okay, now stand straight and brace it against your belly. Easy, huh?" And he, slight of build, demonstrated with a hundred-pounder he lifted from a bin and slapped on the table.

They worked into the night, sliming the final loads of halibut from the *Lincoln,* then piling them in a corner under layers of shoveled ice because the freezers were jammed. There would be a freighter docking in a few hours, Buck said. When they punched out near midnight, he chose several of the men, including Hank, to report back by 5:30 A.M. to move the shipment. They all returned to the barracks tired, but full of energy. Somebody had firecrackers, and they threw a string of them into the girls' dorm upstairs.

Hank shook Pete awake. "Hey man, have a brew?"

"Go to hell. I'm back at that dump washing dishes at six."

Hank yawned, pleased with himself. "I'll wake you as I go." His arms and shoulders ached, and it felt good.

The salmon strike went on and on. Hank at first paid it little attention except as it affected the opening of Swede Scorden's cannery, but the issues began to draw his interest as his friends on the *Rondelay* argued the strike among themselves. It seemed that the salmon runs the year before had been spectacular, with the canneries paying forty-five and a half cents per humpie. This year the biologists predicted fewer salmon, but the canneries were offering a lower price. "Hell," declared Jones Henry on one occasion when he took Hank along to a meeting of the United Fishermen's Marketing Association, "what kind of game do those fellows think they're playing? Don't everybody know the fewer the fish, the higher the price should be?" Jones' voice, as wiry as his body, remained even and firm. "I got the same boat payments, and a new engine on order. The cannery wants to see me crawl to them for a loan so they can take me over, mebbe. Well, I'll fish from a rowboat before that happens." Other fishermen nodded grimly. They sat around on folding chairs, men with weathered faces, wearing deck shoes and heavy work clothes. One of the movements afoot would have had the canneries pay by the pound rather than by the fish—nine cents had been offered in Kodiak compared to ten and a half in Cordova, and the pro-and-con discussion became loud. Hank was impressed with the number of men who spoke articulately. He had not thought of fishing as an occupation that bred public speakers, but these men, whom he admired more and more, appeared as able to pull their weight with words as with work when it concerned them.

One man argued that, whatever the price, the boats should start fishing. "The canneries is making suckers of us. They've got so much king crab coming to their lines this year they don't need the salmon. First thing we know, the salmon runs'll be over, because the humpies ain't going to wait."

"We got to stick with what we started," said Jones Henry, "or the canneries won't ever take us seriously again. You don't think those fellows ain't sticking together? What about all the canneries out in the bays that process nothing but salmon? You think fellows like Swede Scorden figure on closing down?"

"Swede's got his beach sites," said the man advocating capitulation. "The fish we don't catch go straight into his set nets. Bastard's probably running double shift and laughing at us like hell." The comment brought a silence.

"Well," said another, "I'm not for the canneries shitting over us, but I give it about another week and then I convert my boat back to king crab for the season."

"Hope you've got a processor that'll buy from you. The plant up the way's so plugged they ain't buying but from their own ten boats."

The meeting adjourned with no clear decision except to remain tied up. Jones Henry, walking back to the *Rondelay*, said seriously, but without apparent fear, "Last year the season was so good I paid most of my debts, and then got carried away with house frills like the old lady's always wanted and replacing my old Jimmy. The way things are going, I may have to longshore or something just to keep the boat."

Suddenly the ground trembled underfoot for a moment, then stabilized again. To Hank's startled exclamation Jones said, "Oh, when you live in Kodiak you get those. Not enough to call an earthquake."

For Hank, his work at the cannery turned to king crab as soon as the halibut boat left. Buck started him on the shake line, pounding tubes of crabmeat from the cooked and cracked legs. After the freedom and variety of jobs handling the big halibut, it was dull and confining to stand in one place doing one job. At least he had friends around him. They joked and horsed around when Buck wasn't looking. Finally Hank landed a job on the butcher line. It was messy and strenuous in a satisfying way. To butcher, he wore a hard chest protector. He held the huge live crabs, two legs in each hand, pressed their shells against his chest and their undersides against a metal wedge, then with a snap of his arms tore them in two. Crab entrails dripped everywhere, even occasionally hitting him in the face. It took a special twist of his arm and wrist to do the job in a single motion. There was pressure to maintain speed, because the entire processing line depended on the crab halves produced by the butchers. Hank knew if he slacked he would be returned to shaking or some job even duller, one that could also be done by women. His arms hurt and throbbed at night, but he competed with the more experienced butchers and kept pace. The others stopped to wash their skin when parts of crab hit them in places not protected by gloves and rain gear. It seemed unnecessary to Hank—until one day he broke into a painful rash. "That's how it is," said Tim. "I've seen crab rash put guys in the hospital." Hank weathered the rash, learned to wash even if it meant skipping a beat, and remained a crab butcher.

They settled the strike in the second week of July, for forty-four cents a fish, a cent and a half less than the year before. It was hardly a victory for the fishermen, but without ado they began to gear for a Monday opening. The weather remained bad for flying. Buck, at Swede Scorden's direction, put Hank aboard the *Billy II*, a power scow being used as a salmon tender, and suddenly he was cut loose from a world that he had hoped would last all summer, without even time to say goodbye to his friends.

In the boat harbor he could see the *Rondelay*, with Steve's hulk high atop the boom as he rigged something, while Jones, Ivan, and Sven the cook stood on the deck below. He called and waved, but they were too absorbed to notice. As the tender passed around the spit that edged town and the sight of buildings opened and closed to him, he watched the beanery and the bars, the jail, then the barracks, for people he knew. Would they still remember him in two or three months when he returned? The tender entered a narrow channel, with waterfront buildings on the Kodiak side and scrub banks on the other. Gradually they left the town behind until even the twin domes of the Russian church, dimming in the rain, disappeared behind the low hills.

The *Billy II* was not a satisfying vessel. Power scow, garbage scow, it had a high square housing painted barn red and nothing but a large fish bin occupying the entire forward deck. With a flat bow and stern, it chugged and bumped through the water. Roomy enough quarters—the entire engine space, wheelhouse, bunks, and galley of the *Rondelay* could have fitted into half the galley of the *Billy*—but the total of it hardly equaled the feel of the fishing boats he had visited.

The pace of the tender underway was slow. In the galley the cook, whose name was Joe Spitz, sat on a bench at a long table reading, while several fat chops smoked on a stove behind him. The man who was engineer, to judge by the grease on his arms and clothes, lay stretched asleep on another bench. The deckhand, Nick, a guy his own age, cut two quarters of fresh-baked berry pie and shoved one toward Hank. They had already started an acquaintance on deck when Hank had helped him coil lines and lash down some oil drums. In the wheelhouse, which was separated from the galley by a few steps and a door, Hank could see the captain's legs propped on a railing, while at the wheel stood his wife or girlfriend. She wore dungarees and a Mexican vest, with long hair tied in a velvet bow, and this fancy casualness seemed to set the tone.

Scattered radio voices from the wheelhouse occasionally broke the silence. The captain answered a call from Swede Scorden at the cannery to say: "Raining here. We'll come through Whale Pass say six-thirty, wind southeasterly maybe ten or twelve knots. Tie up your place say three or four in the morning. Okay."

"Hear you, *Billy Two*," said the dry voice. "That puts you in Whale Passage near maximum flood according to my tables. Not going to wait for slack?"

Joe Spitz looked up from his book and darted glances at the others in the galley. Nick shrugged.

"I'll judge when I get there," continued the captain. "Good mile of visibility. I'm not one for killing time."

"Jesus!" exclaimed Spitz in disgust. "He's got no judgment, and he'll get away with it."

Swede's voice continued: "Are you carrying the whole load of stores I ordered? Over."

"Affirmative that, affirmative."

"I'll send my unloading crew at the start of the six-o'clock shift. Your men can stand by. See you in my office at eight."

"You slave-driving prick!" shouted the captain, after the radio transmission had ended.

"*Somebody* needs guts to tell that bastard off," declared Spitz loudly enough for the pilothouse to hear. "Now we get no sleep." Spitz had white hair although he was not old, and his mouth seemed permanently tightened at the edges. He placed his black-rimmed glasses on the open book, flipped the chops onto a platter, and slammed dishes of vegetables on the table. "Chow's down if you want it. When we go through Whale Passage like circus monkeys, it may be your last meal." As an afterthought he shook dried parsley over the potatoes. "Swede Scorden blows his nose and we scramble after his snot like it was nuggets."

The engineer rose, yawned, and speared a chop. Nick prepared and delivered two platefuls to the pilothouse, returning to fetch a bottle of catsup. The captain and the woman started laughing, but the men at the table ate in silence. When two dishes touched, the boat's vibration made the edges rattle against each other.

After eating, Hank put on his new oilskins and went outside to watch the scenery. He had hoped for mountains, but if they existed the misty rain obscured them. Only a low strip of land was visible. They passed a rock shoal where waves broke into white spray. Other waves, unobstructed, rose and fell in a variety of undulating patterns, their smooth surfaces striated by the blowing rain. When the boat changed course, he saw an opening between the island and the mainland. "This the famous Whale Pass coming up?" he asked through the galley door.

Nick glanced out. "Only Spruce Island Pass. Nothing special."

"Whale Pass is worse?"

"Just add a bitch of a current to rocks and rough water. Sometimes a boat has bad luck in Whale, that's all."

"Bad luck!" Spitz stopped exploring his mouth with a toothpick. "There's no such thing as bad luck; you're talking bad seamanship. When you reach a place that's dangerous at full current you lay to for slack, even if it costs you two or three hours. We're talking judgment, my friends. That's the second rule of seamanship, the first being knowledge." He looked from one to the other belligerently, as if expecting a contradiction. "You don't knowingly buck into a force of nature you can't control. You bow to it. *Then* you have good luck."

"And the other boats catch all the fish because they get there first."

"Until they crack up some day."

Nick and the engineer exchanged glances and shrugged elaborately.

"You ought to be running your own boat," said Hank with admiration.

Spitz peered over his heavy glasses. "You, my friend, either close that door or come inside."

Hank recognized Whale Passage when they reached it, if only because Spitz appeared at the top of the stairs to the galley entrance wearing a life jacket. (Hank thought briefly about possible danger, decided that the captain's skin was as dependent on safety as anybody else's so that he knew what he was doing, and remained at the rail to watch.) They had crossed a body of open water with little ahead but a low hump of a mountain. As they drew closer an opening took shape, guarded by rock bluffs and a marker to the right and by a light on a rock to the left. The water appeared calm. As the boat passed between the navigation aids it stopped rolling. They glided swiftly, passing close enough to a face of blackened granite for him to see tufts of lichen and barnacles growing in the crevices. The water by the rocks was dark and swirling. No sounds, except for the squawk of a gull and the bounce-back of engine chugs from the rock face. Eddies of water bubbled in places like small creatures tussling just beneath the surface. Suddenly the boat began to be kicked from side to side arbitrarily. They traveled faster and faster, veering from a straight course like drunks. A red buoy passed that was being pulled almost horizontal by sucking and gurgling water. The wake from the buoy swirled downward like the propeller churn of a fast-moving ship. As for the boat, it felt as if hands were pushing from below. The water around them swished in streaks.

"Yahoo!" yelled the captain from a window of the wheelhouse. "Here come the tide rips." Spitz, standing nearby, watched him with unconcealed anger.

Up ahead, a dark line ran across the water almost like a wall, with streaks on the near side and thousands of choppy waves on the others. As the boat hit the waves, it began to pitch wildly. Water splashed in little geysers all over the deck.

When the boat settled into a calm open passage again, Hank regretted the end of Whale Pass. He remained leaning on the deck rails, letting the rain pour over his oilskins as he watched the sea. The busy water stirred excitements he had sensed in himself earlier, staring at ocean waves on a beach, which had never before been ignited. Dusk filtered into dark. No light shone along all the shore. They passed an occasional fishing boat whose lights bobbed in and out of visibility like ghost lanterns. Land and water were indistinguishable. The loneliness and beauty of it clung to his mind like new music.

Finally he became chilled enough to go inside. They were all gathered in the pilothouse, lounging and smoking—even Spitz, who appeared to have weathered his snit. The room had a pleasant combined smell of warm electronics oil and beer. Hank hung close to the door, unsure of his welcome.

"Come in and dry off," said the captain in a friendly voice when he noticed Hank. "Had your fill of poetry? I think we saved you a can from the last six-pack."

Hank laughed as he opened the beer. "Thanks very much."

The conversation resumed. It wandered from the strike and the fairness of the price offered for humpies to the money some fishermen now made in king crab, to a newspaper account of Negroes beaten for riding buses in Georgia, to the way President Kennedy the preceding October had stopped the Russians from putting missiles in Cuba, to speculation over whether the astronauts could ever stay in space for more than a few minutes without dying or going crazy, to the way Swede Scorden manipulated fishermen. Nick and the engineer said little, but the others were full of opinions. Hank told of restaurant sit-ins between Washington and New York to force service for Negroes (without volunteering that he had participated twice himself) and told how people in Baltimore had cleaned the cans off grocery shelves on the day the battleships headed for Cuba. It was pleasant company, although less heady than the activities of Kodiak he had just left behind.

Around midnight the captain and Cindy went to their cabin, leaving Spitz in charge of the pilothouse. Nick and the engineer had drifted to bed earlier.

Hank asked Spitz if he could help. "Brew some coffee if you want." Spitz gave him instructions, and the resultant pot was satisfactory. Hank studied the green needle of the radarscope as it traced the shoreline and tried to coordinate the land shapes with those on the chart. It became increasingly hard, as the strait widened and the images became disrupted by distance.

"Guess you know your away around here?"

"Eyes closed," said Spitz.

"Only dangerous part's Whale Pass?"

"Well, the rest is open enough that you have to be more stupid to hit the rocks. It still happens. Before radar, of course, you pulled over at night. Unless you had a clear moon, or no judgment at all."

"You've been here that long?"

A pause. "Off and on. Okay, friend, if you want quizzes and want to learn, let's start at the bottom. You know port and starboard?"

"Left side and right side, red and green."

"That's something. Go out and check our running lights."

Hank did as he was told, happily. Outside, he slipped on the slick walkway. His legs shot toward open water, although he grabbed a rail long before falling overboard. Nothing but wet darkness beyond the warmth of the boat. He shivered to think of being in the water, watching the only lights anywhere recede.

Back inside he asked if he could steer. Spitz showed him the rudiments in quick order, then continued what became a lecture, leaping from subject to subject as Hank strained to store the information. Rules of the Road. Know your wind and the direction of the current. Don't guess. On and on, as Hank wondered again why Spitz was not captain of his own boat with all he knew. "Know your boat. Each one handles individually. This power scow, for a bad example. Maneuverable as a plow. When you're going to turn, make plenty of allowance, don't take a close shoal and expect God to help if a williwaw hits you broadside."

The night wore on, with Hank at the wheel most of the time. At one point in open water Spitz dozed, but most of the time he talked: always information, never about himself. They entered the wide mouth of the cannery bay and traveled through diminishing arms of water as land closed in again. Hank watched the radar contours eagerly. They passed close to shore, but no forms took shape outside in the dark to show him the terrain.

36

Close to four, as predicted, a misty collection of lights emerged ahead of them. "Well, that's your new home," said Spitz. "Heaven help you." As they approached, the general light separated into bare bulbs with rain halos that etched a series of docks and gabled roofs extending a quarter mile. Spitz directed Hank in the placement of lines, and they moored without waking the others.

4

SOCKEYE
SUNDAY

IT was a village of white clapboard sheds built upward into a hillside, with everything connected by steps and boardwalks. Mist hung so close in the dim morning that it fuzzed around the corrugated roofs and hazed out the structures farthest away. A long windowed building was lighted, and inside he could see people walking with trays and eating at tables.

With tide low, the cannery pier rose twenty feet higher than the floating boat docks. The barnacle-encrusted pilings towered above the *Billy II*. Hank lent a hand unloading the supplies, first with Nick to break them from the hold, then with two cannery guys named Jordan and Ozone to carry them to the store. The two were such a team that when one started laughing the other joined in a near-giggle. They walked with heavy cartons on their shoulders up a gangway pulled nearly vertical by the tide, then up along boardwalks and low ramps. Hank followed the others from the porch of the store to the warehouse, past long shelves of austere staple foods in giant cans. In back, a sallow nervous man marked each carton with a hard stroke that nearly pushed it off his shoulder, then snapped if he put it in a wrong place. When it was over, Hank stood on the porch asking questions of Jordan and Ozone as he watched the faces of people on the walks and wondered what they were like behind their checked shirts and kerchiefs.

"Down below," said Ozone, who with his buddy worked winters in a Seattle filling station, "you spend on booze and pussy as fast as you make it. Don't have nothin' to spend it on up here; store ain't got shit and the pussy's free." The comment started laughter between the two that nearly doubled them up. Suddenly a wiry man wearing a yellow tractor cap strode past. Jordan and Ozone quieted instantly, and started with purpose toward one of the buildings.

"Who's that?" asked Hank, trailing.

"The boss, Swede Scorden. Don't follow us if you're new; go check in the office." Jordan started laughing again as he added "Unless you plan to work for nothing."

Hank followed the main boardwalk, moving against a general tide of people. A whistle blew twice, and a girl in passing used a word that shocked him, coming from a female, as she observed that only one whistle remained before starting time. People stomped from porches and down the hill, hands in pockets, talking little. Their ages varied, although most were young. Some of the girls appeared worth knowing, and he tried a direct smile as each passed. A few smiled back; others stared through him.

The office, a long white clapboard building like the rest, had a sign on the glass: "OFFICE wipe your feet." The door was locked, although a man at a desk bent over papers without looking up. Alongside the door were tacked two mimeographed sheets, one entitled *Crew Shift Hours* and the other *Rules for Bunkhouses*. Each was signed by C. L. Scorden in heavy black script. Hank began to read the rules, which began "UNDER NO CIRCUMSTANCES shall: (1) Alcohol be permitted; (2) Smoking be permitted except in the presence of LARGE ASH TRAYS at least a foot in diameter; (3) Fighting be permitted. There is a cleared area behind the dump for this if you want to risk the bears; (4) Knives and guns be permitted; (5) Food be brought in to encourage rats. During night work, the chow hall will be open all the time; (6) Rowdy noise . . ."

"My husband says the office don't open until eight."

An older man and woman were sitting on a bench alongside the door. Both their faces were hefty and weathered. The woman wore a long print dress and boots, and her iron-gray hair was secured neatly with big amber hairpins. The man's white hair was shaggy. He wore a shirt with string tie and hip boots rolled down.

Hank gladly joined them. "You folks from around here?"

"Oh . . . ten mile up the beach. This is Mrs. Hatcher, and I'm Dan Hatcher."

"More like eight."

"Yes, I'd say eight mile up the beach."

A conversation started easily, with Mrs. Hatcher in particular happy to talk. They lived in their cabin, she said when Hank showed interest, and fished salmon with a set net. Dan had built the cabin himself forty years ago—of course they'd added since then—and they'd raised four children in it. The two boys now had their own seiner together, built by Dan and themselves. One daughter, who lived Outside, was coming to visit, to help with the fish-smoking, and they had boated over this morning to meet her plane. "I'll tell you, with this strike of the seiners—the boys tell us all about it by radio—our nets have caught near everything and we've worked and worked. But for us and a few other set-net folks along the shore that deliver to the tender, I'll bet this cannery wouldn't be open now."

Hank was curious about a set net. Dan explained that you staked it in a fixed place instead of running it like a seine. When the salmon swam into it, their noses went through the web. The meshes were too small for their bodies to pass, "and when the poor fellows try to back out their gills hook in the web, and there they stay caught until Mrs. Hatcher and me pick them and put them in our boat." They owned their site, and nobody else could use it.

They handled the net all by themselves? It seemed natural enough to them. Best to have two people in the boat, one to steer and the other to pick. Although Dan could do it by himself easy, added Mrs. Hatcher. "If there's fish he'll catch them. He hunts good, too. We've never gone hungry. The children try to get us to spend the winters in town, but except when the boys fetch us for Christmas, we wouldn't want to live anyplace else. It's too busy in Kodiak. Not like before the war."

"Dan and Maude!" said a dry voice cordially. "You had breakfast? Come up to the house." It was Swede Scorden.

Hank rose, but Scorden paid no attention to him.

"Well, Swede . . . we came over today . . ." Dan squinted his eyes. "Want to buy five gallons of red paint. Got five ton of herring. Going to pump air into them, shoot them with red paint, and sell 'em to you for sockeyes."

"Good," said Scorden. "At least you're planning to pawn off real fish on me this year. Last season, half of what you threw in my hoppers was stones."

Dan slapped his knee. "I can't help the dull blades on your Iron Chink."

Mrs. Hatcher rose and smoothed her dress. "Charles, we'll eat in the messhall. Mary's not expecting us."

Scorden glanced at Hank. "Who are you?"

"Hank Crawford, sir, came from Baltimore last month, delayed all this time and I know you've been waiting—"

"Go over there to the chowhall and bring to my house—the place up there with the red curtains—four complete breakfasts. Tell the cook it's for Swede, make sure they're covered good so they stay hot."

When the office opened, Hank was given the name of his foreman and assigned a bunkhouse bed and number. Rooms were arranged off long corridors. When he opened one wrong door, a Filipino sprang to attention and grabbed a knife from under his mattress. By the time he found his place, a bleak room of three double-tiered bunks and six lockers, he yearned for Kodiak. Signs on his door said BOOTS OUTSIDE and NO BROADS AFTER TEN EXCEPT THROUGH THE KEYHOLE.

The foreman's name was Joe Cutch. Hank had trouble finding him. A girl in a kerchief, one with big eyes who he thought had smiled at him, pointed out Cutch's burly swift figure in a bright-red shirt through several lines of conveyor belts. By the time Hank had stepped over troughs and around machinery to the moving conveyor of gutted fish bodies where Cutch had been, the red shirt was high on a trestle, pointing out something down on the other side to a man with a pole. Hank climbed the metal stairs to a walkway overlooking bins of fish, keeping his eye on the shirt. Just as he approached, Cutch jogged down another stair and began gesturing to a tall man in coveralls who knelt with a wrench to the underside of a many-bladed machine splattered with fish bits.

Hank paused a minute to appreciate the scene from his panorama. It was busy and interesting, far larger than the halibut line in Kodiak, with a variety of complicated machines. Even with a layman's eye, he could trace the progress of the salmon from deep bins, where men sorted them onto running belts and others lined them head-to-head, into big machines with water spraying in all directions that transformed them from creatures into slabs of food, to lines where people with knives and brushes dressed them further. The fish then disappeared into other machines and emerged as chunks in cans. Farther on, the cans—with lids now on top—went into steaming cookers. Hundreds of feet beyond, fork-lift trucks moved stacks of cartons. Water gushed everywhere. Fish-gut washed along the floor and clung to people's oilskins. The air was saturated with the odors of fish, and the noise of machinery required shouting. Like to try all the jobs, he decided.

He finally caught up with Cutch. Hank towered over him, but there was no question of the foreman's superior energy. Cutch glanced at the slip, and called over the noise, "Henry, is it?"

"Hank, if you don't mind."

"Fine, fine. Have to get you a time card, Hank." He gripped his arm as if holding a piece of goods and darted off, pulling him along between clacking machines. Hank followed to a cluttered small office enclosed in glass. Cutch scribbled Hank's name on a time card, pulled him to a punch clock outside the office and showed him how to use it, then, the arm still in grip, trotted to a far end of the warehouse where an Indian girl stood by a machine. "Audrey, show Hank how to make boxes." And Cutch was off.

Audrey was large and shy. She spoke only in monosyllables. The job they shared, far from the mess of fish and general activity, involved opening flat packets of cardboard and stapling the flaps on a simple machine so that they became cartons. Hank learned the job in five minutes and was completely bored with it thereafter. Audrey murmured that it had taken her much longer, and in fact she still stapled about one out of ten incorrectly. He worked there all afternoon. After dinner, they returned until eleven. Twice Cutch darted by and Hank turned expectantly, hoping to be rescued. But Cutch did not even glance his way.

At coffee and meal breaks he passed through the real work areas. He looked with yearning at the men on the fork-lift trucks, even at those standing in one place by the clacking cans, and envied wildly the men using their muscles to sling fish and push heavy carts. When the work-day ended, his spirits lowered further to find among his roommates the giggle team, Jordan and Ozone. The other occupant of his dormitory was a rough-looking guy his own age named Tolly Smith, who had cut scars on his face and wore a gold earring. Tolly at least asked if he was squared away before he sprayed cologne on his chest, put on a flowered shirt, and sauntered out. Hank lay awake long after the self-generating laughter of Jordan and Ozone had faded into snores. He listened to the rain on the metal roof above and to rats scurrying, and wished close to tears that he could be back in Kodiak.

In the cannery, he continued to staple boxes with Audrey. She was a gentle person, and he treated her politely, but they had no real communication. She lived in a village with her parents, she said, except she lived here for the summer. Summer was nice, here at Mr. Scorden's cannery. Yes, winter was nice in the village too, learned a lot in school. But cannery was nicer, didn't have to work so hard and made lots of money.

At mealtimes and breaks Hank haunted the docks, watching the beautiful seiners that drifted in for repairs or unloading. The men aboard were carefree, marvelous. They lounged and worked joking from deck to deck, oblivious of the cannery workers. The two were different breeds, and Hank was ashamed to be among the latter. When there were no boats, he tried to meet some girls by sitting at various places in the chowhall. Most had already formed attachments. If he could only transfer closer to where they worked! In the dormitory, Jordan and Ozone often chattered about getting "pussy," but it was only Tolly he ever saw with anyone female.

Monday in remote Alaskan canneries is Sockeye Sunday, the traditional day of rest. Seiner crews must by law stop fishing over most weekends. They have delivered their catches by Saturday. By Monday the cannery bins are empty, with a new haul not ready for the tenders until Monday night. By Saturday afternoon, scores of boats had come from the bays to tie up and buy supplies. Hank watched the procession begin as he walked the docks during coffee break. Masts dotted the water as far as he could see down the passage of green mountains that framed the inlet. New faces crowded the platform by the store. He wandered among them, feeling the stink of the cannery on him like a curse. The fishermen all knew each other. Their talk was of web and power blocks, sockeyes and diesel engines. He drank it for minutes, and then the whistle returned him to Audrey and the stapling machine.

At dinnertime he mingled again. For once the sun had been shining, and there was a pleasant warmth in the air. Several shouting

43

fishermen boarded a pontoon plane, ready for a night in Kodiak. The sound of a harmonica drifted from one of the boats. He'd had enough! He jumped over to a deck, entered the cabin, and asked if they needed a crewman. No, and besides, did he have experience? But it started him in motion from deck to deck. By the time the cannery whistle blew, he had taken two friendly slugs of whiskey and had received a dozen negative answers of assorted cordiality. One skipper told him to check back if the weather closed in, since half his crew had flown to town. In an instant the words changed a daydream into a possibility. He returned to the stapling machine elated, paying little attention to the fact that he had missed chow and punched in fifteen minutes late.

"I didn't tell on you," said Audrey. "Mr. Cutch, he come asked for you. I said you run to the toilet."

Hank rushed off and trailed Cutch's elbow from the Iron Chinks to the retorts before catching his attention. "Did you have a new job for me, maybe?"

"No, you're doing fine where you are. That booze on your breath?"

"*Could* you give me a different job?"

"What's that?" Hank repeated the question. Whether Cutch heard was uncertain, because a machine clanked strangely and he dashed away.

Saturday night had the air of a party because of the boats, despite cannery turn-to on Sunday morning. The shift ended at nine, earlier than usual. The Filipino workers, who bunked and ate separately from the rest, had already started an outdoor fire to grill marinated salmon, apparently a regular Saturday rite. Beside the time clock was a fresh notice with Spanish translation: *Cannery employees are reminded that possession of alcohol is absolutely forbidden. C. L. S.*

"In other words, you got to drink it fast," said Tolly behind him. "Come on, if you like, time to wet our throats and maybe our cocks." Hank followed willingly. First Tolly took a shower, as he did every night after work, no matter how late, then doused himself with heavy-smelling lotion and brushed his teeth. He examined his gold earring in the mirror and polished it with his fingertips. Finally he changed to newer, tight dungarees and slipped a black woven vest over a clean flowered shirt.

Hank, also freshly clean on a less grand scale, followed down the stairs of the bunkhouse and down the walkways to the boats. It was about ten in the evening. The sun had gone behind the mountains, although the sky was still blue and the inlet was filled with black and purple shadows. Tolly walked with a happy swagger, beaming at people as he passed and calling comments. Most reacted with a grin. His scarred face might have been sinister but for the good will it radiated. He was his own person all the way, and Hank was pleased to be seen alongside him. Just that afternoon, Swede Scorden had strode into the coffee room with a minute left of the break, and everyone but Tolly had scattered back to their jobs. From the floats they jumped to a deck that Hank had visited that afternoon and walked over several others on boats tied gunwale to gunwale. Tolly hailed and joked with everyone he passed, and they all knew him.

"Well, I figured you'd show," declared a huge man with frizzled hair who was turning slabs of salmon over a charcoal grill placed on his hatch cover, "so I dressed an extra one." A woman with a pleasant face appeared from the cabin door to announce that she had a potful of carrots and potatoes on the stove. "I brought the rest," said Tolly, producing two flat pints of whiskey from inside pockets of his vest.

"Hank, meet the crew of the *Linda J.* That's the skipper in there, Miss Linda, and out here's her poor husband, Joe Eberhardt. I don't see Spiff or Luke around. Hank's got a last name, but I don't know it. I seen him smelling around these boats like a dog in heat, so I figured I'd bring him along."

"Yup, he asked me for a job today," said Joe, and offered a hand so big it covered Hank's. "Any luck?"

"Not much."

"Stick at it." Joe's voice was a low, mature growl, even though he could not have been older than his late twenties. "One of these apes is bound to break his head open some Saturday."

Hank could not have said what he hoped to find by following Tolly, except for company and a possible sexual adventure, but he was surprised and grateful to be included in the dinner that followed. He had never tasted such fish. Joe said they were small sockeyes. The meat was flaky in the manner of the salmon he knew from cans, the color more red for what difference it made, but the flavor of fresh salmon had a depth and richness so beyond that of canned salmon that they could hardly be called by the same name. A thin, succulent layer of fat surrounded the meat. There was such abundance that he ate his fill and more, stuffing piece after piece with ferocious enjoyment.

The cabin was cramped. For Linda to move around the stove, Hank and Tolly had to crowd by a small snapdown table while Joe, in good humor, hunched on a top bunk against a rumpled sleeping bag, a plate on his knees. Linda was a mild, vivacious, lovely woman. It bothered Hank that Joe and Tolly used the same language around her that they would by themselves, and it startled him when she herself said casually, "Tol, have you had enough of the cannery shit?"

Tolly slugged from the bottle and passed it on. "You can tell Chip two more weeks, if you see him on the grounds." Hank learned that a crab pot had crushed Tolly's arm last February, and the cast had not long been removed. On his regular boat with Chip, as the season began, merely pulling the nets from storage had been so painful that the doctor told him to wait. So Chip hired a temporary man. And Tolly, in need of money for all the bills, signed on to do cannery time. Since he had too much self-respect to be seen on a cannery line in Kodiak, here he was, one of Swede Scorden's boys.

"Don't you hurt your arm working here?" asked Hank.

"Son, you've never pulled web in a blow."

Much later, Tolly sauntered back over the decks with Hank in tow. Up on the pier he whistled, and a girl who had been sitting on a stack of boxes hurried over. "Stick around, Hank, but just wander off for a minute." The girl put her head on Tolly's chest. He murmured something, then eased her away with a pat on the buttock. "She'll get a friend for you. Come on, have a brew." Where the girl had been sitting stood a bag of cold cans. Tolly led the way to a padlocked door and opened it with a key. Inside was a dark room that smelled of heavy oils. "Machinist is a good man to know, Hank." There were several flattened cardboard boxes of the kind Hank opened with Audrey, and under Tolly's direction they spread them on the floor. Shortly, two girls slipped in.

Hank was apprehensive. There had been only the one experience, on the beach. What if he failed? Tolly would probably laugh and forget him in the future. As it turned out, he managed. Considered honestly, there was more tension than pleasure in it. He was ready to finish sooner than the girl, who kept roving her tongue in his mouth and placing his hands in areas to continue fondling. But when it was over he felt relieved and happy.

The Sunday workday started at seven, as long as any other. Hank attacked the miserable boxes by rote, whistling at the memory of the night before. He had never seen the girl's face, although her name was Elsie. Which of them was she on the lines? He moved as straight and nonchalantly as possible in case she might be watching. With only three hours' sleep, he was just as glad to have a job that required nothing of him.

That all changed when Cutch appeared and grabbed Hank by the arm without further announcement. He propelled him to a room where an elderly woman kept the rain gear mended and washed. "Issue him hip boots, Sally. Get you a suit of skins, report up to Sam, that Filipino with the pole." One of the sorting belts had broken. Soon Hank stood knee-deep in dead salmon that were encased in green slime, surrounded in the depths of a big fish bin by an unimaginable stench. He wore gloves the consistency of rough sandpaper that gave some grip on the fish. "You hold tail," shouted Sam on top. "One each hand, boy. Go faster." Before long he sweated to keep up with a relentless conveyor belt that carried away the fish he tossed. They grew heavier and heavier. When a new load poured from the elevator, the salmon flopped against his back like sandbags.

By three-thirty he had tossed the final salmon and hosed the bins. A hot shower, then beautiful bed. The rest of the cannery would be working various later hours as the fish progressed through the lines. He hosed himself to pry the worst of the gurry from his rain gear, then wearily peeled down and punched out. Tolly breezed past and delivered a playful punch.

"Hey," called Hank, "that was okay last night."

"Do it again tonight. Machine shop at eleven."

"Great!" He should have been more elated. Maybe after some sleep. Swede Scorden strode along the boardwalk, hunched in a checked wool coat, the yellow visor cap pulled tight. Hank nodded automatically without expecting a return. He had come to realize how little he mattered within the cannery apparatus.

"Crawford."

"Sir?" Remembered his name besides.

47

"Making out all right?"

Flattered, he volunteered, "I'm loading fish now, enjoying it pretty much. Not like—"

"I've seen you keeping bad company, and Mr. Cutch reported booze on your breath. Read your rules if you expect to stay." And he was off.

Bastard! Hank hurried straight to the boats. His inquiries were almost desperate, but many who had been easy before now answered him curtly as they prepared to leave for the Monday opening. He handed boxes of groceries from deck to deck and pitched in wherever he could. Joe Eberhardt was tightening lines, while his two crewmen arranged boards in the cramped hold and Linda pumped the bilge. "Here, put your weight on this while I tie her off," growled Joe. Hank grabbed the line and pulled with all his strength. He stayed, helping with other jobs, so reluctant to leave that he rode aboard as they traveled to get fuel at the far end of the cannery. Finally Joe placed a heavy hand on his shoulder. "Well, old man, we're off. Cast our lines, will you?"

Hank watched their wake in the calm and darkening water. "Look us up next week," called Linda.

He ran from the fuel pier back to the main concentration of boats, still hoping for something lucky. Even a rowboat to escape the slavery of Swede Scorden. The tension of departure grew by the minute. No more singing or music, but shouts, instructions, the thump of blocks and the squeak of winches. Men scampered up masts, braced over the side, and clamored into skiffs as they tightened lines and checked equipment. Exhaust filled the air as engines started with putts and roars. Dominating it all was the sight of nets and corks being readied for action. Take me with you, he wanted to cry. One by one the boats left, steaming up the inlet and disappearing around the mountain bends, en route to the wonderful and mysterious fishing grounds beyond. Would he ever see them? By the time the cannery whistle sounded for dinner, the docks were empty except for the tender *Billy II*.

At chow, Hank shoveled his food without taste and forgot to return for pie. He watched the others dully, feeling his body would explode if he didn't find a way out of the place. There was Audrey, talking to an Indian boy with a smiling animation he had thought beyond her. All different, every bit of what he had figured. Couldn't afford to be

48

fired: hadn't even paid yet for his airfare. There sat Tolly with two girls.
The rare sun through the window gleamed on his gold earring.

He wandered the cannery complex from the dump at one end
to the fuel pier at the other. From the laundry shed came the empty noise
of somebody's rock music. He avoided people. Down where the boats
had left, heavy offal lapped around the pilings. It was too much even for
the seagulls, who dove by the hundreds without diminishing it. Water
from the washdown poured from a dozen scuppers and tore holes in the
scum. The stench at low tide was dreary. Beyond the boardwalks was
coarse grass laced with painfully stinging nettles. He climbed up
through it to gain a better vista of the water. Below, the last processing
steam spouted from the cannery stacks as the crews shut down, and the
odor of cooked fish permeated even the air where he stood. Out far beyond the green mountain spits, toothpicks of seiner masts still remained
etched by the lowering sun.

A cold wind blew on his back. Rainclouds were coming over the
mountains behind him, their swirls snagging on the peaks. The grayness
engulfed the cannery and traveled toward the boats, blotting the gold
sunstreaks as it went. The water kicked into waves, the rain began, and
the boats disappeared in roiling gray. People below, caught without
raincoats, ran the ramps from building to building. The gulls diving for
offal and he were the only ones oblivious of the weather. The rain rattled a din on the tin roofs. He let it take its fill of his shirt and pants.
No way to do it, no way but to stand by himself.

"Ay-EEEE!" he shouted, and began to beat his chest. "Ay-EEEE!
Fuck you all!" He waited for the sound to carry over the roofs, then
drew his largest breath. "Fuck even you, Swede Scorden." Then, hands
in pockets, whistling, he slogged back down to the bunkhouse to find
Tolly.

5

RONDELAY

Hank had come to Alaska in mid-June. By early August he was a scruffy Alaskan type, living in his boots, shaving only now and then, taking the world as it came. At the cannery dump he had been knocked down once in a fight but had not disgraced himself. On weekend nights he could count on a regular girlfriend in Elsie, and he had inherited the key to the machine shop. He worked by rote, putting in the hours. He had spent days on end beside set-faced Filipinos sorting salmon, had spent equal periods feeding tops into the can-making machine, minding the cookers they called retorts, and clearing jams on the can line. Once, when the indexer broke, he sawed salmon heads with a big knife for several sixteen-hour shifts, his oilskins running with fish blood that found its way even into his hair, his tendons so popped that his right arm twitched for a week. Most of the jobs had their tricks (a salmon head can be cut in a neat crescent that follows the bone and saves the meat, for example, or can be clumsily butchered), but every one followed a pattern of dull repetition.

Tolly had rejoined his boat, the *Olaf,* and left the scene. The *Rondelay* had been fishing Alitak in the southern part of the island and had then moved around to the western bays and started delivering to Swede. It was great to see Big Steve and Ivan and Jones Henry. But each weekend passed, and no boat needed a green hand. It was a poor season. A few men quit, but their boat crews chose to work shorthanded rather than replace them, so that each individual's share of the small take could be larger. Hank even flew to Kodiak one Monday to scout the harbor. He had a fine visit with some friends at the barracks (although Pete had disappeared and even Jody was gone from the beanery), but he found a dozen guys his own age wandering the docks looking for a berth.

As for Swede Scorden and Cutch the foreman: you did your work dependably, disobeying the rules only in the dark, and you got along. Merely doing your work stood you out from the rest.

Ozone and Jordan, for example, made a cult of idleness, and their laughter gained momentum whenever they bested Scorden of an hour's wages. Hank followed Tolly's example. When he had earned a break, he took his right and fixed a cool stare at anyone who tried to hustle him back to work.

Suddenly, one Wednesday midday as he was minding the rows of cans and joking with the girls on either side of him, in hurried Big Steve with the announcement: "Get your gear and come fishing." Jack, of the *Rondelay* crew, had fallen down the hold and broken his leg. A plane was just coming to evacuate him to Kodiak.

In his excitement Hank hardly knew where to start. He swept the girl closest to him off her feet and twirled her around, then found Cutch, and—pounding gleefully on his shoulder—quit. Cutch smiled with his mouth as he said: "If you can't finish the day and the washdown, don't come back." Hank became serious for a moment. "Guess I won't, then. The boat needs me now. No hard feelings." He held out his hand and Cutch, with the same peculiar smile, shook it loosely. "Punch out and take your card to the office if you want to get paid."

He stuffed his clothes into his duffel bag without order, dirty and clean intermixed, and started at a trot toward the office, then paused to return to the cannery. Elsie was working on the patcher line. He touched her shoulder. "Hey, Else, I'm going out on a boat." She looked up at him, and her big eyes were full of tears. "I know."

He had not expected her emotion. "Well, look, it's okay, I'll probably see you on weekends..."

"Goodbye, Hank," she said sadly.

She had actually cried over him! The notion gave a new bounce to his step as he hurried to the office with his time card, although he quickly forgot Elsie herself. The clerk gave him a termination form. Swede Scorden's voice came from the inner office, talking by radio to the *Billy II* as he asked for the size of their load and told them the time to be at the cannery. As Hank filled out the form he debated, and when the transaction was finished he unlatched the gate and walked through the office to the hidden room.

"Mr. Scorden, excuse me, I just wanted to say—"

Scorden, the yellow tractor cap perched on his head, sat in a swivel chair at a desk full of papers, facing a window that overlooked the cannery and docks. Without turning he snapped, "You'll get into all kinds of scraps with that hopheaded crew of Jones Henry's."

"News sure travels fast, sir. I just wanted—"

"*I've* seen you nosing around the boats. Okay, Crawford. You worked harder than some, and you broke more rules than most. Good luck. Don't come back." By the way Scorden resumed scribbling notes, he had ended the interview. Without ever looking up. Hank left with less confidence.

But there waited the *Rondelay*. The paint on her white hull and blue gunwale was chipped, the cabin boards were worn to the gray bare wood, the anchor was rusty, a jumble of boxes and broken gear littered the cabin roof where Jones Henry stood at the wheel, and she was fabulously beautiful. Sven the cook had hailed him as he passed the store and loaded him with boxes of groceries. At the boatside he passed the boxes to Ivan, who caught them without spilling an ash from his pipe. "Let's get fishing," said Jones. Big Steve unmoored one line and Hank the other. They leaped aboard, and with a roaring cloud of blue smoke the *Rondelay* chugged into open water.

Hank remained on deck, watching the nest of low clapboard buildings recede. As the distance increased, snow-streaked mountains rose above the lower green ones like targets on a shooting range. He licked his lips, trying to contain the wild grin and shouts inside him. Whenever Ivan or Big Steve or Sven went to coil a line or tighten a turnbuckle, Hank raced to help. Not enough work. He feared they might ignore him, do all the work themselves. Finally Sven sat him on the hatch cover with a bag of potatoes to peel and told him not to get up until they were finished. Hank peeled avidly, and started to whistle.

Sven threw a wet rag that hit him in the face. They all turned on him at once. "What kind of stupid bastard," roared Big Steve, "whistles on a boat?" He swerved his arm in an arc that embraced the sky. "You want to whistle up a fuckin' storm in this nice weather?" Hank stared up, startled. Steve's anger was real. "You ever whistle on here again, I'll throw you overboard. Got it?"

"Yes, Steve."

Steve turned to the others. "Nobody ever told him, so forget it."

"Everybody got to learn," said Ivan.

Sven wagged a finger at Hank. "I just made a cake in the oven, to welcome you aboard. If it falls . . ."

"Sure, Sven, I'm sorry, I just didn't . . ."

"Ja, ja, okay, Hank," he concluded with gentle, singsong inflection.

Hank, sobered, finished peeling the potatoes. The cannery was now far down the inlet, separated by waves of wake. White puffs of fog lingered around the mountaintops and clung to individual spruces and ravines. The skiff bobbed astern with Ivan, who was arranging gear. Jones Henry, oblivious of the rest, stood by his wheel on the open deck above the cabin that he called the bridge. Inside, Sven sang tunelessly to himself as he fixed dinner and merely nodded when Hank delivered the potatoes. Big Steve sat on the pile of corks, a section of net drawn across his lap. When he said, "You can give me a hand," Hank hurried over.

"Spread the web in your fingers so all the squares is open alike, then hold it tight and even." Hank did as he was told. Steve's thick fingers held a heavy white needle that he worked with flashing dexterity among the torn strands of netting. He payed out the cord inside the needle in a series of knots, twists, and open lengths that became new mesh, indistinguishable from the old except by its whiteness. When he had emptied the needle, he pointed to a ball of cord and told Hank to wind him a new one. Hank examined the foot-long needle and figured it out as quickly as he could, before Steve might grow impatient. As he held open the meshes again for Steve to finish the job, he asked what the difference was between net and web.

"You're holding web. Net's the whole seine—cork, web, lead." He pointed in turn to the three separate piles around them on the stern. Web formed the center pile, but also intermingled with the other two. "Now pay attention." Steve picked up one of the flattened circular corks, and some attached line and web pulled up with it. His big hands barely reached around the perimeter. "Corks float, right? Your cork line here holds up the top of the web. Lead weights sink, right? Your lead line over there" (he pointed out of reach to a pile of snaky thick line that had weights attached) "she holds down the bottom of the web." The snaky line was hooked at points every few feet to brass rings that were pushed one against the other on a horizontal bar. "Purse line draws through them rings, and if your rings ain't stacked in sequence when the seine pays out, you've got two hours of snarls." Hank nodded.

"Now, one end of your seine's attached to the boat and the other to your skiff. When the skiff casts off and draws out the seine, you've put a wall of web in the water. If your skipper's smart enough to lay out the wall in front of the fish, they swim into it. Then you close the seine around in a circle by bringing the skiff back to the boat, and you've got the buggers trapped. Fast before they find a way out you start pursing. You pull your purse line through the rings—they're with the leads at the bottom of the web—and it draws the bottom tighter and tighter like one of them drawstring bags. Purse seine, right? Then you start hauling one end of the net back aboard, and the more you pull in, the smaller you make the circle. Finally you've got the circle so tight that you've crowded all your fish in one place. That's your moneybag if she's full. You haul it aboard and empty it."

Steve wore a new flannel shirt cut off above the elbows, with dirty underwear hugging his arms beneath. Hank asked why so many fishermen he'd seen wore shirts that way. "Sleeves get caught in machinery. And when they pick up gurry they rot and stink like hell."

"Any scissors around? I'd better cut mine."

"Where's your knife?"

"Don't have one."

"Hooee, some fucking fisherman. Follow me." Steve went to the cabin, pulled open his drawer beneath the bunks, and handed up a worn sheath knife, ignoring Hank's expressions of gratitude.

The small space of the cabin combined engine, galley, and bunks. A plyboard cover over the engine served as the table. The triple-tiered bunks were little more than slots against the side, with one end tapering in the contour of the bow. Steve patted a top bunk that practically met the ceiling and kicked a bottom one on the other side that was stuffed with gear. "Take your pick."

Sven was crowded in the space between sink, stove, and engine

cover, cursing with a cheerful lack of venom over the contents of a pot.
As Hank cleared the lower bunk and stowed his gear, he asked Sven if
he could help. "Oh, ven I finish making the mess you clean it up. Ja?"

"Sure. Right now I need the toilet, but I don't see it."

Sven called out to Steve, who had returned to deck. "This fellow
vants to see the toilet, har har har!"

Steve, equally amused, showed Hank the ledge where they kept
paper and the rail they gripped to hang over the side. Hank's face must
have shown his shock, because even Jones Henry above him grinned
down. "Wind's coming portside, so you'd best shit to starboard today."

Hank returned the paper to the cabin. "I'll wait awhile."

"Suit yourself." Steve squeezed into his bunk with booted feet
sticking out and was snoring within a minute.

Hank wandered aft to where Ivan still worked in the skiff. A heavy
chain secured the skiff's bow tight against the stern of the *Rondelay*.
Hank balanced on the pile of web and started to enter the skiff. A sudden flicker in Ivan's eyes cautioned him. "Okay if I come help you?"

Ivan's high cheekbones rippled as he chewed his pipe stem. "I'm
fine," he shouted over the noise of the engine.

Still angry over the whistling? Hank watched with hands in
pockets as Ivan payed a small length of cork and web from one stack to
another, inspecting it as he went. The pipe between his teeth seemed as
much a part of him as his black pea-soup hair or his camelback nose
(earned from too many fists in the puss, according to Steve that night
in the Kodiak jail). His arms stretched from thick shoulders to grab even
the farthest object, so that he seemed to occupy the skiff completely.

The boat turned a bend and passed along a shore of gray beach.
Smoke puffed from a cabin on the inshore flats. Behind rose a high
green mountain, placing the building's smallness exactly within the size
of the universe. Hank wondered at the loneliness of such a place. Who
lived there? He asked Ivan but received only a shake of the head.

The engine slowed and quieted. Up by the wheel, Jones Henry
leaned over the side to call down to someone hidden from Hank's view
as he maneuvered the boat around a single spot. Hank went to look. A
skiff with two people in yellow oilskins bobbed alongside. A section of
web was pulled inside the skiff, and one of the people (whose gray hair
beneath a slicker cap resembled a woman's) was twisting free a salmon.

The muted engine still drowned the conversation. "Runs not much" came through, and "Penny more a fish," and "Bursitis not so bad in the heat." After a while they all nodded to each other, and the *Rondelay* resumed speed. As the skiff passed close Hank recognized Dan and Mrs. Hatcher. He called and waved, excited to be seen at last as a fisherman. They peered at his figure and waved back vaguely, but they were already absorbed in pulling other fish from the web.

Hank climbed the ladder to Jones Henry at the wheel. "I know them! Nice folks. Is that their cabin?"

"That's it." Jones' voice had an assured, reedlike quality that made Hank feel at home. He was a wiry man, with big hands like the rest, and a chin that pointed at the horizon. His eyes had a permanent squint. "As you say, nice folks. They've set-netted off this point for all the years I've fished here, since before the war, and I expect they will until they die. See if there's coffee down in the pot. I take it black."

When Hank returned he sat on the end of a long storage box that also served as a seat for the helmsman, and resumed the conversation. "The war was nearly twenty years ago. You started fishing young."

"I've fished longer than that, and I'm older than you think. Kids never get ages straight."

"How old are you?"

Pause. "Not much past forty."

"Wow," said Hank sympathetically.

"What the hell's that mean? Stand up here and punch me in the gut, hard as you can."

"Come on, you're my boss."

"Your boss says punch him in the gut."

Hank hit Jones' stomach gingerly. Beneath the loose flannel cloth was rock hardness.

"Can't you hit harder than that?"

Hank grinned, impressed. "Don't want to break my hand."

"Better believe it," said Jones with satisfaction. He adjusted the brown canvas hunting cap he always wore so that the brim shaded his eyes. It gave him a jaunty look.

"Guess you were born in Kodiak, to fish here all that time."

"No, Ketchikan, down in southeastern Alaska. Ever been there? Not like Kodiak. Place has a little class, big houses on the hill, a real

downtown. A shame the way their salmon's petered out. Adele—that's
the old lady—wishes we were still there. But Kodiak's where the fishing
is. See that eagle's nest in the dead tree yonder?" He handed Hank his
binoculars. "No, to the right of the mountain. You can see their white
heads sticking from the mess of twigs."

"Yes! They're beautiful!"

"Garbage-eaters. Go out to the cannery dump if you want to see
eagles at work. No, my daddy trolled for salmon all the years down in
Ketchikan, took me out with him from when I was ten. Had my own
troller by the time I was eighteen. That was the late thirties. Trolling,
now, that's a good life if the woolies don't blow you to pieces. Just
yourself, mebbe your dog for company, and four lines of baited hooks to
drag through the water. You'd be surprised how sly you have to be
with them cohos and kings, adjusting depth, changing lures and baits
until you've figured what they want that day. But I'll tell you why I
launched in Kodiak. I like the action of the nets, and when you can fish
king crab the rest of the year you've got a living. Mebbe I like having a
crew, too, because I don't mind hearing talk around me."

"I think Kodiak's pretty nice."

"How long were you there—three weeks in the summer? Long
days, and the sun shines now and then. Days are short in the winter;
she only stops blowing forty when she gusts to ninety, and the only
time it don't rain's when it snows. Want to get in the pickup and take a
drive? About twenty miles of road, mostly potholes, and it don't lead to
much but the Navy Base with a guard at the gate. Not that I need
to go in. I was Marines all through the war, and don't ever show me a
uniform again." Hank asked where he had served. "Guadalcanal to Iwo,
all hell and gone, and never tell me to be nice to a fuckin' Jap. The way
we let 'em fish off our shores now? Shit!"

Hank listened in awe. His own life was trivial. All the opportunities for such adventure had happened in the past.

Jones began to talk about his father. "*He* was a fisherman! In
bad salmon years, or when he figured it was time to free himself for a
while, he'd sign on with the cod fleet from Seattle that went to the Bering
Sea. I went down with him once as a kid; guess Ma wanted to wave him
off, since the trip lasted a few months. Three-master called the *Wawona*,
in about nineteen-thirty. Oh, I wished I could go. A sailing ship has

a creak to its timbers that's hard to describe if you don't know it. Whenever I smell creosote and coal oil it still brings back them old schooners. They dory-fished. Don't see that on the West Coast any more, and that's a few less fishermen dead. Each man got issued his dory, drew lots for the best at the beginning of the trip. Rough bunch of buggers. Fellows drifted from logging to fishing and back again by season. That was the Alaska fisherman back then, a drifter. They'd kid people like my old man who'd finally tie himself to one place and raise a family. I missed out on some adventures back then. Lot of tales he told, and I expect some he didn't."

"What happened to your dad?"

"How do you mean?"

Hank had been thinking of loss at sea or some such dramatic event, but was reluctant to say it. "I mean, how's he doing now?"

"Well, if he was living he'd be eighty-something—I came late—and he'd still expect his half-dozen snorts a day. He went down on his troller three–four years ago in Clarence Strait near Ketchikan. Must have caught a woolie near some rocks. Well, he didn't mind going that way, and I didn't mind for him. Out fishing by himself, except for his dog."

They both remained silent for a while, watching the calm wilderness around them. Birds flew past. The sky was patched with gray and open blue. Pieces of fog clung to the mountain heights despite the intermittent sun, moving in strips from one tree clump to another. Once Jones pointed out two sea otters in the water, but despite Hank's interest the best he could see was a black ripple.

"What's a woolie, Jones?"

"If it ever got in a book they'd call it williwaw, but nobody says it that way. Wind builds on the opposite side of a mountain and crashes down, sometimes a hundred knots—no warning, no direction you can figure in advance. Can tear a boat apart. You stay around here long enough and you'll feel a woolie."

Suddenly Jones stiffened, grabbed the throttle, and slowed the engine as his eyes squinted into slits. The engine noise dropped from a steady roar to a pock-pock. Big Steve, whom Hank had left sleeping, appeared on deck almost instantly. Sven followed, wiping his hands. Ivan stood at attention in his skiff with the engine sputtering a white cloud.

58

Within seconds they had pulled on their rainpants. Steve stood by the taut line that connected the skiff to the boat, a mallet in his hands, looking up at Jones.

Hank felt the tension, feared they would forget him. He tumbled below, barely touching the ladder, tried to leap into his oilskins in a single motion as Steve had done, and struggled with a foot in the wrong leg. "Keep clear of the pelican," growled Steve, and Sven motioned him to a corner.

Ready in position, the crewmen squinted over the water in the same manner as Jones. Hank watched as best he could without being sure what he should see. A splash, accompanied by others. "Fish!" he exclaimed, and pointed.

"Only feed fish. Keep looking."

They peered and peered. At length Jones announced, "Certain I saw a jumper, a humpie, but he don't seem to have brothers. Place I'd planned to lay out with the tide's still a half hour away, so let's eat. Hank, don't get in the habit of pointing. Just shows other boats what you've found."

Steve motioned Hank over to show him some running gear. A pelican hook connected to the winch the line called the painter that held the skiff's bow snubbed against the boat's stern. When the hook was opened with a mallet blow, it released the skiff and snapped the heavy hook across the deck. "So always stand clear," said Steve. "Now, as soon as the skiff goes, it starts paying out that few feet of net on board that Ivan's always working over. You call that the leed; it's a shallow net so the skiff can maneuver close to shore without catching snags. The leed's attached to the seine, so as soon as it's out, the skiff's pulling the seine over the fantail, and all kinds of lines are running on deck. Watch your feet, never catch them in a bight, or you'll get pulled overboard. Right?"

Next, Sven summoned him to the galley to show how the dishes and condiments were packed in the cabinets against heavy weather. He pointed to the mugs hanging from hooks. "And I tell you this before you make some crazy mistake. All cups face outboard. You put 'em which-ways and a storm kicks up."

Hank wanted to laugh, but he said gravely, "I'm trying hard to remember all these superstitions."

"No superstition," said Sven crossly. "It's what happens, so don't forget if you want to be fisherman, ja?"

Sven heaped a plate of food for Ivan and sent Hank to call him. "Skiffman always eats first, since he might be off in water any time." Ivan glanced from the confines of his skiff and told Hank just to bring it and set it on the bow.

"Skipper next," said Sven. "Take it to him on bridge."

"Guess I eat last."

"Nooo. Cook eats last. Get your plate." When Hank said he thought that screwed the cook, Sven said mildly, "Ja, but cook don't have to pitch the fish at night to the tender."

Hank took his plate to sit beside Jones at the wheel, since Jones seemed glad to continue talking. He asked what Jones had seen in the water to stop the boat.

"You got the humpie salmon this time of year, about four-pounders, and the dog salmon starting their runs, about seven–eight-pound fish. With both kinds, when they're running in schools, one or two are going to jump out of the water and then you see where they all are. So what you look for is jumpers. Sometimes humpies just rise halfway and show a fin, but finners are hard to see in open water with any kind of ripple blowing. Now, a humpie leaps straight from the water and back in a clean circle, but a dog salmon jumps out at an angle and skitters along the surface for a bounce or two. That's how you tell them apart. And it ain't just that he jumps. You want to see which way he's jumping, and, if he comes up again, which way he travels. Does no good to lay out your seine where they've been, you've got to get ahead of 'em so they swim into you. Then, of course, you've got to keep your seine set so they don't back out on you or escape around the edges. And you've got to figure it all with the way the tide's running." He winked. "There's tricks to every part of it. Here, I need to take a crap. Can you steer?"

"I had the wheel most of one night on the *Billy Two*."

"You got her."

Hank remembered his instructions from Spitz. "What course, sir?"

"Course? Just steer for those trees way down the inlet."

Hank wrapped both hands around the chipped wheel and took control. He checked himself about to whistle, licked his lips instead.

Rain blew into his face, even though ahead he saw blue sky through gaps in the clouds. The sweet smell of spruce gusted over him. Unfamiliar birds flew by, cawing above the engine noise, and dipped toward the water so close their wings splashed. Other birds, fat and black, seemed held so heavily by the water that all they could do to make way for the *Rondelay* was paddle like a riverboat and flap their wings. Was that the head of an otter that dipped from sight? Oh, the world was beautiful! Sven's voice rose through the galley vent, singing tunelessly in Norwegian. All around were the trappings of a boat built for work, the wood patched with tin and covered by white paint chipping gray, the ingrained odors of oil and fish, the swabs and buoys and coils of line lashed in place, the weathered ropes that stretched mastward in complicated rigging. All tangible so he could touch it, all unbelievable. That lazy crowd on the beach back home, if they could see. He whistled several notes before he caught himself. Skiffbound Ivan, the only one on deck, lifted no outraged face from his mending. Saved by engine noise.

Hank peered ahead and rose, frightened. His clump of trees had drifted far to starboard. He turned the wheel sharply, then sharper yet until the bow responded. But when he straightened the wheel again as the bow pointed toward the trees, the bow continued a steady arc to port. The boat was heading straight to the nearby beach. He slammed the wheel in the other direction. With a shudder the boat arrested its port circle and started inexorably again in the opposite direction. This time he slacked the wheel before the bow reached the tree clump, but not enough to stop a swing almost as wide. Call for help? He glanced back at voices. Ivan, red-faced and shouting, clutched support as his skiff slammed and bumped sidewise against the stern. Their wake looked like a corkscrew. Back moved the bow with a steady swing and he spun the wheel to meet it.

Jones Henry bounded up the ladder, clutching the rail with one hand and supporting his trousers with the other. A roll of toilet paper trailed behind. His calming grip on the wheel steadied the boat almost instantly. Hank stepped away, panting and humiliated. "I'm sorry."

"Finish your dinner," said Jones without heat.

"Everything okay?" asked Big Steve behind them.

"Couldn't be finer," said Jones. "Here, take over while I finish wiping my ass."

61

Hank remained standing, his back pressed against the rail, eyes on deck. Would they return him to shore?

"You, Hank," said Steve. "Get back here and grab the wheel. Nothing worse than a dumb hand that can't take over."

Steve showed him how to compensate slightly, without the over-reaction he had given. "On the *Billy Two*," murmured Hank, "you had to turn the wheel hard each way to make her move."

"Yeh, well, every boat's different and you don't play 'em the same. Watch your heading." A touch of the wheel was all it needed. Hank's steering became competent within a few minutes.

They rounded a gray gravel spit. One by one a line of tents and shacks came into view, erected on a plain of scrub grass in front of a sharp-sloping mountain. "Village way out here?"

"Summer beach net site. Bunch of hippie families."

Some of the makeshift buildings were painted bright reds and blues. Wash flapped on a line beside a pink tent. Hank attended to his steering, but glanced enough to see men and women lounged around a smoking fire. They wore hip boots and held beer cans. Children and dogs played around them. Their smoke drifted in horizontal streaks, undeterred by the patchy rain.

Hank felt intruded on, possessive of his wilderness. "Damned place for hippies to camp. Why come here?"

"Catch the salmon, same as everybody. With the right tide, you'll see them out there, holding one end of their net to the beach and the other out with a boat, and then pulling it in mostly by hand and sometimes working ass-deep in water. They work hard enough." Steve said it with the calm of a man whom nothing threatened.

"At least they have the right idea between work. I could use a beer myself."

Jones Henry had returned and stood beside them. "You'll never have one on my boat at sea. Boozing's for land and dockside, even beer." He studied the water as he took back the controls. "Last year we made some good sets here, close into shore."

"I remember," said Steve. "Thousand-fish jag."

There were at least a dozen other boats around in the wide mountain-hemmed inlet to which the bay had narrowed. Jones and Steve discussed where they might best set at the tide change without being crowded, as Jones cruised the shoreline squinting at the water.

A humpie jumped in an arc straight ahead. Another followed. Jones bore hard on the throttle to maneuver into position as the others leaped to deck. By the time his hand came down a moment later they were all in position. Steve's mallet hit the release, the pelican hook clattered back as the line separated and the painter sprang free, and the skiff moved off with Ivan paying out his leed. The boat gunned ahead while the skiff pulled the opposite way. Sven guided the purse line so that it ran through the rings without snagging. The seine on the fantail started slipping overboard a layer at a time, the leads clanking and the corks thumping, the web between moving with a hiss. One by one the rings clattered off the bar. Within a minute Ivan was far distant, practically on shore, while hundreds of beadlike corks filled the growing distance between them. On the bridge, Jones pointed the direction he wanted Ivan to steer the skiff, using wide gestures.

Before long the seine was fully in the water, its cork line curving as the boat and skiff each pushed their ends against the current with engines running. Ivan had the skiff nosed practically into the beach. It was the first time Hank had seen the fantail empty. Seaweed and small dead fish covered the deck. Without prompting he found a bucket on a rope, drew seawater from over the side and started sloshing down.

"Plunge!" yelled Jones. "Them buggers are working around."

Steve pulled from against the housing a long pole with a metal cup attached to one end. He rammed the cup into the water between the seine and the boat. It made a loud pop and spewed foam and bubbles as it went down. He kept repeating the process until Hank had finished cleaning, then called him over. "Here's the plunger and you're the plunge man. Take over." On the first try Hank nearly lost the pole as the water in motion pulled it from his hand. He gripped more tightly and put all his energy to the job. He thought he was doing well when Steve said, "You ain't rocking the fish to sleep," and showed him how to pop the cup into the water with a sound like a gunshot. "The idea's to scare them back so they don't swim out in that gap between the seine and the boat. Ivan's plunging on the other end, too."

The taut cork line stretched from the water up over the stern and back to the winch where it was secured. It made a cablelike division down the longitudinal center of the deck. When Jones shifted direction, the line swept across deck with the force of a closing wall. Before Hank learned to watch, it almost eased him overboard as he worked the plunger.

Slowly, during a half-hour period, Jones began nosing the boat toward shore, so that the seine as delineated by the corks formed more and more of a circle. At a signal from Jones, Ivan headed his skiff straight toward the boat with the seine in tow, closing the corks into a circle. He stopped long enough to detach his leed, then delivered a mass of lines joined together by a grouping of shackles. Steve and Sven deftly separated the lines as Steve said on the run: "This here's called a Canadian release that holds 'em together, important as hell. Show you later." It all happened too fast for Hank to follow, but soon Steve and Sven were pulling aboard opposite ends of the purse line, having wrapped them around the winch's revolving drums that Steve called niggerheads. The lines came dripping with jellyfish tentacles.

Jones appeared on deck and took charge, darting like a mosquito from job to job as he operated the winch and shouted directions. They all worked on the run, with Hank helping where they told him. As the unseen purse tightened, the orderly circle of corks disintegrated into a jumble around the bow and stern. Jones showed Hank how to pull the back ones and pile them astern to keep from fouling the screw. Under Jones' direction, Ivan in the skiff held the *Rondelay* off the beach and slowly pulled it clear of the cork jumble. When both ends of the purse line had been winched aboard except for the center bight, the rings all hung together. They brought the rings aboard, and then by means of a messenger line drew the end of the seine up through the wide sheave of the power block suspended above deck.

The seine traveled up through the power block as a thick, dripping snake of web, cork, and lead line. Each cork screeched as it passed over the sheave. Steve and Sven took positions on opposite sides of the fantail and placed Hank between them. Steve drew off the corks and began to stack them in a neat horseshoe pattern, while Sven pulled the lead line free and tossed each ring in turn onto a long bar with the line snaked beneath it. Hank's job was to ensure that the mass of web falling between was distributed evenly back and forth. Steve showed him how to stiffen his hands and bear-paw the web from side to side for speed.

Hank had to work directly under the web. As it descended it covered him with cold seawater and with globs of jellyfish that stung his wrists. He transferred the sting to his face as he wiped sweat from his eyes. "One of the webman's jobs," said Steve smoothly as they worked. "He watches for rips and other shit. Like this." He reached over and pulled a large stone from the web. "Hole!" he called, and Jones stopped the block. He and Jones converged with a needle and in a minute had rewoven several meshes. It went on and on. Hank began to glance at the water, because it seemed certain they should have finished, yet more corks still floated. During a pause to pull loose a small branch, he asked and Jones told him that the seine was 1200 feet long and 250 meshes deep. Up came a thrashing silver fish, its gills hooked in the web. Hank grabbed it out, and felt with sudden excitement its slippery strength.

"Ha, over there!" said Jones. The water was splashing within a circle of corks, and several of the corks bobbed. Sven chuckled unexpectedly. Other single fish began to come in by the gills. The ones Steve identified as humpies were splendid enough, but Hank gave a yell when a dog salmon—twice as big—rose flapping over the block. Agitated dark shapes flitted in the water. As the ragged circle of corks diminished and came closer to the side, the surface of the enclosure started to boil with shapes.

"I judge we'll have to brail," Jones said, grinning.

Steve pounded Hank on the back. "First time this year. Must be the greenhorn."

Ivan now had his skiff alongside the remaining enclosure. He calmly lifted out a dozen huge red-veined jellyfish with his bare hands, indifferent to tentacles that plastered themselves along his thick wrists.

Jones sent Hank to fetch the brailer, a hand net nearly four feet in diameter. He said to Ivan, "I'm sending Hank to help you."

"He ain't ready."

"Teach him."

Ivan chewed on his pipe. "He better not whistle in my skiff." Hank assured him he would not. Ivan held out his hand, scowling. "Don't slip."

Despite the precaution, Hank's foot touched slime on the railing and shot out as he jumped. He grabbed Ivan's arm, which budged as little as a tree limb, and swung aboard.

The others attached the brailer's rim and long handle to support lines, then sent it over. Hank grabbed the rim and helped Ivan push it down through the resisting fish bodies. They churned the water and leaped at his face. As the brailer lifted, its net bulged with the silver fish.

They made four loads and were preparing to take a final one when Jones muttered, "Sven, stow the brailer. Hank, get back aboard. Here comes the *Linda J* and the *Olaf*. Quick!"

Hank had little time to think of the pleasure of having friends discover him aboard before he was bending over the boat side with the others. While Ivan, still in the skiff, gathered remaining corks to keep the fish from leaping out, they dug their fingers into the web and, with a grunt in unison, pulled. The full net below rose slightly. After each heave, they pressed their knees against the web to belay it, then leaned over again. No matter what strength Hank gave, it seemed to require more to raise his share. His long johns had become a soggy mat of sweat beneath his oilskins. Each inch gained was painful. At last, the salmon started slipping over the side against their legs. It happened faster and faster, an avalanche of fish as they gripped the bottom of the bag and heaved it in. Fish slapped around Hank's feet. Their slime covered him, its odor clean and astringent compared to the smells of old fish at the cannery. Silver and gray glints caught in the light as they arched their backs. Some even leaped from the deck. He could feel their force through his boots. "My God, they're beautiful!" he cried.

The others grabbed the salmon by the tails and tossed them through the hatch. It needed a tight grip or the fish would kick and slither away. At one point Jones exclaimed and pointed close to Hank's feet, where a salmon was flapping to freedom through the scupper. Nice try, thought Hank, and slung him grandly in the air and down the opening. He looked up and there was the *Linda J* close by, with Joe Eberhardt and Linda standing together at the wheel. "You sure meet strange people out here."

They recognized him. Linda gave a shriek, and they both started laughing and exclaiming. No moment had ever been pleasanter. Close by on the *Olaf* stood his old friend Tolly, grinning in equal disbelief. Hank bent to stowing the rest of the salmon in the most businesslike way he could muster.

"Say you pulled a decent jag," said Joe.

"Middling," drawled Jones Henry. "You folks been doing good?"

"Oh, can't complain. Looks like they're running close in. You plan to set here again?"

"Pretty soon."

Indeed, as Hank glanced around, he saw that Ivan was already zooming to retrieve the leed, while the others scurried to ready the gear again.

"Guess you pulled two–three hundred pinks in that set," said Joe.

"Mebbe," said Jones vaguely. "Looks is deceiving."

"But, hell," Hank volunteered, full of the pleasure of it, "we brailed four loads before you came."

His crewmates stopped and turned toward him in silence. On Big Steve's pirate face a flash of black anger softened to open-mouthed wonderment. Aboard the *Linda J*, Joe Eberhardt began to guffaw, and on the *Olaf* Tolly gave a whoop that his skipper echoed. Linda's voice rose above it, saying "He didn't know. Now, come on!"

At length Jones Henry said "Oh shit" and began to laugh himself. Neither Sven nor Steve joined him.

Joe Eberhardt varoomed his engine and announced cheerfully, "I'll just lay out downstream from you. See you later, Hank." Off they went, Linda waving. The *Olaf* was already preparing to set just in front of the *Rondelay*.

"Well," said Hank, to get it over. "I fucked up."

"That is correct, my friend," said Jones, still smiling but without humor. "When a fisherman's on to a big haul he don't broadcast it. Why'd you think we hid the brailer? Now we have to wait our turn with that goddam *Olaf* or find ourselves a new place."

"Ja," burst Sven. "Maybe you come fishing to have good time and go back home ven season's over, but we come here to feed our families."

Jones sighed. "Okay, Hank, we've got all the fish stowed, so put the hatch cover down." Hank, trembling, grabbed the cover and was about to replace it when Jones' hand blocked the way. "Now, call it superstition or not. But a fisherman never puts his hatch cover upside down, unless he wants the rest of the boat to follow."

"You'd better put me ashore before I really screw something," Hank murmured.

"Not that simple this far from any place. We're stuck with you, and vice versa. So you'd better learn, and blubbering about it won't help." Jones then softened it by saying, "You're doing all right. Just pay attention." It lifted the weight.

Hank drew a breath, and looked around for work. He grabbed a bucket and sloshed the gurry from deck. When he glanced at Steve and Sven, they had no anger left on their faces. Soon they made another set, and he was plunging again, a job he knew. He rubbed his wrists. The sting at least made him feel he'd pulled his own with the web. Around him the mountains throbbed with green. Purple shadows flickered along the water, and birds dipped past. They said he'd brought them luck. All those salmon flapping over his legs, going to happen over and over. He'd make it. If that play crowd back on the beach could see him! He started to whistle exuberantly.

It happened fast. Steve tossed a line around his leg and threw him overboard, lifting him as effortlessly as a single fish. The water was so cold that he could feel his testicles crawl. The weight of his filled boots and clothes under oilskins was startling—his legs dragged down, and all he could do was flail. Steve hauled in the line, grabbed his leg, and pulled him back to deck like a crab, sprawling and dripping, then patted his head.

"If you don't have extra boots or nothing, take the extras by my bunk. Move your ass, we got a set to finish." And he and Sven jumped to the business of receiving Ivan's skiff.

No more was said, and Hank took it in stride. They made three more sets, the final one in the dark. Ivan never left his skiff. The minute they secured its bow, Jones headed back to the beach and gave the signal to set again. No haul repeated the abundance of the first, but each time the fish poured over them after putting their backs to the final heave, Hank experienced the same thrill. On the final set the web pulled up lightly. At first Hank thought his muscles had settled in. The bag lifted with nothing but seaweed and jellyfish. "Fuckin' waterhaul," muttered Jones. "We'll call it a day."

"Goddam," Hank exclaimed. "After all our work!"

"Vell," Sven said mildly, "God sure didn't promise fish every time."

When the skiff was safely secured, Ivan strode past them straight to the cabin without a word. Jones gave the boat full throttle, and spray began to kick around the sides. Hank's legs were heavy just to lift. Maybe open the sleeping bag, maybe find that much energy before crawling in.

"Get to the dishes from lunch, Hank. Shake it! I got dinner coming."

"Oh. Sure, Sven." The sweet odors of a roast filled the living space. All that showed of Ivan were two huge dirty socks sticking from the shadow of his bunk. There were no shortcuts to washing dishes on the *Rondelay*. The only fresh water came by pumping a handle that kept slipping its screw, and hot water had to be heated on the stove in competition with Sven's pots. Moreover, he could use only a trickle for the big soapy dishes since the boat carried a small tank. It made luxury of the washtubs at the Kodiak beanery.

"So, how you like svimming in dis vater?" Hank laughed, grateful to have it become a mere joke. Sven sang a Norwegian song in a high voice that penetrated over the engine noise. Evidently singing and whistling were not the same. Hank's clothes from the dunking hung over the stove. The dungarees and flannel shirt were still wet. The rest had disappeared. He looked around, fearing Sven might have slung them outside or in a corner, and found them folded dry on his bunk.

Hank had just wiped the last dish when the engine slowed. Ivan in one grunting motion slid upright into his boots and went on deck. "Better hurry put on your rain gear," said Sven.

"Aren't we through for the night?"

"Get out here, Hank!" yelled Steve.

In the dark they approached a cluster of masts and lights that shimmered in the water. The night was vast except for this patch. "Here, pump the bilge," said Steve. Hank dutifully took over a long pipe handle as Steve and Ivan coiled mooring lines to throw from the bow and stern. The fish bilge slurped up with a sharp stench. Ahead, mast and deck lights separated from the mass as they came closer, but the dark spaces between still made it hard to define individual boats. Around the center climbed one man in a plaid shirt and watch cap, another in a red T-shirt.

A large brailer of fish rose in the air, stayed suspended for a few seconds, then swung over and dropped out of sight.

"Put your fenders to starboard," called Jones.

The main vessel was bargelike, with square housing aft and a long foredeck fenced by boards. "She's built like the *Billy Two*," said Hank.

"Then I guess it is the *Billy Two*."

Hank strained to see faces he recognized. There stood Spitz outside the wheelhouse operating the controls, his white hair and tight-set mouth recognizable even in the shadowed lights. Beside him stood the captain's girlfriend.

"Hey, where's Nick?" he called to the red-bearded man who received their lines.

"Quit. I took his place. Don't I know you?"

"Your voice is familiar but the light's bad. My name's Hank Crawford."

"Well, shit, man, I'm Pete Jorgenson. You didn't think I was going to wash dishes back in that beanery all my life?"

Hank leaped over to shake his hand and pound his back.

To unload, he joined Steve and Ivan in the cramped hold among the fish. ("Cook don't have to pitch fish," as Sven had said.) He knew the rancid green odor from the cannery, but it surprised him that the beautiful salmon should have acquired it so soon. Their bodies were now hard and stiff, and the silver had disappeared. A brailer lowered through the hatch as they backed against the sides of the hold to avoid being hit.

"Okay," said Pete with authority, "we'll take 'em about two hundred at a time, and make sure you separate out the dogs."

For once Hank knew what he was about. From experience in the cannery bins he slung the dead fish by their tails into the brailer as fast as the others, tossing an occasional dog salmon aside as he worked, and counting as he went. He strained to be the first to load his quota of seventy-five, but even though he was the only one racing they beat him each by at least eight fish. For the final loads, Hank crawled on all fours into the slippery corners under the deck boards and pushed out the fish with his hands and feet.

With the salmon gone, several inches of gurry still sloshed around their feet, and red clots of it clung to the sides. Sven handed down a pressure hose from the tender. They first scrubbed the hold until the white enamel walls shone clean, while the bilge pump sucked the mess away. Then they climbed back on deck to hose and scrub each other.

Pete, standing by the high boards on the tender that enclosed the fish, watched Hank with detachment. When Hank finished he sauntered over. The two looked each other up and down, grinning.

"Guess you like slopping in that muck," said Pete.

"You must go ants, doing nothing but counting other people's fish on that little gadget."

"Getting paid overtime right now just to stand around and talk to you. Got a stateroom to myself, and you've never seen such grub."

"If you ever miss not being on a real boat with a bow and stern, come visit us."

"That one of those putt-putts where you dip your ass over the side to shit?"

Sven sent Hank to the tender's cook to fetch some groceries he had ordered. Hank remembered well the big galley and the array of pies with oozing berries. Spitz recognized him, but said without interest "Turned fisherman, eh?"

"Yup. And I'm grateful for the things you bothered to teach me in that wheelhouse."

"Help yourself to pie."

Hank in leaving passed around the flat stern of the tender, where there were toilets and showers for the fishing-boat crews. He wanted to use both, but not after Pete's cracks about the *Rondelay*. Pete threw off their lines, and the two friends exchanged final insults as the black water stretched between them.

After a few minutes' cruising, Jones anchored the *Rondelay* with the *Billy II* in sight. It was past one-thirty in the morning when they sat on their bunks around the engine cover and speared into the roast. With the engine off, there was no sound except the click of forks and the mouse-roar of the stove. Hank was reaching for thirds of the meat when Ivan declared: "He don't steer zigzag from the plate to the pot, all right."

"Hawl!" said Sven. "Ve almost lost Ivan in de loop-de-loops. Hank tink he give you a fun ride, eh?"

"Going to put one of them megaphones around his neck so he can broadcast a little louder what we catch," said Jones.

Hank smiled and continued chewing. No place in the world

would he rather be. When Sven produced a peach upside-down cake in his honor he knew it again.

He was not used to stuffing himself and then going to sleep immediately like a bear or dog. By the time he had finished the dishes the others were merely heads and feet in the shadows of their bunks, their clothes folded on the engine cover, their boots peeled down and lined by the stove to dry. Better face the bathroom arrangement and get it over. Outside in a light drizzle he lowered his pants and grasped the railing. In the distance he watched the haloed lights of the *Billy II*. She was moving out, taking the fish he had caught back to Swede Scorden's cannery, where twenty-four hours ago he had slept in a dull bed dreaming dreams. Goddam this was good. Goddam! Why would you ever want to be anything but a fisherman? As he thought about it, he even liked this way of taking a crap, straight into the water.

His bunk was practically on the deck, with only a two-foot clearance beneath Steve's sagging mattress above. To enter, he had to brace his elbows on the deck and first slither his feet in, then the rest. However he turned, one side of him pressed into the curve of the bow. The water lapped quietly against the hull, an inch away. Inside, the air was close with fish and sweat. Somebody began to snore. It rose in a choking crescendo, then mercifully sputtered and subsided into heavy breathing. He heard the tattoo of rain on the housing, and again the persistent lapping of water an inch away. Beautiful.

6

THE FATED
SALMON

Hank dreams his dreams, and the *Rondelay* rides gently at anchor in a summer harbor. Underneath, in the world that fishermen invade with nets, pots, and hooks but never see except through the ravaged tatters they bring to the surface, swim the salmon.

It would be sentimental, and dangerous to the economy, to humanize a species of fish. Yet the salmon, by its fight and strength when hooked, by the beauty of its colors and by its flavor in the pan, is among lower creatures at least one of the most respected by man.

The Pacific salmon bears—rather, has had imposed on it by Nature—an aura of tragic destiny. A cruel instinct drives this creature in from the ocean at spawning time, then goads it to beat upstream against all odds and pain, to reach again the identical area it swam as a fresh-hatched fingerling years before, there to lay and fertilize its eggs, and die.

As with humans, some Pacific salmon have it tougher than others. Those whose karma it is to be hatched in the gravel of the upper Yukon River must fight their way from the ocean, where they have lived, back against two thousand miles of swift-flowing water. Columbia River salmon make at least a thousand-mile return through the connecting Snake and Salmon rivers of Idaho. What other creature has the cosmic tuning to perform so specific a final act?

To the salmon's peculiar instinct is applied the word *anadromous*, a term that derives from the Greek for "running up." According to one dictionary, it means those fish "which spawn in fresh or estuarine waters . . . and which migrate to ocean waters." Other anadromous fish include steelhead, smelt, green sturgeon, and Atlantic salmon, but all of these return to the sea after spawning, while Pacific salmon die.

The life cycle of Pacific salmon spans two to seven years, depending on species and location. It starts with the egg and ends with the parents who deposit and fertilize the egg. The parents' adult lives have been spent in the sea. Both the beginning and end occur in the fresh running water of a stream or river.

To start, with her tail and body the female digs a nest, or redd, in the gravel of the stream bed and deposits several hundred eggs at a time, then covers the hole with the talus of the next she digs. The male twitches and darts alongside, guarding against predators and other males. During the actual spawning process both move close together, and their mutual body vibrations release eggs and sperm simultaneously. Neither parent has been able to eat since leaving the sea to enter fresh water. They have beaten themselves to the popped-stuffing consistency of rag dolls. After their final mission they simply float with the current. Within hours or at most days, both are dead. Their bodies provide food for other creatures, including those their offspring will eat in turn.

The protected eggs winter in the gravel of the stream bed. They hatch in 120 to 180 days, depending on water temperature, into big-eyed larvae or alevins. These are nourished from the attached yolk of their birth egg. Weeks later, in early spring, they struggle up from the gravel as fry (or fingerlings), still big-eyed but shaped like fish. As the fry swim in free water they feed voraciously on plankton and small insects. In the process they become smolts, fully formed little salmon ready to enter the sea.

The time span of development differs greatly among the species of Pacific salmon. The pink or humpback becomes a smolt and goes to salt water within a day of hatching, while the red or sockeye first goes to a lake and takes as much as two years for the same process. Most of a salmon's life is spent in the ocean, where it travels, feeds, and grows. The pink operates on an exact cycle that returns it to its birth stream just two years after being deposited as an egg; the sockeye spends two to four years in the ocean. The king or chinook's cycle takes up to seven years. The longer the span, the larger the salmon at maturity, with pinks about four pounds, sockeyes seven or eight, and kings twelve to forty or more pounds. Whatever their annual timetable, all salmon smolts

74

enter the sea during late spring and return to spawn in summer or early fall.

During their life at sea the various species of salmon are generally silver, with bodies shaped smoothly like bullets. The return to fresh water changes them. The males develop hooked snouts (making it easier to defend their nests but impossible for them to take food) and humped backs, the hump in the case of pinks being pronounced enough to earn the subname humpbacks or "humpies." The digestive system degenerates and stops functioning. The bright silver turns to mottled browns, blacks, and greens except in the case of sockeyes. These transform most dramatically of all, to a glowing magenta with dark green around the mouth. From a human viewpoint the spawning fish become inedible: the meat turns watery and loses flavor, along with the appetizing pink and red colors, as the fish draws on his stored oils and minerals for nourishment in place of food. The bears who station themselves in the stream mouths to scoop the massed fish with their paws appear not to mind.

Fishing boats harvest salmon during that period in summer, just before spawning, when the fish leave open sea and travel the waterways that lead back to their destined rivers or streams. Year after year each race of salmon swims the same migration pattern (even though as individuals they travel the route only once), following the contours of bays and capes, moving with the tides. They even keep the same time schedule as their parents, with runs predictable almost to the day no matter how far they must travel to meet the appointment.

The ocean course of salmon is hidden to humans, who can only tag them as smolts and then chart their migrations through the random hauls of research nets. Their trips homeward along the shorelines are visible to a well-tuned skipper as finners, jumpers, and various ripples. When they reach the streams for their upward struggle, they may keep their mystery intact but their privacy is over. The sight is one of Nature's great ones. Remember that freshwater streams composed of springs, rain, and snowmelt flow downhill from mountain to ocean. In salmon country you will see a falls of white-churned water tumbling several feet to break with hammer force over rocks. Suddenly black fish shapes emerge within the white. Their tails wriggle but they are otherwise stationary, heads up, as the water pours over them; they are actually swimming fast enough to hold their own against the flow. Occasionally they leap into free air and re-enter the falls a foot or more higher. If the water force crashes them to the rocks they start again. Over and over they move against the force until they make it to the top and can rest exhausted in one of the backwashes of the falls before continuing.

The term *salmon* is used ambiguously to cover all three members of the biological family Salmonidae: trout, genus *Salmo*; char, genus *Salvelinus*; and Pacific salmon, genus *Oncorhynchus* (Greek for "hooked nose"). The three have in common an exclusive natural habitat in the northern part of the Northern Hemisphere. All bear a family resemblance—sturdy, rounded, muscular, spirited fish—while differing in fin and scale structure as well as some habits. For example, the legitimately celebrated "salmon" of Nova Scotia and Newfoundland are actually trout, as are other Atlantic salmon. They follow the same anadromous cycle as their Pacific relatives but do not habitually die after laying eggs, often surviving for three or four separate spawnings. The Pacific salmon, genus *Oncorhynchus*, occurs only in the North Pacific Ocean. The five species in American waters are *Oncorhynchus nerka,* the sockeye or red; *O. gorbuscha,* the pink or humpback; *O. tschawytscha,* the chinook or king; *O. keta,* the chum or dog; and *O. kisutch,* the coho or silver. These five also occur on the Asian side of the Pacific along with one other, *O. masu.*

North American runs of Pacific salmon are shared by northern California, Oregon, Washington, British Columbia, and Alaska, while Japan and Russia are the main Asian beneficiaries. The salmon spawn in thousands and thousands of streams and larger waterways that flow from the mountains to the sea along the entire rugged Pacific coast. The greatest American abundance is in Alaska, where the coastline is as uneven as an ink blot on porous paper and every spur and cove represent the mouth of at least one stream. Hardly any part of coastal Alaska lacks salmon. They even run in the streams of the far Aleutian Islands and in the rivers of the lower Chukchi Sea above the Arctic Circle. On Kodiak Island alone there are some forty salmon-breeding rivers and three hundred streams. The largest individual salmon waterways of North America are the Columbia River that separates Oregon and Washington, Puget Sound in Washington, the Skagit and Fraser rivers of British Columbia, Bristol Bay off the Bering Sea in Alaska, and the Kuskokwim and Yukon rivers of far-northern Alaska.

The only predictable factors in salmon fishing are the general part of the year during which each species runs and the two-year cycle of pinks. Not all species swim all waters, nor do all groups of a species school simultaneously. Some streams have two and three individual runs of, say, sockeyes or pinks; some rivers have separate runs of each species in its time. In the Kodiak area, sockeyes run in June, pinks in July and August, chums (locally called dogs) in mid-August, and cohos (silvers) in September. The Bristol Bay sockeyes appear in early July. Off Ketchikan, the kings begin running in May, the cohos in August.

Nets in the overlap periods can be counted on to yield a mixture. A Kodiak purse seine in early August may pull about 75 percent pinks, 20 percent chums, and 5 percent sockeyes and cohos.

The different salmon have distinguishing characteristics by which fishermen and cannerymen tell them apart. Hank, sorting fish in the hold, won't need his college education to identify the thick, mottled chums, which are twice as big as the clear pinks. But to cull from the pinks the incidental sockeyes and cohos, especially if they are small, will be quite beyond him at first in the bare-bulb shadows. Among a fisherman's guidelines: Male chums have big teeth and plierlike snouts, male pinks have more pronounced humps (although all mature male salmon share these characteristics to some extent). The tail fins of pinks are spotted; the others' are striped. Chum tail fins have milky stripes. Sockeyes have similar stripes on a darker tail with thin lines of silver that sparkle at some angles. A chum's tail is more tapered and a pink's scales are smaller than those of the others. Only a king's lower inside mouth is black. Chums and cohos have larger eyes than sockeyes and kings. The inside gills of a sockeye are reddish, those of the others white. A coho's fins are frequently (but not always) tinted with orange. There are large, dark regular spots on the back of a pink, small ones on a coho, irregular ones on a king (including his dorsal fin), none on a sockeye or chum. But don't stake your life on any of the above. The characteristics are not always that pronounced with the fish in hand. As soon as a novice memorizes a rule and begins to apply it, his seniors will generously shower him with exceptions. Then, one day, if he commits himself to the profession, he will suddenly find that instinct has taken over, and he will wonder how he could ever have failed to tell the salmon apart.

The water performance of the different salmon also varies. A line fisherman knows whether he has a king or a coho before either surfaces, because a king characteristically makes a first strike at the bait (which he mistakes for a live fish) to stun it. A hooked coho leaps from the water, while a king is more likely to sound. Neither of these two large salmon nor sockeyes play on top of the water while swimming free, as do the finning and jumping pinks and chums. As noted by Jones Henry, a jumping pink arcs straight out of the water and down again, while a chum jumps a narrower angle and flaps his tail once or twice. But again, don't count on any of it.

Man as sophisticated predator likes to elevate his kill of exceptionally spirited creatures. It helps explain his blood lust. For years Ernest Hemingway had us convinced that a bull's bravest calling is to participate in the corrida, where he is mutilated into a furious state and then murdered by a courageous and graceful man in costume. I used to buy that. But it is no longer so clear to me that the hunted creature, whose odds of getting away are about one in five hundred, and odds of escaping unmaimed even less, shares the mystical communion. Nevertheless, I remain guilty of loving to catch salmon. And I feel an affinity for the doomed creatures as I bring them in either as individuals on a hook or in the abundance of a seine. My own rationalization is that they are part of my food chain. After all, by eating hamburger I silently consent to the trussing and slitting of steer, so why not the fishing of salmon on their way to inevitable death? I can still work to prevent the depletion of a wild stock through overharvest, and I can still hate the slaughter of creatures for entertainment on whatever mystic level. But Nature made me a carnivore, just as she gave bears and eagles the taste for salmon and gave salmon the instinct to feed on herring. I am a predator once removed from the jungle, and so are you.

The natives of the Pacific Northwest had no more compunction about living off salmon than did the bears. The Haida and Tlingit tribes which occupied (and still do in diminished numbers) the river-cut coasts from present Vancouver to present Yakutat had cultures based on salmon fishing rather than hunting. If the runs fell off, the tribe migrated to a new set of waterways and sometimes starved before finding new grounds. The oils in chinooks and cohos made them perfect for smoking, and the lack of oil made chums equally good for sun drying. (Chum salmon acquired their second name because they were dried to feed dog

78

teams.) Both methods permitted the storage of a food supply throughout the winter and also the accumulation of fish as the property that sometimes led to extravagant potlatches. Farther north, the salmon was prized by the Aleuts and Koniags and the Eskimos who inhabited western Alaska from Kodiak and the Aleutians up past the Yukon River and the Arctic Circle. The splendid fish sustained tribes along river systems far from the coast. The Lewis and Clark expedition in 1805 stumbled starving from the Rockies into the Snake River country of present Idaho, and would have made it no closer to the Pacific had it not been for the dried salmon of the Nez Percé Indians.

The first white men to think in terms of salmon were the Russian fur traders who in the eighteenth century began to sail from Siberia. In 1785 a group of Alexander Shelikof's men wintered on lower Kodiak Island by the Karluk River, and here began a Russian traffic in salt salmon. In the late 1820s the Hudson's Bay Company began exporting salt salmon from the Columbia River, and soon other commercial salteries were established in Puget Sound and the Fraser River. The site of the first salmon cannery was the Sacramento River, in the 1850s. After the Civil War the pioneer of this enterprise, William Hume, moved north to the Columbia River. Others followed, establishing scores of canneries progressively northward as each river became overfished. By 1901 there were seventy canneries along the Canadian coast that separates Washington from Alaska. In Alaska itself, the first cannery opened in 1878. For two decades starting in 1882, the Karluk River on Kodiak Island had such huge runs of sockeyes that it supported one of the largest fish-cannery complexes ever built.

The farther north and into the wilderness the salmon entrepreneurs went, the wilder was the life of following the salmon. The money was sometimes big. A few cannerymen made fortunes. More went bust. The men who caught the fish and those who cleaned them survived from season to season, a rough lot living in a world of bull work, small expectations, and extravagant steam-letting. Whether the history and mythology of the salmon fisheries is yet recognized outside Alaska as part of the American saga equal to the railroad push, the gold rushes, and the Pony Express, and whether or not it produced a Paul Bunyan or a John Henry, it was still a hairy time, a legendary time.

Rudy Anich, a man in his sixties who still fishes the salmon in

Kodiak waters, recalled his salad days in the nineteen-thirties when he fished both Puget Sound and Kodiak. He spoke slowly and gracefully as he steered his seiner *Naknek Made* from the Kodiak boat harbor to the fuel pier. "Well," he said, "from all the gripping and pulling web with your hands, your fingers would be locked tight each morning. Couldn't open them, couldn't hold a thing. We learned from the old-timers to urinate on our hands, and that would start them moving. Whether it was the warmth or something else, I don't know, but it helped the pain and started them opening. Your thumb and forefinger would open first, you'd start gripping with those. But oh, pulling that raw Manila! Men would cry in the morning as they hooked their claws around the cold rope to haul the anchor. And of course there was no refrigeration. If the cannery tender brought us meat, we'd have to scrape the mold and maggots off it. You'd make a stew and she'd be white with maggots." Part of a boat's regular dried stores would be quantities of raisins. The boat crews would keep five fifty-gallon cans going with a fermentation process to produce raisinjack. "We'd drink it with each meal, gallons of it, about eighteen percent alcohol. Keep us drunker than a skunk. That way we kept working, and didn't feel the work so bad. But, young kids were so strong from pulling those enormous nets by hand! At one time, I could do pushups on one hand balanced by two fingers, keep doing them easy as breathing. I remember one kid, Murphy, weighed only a hundred forty pounds, he'd eat fifty pancakes at one sitting. I don't mean little ones. We'd all shovel in the food like that whenever we stopped long enough to eat. You'd burn it off soon enough."

Hank toughs it a bit for a youth of the sixties and seventies. He follows the pace of his crewmates to exhaustion, and he faces the primal wind and water. But technology eases his way. His boots and rain gear, thanks to chemistry, are less likely to stink, stiffen, remain clammy, or crack apart than those of past fishermen he never knew, so that he is warmer and drier than ever they were. He does not have to row his skiff when making a set. His engine, being diesel, will not explode in his face and burn his boat from under him. Radio gives him a voice to people beyond the wilderness, and aircraft the means to reach him in the event of emergency. (Disaster, of course, still leaves him on his own.) The nets he pulls are made of synthetic fabrics that weigh less than cotton web, both of themselves and because they do not absorb water.

He even no longer must dry his net to keep it from rotting. And, above all, to bring the tons of net and fish aboard during each set, he need not use his arms and back for every inch of the way: a hydraulic power block does the heaviest pulling for him. This development, invented by a fisherman named Mario Puretic, was introduced to the salmon fleets in 1955 and perfected by 1958. It might be the single most important development in fishing since the contrivance of the first net many years B.C., freeing fishermen from being beasts of burden just as the tractor freed farmers.

The fish business has never been a sure thing, even now with the wisdom of biologists. Salmon may return to the stream of their hatching, and they may follow a mystically predictable route around this cape or that point. But where they go as adults in the great ocean remains their secret. Therefore mainly unknown are those creatures, currents, temperatures, and food supplies which act together to decimate or preserve them. Biologists can predict through valid pragmatic devices, and canneries can tool for big or small seasons, but it all depends on what comes into the boats. Fishermen must still wait for their salmon at the gateways, never knowing for sure whether the season will be one of feast or of famine until they haul their nets and lines from beneath the surface.

7

HANG
TOUGH

Aᴜɢᴜsᴛ was nearly over, and they had found only a couple of brailer sets since the one of Hank's initiation. They now ate hamburger or fish rather than roasts. True, on most days they delivered four or five hundred fish to the tender (one day only thirty) at forty-four cents each for pinks and seventy-five each for the chums, which were twice as big. However, with the division of proceeds into 11-percent crew shares and with the cost of fuel and supplies, Jones was mainly breaking even, and nobody had made an adequate winter stake. "Have to fuckin' longshore next winter to pay the booze," Ivan grumbled.

Jones was a man of calm demeanor except in the heat of a set, but the strain began to show on his face. After all, his was the investment and the mortgages. At the end of each thin week, as the allotted weeks of the season diminished, he looked older, partly from the grayness of his stubble as it grew out before the Saturday shave but also from the hours of squinting and straining for the sight of fish. Jones did not like to waste his men or other resources, so his habit was to search, even for hours, until he saw sure signs of fish, rather than to set on the mere chance of fish as many other skippers did. Now, however, they all became restless if the search took too long, so that they sometimes persuaded him to set in areas of previous good hauls, regardless. It seldom produced enough fish to reward their effort.

Mid-August brought fogs and blows. There were days when the mountains might have been plains for all they saw as they worked the nets, times when the wind penetrated Hank's oilskins and every pullover he could find. The others worked without ever altering their basic clothes. For a few days the sky opened and the sun beat down, while the temperature rose gradually from fifty to seventy-five. Hank found the heat exhilarating. He stripped to his back and reveled in the prickle of sunburn. The others acted like old men, remaining dressed as before. They in fact only changed if a garment started to rot from gurry or to tear apart. During the first weeks on the grounds Hank's own sour odor bothered him at night, especially as it drifted from his long johns. But by the second week the smell was barely noticeable. He had also settled in so well that he no longer even thought of whistling.

When Hank helped Steve mend web, Steve sometimes handed him the needle, even when it slowed the work and produced less perfect meshes. He took tricks at the wheel whenever Jones Henry wanted to duck below, and nobody needed to monitor. Sven was glad to teach him things on deck, although he was as possessive of his stove as Ivan was of his skiff. After a while, Ivan consented to let him join the skiff as second man. This opened an entire new literature of duties. He learned to work the leed while Ivan handled the tiller, and to help maneuver the skiff in a tight place by the way he threw his weight on the taut cork line. However, Ivan never relinquished the steering or other skilled jobs, and Hank's major skiff duty was plunging. He liked the skiff. Sometimes seals and otters swam close, and they saw more of the shore than aboard the boat, although whenever they came close to land blankets of mosquitoes descended.

His favorite part of the skiff job came when they brought back the encircled net. He heaved the line to Steve, then leaped back aboard the *Rondelay* with split-second timing, often while both vessels were in violent motion and geysers of spray shot up between them. As soon as he touched deck he hustled with the others to rig the two purse lines and speed them aboard before the fish panicked out. He could work the winch himself if Jones was occupied, and, after weeks of practice, could coil the hundreds of feet of a purse line at high speed without fouling it into twists and "assholes." Then, when they finished stacking the seine and hauling the catch, he leaped back into the skiff to help Ivan recover the leed. Eventually, in calm weather, with many cautions and instructions, Ivan began to let him bring the skiff back home, even to the delicate maneuver of nosing the bow into the stern of the *Rondelay* for tie-down. All in all, he was becoming an equal hand among them.

Thus with all his duties, which seemed to continue after the others had finished theirs, Hank started to chafe at washing the dishes and all Sven's greasy pots under the miserable cold-water pump. Before he came aboard the others had taken turns. At first he tried random grumbles. Finally, once when they had all fished especially hard and he had pulled his weight without question, he declared after eating that he figured it was somebody else's turn. Jones Henry replied without hesitation that cleanup was his job until somebody greener yet, heaven forbid, signed aboard the *Rondelay*.

A few other things went wrong also. There were days when they called jokes back and forth, then days, especially close to the end of the week as the season wore on, when they snarled at each other over petty things. Jones sometimes shouted when they moved too slowly, sometimes almost screamed. It surprised Hank that Big Steve, particularly, took it. He himself had little choice. As the excitement of fishing on the *Rondelay* became routine, Hank wished for occasional privacy. On a day too stormy to fish, there was not even room to stretch without knocking a bunk or a shoulder. At night, Steve and Ivan snored like hogs.

And Ivan, who slept head-in directly across from him with feet no more than two yards from his face, had feet that stank above any other odor in the cabin. Hank decided to be cool about it: one weekend at the cannery store he bought three new pairs of socks and left them on Ivan's bunk.

Ivan placed them on the engine cover when he crawled in to sleep, obviously assuming they belonged to someone else. So Hank presented them to him. "I *got* socks," said Ivan, looking up from his bunk with the innocence of a man at peace. Hank made a joke of it as he explained the reason. He might better have made a filthy suggestion. Slowly, Ivan put on his boots and went outside. Hank turned to the others, but Steve frowned reproachfully, and both Sven and Jones looked away. Hank went on deck in the dark. Ivan was standing in his skiff with arms folded. He gave no answer to Hank's awkward apology.

After this, Hank ceased to exist for Ivan: he stood in the skiff, hands dangling, as Ivan assumed all the jobs himself. If he started to work the plunger, Ivan removed it from his hands as impersonally as he would have picked it from the rack, and if he hauled on the leed his hands would be flicked off like the jellyfish.

84

It grew worse. Once, as the others gathered around Jones Henry at the wheel to search out jumpers, Hank joined them in time to hear Ivan declare in his deep voice: "Let a sissy college kid aboard and next thing, everybody takes baths instead of catches fish!"

That night, as Hank scrubbed the hold with Steve after delivering the fish, he asked what he could do.

Steve took the question seriously, lowering the pressure hose as he pondered. "Well, you got contacts at the cannery. Old Ivan, he likes Demarrara, that's the black rum. But don't give him none unless I'm around. You never shoot a bear with a BB gun."

Their normal weekend routine started with offloading to the tender, followed by a long scrubdown with disinfectant of all the boards in the hold, then a personal shower and shave aboard the tender. (Only Steve and Hank let their beards grow. The others accumulated a week's stubble as an expedient and were glad to be rid of it.) They ate and slept as they traveled through the inlets, and tied to the cannery floats by Saturday afternoon. After performing any repairs necessary to the engine, seine, skiff, or whatever, they spent the evening visiting back and forth between the boats. Hank still had Elsie, who clung to his arm as they partied from deck to deck. The Sunday routine: stock groceries, take fuel, return to the grounds in late afternoon, anchor, eat, sleep until about first light, seine in the water by the six o'clock opening, and start a new week of fishing.

That Saturday, Hank found his Demarrara, after a long search by many words of mouth, in one of the Filipino bunkhouses. Two bottles cost him thirty dollars apiece.

Ivan examined the labels and held one of the bottles to the light. "What you do, stuff socks inside?"

"Open the fucker and pass it around," said Steve.

With only two bottles among them it wasn't much of a drunk as such things go, but it took Ivan through the necessary phases. By the end of the first bottle his dark silence toward Hank had ended, replaced by an angry roar. "Som' bitch, if a man ain't free to wear his feet like he wants, ain't free to keep a *man's* feet"—the huge hand banged on the engine cover—"then kids who don't like it can piss off the boat and go live with the goddam women who keep their feet in *buckets of water!*" Hank tried to explain, but Jones winked and shook his head. As Ivan's fists began to emphasize his words, Big Steve shifted casually to place himself between Ivan and Hank. The support filled Hank with gratitude. He endured the tirade, which enumerated his every mistake aboard the *Rondelay,* including the loss once of a dozen forty-four-cent humpies ("five hundred sockeye fuckers worth two dollars apiece," as Ivan put it), and the hours each of them had sacrificed to teach him what little he knew.

At length Ivan stopped. His brown-leather face became peaceful as he uncorked the second bottle, sniffed it, took a long slug, and passed it to Hank.

"That kid's sure on your shit list," said Steve, returning to his bunk.

Ivan shrugged. "Kid works hard enough when he ain't talking."

And it was over. Later they were all asleep as usual, with Steve and Ivan snoring loudly, and Ivan's feet dangling comfortably not far from Hank's face.

The *Rondelay* slept that night, and other Saturday nights at the cannery, tied deck to deck within a visible community. The community, while remaining nests of individuals the like of which the clock-punching world has never seen, was no less bound to each other while scattered on the grounds. Every man in it was as eager to make his winter stake as those on the *Rondelay,* and he grabbed what he could. But within the apparent anarchy of the fish business he followed the rules. Rule one, of course, was to render assistance to a boat in trouble, friend or enemy. Twice, to Hank's impatience until he understood, they had stopped fishing, once to hoist the stern of the *Teddy Ann's* skiff so that the two men aboard could laboriously free a fouled net from their screw, once to tow the *Fraser Bay* several miles to a cannery in another inlet. One day, however, when he was in the skiff with Ivan, their engine died and a strong northwesterly started gusting them toward a rock. Ivan set Hank to rowing and fending off with an oar while he frantically tore into the engine. Hank could smell the kelp churning on the rocks a few feet away, could hear the roar as if he were a rock in the surf himself.

"Want a line?" called Sonny from the skiff of the *Olaf* as he appeared alongside.

"Wouldn't mind," said Ivan.

The community had other rules. Once, tied deck to deck at the cannery floats, Hank grabbed a bucket to wash the remains of a silver he had just cleaned and, in his hurry to get ashore where he saw Elsie waiting, he left the bucket in the middle of the deck. The others had gone visiting. Men were already walking from boat to boat to get ashore, and the *Rondelay* had taken its place as a piece of the boardwalk. Hours later, in the black, foggy morning, Hank stood on the pier above the floats, turning the machine-shop key in his pocket and giving his last thought to Elsie for another week. The boats below were mostly silent, although sounds of an accordion and raw Norwegian singing came from one. A man staggered a slow course over the decks, across the *Rondelay*. Suddenly he fell with a clatter and roared in pain. By the time Hank arrived, jumping from cabintop to cabintop to make better time, Jones and Steve in their underwear were pulling the bucket from the man's foot as he writhed, cursed, and spat blood. Angry rough voices followed Hank's wake, one demanding a fight for having his head stomped overhead. The victim was Oslo Johnny from the *Helga*. He had sprained his ankle and cut his mouth on the hatch cover as he fell. Steve and Jones helped him to his boat, then returned to lay it on Hank. Did he need a map for every way he could fuck up? When you tied boat to boat you kept clear decks. And, in case he didn't know, you never jumped onto cabintops—it was noisy enough to have people stomping across your deck at night, let alone the boards over your head.

As for Oslo Johnny, whom Hank agonized that he had deprived of a livelihood for the season, he limped glumly across the decks next afternoon carrying a box of groceries. His lip was scabbed and swollen. Letcher John from the *Goodluck* commented on it, and Oslo answered vaguely, "Must have been some fellow hooked me, damn if I remember."

A fisherman might have his obligations to the community, but they did not include sharing his fish. A few of the skippers worked together—men who in the winter lived side by side in Kodiak or in places below like Anacortes and Bellingham—and these would exchange discreet prearranged signals if they fell on a good run. But either as pairs or individuals, the boats hid their fortunes as best they could. Hank had learned early never to point if he saw a jumper. When boats visited alongside, Jones lied cheerfully about the fish in their hold, increasing the number on a bad day and drastically diminishing them on a good one. (The numbers might become common property for anyone lounging around the *Billy II* during the nightly delivery and tally, but each day was its own affair.)

Jones, on the other hand, spent considerable energy trying to figure the catches of others. If they were fishing a poor run and another boat appeared to be hauling them in, he was no better than others in the way he raced to lay out his seine before the lucky boat could claim the next set. The danger of sharing a good run was apparent enough. If several boats converged on the same territory, they had to take turns, since simultaneous sets would only snag all the seines together.

Sometimes a boat jumped his turn, and the boat whose turn had been usurped felt honor-bound to cork him: set in the current ahead of his net to block off any flow of fish. This happened especially as the season progressed with thin results.

One day on the *Rondelay* Jones discovered a run of chums after two hours of patient cruising. They were heaving a good jag as Jones maneuvered the *Rondelay* to block the view to other boats. Over started the *Linda J* just as they sneaked up a brail load. Quickly they rushed up a second brail, then stowed the brailer out of sight as they kicked the fish into the hold and strapped up the rest. The play failed to deceive Joe Eberhardt, who circled them once, his ruddy face beaming behind his frizzled hair, and then laid out his seine exactly where they hoped he would not. Joe's fishing partner, Chip Hansen of the *Olaf,* started across the bay toward them.

Cursing and sweating, the *Rondelay* crew readied their gear again. Jones throttled to the one remaining spot. It was a race with the *Olaf,* and both boats were kicking spray to make it first. The *Rondelay* made it by twenty seconds. But the *Olaf* started setting before she arrived, reversing the usual procedure by leaving her skiff stationary and laying the seine toward the beach with the more powerful main boat.

Jones Henry was furious. To make it worse, three jumpers leapt in quick succession. Hank watched with the others, his head pounding with their shared outrage. There was his old cannery friend, Tolly Smith, the bastard, his gold earring glinting from the deck as he grinned while plunging *Rondelay* fish into the *Olaf*'s net.

"Goddam it, stand by to cork that son of a bitch!" cried Jones, and no crew of John Paul Jones ever hustled to battle stations with greater will.

88

They set exactly along the enemy net, no more than five yards away, to include the jumpers, and then roundhauled—brought the seine full circle immediately. Hank had never seen Ivan handle the skiff with such speed and delicacy. Nor had he ever seen Ivan more animated, laughing and cursing, with Hank included in all of it. Their skiff practically sideswiped the *Olaf*. The *Olaf* crew on the deck above shouted vituperations and flung out their fists. Tolly's face was so dark with anger that his cut scars glowed.

The *Rondelay* did indeed grab the fish. Their haul required the brailer and produced the best catch in many days. The *Olaf* waited a half hour to purse, and then, as the *Rondelay* crew watched through binoculars from a distance, brought in virtually nothing.

"Ha, that fuckin' Chip Hansen," crowed Ivan hoarsely as he danced like a boxer, "you shoulda seen the popeyes on that halfbreed bastard's face when we corked, *wasn't* it, Hank?"

"You're breed yourself," said Jones easily.

Ivan turned serious. "Some Aleut and plenty Russian and American, sure, but who ever heard of Aleut and Norwegian and ten other things besides? Chip, he don't even go to Orthodox church no more."

That afternoon they delivered early to the *Billy II*, treating themselves to a rest instead of scratching in heavy tide. Spitz called down from the controls that it was the best haul any boat had brought all week. To celebrate, Steve and Sven decided to take midweek showers. Jones, after entering the tally in his record book, sauntered to the tender's wheelhouse, where the captain and his girlfriend held continuous open house for skippers alone.

Hank joined his friend Pete. They laughed over the corking as they sat with their backs against the boards of the fish bin, stroking their beards and smoking the pipes they had both adopted. Fine drizzle softened the mountains, and puffs of vapor lingered on the tops, while birds made black ripples that moved lazily across the calm water.

"Made your winter stake?" asked Pete.

"Not by half. What about you?"

"Shee-it. For living high in Seattle? I'll probably end up back in the woods near Spokane, busting my ass setting chokers where my old man works."

Hank glanced at the rich clumps of spruce trees along the mountains. "Logging doesn't sound like a bad life."

"Hank, buddy, you talk like a jerk. You've got college, and then the rest of your life in some office, so all this dirty-hands stuff one summer tastes like candy."

Hank pondered the truth of it, and the desires he could barely trust which might make it not true.

An outboard skiff came alongside with two men and a girl. Hank recognized them from the beach net camp, especially the older man by his red flannel shirt and battered felt hat. They looked scruffy even by his own present standards, with hip boots torn at the top and holes in everything they wore, including their raincoats. The lusterless salmon around their feet sloshed like logs in the bilgewater.

"How many you got today, Sut?" asked Pete as he rose and took their line.

"Hundred seventy-three dogs, forty-eight pinks, three reds, and a silver," said the older man in a deep, comfortable voice as he stepped from the skiff. "Load 'em up, kids."

"Right, Sut."

Hank had never met him, but Sut said, "Corked the *Olaf*, eh?"

"We got there first."

"So you did, and served 'em right." The statement relieved Hank. He introduced himself, and learned that Sut lived all year at the site, in the largest of the seemingly makeshift structures back near the mountain. Half his workers were married in one way or another and came back year after year. Others were just kids who drifted from places like Frisco. If they got themselves as far as Kodiak, Sut staked them to the flight over against wages. "Only the regulars get shares, but she's a good life, requires hard work now and then, plenty of nature in between. Drop in. Always a bottle open."

Behind Sut's skiff arrived another with Hank's friends Dan and Mrs. Hatcher. He hurried to catch their line, then to give his hand to Mrs. Hatcher, who, despite her rain gear and fishy boots, could step from a bouncing skiff with dignified agility. He had now chatted with them several times as Jones pulled alongside their site in passing. "Good day, Dan?"

"Running slow, Hank, I don't know. Wish these chums'd look sharper."

Hank slipped into the skiff to help Dan unload, although Dan insisted he was doing fine. Hank's admiration for the Hatchers had grown steadily. After the Elsies had come and gone, he wondered if he himself would be lucky enough to find a partner as true to his own life.

"Corked the *Olaf*, did you? Rough bunch."

"News travels." Hank remembered Tolly's dark anger. He tried to be casual. "When boats cork, do crews ever fight?"

"Oh . . . Young fellows like to stretch their muscles. But fishermen don't like to bust their hands during the season, so you don't have no rule."

The rigging of a fish boat glided up on the other side of the tender. It was the *Olaf*. The whole crew stared grimly at the *Rondelay*. Hank caught Tolly's eye and nodded, but received no acknowledgment. He went up to the wheelhouse, where Jones, Sut, and the Hatchers were sharing a bottle with the captain and his girl.

"Want something?" asked the captain.

"Just to tell my skipper the *Olaf*'s in."

"That so?" said Jones calmly. "Wait for me."

Hank paced in the galley and watched below. The *Rondelay* and *Olaf* were tied on opposite sides of the central fish bin. All the *Olaf* crew stood on their deck together. Ivan on the *Rondelay* deck smoked his pipe as he absently hit his fist into his big hand. Steve and Sven were just coming aboard from their shower, wearing their same heavy gray undershirts. The muscles of their arms and shoulders bulged beneath. Should he sneak somewhere and do exercises, to be in better shape for whatever came?

Jones left the wheelhouse and started below. Hank fell in behind. "Where you think you're going?"

"I'm part of the crew."

"You stay here, and that's an order."

Hank returned to the galley, humiliated. He might have been afraid to fight, but now he wanted to desperately. There from the *Rondelay* sauntered his crewmates, following Jones around the fish bin to the *Olaf*.

91

Both crews stood with arms folded, apart from their skippers. Chip Hansen, florid and beefy, stepped to the tender alongside the wiry Jones. The tender's brailing operation had stopped, and Pete stood watching. It started with angry gestures from Hansen. Jones, his cap pulled close as usual and the week's gray stubble outlining the rest of his face, barely moved. The *Rondelay* had one man less than the *Olaf*. Hank decided that when it started he would join, whatever Jones had said.

Nothing further happened. Jones and Hansen, their faces hard, returned to their own boats. The *Olaf* crew climbed into their hold, and soon a brailer full of salmon swayed up under Pete's direction to be emptied on top those of the Hatchers, Sut, and the *Rondelay*.

Next evening, as the *Rondelay* delivered a puny load after a day of virtual waterhauls with tons of kelp and stingers, Peter said to Hank: "You've got a cool skipper, man. He took no shit."

The following day was equally as bad. At last Jones managed to encircle what appeared to be a smart jag of chums, and all their moods improved. Suddenly a dark shape rose within the purse, and a tan snout emerged holding a salmon. "Fuckin' sea lions!" roared Ivan. Jones rushed inside to pull a rifle from over his bunk and came out loading cartridges. The tan snout had already tossed the first fish in the air with a half-moon bite taken from it and held another as it dove. The sleek brown body seemed as huge as a submarine. To Hank the sea lion appeared a joyful creature as he tossed the salmon. He asked Steve if Jones really meant to shoot it, or just scare it away. The answer was garbled with anger.

Jones held aim and waited until the sea lion's head appeared. The first shot kicked the water, the second hit. The heavy lumbering motion continued, and another bitten salmon sailed into the air. Jones shot again and reloaded quickly. The creature reared, then struggled toward the far edge of the corks. The men fell silent. "Jump the corks, you bastard," muttered Jones, and fired. Instead, the sea lion disappeared, and the corks began to bounce and pull under violently. Sven and Steve groaned, and Ivan shouted a steady stream of curses. Jones stood erect with the spot in his sights. When the sea lion rose it received another round. It sounded in a new area and the corks went wild. Jones' face flushed dark red.

When it was over, all the salmon that were not floating mutilated had escaped through the holes the sea lion had ripped through the seine, while the sea lion carcass remained for them to disentangle. It took more than an hour. The bristly warmth of the freshly dead creature bothered Hank. But when he saw their net ripped like fisted cobwebs, and as he sat with the others at anchor, taking turns for the next thirty hours mending web while other boats fished around them, he freely joined the others in their hatred.

The fishing grew worse rather than better. When boats pulled alongside each other and skippers chatted back and forth, they talked glumly of nothing else. Some of the boats left to try other bays but drifted back to report the fishing uniformly slow. Many boats hosed their nets, stowed them in the scrubbed fish hold, and headed home.

Jones Henry intended to fish king crab later in the year, and he began to talk of calling the salmon quits and going to Kodiak to ready his pots and crab block. Hank listened with trepidation. It would be the end of the season for him, since crab boats operated with four, including the skipper. He wasn't ready to go. He began to wander the *Rondelay* and, when no one watched, to pat its boards and rigging. When he left he'd be forgotten, and the fishing cycles would continue as in the years past.

With the scarcity, other tenders than the *Billy II* appeared in the bay, flying the green pennant that proclaimed them in the market for fish. "Cash buyers," Jones called them, and his eye wandered to them more and more. One had a canvas sideband with the message in block letters: PINKS *80¢ apiece*—DOGS *$1.20:* a price nearly double that Jones had contracted to receive from Swede Scorden. The whole crew became restless when another cash buyer appeared and the rumor passed from boat to boat that he was paying 83 and 1.30 and throwing in free beer and beef roasts besides.

On the final morning of the week, Jones laid their slack-tide set in deep black water near a rock bluff that had yielded them nothing so far but which he remembered for late-season luck in years past. One netload brought up some five hundred dogs and a few pinks, and the next load another three hundred. After that the run stopped, although they set twice again.

The new cash buyer on the scene had selected a cove well shielded from view of the main bay and any eyes on the *Billy II*. Jones took two hours to meander to the site. The man who was cool in facing down a fistfight suddenly became nervous. They made an unnecessary set in sight of the *Billy II*, one that yielded them only kelp. Then, while Ivan ran the skiff slowly to gather the leed, they ducked at full speed into the cash buyer's cove as Steve and Hank leaped into the hold to make ready. Under Steve's direction they threw a few dogs and pinks into a separate bin for the *Billy II*, then bent their backs to filling the brailer when it lowered. Hank had no time to see the faces of the men aboard the cash buyer until they were headed away again, dumping buckets of water over each other to remove the telltale gurry.

"Hank!" called a woman's voice.

He looked up to see Jody, the waitress from the Kodiak beanery, waving from the cash buyer's deck. All her sour reserve was gone. She was snuggled against one of the men he remembered from the Kodiak bars—a big, mustached guy with sleepy eyes—and she was smiling. He waved back cautiously, not sure whether in some way he might be betraying their position, but flattered that she remembered him, and in sight of his crewmates at that.

They pulled the skiff astern within sight again of the *Billy II*, fifteen minutes after they had left. Jones cruised the *Rondelay* to the opposite shore. In the cabin he counted out a roll of bills. Hank's share was nearly a hundred dollars. Sven put the free roast in the oven, and they covered the two six-packs in one of the bunks for sometime at dock.

"Is it that bad to sell to a cash buyer?" asked Hank of Steve as they drew in the purse lines of their next set.

Steve stood straight and stared ahead as he said, "Skipper probably gets a bonus at the year-end that ain't our business if he delivers exclusive to Swede, and he might lose it if Swede catches him selling outside. Any number of ways Swede might fuck him, use it against Jones next contract time, maybe not renew if there's too many boats. Swede's tender looks out for us over the season the way you couldn't expect from a cash buyer, and he guarantees to take your fish. You'd know what that means when there's good runs like last year and boats lined up waiting to sell before their fish goes bad, and canneries limited on how much they'll buy to pack through their lines."

"Well, look, who do the cash buyers deliver to?"

"Other canneries. You think Swede Scorden don't run his own cash buyers to other bays? Sure, paying money he'd never give his regular boats, to steal fish from under somebody else's nose." Steve laughed easily. "Shit, there's more to catching fish than hauling them in. You'll never see me a skipper."

That weekend the Alaska Department of Fish & Game announced an unexpected opening in a bay across Shelikof Strait on the mainland. It was to last forty-two hours, from six Monday morning to midnight Tuesday. The bulletin came down to the boats tied at the cannery dock on Sunday morning, and the frenzies of departure started at once. Hank, carrying a heavy box of groceries, waited twice to reach the *Rondelay* as boats slipped under each other's mooring lines to leave. The excitement caught him easily. He had seen the same spits and bluffs day after day, and now they were headed for the great snow-capped mountains that dominated the far horizon.

Since a northwester was building and they would kick into it to cross the Shelikof, the boats traveled in convoys of two and three. The *Rondelay* teamed with the *Linda J* and the *Olaf*—no visible angers remained from the corking incident. They began to pitch a half mile before the mouth of the bay, with white-capped water visible beyond the bar. Hank helped the others tie fast everything in sight. They entered Shelikof Strait and the boat went wild. It leapt into the air, then pounded back into the water with a shuddering thud. Waves rolled toward them, then split over the bow with sheets of spray. Hank stayed on deck enjoying his first time in heavy seas. He had worried that he might not see any.

"Come inside. We don't have time to fish you back aboard," called Steve, and made Hank join the others inside. Jones steered from the cabin wheel. When the bow plunged, bubbling seas shot over the window to obliterate their view. Ivan smoked his pipe as usual, and Jones had a cigar in his mouth. The smoke, the engine fumes, the motion —suddenly Hank rushed to the door and vomited as the others laughed. After a month aboard! He explained over and over how he'd felt sick since yesterday, until he himself began to believe it as nausea took over and he rushed for the door again.

Sven tapped him on the shoulder and said sympathetically in his singsong Norwegian accent, "Here, Hank, I got a present to make you feel better." He handed him a hideous piece of fat attached to a string. "You svallow it, den pull it back up easy and grease the tunnel." Hank tossed it into the sea as the others roared.

For a while the mountains ahead loomed white and spectacular. Then they gradually disappeared beneath closer mountains of gray rock. The nearer they came under the lee of the other side, the less the wind blew, until they entered the new bay in relative calm. There were grassy spits on either side. Hank, who had begun to think himself doomed to indefinite misery, recovered with an alacrity he could hardly believe. The farther they moved into the bay, the milkier green the water turned. "That's what melts from the glaciers," said Jones, and in fact they could see a blue-shadowed cliff of ice in the distance.

There were at least seventy other boats crowded in the small bay, with more arriving all the time. Hank counted as they cruised among them: ones he knew and dozens he had never seen before, passing so close that he could converse in a speaking voice with other crews. They glided by the cash buyer, and he said hi to Jody. Boat to boat they were the oldest of friends. She was cook, and told him to come over for dinner some time. They circled the *Olaf,* and Tolly with his dark gypsy grin said, "Nice blister. Introduce me, buddy." Hank's returning grin was noncommittal. He had begun to wonder about his own chances with Jody.

He barely noted the water-slaps around him until he saw others peering over the side. Salmon jumped everywhere—big chums. He started shouting, to Steve who stood nearby, to himself. Unbelievable! The water churned with their green-and-silver bodies. The others took it calmly. Except for Jones at the wheel, they were soon in their bunks asleep even though it was only afternoon. Hank sat alongside, chortling at the fish, as Jones steered a zigzag course in search of an area he might call his own while talking to other skippers and cursing the number of boats. "The State ought to license only boats owned and fished by Alaskans. More'n half these boats come from down in Puget Sound and Columbia River and that's where they belong."

Hank found sleeping difficult that night at anchor. Salmon thumped against the boat a few inches from his head. What if they all had disappeared by morning? When he woke before five in the dark as the others moved around him, Sven had already made the coffee and was juggling pans of eggs, ham, and flapjacks. They ate heaping plates in silence, far more than on other mornings. When Hank asked only for his usual portion Sven shook his head, and Steve said, "Eat while you got it."

The morning was sluggish and gray, with a cold drizzle. A full fifteen minutes before six the men in all the boats stood in position, like an army at the ready. Jones and Ivan conferred on the maneuvering of the skiff, but there was very little sound except the steady slap of fish. On a Fish & Game boat a man raised a pistol and began to fire. The skiffs —more than a hundred now—churned into the fish with their seines.

They roundhauled. Thus each encirclement took only a few minutes. Then they pursed with all their might. Sometimes it was not fast enough, and the dog salmon sounded out the bottom. Other times they had to brail, and the big dogs poured and slapped over them. As soon as they emptied each moneybag they set instantly again. Through the day, rain blowing, other decks close enough to shout back and forth (mostly warnings to stay clear), they set and hauled. Their first work-break came at three in the afternoon, when they lined up to unload on the *Billy II*, which had followed the fleet. Spitz signaled them alongside, forcing other boats not contracted to Swede Scorden to make way, and they lost so little time there was none for rest and barely enough to gobble some cold pork and beans from open cans.

They only went to the tender when fish had filled the hold and were scattered so high on deck that they slipped and fell over them. The second delivery came after midnight and eighteen hours' straight fishing. Hank's hands, which he thought were toughened completely, had torn open in sores and cuts. He was shivering and groggy, and the hard touch of the net had become agony. As he emerged from the hold with gurry dripping even from his eyes, having just pitched over two thousand eight-pound fish by the tails, he asked Steve when they were going to rest.

"This is our winter grubstake," Steve said roughly.

Hank's hands emerged with fresh pain from the thick nubbled gloves he had worn to heave salmon. Some of the frayed skin had scabbed against the lining and then torn loose. He glanced up at the tender where Pete stood wearily, counting fish by pressing his gadget. For once Hank would have traded places.

97

"Here," said Steve, and set a bucket of fresh-drawn seawater to one side. "Soak your hands in this whenever you can."

Jones raced back to the grounds and they set again at once. The loads were diminishing, and the fish no longer jumped in the water, but they still pulled more fish every few hours than in any previous week. Long before, they had eaten all their candy bars and apples and salted peanuts, and finished the cases of soft drinks. Sven ducked into the galley long enough to make coffee and to open more cans. When food came in any form they wolfed it down.

The rain grew heavier at the start of the second morning. Hank occasionally cried from pain and fatigue, without shame, while continuing to work. Other than renewing his bucket of seawater, nobody acknowledged his misery. If he lagged, Steve or Jones told him to shake his ass. All their voices were hoarse. When their net snagged with that of the *Linda J* even Hank shouted vicious accusations across the water. By the time they delivered their fourth load, around noon, after thirty hours, Hank had entered a phase of numbness.

"Okay," said Jones, his face haggard, "I figure we've made our winter stake, and I see boats pulled over and given up. I ain't pushing anybody further. It's up to you boys whether we hang tough or get some sleep. Another twelve hours of opening, so we could mebbe snooze a couple hours, then go back to it."

"Nah," said Sven, "ve lay down, nobody gets up. How many times you get fishing like this?"

"Has to be everybody at this point," said Jones.

They glanced at Hank, who had his hands in the salt water. "We'd better hang tough," said Hank.

"Good," said the others, and back they all went to the nets.

8

SPITZ THE
PROPHET

BY THE final count from the two-day opening, they had made their winter stakes and then some. As did most of the other boats, they delivered their final load, scrubbed the hold, anchored, and slept for an entire day.

None of the *Rondelay* crew cared to scratch-fish any more back on Kodiak Island. Next day they found a cove out of sight of Fish & Game and Jones and Steve went hunting with Hank in tow. They walked through marshes and over rocks, saw the glacier, and watched bears from a distance. That night the smell of deer blood and carcass dominated the *Rondelay* deck. Hank marveled at the glinting knives the others handled so expertly. He had not thought of them as total outdoorsmen. As for shooting off season, Jones observed: "Those rules are for rich fellows who fly in with a guide. We're taking meat for the table, and if that ain't why the Lord put it there, you tell me."

On the third morning, with Shelikof Strait calm and sun catching the ripples, they returned to the cannery. The atmosphere had changed. On the high pier, crews draped their seines to dry before stowing them. A skiffload of shouting men and duffle glided to a pontoon plane, and soon the plane roared across the water and lifted over the green mountains. On an inner float, several boats bobbed together like dead things, their skiffs battened to the bare deck where the seine had been and the cabin doors padlocked. Hank felt a pang to find the *Linda J* among them.

The mood of departure caught them all. Jones noted a northeasterly breeze and declared the salmon would disappear anyhow until

99

it stopped. "Let's get to town and tie one on," said Steve. "I'm ready for a three-day piece of ass." Within the hour they were hosing the seine. Hank handled the web and corks lovingly. Unbelievable that a few days before he'd had his fill. While Jones completed paperwork at the office, Hank wandered the cannery to say farewells. Elsie had quit and gone home. Cutch the foreman grabbed his arm in passing. "Too bad you didn't stay. I'd have you running your own machine by now." On one of the boardwalks, Swede Scorden stopped long enough to growl, to Hank's shock: "Tell your skipper I'll overlook his selling to a cash buyer one time, but not again." Audrey still stapled boxes. "They give your job back?" she asked. "That's too bad. Maybe next year."

The *Billy II* was tied to the fuel pier. On the stern Spitz and Pete were reeling in small fish. "Guess you guys *do* get jealous of real fishermen," said Hank expansively, "but can't you do better than that?"

Spitz for once was relaxed. "As for these, my fisherman friend—nations have risen and collapsed on herring, and wars have been fought. The rich afford salmon, but herring feeds whole populations. Come back when I've fixed some, and you'll taste the fish of the ages."

"Not for me when there's meat around," said Pete. "I'm catching mine for crab bait."

Hank said he'd try herring any time, but they were leaving.

"Hey, we're headed for Kodiak ourselves," said Pete. "Swede's sending over the fish he can't handle from the big opening. We're just waiting for the captain."

"I'll kiss the ground," declared Spitz, "when I pay off from this so-called captain and his Cindy. Some men spend their lives around the water and know all the information, yet have no more sea sense than a horse behind a plow."

"Ah, Spitz, you're pissed because they ride your cooking."

Spitz ignored Pete. He threw his herring into a heavy tub that was half full and started away with it, obviously a stronger man than he appeared. "I'm going to brine these, Norwegian-style," he said to Hank. "Incidentally, you can tell your skipper that according to my tabs he was one of our highliners for the season."

After Spitz had left, Pete said: "That guy's a pain. Captain told me he put a boat on the rocks a few years ago and lost a man, and that's what's spooked him. It's a fuckin' circus. Spitz bitches to everybody else, but when they're face to face the captain raises his voice and Spitz backs down."

"Yeah. You hear that, you slob? I'm a highliner."

On the way to tell his crewmates, he found his source and bought three bottles of black Demarrara, at a ten-dollar closeout price. They received the news and the rum with equal glee. Ivan immediately opened one bottle and passed it around, then rubbed his knuckles into Hank's scalp. "Ha, you highliner kid, you a rich fisherman now, hah?"

Sven was singing in Norwegian at the top of his voice. As soon as they reached Kodiak he would fly home to his wife.

Jones looked at a red streak in the otherwise clear sky and predicted bad weather. "I'd had us going through Whale Pass on noontime slack tomorrow, but mebbe we ought to go all night to make early-morning slack, get through while we can."

"Whatever you say, boss," said Steve expansively. They all swigged once more from the bottle, corked it, and started clearing the gear for storage.

The *Olaf* came alongside. Hank secured the line that Tolly threw him. Tolly had obviously tapped his own source of booze. His eyes were red and half-lidded. "Grabbed all the fish, eh? And now you're running home."

"Hope you guys did well on the mainland."

Tolly's rough face was sullen. "We always do good when some son of a bitch don't cork us."

Hank tried to alter the subject. "Ass-buster over there, wasn't she?"

"Ass-buster?" Tolly mocked. "When you're a fuckin' fish thief you better stop with big-fisherman talk."

"Get your fuckin' story straight," barked Hank. "*Our* skipper found those grounds, and you came like sharks when you saw us brailing. You couldn't find your own fuckin' fish in an *ocean* of jumpers!"

Tolly leapt across the gunwales and grabbed. Hank swung. Like hitting a post, and a chest blow landed him on deck. He felt sick and dizzy as he gathered his legs and raced into another of Tolly's fists. From deck again he saw a swirl of his own crewmates mixing with those from the *Olaf*. Steve swung on Tolly. Ivan and Chip Hansen roared into each other as if a rubber band pulled them, while Jones and Sven squared off on the others. But it was five from the *Olaf* and only four of his own without him. The extra man had joined Tolly's defense against Steve. Hank wobbled to his feet, waited a moment to think it through, then ducked in beneath the prevailing fists to slam Tolly in the gut. In a moment he himself crashed to deck again with teeth through his lip, but Tolly now sprawled alongside. They punched at each other automatically, like crabs in a mating dance, until Steve pulled them apart.

The fight subsided as quickly as it had erupted. Hank and Tolly sat on the deck and spat blood as they counted their teeth, while others paced and cleared their heads. Ivan and Chip, both bleeding and still erect, continued insulting each other. By the time Swede Scorden appeared to order them off his float, another bottle of rum was open and passing the rounds of both crews.

"Where'd you get that booze?" Swede looked accusingly at Hank. "Better not be from my people."

"Help yourself," said Jones.

Still scowling, Swede swigged from the bottle and handed it back. "If you're through fishing, get back to Kodiak. Have a safe trip and I'll see you next year."

Shortly they were underway, singing and joking about the fight as they dabbed antiseptic on each other's cuts. They stopped at an abandoned saltery to hang their seine for the winter with many others, then ate as they continued out of the bay. By nightfall Steve, Ivan, and Sven were asleep. Jones had only nipped from the bottle. He stayed on the bridge under the clear night sky. Hank brought mugs of coffee and settled beside him.

The mountain shapes slipped by. A harbor buoy flashed, and Jones altered course to steer close between two islands. The spruce smell drifted over them. Above the engine throb Hank could hear some creature squawking as they passed close to land.

"Jones? Will you call me next year if your other guy doesn't come back?"

"Glad to."

Hank rocked back and forth, smiling to himself.

They entered Shelikof Strait to a gentle roll. A large orange moon, nearly full, was rising, and its light pecked at the crest of the small swells. Other boats traveled with them. Jones chatted with a few over the radiophone, easy bantering conversations about runs and gear and relative luck.

"You sober?" asked Jones.

"Yes. I only had a couple of swallows."

"And your head ain't joggled from that fellow's fist?"

"I feel just great."

"Take your watch for two hours, then, and I'll get some sleep." Jones gave him exact course instructions. "But if you see anything you can't account for, stop the engine and I'll be here before your hand's off the stick. If the land fogs up, call me. I'll hand you more coffee."

Hank had taken the wheel often, but never underway at night while the others slept. Nor had Jones ever waited on him. The white moon blazed on the water and outlined the black mountains. The world was incredible, just incredible!

The radiophone crackled with the conversations of other boats. Somewhere in front of them rode the *Billy II*, which must have slipped away shortly after Hank left. And behind followed the *Olaf*—Jones had actually swapped jokes with Chip about the fight.

"Yeah, *Billy Two*, this is *Teddy Ann*, do you have parts on board for a number three—" Static obliterated the rest.

"*Teddy Ann*, this is *Billy Two*. Can't hear you, switch to the next channel, okay." More static followed. A few minutes later, the captain of the *Billy II* was back chatting when he interrupted himself to say, "Sky's dark ahead, looks like a squall coming." A few minutes later, the voice announced, "Got a thundering bastard of a squall."

Hank could see for himself the approaching clouds. Land was distant on all sides, but he decided to take no chances. He thumped on the deck, and in a few seconds Jones stood by his elbow.

The wind had already begun to increase. Moonlight at their back silvered the edge of a tangible blackness that raced toward them, erasing mountains and shoreline along the corridor of the Strait. "Shit," said Jones, "I said she might squall, but I didn't figure it this soon or I'd have stayed back in the bay. Bucking this we don't make Whale Pass by early slack." Hank fetched their oilskins. They watched the squall move over them like a huge hand: first came the wind with iodine seasmells, then isolated drops as hard and big as raisins, suddenly a torrent of rain. Behind them the white moon still glowed intact, but as he

103

watched, layer upon layer of rain obscured it like veils until it disappeared.

The rain was so thick around them that it reflected back the running lights like a close wall. Jones slowed and started blasting their whistle at intervals.

"Never saw rain like this," shouted Hank admiringly.

"She's a dumper. You want to listen to the way our whistle travels. If the sound bounces back, you're close to something. Want to listen for other boats, too, because you ain't going to see them." Jones switched his controls to the cabin and left Hank on watch. Around one in the morning, Steve relieved him and insisted he go in. By then the pleasure of a lonely watch in the rain had grown thin, and Hank was glad to oblige. He fell asleep quickly despite the activity of Jones at the wheel between the two sides of bunks, the light on the chart spread across the engine cover, and the crackling voices on the radio.

When he awoke it was daylight of sorts—a gray half-light sliced by rain. The boat had a steady, heavy pitch that creaked the woodwork over his head. From his bunk he gazed through the open door as the line of the stern rose against the sky, then plunged with a thud that made everything shudder. After each thud, the stern scudded sidewise and seas washed over the deck, while the horizon tilted. Then the stern shot up again with sickening speed. The water itself, seen only on the plunge, was turbulent and sluggish, with green-brown swells that had a dirty white foam on top. He closed his eyes, feeling sick, then opened them again, unable to keep from watching.

Around ten in the morning they tied alongside the anchored *Billy II* in the lee of Whale Island. It was difficult to believe the calmness. Within sight of the cove where they lay flowed the whirlpool currents of Whale Pass. A few other fishing boats were also standing off, apparently waiting for slack.

Pete received the *Rondelay*'s lines from Hank with a crack about their slowness, and the captain waved from the pilothouse for Jones to come join him. It was like neighbors encountering each other in far places.

"Who'll have some fresh salt herring?" asked Spitz, as they all settled in the warmth of the tender's big galley.

"Give my friend Hank some," said Pete magnanimously. The

herring had a sweet, rich, stinking-fishy flavor that Hank could at least abide. He pretended to savor it, with his eye on the berry pies as soon as he had earned them, and bugged Pete by asking for seconds.

Spitz watched with approval. A while later he called Hank outside to show him the current through Whale Pass. From the raised deck, they could see a long stretch of the turbulent water. "She's on max ebb right now," Spitz declared quietly. "Take a look if you ever want to see devil's water."

With the proximity binoculars gave, the water had the primitive drive of a thunderstorm. It flowed in glistening ribs, broken by whirlpools but never diverted. As Hank watched a huge log floated from the straits they had just traversed, entered the current and suddenly accelerated to four times its original speed, then was sucked under and disappeared. He whistled appreciatively.

"What did you expect?" said Spitz with satisfaction. "You've got Kupreanof Strait, where you just came from, on one side and all of Marmot Bay on the other, connected by a pinhole at Whale Pass where millions of tons of water have to shoot through at each tide change. Nothing surprising about the force. It's what happens out of sight that bothers you. Think about it. Nature moves the tides on such a regular clock with the moon that anybody with an adding machine can tally it for a century in advance, and we publish it in tide and current tables. But then, my friend, Nature exercises her prerogative of chaos over the symmetry. You can't predict her all the way. You can say, uh-oh, northeasterly front building five hundred miles away, she'll do this and that, to judge by past experience. But you'll never know for sure until it's hit, till it's happened and over."

"Not necessarily chaos when we can't figure it."

"Maybe," said Spitz reasonably, "but it'll do for chaos. Where's that log now, the one you watched suck under? Is it bumping along the bottom a few feet from where it disappeared, did it pass safely to be floating free now out in Marmot Bay, or has it been splintered into five thousand pieces and redistributed? It's already happened, yet we'll never know." After a pause, Spitz said in a low voice, "I'll admit it, that chaos water scares me like none other. It has forces beyond the hope of human control."

An hour or more passed in conversation and with the reading of comic and girlie books at the long galley table. Sputters of radio dialogue came from the pilothouse, where the two skippers were visiting. The engineer passed through, announcing that he had fixed the trouble that had made them miss the previous slack. This brought out the captain. "Okay. We're getting underway," he announced.

Spitz looked sharply at the clock. "It's another two and a half hours to next slack."

"The marine forecast says this little northeasterly's going to make into a gale, and I plan to get through before it starts blocking the mouth of the pass."

Spitz grabbed his binoculars and peered at the current. "We're only an hour past maximum ebb. You can see it still running."

The captain ignored him and said to Jones, "I wouldn't run ahead of slack like this on a dark night in a storm, but shit, we've got visibility. If I holed up in a cove as many times as the wind blew"—he winked— "I'd still be nothing but a cook or a deckhand."

The jab reached Spitz. His face reddened.

"Sam, rev her up. Pete, haul anchor. Away we go." The two nodded and left, without question. "You boys on the *Rondelay* can trail us."

"I reckon we'll wait a bit," said Jones.

"Suit yourself. This scow's got a real horse of an engine, and that makes a difference."

"But she maneuvers like a barn," snapped Spitz.

The captain winked again at Jones. "Depends on who's behind the wheel."

"Jones," said Spitz, "look at the current yourself and tell this numb-nut it's still ebbing too strong."

"It ain't my judgment."

The engines started, their vibration shivering through the boat. "I'll tell you guys how it's blowing on the other side of the pass," said the captain, his voice tighter than before. "You can just stand by your radio."

"We'll do that. Mebbe see you in Kodiak tonight."

"Might not. You could still be here."

Spitz was sweating. "With that northeaster blowing since last night it doesn't have to make into a gale. You could already have a tide

106

rip a dozen feet high waiting at the other end of the pass, one this cur-rent'll slam you into head-on."

"I've handled through some seas before, Mr. Spitz. I've never piled a boat on the rocks, like you have."

"Then take it from me," Spitz cried, "it's not worth the chance!"

"In these waters, you don't survive if you don't take chances. Now that's the end of the argument." The captain started back toward his wheelhouse. "But, Spitz, if you want to snivel aboard the *Rondelay* I can get on without you."

Spitz stared, his thin mouth working, his fists clenched.

"You're welcome to ride with us," Jones said calmly in passing. They boarded the *Rondelay* and waited, but Spitz did not appear. Pete threw them their lines, laughing. "I'll tell you," he said to Hank, "we never need TV up here with those two swiping at each other. Hope your putt-putt boat makes it through before winter."

Jones started their engine and trailed the *Billy II* as far as possible without leaving the sheltered water. They had a partial vista of the pass. The current no longer appeared to streak with the same intensity. Other boats around were still laying off.

"Are they really taking a chance?" asked Hank, settling beside Jones on the bridge.

"Ah, no more than most."

"Then why don't you go through?"

"I'm never in that much of a hurry. This boat's got to see me into old age."

The *Billy II* moved slowly around the spit. With its square red housing and blunt ends it resembled a boxcar on a barge.

"She's a solid old workhorse; that power scow got a sturdy en-gine," said Jones. The *Billy II* delivered a lively series of whistle blasts and Jones tooted back. A waving of arms followed between the two skip-pers. "Yep, I've known John there about ten years. He ain't the best and he ain't the worst."

Spitz opened the galley door and leaned on the rail, looking down at the water. The captain's voice came up on the radiophone. "Yeah, *Rondelay*, better trail on behind, she looks calm and cool, okay."

"*Billy Two*, read her out for me on the other side."

"Will that, *Rondelay*, will that. Oh boy, we're entering the old roller coaster." They could see the *Billy II* dip forward, then start to move two or three times as fast while its stern scudded sideways. "Ah, *Rondelay,* you don't get these fun rides when you play it with the slack." A pause. "I'd judge this current's still as much as seven knots. And I'm doing another three or four minimum just to keep way. Be through here in less than ten minutes. *What* a ride! Little tricky, so I've got the wheel and Cindy's holding the mike up to my mouth. I'll play radio announcer. Ever go down a big ski slope, Jones, and get to moving so fast in the middle you asked yourself what the . . . ? Little tricky here. Just feel that bastard kick." He laughed. "Like some kind of Loch Ness monster kicking us around from underneath. Yeah, bet you didn't know I was a slim, trim skier in my younger days, out at Snoqualmie. Girls still find I can . . . *Jeez,* a little tricky."

Jones had edged the *Rondelay* out as close as he dared, and they were all watching. Their vista included a grass-covered island with a buoy riding nearby. The *Billy II* darted past so close it looked like they might have clipped the buoy, which the current pulled sideways.

"Current wanted to take me right over there. She's . . . uh . . . still a little strong."

"He should have taken Koniuji Islet wider than that, and he knows it," said Jones quietly.

"Maybe he ought to come back," said Hank.

"He can't. Even if he had power to buck against seven knots of current, no boat could turn in that channel without being smashed on the rocks. He's got to see it through."

The radio voice resumed after a long pause, this time more soberly. "Well, friends, here we are back with Lowell Thomas, shooting Niagara in a barrel." Pause. "She's a little rough, little hard to control. We'll make it easy, but . . . Here, hold that mike steady, honey."

Pete'll have some ride to bullshit about, thought Hank enviously.

The *Billy II,* hazy from more than a mile away, glided from sight behind the rocks and trees of Whale Island.

After a while Steve said to Jones, "Why don't you ask him how he's doing?"

"He don't need to hear from me."

The voice of the captain said quietly, "That northeaster's blowing. I can see whitecaps out beyond the end of the pass, and I can see trees on shore bending. There's white water around Ilkognak Rock. I'm steering my way clear of it, of course, but this current's really a kicker. Jones, if you're still listening, I don't advise coming through right now. We've got good power, there's no problem, of course, but with you . . ."

A wondering voice that sounded like Pete's said, "Skipper, it looks like a wall of water ahead."

Jones Henry groaned.

"Give us binoculars, Pete." A pause, and the captain said in a steady voice, "Jones, if you're listening, it looks like we're going to hit a bitch of a rip tide, maybe twenty feet high. If you're listening, you might . . . Pete, help me hold this wheel. Just throw down the binoculars."

Jones scrambled below. From the cabin they could hear his voice demanding Kodiak emergency on the second radio.

"This . . . wheel . . . won't respond." The voice grunted with each word. "Pete, with me. Uh! We've cleared the rock, thank God, but oh, my Lord! Three times higher than we are, my . . ."

There was a high male scream that sounded like Spitz's.

"The rip's turning us upside . . . Uh, *uh*. Mayday, Mayday. Whale Pass. *Billy*—" There was a roar, then nothing but static.

They waited on the *Rondelay* for more, but no more came.

9

BOATS THAT GO DOWN

T HE last transmission from the *Billy II* had occurred close to noon. By midafternoon, Swede Scorden was flying overhead in a chartered plane, while a seagoing tug and a Coast Guard cutter from Kodiak cruised the coastline. A boat in the eastern mouth of Whale Pass would never be more than a third of a mile from shore, but the searchers could report no evidence of the *Billy II* on the beach: neither boat, oil slick, debris, nor people. Despite the lee where the *Rondelay* rode calm, it was blowing fifty and gusting higher on the other side of the pass. Jones sped the *Rondelay* across the strait to moor it in the shelter of the Port Bailey cannery dock. Swede landed his seaplane to take Jones aboard. A Navy plane picked up the others and distributed them on the various search craft to help identify anything that might be found.

Hank, his throat still tight five hours after the event, became a passenger aboard a Coast Guard buoy tender. For the remaining hours of daylight he huddled on the bridge wing with the watch as wind and rain tore about him, peering through binoculars without rest for some sign among the hazy rocks, refusing food, occasionally coughing to hide a sob as the immensity of the event returned to mind.

It was a relief when darkness came to relieve him of the obligation to search. He was hungry and cold. Gladly he followed a sailor named Mack down the steel stairways and through steel corridors to the crew's messdeck. In the clothes which had practically grown to his body, he felt scruffy among the men in their clean-bleached dungarees. He even began to sniff his own odor.

After eating, Mack took him below to a dark berthing deck where the bunks were stacked in tiers, assigned him a bunk and a locker, and issued him bedding. He took a shower. Mack loaned him clothes and he washed his own, then hung them at Mack's direction on a line in the engine room. He watched a movie on the messdeck. Thoughts of Pete and Spitz returned often in a guilty wave, but the event was so unbelievable that the movie pulled him away. Later the captain asked him to the wardroom, where he sat among the officers at a felt-covered table and repeated the whole story of the *Billy II*.

The high bunk where he finally stretched was more comfortable than any bed he had slept in since leaving home. The ship rolled and pitched, but he had hardly noticed it, so far removed was it from the slap of the sea. He thought of the raging top of the water, and the cold depths pulled by currents and inhabited by dark forms of creatures. I might have been there, he thought. Wherever they are. Our Father Which art in Heaven. . . . He stretched his body and wriggled into the warm mattress.

The next sound he heard was a tinny shriek that rose and fell in pitch, and then over the same loudspeaker a voice droning: "Now oh-six-three-oh, reveille reveille reveille, all hands heave out and trice up. The smoking lamp is lighted in all authorized places." Groans and coughs followed from the bunks around him, and a light snapped on in his eyes.

He had not even dreamed! He lay thinking of the salty, regimented reveille call as he watched the men in their clean white skivvies stand on the metal deck and pull into their dungarees. Different kind of seafaring altogether. He'd take the cramped, dirty *Rondelay* with its wooden deck. But, putting from his mind why he was there, he dressed with the others and gladly ate a huge breakfast in the knowledge that he would not have to wash the dishes.

On the bridge, the watch officer showed him the chart and explained their search pattern for the day. Mack appeared, saluted the officer, then took a microphone and blew a little whistle around his neck that shrilled with the same noise as the reveille. "Now all hands turn to, foul weather gear on the buoy deck." Hank stood admiring the performance, as Mack strutted past and winked.

"Object on the beach, sir," called the lookout.

Everyone crowded outside to look with binoculars. In a break of rocks, on a narrow gray shore, the water broke against a round white object half submerged, while a red board bobbed close by. Hank had seen endless driftwood while fishing, but a bad feeling gripped him.

A voice over the speaker said sharply: "Now, deck crew muster at number two boat on the double, boat crew prepare to launch the ready boat." The officer tapped Hank's shoulder. "You go along." Blocks clattered and men moved everywhere as he hurried down the metal stair from the bridge to the boats. A seaman strapped him into an orange life jacket. No one spoke except to give directions. In the boat Mack stood by the tiller, and another man had started the engine. Hank stepped in. Mack told him to grab a monkey rope for support, nodding toward several ropes from an overhead sling with knots tied at intervals. The boat lowered, slapped the water with a bounce, rose, slapped again as spray kicked over them and water surged between the boat and the ship. Finally they rode firm, and Mack shouted commands for releasing the falls and sea painter. As they bucked toward shore they all hunched against breaking seas except Mack, who remained straight and grave by the tiller.

Hank jumped to the beach through breakers as Mack nosed the bow as close as he dared. He ran over the hard gravel and waded among the rocks. The board had the red of the *Billy II*. He tossed it on the beach and pulled at the white object. It stuck in the gravel beneath the water, then with slow sucking yielded the face of a large scale, with shards of red board attached.

"Recognize it, Hank?"

Hank nodded, unable to speak. Other tenders had scales, other boats were painted red, but these. . . . He waded above his boot tops among the rocks as the others cautioned him not to go too far. The water pushed and surged around his legs like a live thing.

Under the water, in the rocks, he grasped the fingers of a hand.

They all unwedged the body from the rocks and dragged it ashore. The face was scraped and bloated and turning black, but it had Pete's red beard, his red hair slapped against his head, the vestige yet of the sassy carefree expression. As the water drained from the beard it fluffed out.

Hank vomited and vomited, then walked by himself into the spongy woods.

They found no other bodies. But the seagoing tug, with Steve aboard, had found a piece of lifeboat with the Y II part of *Billy II* stenciled on it. The currents and the sea had claimed the rest.

At the end of the third day the search was abandoned. Hank returned to Kodiak aboard the cutter. Along the way they passed the *Rondelay,* manned apparently by only Jones Henry and Ivan, the two who had ridden planes. They all waved gravely. Hank felt desolate not to be aboard his own boat among his own people, to talk out the experience.

The *Rondelay* entered Kodiak through the narrows, but the Coast Guard ship took a longer seaward route. As Mack explained: "Russian trawler cocksuckers are dragging nets practically across the harbor, and the best we can do is route all the time to keep watch." Hank saw them: black, rusty ships the size of freighters. A few hours later he had also seen part of the Navy Base where the Coast Guard docked—a dreary place of long gray buildings—and had ridden a bus along ten miles of pockmarked highway, past the airport that seemed part of his prehistoric past. Where the road skirted the coast he could watch the Russian trawlers again. As they rounded a promontory he had a vista of Kodiak: the cannery buildings puffing steam, the frame buildings of the town topped by the dome of the little Russian (Russian!) church, the crisscross of floats with boats tied in. He reached the harbor, sighted the *Rondelay,* and broke into a run.

The rest were there, to his grateful relief. Ivan passed him an open bottle without a word, and he settled on the engine cover among them.

One by one they recounted their experiences during the search. As Hank told how he had discovered Pete's body, he found that the passage of days had lessened the impact enough that he could speak of it in a steady voice.

"Aye-yup," sighed Sven, "'ve all got to go some time, and if you stay around de vater, maybe you die vet." He told of his own brother, lost only a few years ago with the rest on his halibut schooner as they fished Albatross Bank in late season. The last message anyone heard from them anounced that winds and freezing spray had begun to ice their rigging, and they were underway full speed toward shelter in lower Kodiak Island forty miles away. The Coast Guard and Navy hurried out

113

to help, taking ice themselves, but they found nothing. "It's no joke, ice," Sven concluded. "It comes so sudden in vinter if she blows from north." The others agreed.

Jones added that once ice accumulates so thick that your boat can't right itself in a normal roll, "you can frostbite yourself out there hammering it off but your chances ain't better than fifty-fifty unless she stops." But then, remember the *Pequod?* They all nodded. "Covered with ice and likely to turn over any second, and two days later they found her still floating with a list, ice in the shrouds so thick the plane first thought it was a growler from one of the glaciers. Full mugs of coffee still on the galley table." Jones turned to Hank. "The boys could have ridden her out, you see, but they guessed wrong and abandoned her. Found the bodies not far away in a life raft, caked in ice, just like the boat. That was a bitch of a winter."

"Yeah," said Steve quietly. "It's a hard decision to make when the time comes. Ten years ago near Cape Igvak we grounded the old *Olga Bay.* Fellow named Dave Snyder and me took our chances with the rocks and made it ashore, near froze and starved for two nights before a plane spotted us. The others went down when the *Olga* fell apart. You don't sometimes have but a second to decide, and if I hadn't seen a rockhold when the water surged away for a minute, and committed myself by jumping, I'd have probably taken my chances with the others. And Dave, he just followed. I don't think he'd have jumped by himself."

It had happened just the opposite, Jones recalled, with the fellows out shrimping off Mitrofania on the *Dolly R* when she grounded. Charlie Harris, who now fished aboard the *Morning Glory,* chose to stay aboard while the others decided to rush it the hundred feet to shore before the boat might break apart and hit them with debris. Charlie watched in broad daylight, helpless to do anything, as his crewmates weakened, froze, and died halfway to shore in the grip of a current. The *Dolly R* stayed fixed to the rock.

The way fellows piled their crab pots too high brought a whole new set of problems, Jones continued. "I myself saw Sam Dietrick sail from this harbor in easy weather with his pots strapped six high on deck —didn't want to make that extra trip, you see. Couldn't blame him. Cruised up to Marmot Bay and one of them northeasters we just saw hit him sudden. He reported that much by radio, and said he was heading for shelter. Wave must have tilted him too far, and the pots topheavied him the rest of the way over. Not a trace, ever, not even as much as we found of the *Billy Two*."

Before he came to the *Rondelay*, Ivan said as he leaned heavily on the engine cover and handled the bottle, he was king-crabbing on the *Miss Jane* within sight of Kodiak and a young fellow—named Pete like the one just drowned—had crawled into the pot to change bait when a heavy sea washed the pot overboard. "Oh, shit, we brought that pot back fast, but the kid was gone and nobody ever found him. Last year his old lady married Led Freeman in town, fellow runs the store. She told me once on the street she wouldn't never marry a fisherman again, not with the worry it give her every night he was on the water."

Steve cursed mildly at the hour as he rose and started undressing. While they continued to talk, he poured stove water into the galley sink and sponge-bathed.

"I guess my old lady has a bad time," said Jones. "The more you fish, the less you see them, and after a while you don't think about the same things any more."

"I was married once," Steve volunteered. "Never again."

Ivan puffed at his pipe. "Goddam, some girl come along, I'd take her. She give me lip I'd hit her, but with a girl waiting, maybe my money wouldn't all piss down the barstool."

Sven smiled. "I got a real fisherman's vife from old country, knows the man goes fishing and the voman keeps ready the home."

Steve pulled from his drawer beneath the bunks a pair of dress pants and a western shirt decorated in mother-of-pearl sequins, and then began to slap scented powder over his chest. Suddenly everyone became restless. The bottle was empty, and Ivan was turning it over and over. Jones said he guessed he'd go home and face all Adele's questions about the *Billy II*. Ivan declared gloomily that he might as well start his drunk, and if Jones didn't see him in a couple of days, try the goddam jail. Hank listened with increasing dejection to their plans that had nothing to do with him. He rose quickly when Sven said, "Come along, Hank, ve go up and have yust a little beer."

"We'll start mending and stacking crab pots first thing Monday morning," said Jones. "Every ass better be down here." Hank glanced anxiously, and grinned with relief when Jones added, "Your ass in-

115

cluded. You're part of my crew until you go home, and you know where your bunk is."

Much later, after leaving Sven, Hank found the address of Pete's parents and phoned them. Their desolation choked him. They had learned all the details from both Swede and the Coast Guard, but they thanked him again and again for calling. He thought about it, then phoned his own parents, and felt guilty at their pleasure in hearing from him.

Afterward he walked through swirls of windy rain to the hills above town. Lights below glistened on the few blocks of weathered storefronts and formed halos around the bare bulbs of the harbor floats. No sound penetrated through the wind. Occasional figures staggered or walked, mostly from bar to bar or back to the boats. In the narrows a buoy blinked, and far out the dim massed lights of the Russian trawlers moved in slow banks.

He walked and walked, hoping for some revelation: not to explain—that oceans ran their mystic cycles and that men died in them was perfectly clear, and he did not need to know why as long as he was busy in the middle of it. But, given his life, how was he to use it?

10

RUSSIANS

ARLY Monday morning, Hank and the rest started work on the crab pots. Jones stored his pots in an open clearing off the road to the Navy Base, where he and others left them unmolested when not in use. Most of the pots, including Jones', were circular like big doughnuts six feet across and weighed about two hundred pounds. They were built with steel framework and webbing for the walls. A couple of boats had stacks nearby of square pots that weighed three times as much—seven feet square by three feet, which Jones said were the latest thing. No current could drift them from the bottom, and they held three times the crab, did a better job all around. But he lacked the capital to junk his existing pots for the expensive new ones, especially in a marginal salmon year.

Hank's partner was Ivan, who after a weekend of boozing to near-stupefaction spoke virtually never. However, he used his bull strength on the pots in a way Hank could not. First they inspected each, and repaired rips in the webbing with the big needle. Then they hefted the pots into Jones' pickup and took them to the pier, where they attached numbered buoys and a long coil of line to each. Meanwhile, Jones and Steve had remained on the *Rondelay* to remove the seining tackle and to rig a special hydraulic block for crab pots. When they loaded, the pots had to be stacked one on top of the other and lashed together. Soon there was practically no deck space to walk.

After loading, they bought frozen herring and fishheads from a cannery, then proceeded beyond the breakwater into an area practically within sight of town. Jones cruised among hundreds of floating markers lettered like those inside each of the *Rondelay* pots. Not far away, the fleet of Russian fishing ships moved slowly in the water. Hank chopped the herring in a tub and stuffed the pieces into an assortment of cans and plastic jugs punctured with holes. It was near sunset when Jones finally chose his grounds. One by one they bumped each heavy pot to the rail, emptied the buoys and line stored inside, snapped in a can of bait, then heaved it into the water. The pot sank bubbling while the attached line uncoiled and the buoys held it to the surface.

The lights of town twinkled pleasantly as they returned in the dark. "Goddam," said Ivan glumly, "I'd like it we anchored outside for the night."

Jones brightened and slowed the throttle. "Wouldn't bother me."

"Cut the shit," said Steve, "somebody's expecting me."

So they moored as before. Jones returned to his wife and Ivan to his bar with the slowness of men shouldering heavy sacks, while Steve quickly sponged himself and sauntered off in a trail of manly perfumes.

Hank wandered the town. It was his next-to-last evening: perhaps with the goodbye dinner tomorrow at Jones Henry's, his last look on his own. He said hi to many people, but saw more who were still strangers. He knew the insides of the bars and eateries and many of the boats, but Kodiak itself was far bigger than he had first imagined, far more a complex of businesses and interests beyond fishing. He only knew the segment that had involved him. Suddenly he wanted to possess it all. There were lights along the hills. For every threshold he could cross or face he recognized, there remained a hundred strange ones.

"Hank!"

He turned at the woman's voice and there was Jody, wearing a dress rather than dungarees, her hair groomed and soft.

"Well, fisherman, you never came to claim that mug-up. Afraid Swede would see you?"

He found himself admiring her wide mouth and direct eyes—the kind of woman who really attracted him, not one of the mouselike Elsies who waited for a scrap of attention. "Guess you'll sling hash again now that fishing's over?"

"Not likely!" Her laugh was feminine but pleasantly husky.

He felt he should have talked about Pete, but he began to have different hopes and notions about the evening. "Say, I'm a pretty rich salmon fisherman. Why don't we—"

A big bearded man Hank had seen on the grounds popped his head from a nearby tavern and shouted her name. With a broad smile and a wave, Jody left him.

In the morning they stacked a new deckload of pots and headed out. The ones they had set the night before would not have soaked long enough to be full, said Jones, but they'd haul a few so that Hank could work the gear and grab himself a handful of king crabs. Mrs. Henry planned to cook the crabs that night for Hank's farewell party at the house.

Their first sign of trouble was a buoy marked with the *Rondelay* R wedged in the rocks of the breakwater. Farther out they saw another of their buoys afloat. They continued toward Cape Chiniak and there, in the midst of their pots, steamed the Russian trawler fleet. One ship moved slowly over their grounds as it let out its trawl, the taut moving cables visible astern. Even as they watched, the high rusty bow cut a path through *Rondelay*-marked buoys, and several bobbed loose with the current as the propellers severed them from their pots.

Jones Henry turned crazy.

He throttled the *Rondelay* to the ship and emptied his shotgun point-blank into the black hull towering above them, while the others shouted curses and invective. It was as futile as kicking a mountain. A few curious faces appeared at the rail high above them, and a dead fish slapped down on the *Rondelay*'s deck to the accompaniment above of laughter and foreign words. Although Steve tried to restrain him, Jones loaded his gun and fired close to the faces. The men disappeared. The whistle of the ship blew. Jones Henry maneuvered the *Rondelay* astern of the ship and started firing at the cables with Ivan urging him on. A ship that had no trawl in the water left the fleet and headed toward them. Steve and Hank pointed it out, but Jones, now grimly calm, paid no attention. His hand left the gun only long enough to reload or to edge his boat closer to the thick, taut cable.

"Jones," cried Steve, "pull out of it. Nobody could snap that fucker with a shotgun, and suppose you did, what about backlash?"

"Fuck it, Boss, fuck it!" countered Ivan. "Shoot 'em again, maybe just by luck—"

Jones returned his shotgun to the storage box. "Don't often lose all judgment." He shook his fist as he backed the *Rondelay* and started off. "No better than Japs, you cocksuckers," he muttered with a tight mouth. "I'd give the rest of my pots to get you."

The Russian, which had just been setting its trawl as they arrived, began to draw it back, all the time blowing its whistle. "At least," said Hank, "they must *think* you can shoot their cable whether you can or not."

The other Russian ship still approached. They were a mile from land. "I don't know whether to stay and protect the rest of our pots or whether that bugger coming toward us really means . . ." Suddenly Jones chuckled and winked at Steve as he altered course and headed for a different part of shore. The ship changed direction to follow, coming with twice the speed of the *Rondelay*. "We're too heavy. Dump some pots. Quick. Open lids if you can, mebbe the buoys'll float, but dump! And hold tight. I might turn sharp."

The bow of the Russian ship had a sinister height as it bore down. Hank saw it only through the sweat dripping into his eyes as they struggled with tieropes on the top layer of pots, then upended them directly over the side.

However Jones turned, the ship followed. No question of its intent. Hank glanced frightened at the distance yet to shore. He could hear the hiss of the high bow through the water. Jones stood on his open bridge, straight and proud. Going down like this? Hank wondered. Not even a life jacket? Neither of the others seemed concerned, except that Steve kept telling him, "When Jones gives the signal, hold tight," as if he knew something.

"Dig in," yelled Jones, and veered to port, then to starboard, each time forcing the Russian to a sharp alteration. Hank bellied down on the circular top of a crab pot and clutched his fingers into the webbing as the pots jiggled and shifted. "We can't do this all the way to shore," he panted to Steve. They jettisoned two more pots, and then Jones called for them to stop and get off the pile.

Suddenly the Russian ship began to blow its whistle stacatto and to back engines with a great churn of water. Jones slowed his own engine and circled, his face calm. They heard the screech of steel crunching as the Russian ship jolted and its whistle blasted louder.

"I remembered them uncharted shoals just when you did," yelled Steve as he hugged Jones and danced around.

The Russian ship escaped serious damage, but it had to hire a tug from town to tow it free.

The projected quiet farewell gathering that night at Jones Henry's house became a wild bash. Throughout the fishing-boat community, Jones was the hero, but there was glory to spare for the other members of the *Rondelay*—even Sven, who had returned from Seattle on the afternoon plane. A passed hat collected a huge sum: enough to buy Jones new crab pots. He declared he could now convert to square ones like the big fellows.

Hank at one point was carried on other fishermen's shoulders. Dream of dreams, Jody took him over. She began to match his drinks with her arm around his waist. He ventured a kiss, and she accepted with such a ready tongue that he soon led her, or followed her, to the skipper's cabin on the cash-buyer boat. With all the alcohol he had consumed he wondered if he could manage. But with the first brush of her naked body he found himself responding as he never had before. Never had he held such a woman! They went at it happily. Later they rejoined the party, and her head found its way to his chest even as they stood together. Near daybreak they returned to the cash-buyer's cabin, but the owner now occupied the bed. Jody, laughing, led him to the crew's quarters. She seemed inhibited by nothing, a natural creature, beautiful in every way.

When he left reluctantly on the morning plane to Anchorage, Jody and the Jones Henrys and at least twenty others waved him off noisily. The party was only taking a breather, and if college registration deadline had not been three days hence and all other flights filled, he would have remained. As the plane taxied, he strained through the clouded window for one more glimpse of Jody's long auburn hair and the wide smile that brought her eyes and the rest of her face to life.

Part 2:
1964, SPRING

11

WINTER
POTS

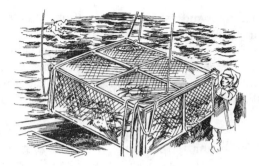

ANK spent a restless winter. Chemistry, the Europe of Metternich, literature in French—they were inconsequential compared to the world he had brushed in Kodiak. Nancy quickly retreated when he tried to sleep with her, and his friends found him too full of enviable adventures: it forced him to tone down to the general level, chafing all the time. Reluctantly, slowly, he settled back into the social patterns of hops and beer busts, and into the study patterns required for good grades. He took up fencing, and on winter afternoons played basketball ferociously.

The breakaway from his parents' influence had begun when he first left for college, but the summer in Kodiak strengthened it. All in all, he felt a cheerful and heady independence about his life. As for the future, his daydreams no longer seemed to carry him beyond the nets of the *Rondelay*. Certainly not to the summer in France his mother still advocated, or a job next summer his father could arrange which might lead to a career with one of the major stockbrokers.

The assassination of President Kennedy in late November stirred his empathy with larger forces. As he watched the replays on television and the actual murder of Oswald, he smelled and saw again Pete's corpse, and heard Spitz's arguments on cosmic disorder. At night he dreamed of mountains. But the ceremonies of death ran their course, and shortly after the burial a chemistry test forced him back into his own present tense.

The pace changed abruptly in midwinter. Jones Henry wrote that the State Department had officially reprimanded him for harassing Russian ships and risking an international incident. Coincidentally, the State of Alaska, without explanation, denied renewal of Jones' fishing-vessel license. Jones' letter, written with occasional *x*ings in a wiry hand, concluded: "Well, Hank, I don't know except that you had better ask around for another boat next summer the way the rest of us is. When the U.S. gvt starts to stick up for the Russian buggers over its own people, it's time to ship for Australia."

Hank, nervous at his own temerity, took a train from Baltimore to Washington the morning after receiving Jones' letter. He went to the offices of the two Senators and the Representative from Alaska. After long waits, an aide at each place hurried out to half-listen, then suggest he write a letter. In his room back at Hopkins, Hank spent half the night drafting the letters, then banging out clean copies on a friend's typewriter. He described the continuing provocation of the Russian ships and the way they had torn the gear of Jones and other crabbers, and told what had happened to Jones. Each letter closed with: "I think this is one hell of a thing to have happen to an American fisherman!" He mailed copies to Jones, to let him know that at least he had tried, as well as to *The New York Times* and the papers in Juneau and Anchorage. Polite letters came back eventually from each of the congressmen through an aide, nothing from the papers. Hank felt angry, helpless, and cynical.

Several weeks later: "Son of a bitch, Hank!" Jones Henry's voice shouted through the crackling long-distance wires. "You're a smart guy! Know what I've got in my hand? My license! Bastards pretended it was only hung up on a technicality." Besides the news itself, it dazzled Hank that he was talking to someone actually in Kodiak. "What's it like up there now? How are Steve and Ivan and Sven? Ever see Jody?" He needed to repeat everything, because one voice had to stop altogether before the other could transmit.

"All fine, fine, old Ivan drunk as ever. Snow got through dumping a while ago and now she's slush and the winds gusting sixty. I just come back from crewing on a shrimper, figured I'd better grab pay when I could without a license, freezing a bitch out there. Now we got the license, I'm taking the *Rondelay* out king-crabbing first of March, work her till the end of May before I gear for salmon. Too bad you can't see my new square pots, mebbe feel what real winter's like."

"You only need three on deck for crab or I'd be tempted to come up over spring vacation."

"You come up. Sven's not that hot to crab all spring with his family in Seattle. In a week you could make your fare."

Hank found a schedule, trying not to sound excited. "Hopkins lets out for Easter on—I'd cut Thursday and Friday classes the week before, maybe more—I could get up there about March nineteenth and stay until the twenty-ninth or thirtieth." In his mind he was already canceling a trip he had promised to take with his parents and a date for the big dance after Good Friday.

"Buy some thermals," was Jones' parting advice. "Not just long underwear. Because you ain't a Norwegian yet."

Hank arrived back in Kodiak on Friday the twentieth, having placed himself in hot water with his date, his lacrosse coach, two professors, and his family.

Jones and Steve were there to meet him and poured him on the back. They collected his bags and soon were bouncing toward town in Jones' pickup. The green mountains of summer had turned brown and snow-covered. The smells of fishy steamed crab blew into the window as they passed the canneries. "Oh man," he declared, "I'm home again!"

Adele Henry threw her arms around him at the door and fixed a fine meal to celebrate his arrival. She was a vigorous and outspoken woman, and although Hank had met her only twice before, they were now suddenly old friends. On the wall, in a frame that apparently once had held a photograph, hung his letter to the Anchorage *Times,* which had been printed without his knowing. Hank described until even he tired of it his visit to the halls of Congress and his opinions of congressional aides. Mrs. Henry pressed him for details of the Kennedy assassination and funeral. Jones then delivered his opinion of the State Department and the way it could even corrupt the State of Alaska. For Hank it was the finest evening he had spent since leaving Kodiak seven months before. Later, he could barely sleep. They had printed his letter, and one of the congressmen had responded with action. What power waited to be used when you grabbed an initiative!

Next morning it was snowing and still dark when Jones shook him awake in the guest bed and they left the house quietly. No sight of mountains, barely of the town, as they tracked through the slush around the silent stores and down onto the floats. A wind blew. It chilled him even through his thermals. As for the *Rondelay*, which had occupied so much of this thought during the winter—she looked smaller and shabbier than he remembered, and, slicked with ice and shrouded in snow that glowed dully in the blue half-light, more vulnerable.

Steve and Ivan were snoring as they entered the warm cabin, but Jones had only to start the engine and they swung automatically into their boots. The stove had been puffing a small jet of flame all night, so the coffee pot contained steaming water. Steve showed him briefly how to adjust the stove—a trick Sven had guarded throughout the summer— and Hank began at once to take Sven's place, starting coffee in the pot and slabs of bacon in the pan as he peeled potatoes and broke eggs.

They shoveled their food with early-morning glumness. It soon became obvious that, aboard the *Rondelay*, Hank's ability to write letters to newspapers gave him no more privilege than before. Jones declared the coffee too weak. Ivan grumped that he hadn't fried enough potatoes to feed a fish, and Steve wondered why the hell he'd spooned the bacon grease into a can rather than leaving it with the eggs and spuds where it belonged? Jones told him to hurry with the dishes as the others went out to get underway.

The boat started pitching as soon as it left the breakwater. Hank quickly understood the reason to hurry. A dish he had left on the engine cover smashed to the deck, a bottle of catsup fell from the cupboard, and the disputed can of grease overturned. As he cursed and mopped, he felt stealing over him the sinister headache and taste of half-digested food that heralded seasickness. Steve yelled for him to get his ass outside and start chopping bait. Had he been crazy to come back like this? The whistling wind had blown the rigging and deck clean of snow, but an ice slick remained. With each roll the sea washed over the rail and gurgled around their legs. He hunched against the cabin housing and, with teeth chattering and hands already numb even in heavy rubber gloves, started to chop at the herring in the tub.

Above them on the open bridge Jones tooted the whistle. Ivan, his feet spread firmly and his face taking slaps of seawater, stood by the rail holding a hook on a line. The boat approached one of the buoys with *Rondelay* markings, visible only on the crest of a wave. Ivan threw the hook hard into the water close to the buoy, then yanked it back with the buoy and pot line it had snagged. He worked quickly, passing the buoy line through a hydraulic block rigged over the water. Hank gave him a hand: the line felt weighted to rocks, and as the boat rolled the water pulled the line out of their hands like an adversary in a tug of war. As soon as they had managed a turn over the sheave, the block brought in the line easily. Hank had seen Ivan so much in drunken helplessness that he had forgotten his ability as a fisherman. Ivan stood as easily on the pitching, icy deck as if it had been a grass plot, coiling fifty or sixty fathoms of line in only a few minutes.

Steve motioned Hank to stand by the rail. A cold sea drenched them, and Hank grabbed the rail for support.

"Move your hand," Steve shouted. "Want it smashed?"

Out of the water in a foam of bubbles came one of the new square crab pots. As it swayed with the boat's motion it thudded against the rail just where his fingers had rested.

Hank hooked up the pot at Steve's direction. Then Steve operated controls that lifted it dripping onto deck as Ivan and Hank steadied the steel frame. It had an inexorable weight. As Hank tried to brace it he lost his footing on the ice and fell as the pot swung past and nicked his head. In a dizziness of pain he saw it returning aimed full at his face and flattened on the deck as Ivan with a grunt diverted it to crash against the rail above him. Hank scrambled automatically to his feet and helped bring the pot to rest. As he followed Ivan's example, untying the cords that secured the lid, a sea that stung his forehead broke over them. He found blood on his fingers when he rubbed to ease the pain. Ivan called Steve and they examined the cut as Hank insisted on its inconsequence. His eye had wandered to the pot, where dozens of big spiny purple crabs were crawling slowly over each other. Bigger than any he had ever seen. He forgot his miseries and started to laugh and shout. Steve and Ivan grinned at his reaction, and they all forgot the cut.

Ivan, with effortless efficiency, bent into the pot and slung out the crabs like a dog scratching earth, some into the hold and the rest onto the deck or over the side, barely seeming to choose between them. Hank lifted one out by a leg and admired its slow-moving, grotesque splendor, then started to throw it into the hold. Steve stopped him with a shout. "Don't you know a female?" He showed him the wide, egg-laden apron on the female's underside, then handed him a bar to measure the minimum size of males. "It don't help anybody to keep crabs that ain't keepers, gets us a bad reputation at the cannery, so don't sort until you know what you're doing."

They replaced the baited can inside the pot with a fresh one, secured the lid, straightened the attached coils of line and buoys to pay out smoothly, and dumped the pot back into the water. Within seconds, Ivan had grappled a new buoy and they were pulling again.

Jones Henry stood alone on the bridge, above the spray but exposed to the cutting wind, his face a vertical slit in his fur-lined parka. He maneuvered the boat from buoy to buoy, replacing one pot with the next as they worked down the line. On deck, Hank learned to creep at high speed on the deck ice, knees bent to give a surer balance. But the pots seemed endless. Even slinging the fruity ten-pound crabs lost its novelty as his arms found them heavier and heavier. After several hours he gladly accepted Steve's order to fix chow as a chance to rest, but the struggle in the galley was even worse. The canned stew rolled from the pot. As he cleaned the mess and started again he began to laugh through his curses, it was so miserable.

"Hank, get your ass moving!"

After a few days, Hank had settled in. They started him running the line. He found that it was simple enough to aim the grappling hook and catch the strap between the two buoys. To coil the line once it began racing through the crab block was a different matter. Steve patiently coached him, but even with the block turning at a third its regular speed his coils were haphazard and often fouled. Yet he worked at it with such intensity that at the end of a haul his gloves had flown off and he was panting. He watched Ivan do the next one: the line zipped in and laid in a perfect stack of symmetrical coils, while Ivan himself appeared relaxed enough to have fallen asleep. Hank tried again, with no better results. After the third time, as his pile of coils flopped across the deck in an agonized jumble, he muttered, "I've stopped us dead. Better go back to the bait tub where I belong."

"Okay," said Ivan, moving to take over.

Steve looked up from baiting, surprised. "Everybody's got to learn. You ain't stupid. Get back there."

130

A week after his arrival Hank was marginally adept—and very tired. They had worked through the preceding weekend, and Jones suggested that, what the hell, they sleep in on Good Friday and Easter. It turned out that both he and Steve wanted to drop in on church services. "Not for me," said Ivan. "Russian Easter comes in May. That's when you see me in the pretty little church." It surprised Hank, not being a churchgoer, until he thought of the shadow of death over the heads of fishermen. As for resting, he welcomed it. On Monday he would fly home. He had made enough to pay his planefare, and if he never saw another decomposed herring from a pot that had soaked for several days, that would be all right. On Thursday after unloading he followed Jones home, took a long hot bath, and settled with a drink in the Henrys' small, overstuffed, cozy living room. He chatted with Mrs. Henry about President Johnson, the time it would take to fly to the moon, and, when she discovered he read French (that he did it badly she refused to believe), about Rimbaud and Baudelaire, whose poems she had in a bilingual volume. He read her the first few lines of *"Bateau Ivre,"* paused to close his eyes, and fell asleep.

"There," he heard Jones say quietly as he drifted back for a moment, "you've talked him to death, and there he goes."

"Poo. You've worked him to death. First fellow I've met in years who can talk anything but fish. He did all right out there with the pots, did he?"

"Oh, I could make a fisherman out of him. But not the way he runs back and forth to school and reads French all the time."

12

WAVES

NEXT morning, when Hank woke around noon, the sun shone
against the curtains. The bed rocked with the easy roll of a boat
at sea, and for a second he could not figure where he was. Then
he rose, opened the curtains on part of the harbor and town, and returned to bed with his pillow adjusted to enjoy the view. The sky was
blue for a change, and patches of snow gleamed on the mountain slopes.
Boats lay moored along the T-shaped floats. Other boats arrived and left
through the opening in the rock breakwater that otherwise boxed the
crescent-shaped waterfront into a harbor. There were two arms of the
breakwater—one extending from the narrow channel between the side
of town and Near Island, which boats used when traveling via Whale
Pass, the other reaching out from close to the canneries on the Navy Base
road—and kids free from school were playing on the rocky tops of each.

 People moved along the docks and floats. It was difficult to make
out the *Rondelay* for sure, since many boats like it were tied close together. By the little harbormaster's building a dozen cars and pickups
caught a gleam of sun. One man in hip boots strode down the ramp
connecting the pier to the floats with a box of what appeared to be
engine parts on his shoulder. A crew at the far end of the pier were loading crab pots aboard their boat. The waterfront, with its plain houses
and stores facing out, had nothing but the business and pleasures of
fishing about it. Outside Breakers Tavern two men holding beer cans
studied the boats as they squinted into the noon sun, then returned inside
again. A block up from the waterfront he could watch over the low roofs
the activities of people on the main street. There was the roof of the

beanery and the bar beside it. He stretched again, and wriggled against the sheets to remind himself of the luxury. But he was already restless to be walking in town and among the boats. He'd had no chance all week with fishing. And what about Jody? He dressed quickly.

Jones and Adele had gone to Good Friday services, and a note told him to help himself. He found juice and hard-boiled eggs. He strolled on their little porch as he ate, marveling at the way the boat's motion remained to affect his equilibrium. The sun might have looked warm, but the air was cold. The noises of town now blended with the view: car horns and squeaks of machinery and dogs and shouts. Building by small frame building, the town was ugly, but as an entity, filling the apron of land between the narrows and the boat harbor and then stretching beyond the Russian church over the hills, he found it beautiful. A town so open to the sea and accessible to boats had to be beautiful.

In town he stopped at the beanery and some bars, asking about Jody, but no one knew except that she was "around." He wandered down to the boats. On the *Rondelay*, Ivan paced and sweated and swore, his clenched pipe billowing smoke, while Steve nodded in the sun. "Shit," Steve muttered through his teeth as Hank sat beside him, "Ivan wants to lay off the booze and asked me to make him do it. Now I'm the fuck stuck here for the day, and all kinds of little blisters waiting for me up town."

"I'll watch for a while, if you want to—"

Ivan jumped to the float and started toward town. Steve strode after him, rammed his fist into Ivan's stomach, which calmed him, then shoved him back aboard. Ivan went gloomily into the cabin and lay in his bunk.

"*You* watch him?" Steve grinned as he sat in his place again.

"Booze wouldn't be any worse for his gut than that, would it?"

"I'll hate the day old Ivan goes hopheaded for good. I'm as glad to help postpone it."

"You make it sound inevitable."

"The way I've seen it with others who hit the booze like that, I figure it is."

In the cabin, Ivan shouted a string of obscenities which dealt impartially with motherhood and the church. Hank could still hear him from the harbormaster's shack on the way back to town. He wandered the two-block main drag—it seemed uglier in the sun than when rain softened the bare low edges of the buildings—and then walked uphill by the Russian church to look out over the darkening blue water and the snowy mountains turning pink. Past five by his watch, and sunset came around seven-thirty. He could identify Jones Henry's house across the harbor, already covered in shadow by the hill behind it, and the *Rondelay* among the clusters of little masts within the breakwater. Steam rose from the crab canneries, both the one directly downhill to his left along the narrows and those beyond the boats and breakwater along the road to the Navy Base. The heavy odors of ammonia and cooking crab obliterated all others. Nothing mellow about Kodiak: a raw place with heavy stenches. Yet, *"Damned* if I want to go home," he muttered. He started back down with hands in pockets.

"I can't believe it!" said Jody's voice, and there she was. They stood grinning at each other. Her eyes were lively, her mouth wide and full, just as he remembered. "You've shaved your beard."

"It scratched when I played lacrosse." The mention of his demanding sport brought no reaction. Could he touch her, or should he wait? Her reddish hair, which had been shorter last summer, was now tied in a loose ponytail. He commented that he liked it.

"Keeps it out of the soup."

"You mean you're back as a waitress?"

"No, I cook for the jailhouse when I'm not traveling on a boat. What brought you back?"

"Been out crabbing on the *Rondelay*."

"Jones Henry bust your ass?"

Not what he wanted her to say, but he interpreted the freedom of language as a go-ahead, and reached for her arm. She started down the hill, and his hand brushed off. "Hey," he said, "that was a *great* party, the night before I left." He took her arm firmly, and brought his face close enough to smell her hair. "Come on, Jody, let's—"

"Hey, Chuck, a great party, but then you left the scene."

"My name's Hank."

"Hank, yes. Well, Hank, I'm on my way to Solly's to meet a guy who sticks around. Walk me down."

He held out his hands. "Hell, Jody, all the times I've thought about you . . ." As soon as he said it and saw the amusement in her face,

134

he felt like a movie cowboy. They walked in silence until she asked if he wasn't going to school or something and drew from him a series of half-hearted answers. At a small frame house on a hill overlooking the business district a woman called, and she went over to chat, with Hank in glum tow. She was so vivacious, so unconcerned!

Her friend had two small children playing inside, with the television going full blast.

From somewhere in a distance came a faint, whooshing roar. A moment later, the ground started unbelievably to shake beneath them.

"Help me get the kids," cried the woman, and rushed inside. Hank and Jody followed, with Hank unsure what was happening. Like walking on a vibrator. A vase danced off a table and crashed. The floor itself was moving. Books flopped from a shelf. He grabbed a crying child and held her close. In the kitchen, cans rolled and jars smashed open, while from the bedroom a glass fishing ball bumped toward him in small leaps like a frog.

He started to run outside. "Stand in the doorframe," commanded Jody.

They all squeezed together as the absurd motion grew worse. "Is this an earthquake?" he asked excitedly. Jody nodded. The woman soothed her children. Neither she nor Jody appeared frightened. The shaking subsided as quickly as it had begun. The television jingle continued at high volume, then stopped abruptly.

"See, Angie?" said the woman. "All over."

"Bigger than most," said Jody, and strolled outside. Hank followed as he joggled the child in his arms and reassured her gently. She quieted to watch him with big-eyed suspicion and to announce that he wasn't her daddy.

Suddenly the ground started rolling—*rolling*. It felt like a deck at sea, and he needed sealegs to keep his balance. Overhead the sky became a wild jumble of telephone poles that bent and whipped with the abandon of saplings. A tree crashed and fell. They struggled back to the doorframe, the child screaming. The house boards groaned and cracked like a matchbox being crushed underfoot, and the windows began to shatter. Outside the ground twisted and heaved in clouds of dust, and a parked truck bounced as if on a trampoline. The road and brown lawns undulated like waves. If they had not all been wedged against each other they would have fallen.

"How long does it last?" he shouted.

"Never gone on this long," said the woman.

"Real bitch of a quake," said Jody appreciatively. "You ever think poles could bend that far without breaking?"

The child now clutched Hank's neck and burrowed her face in his chest. He patted her head as he watched what was happening. The walls of the house swayed like a boat in seas, and broken objects danced along the floor. Outside, a car, its driver wide-eyed by the wheel, bounced upright but sideways down the road. It was so grotesque that the two women started laughing. He joined them dubiously. Parked cars, he now noticed, had mounted each other and were jiggling together in clumps. His own vision of it was blurred from the motion, unreal. Cracks appeared in the road. A pole fell, bringing with it a jumble of wires.

"When will this *stop!*" said the woman. "If only the foundation holds. Jim worked so hard to make it firm."

"Where's he now?" asked Hank.

"Civilian electrician at the Navy Base. Hope he's got sense enough to take shelter."

A geyser of water shot up from a fissure in the road.

"There goes the water main. Pray to God we don't have a fire. This is going to be a *mess* to clean."

The motion seemed to continue forever, then subsided and stopped. "Well, that's *got* to be the end."

"Best one I ever saw," said Jody. "Let's turn on your radio or TV and see where it centered."

The woman picked her way through the mess and announced after flicking switches that the power was out. She and Jody started sweeping. Hank disengaged the child and eased her down. "Shut up, Angie, it's all over now, honey," said the woman as she gave a swoop through jangled glass with her broom. "So much for the good stuff we bought in Seattle." She picked up the phone to reach her husband; it was dead. "No phone, no electricity, only an hour and a half left of daylight. Oh! Better find all the flashlights. Let's have some coffee, I always think better with coffee." From the kitchen she said with a tight laugh, "It's an *electric* stove. Thank God the kids are off formula. Does an oil burner run on electricity? Shut the door, keep the heat in; it's supposed to go into the twenties tonight. I'd better find all my blankets."

Hank righted the furniture and stared unbelieving at the rest. "Where should I help?"

Jody stopped. "Oh God, the boats. You're on the *Rondelay?* Go down and help Jones." She touched his arm. "Look, if you see water coming and you're not on high ground, don't race it, jump on the nearest boat. Understand?"

"Water?"

"Tidal wave, stupid."

"They're supposed to start a siren if they sight a tidal wave coming," said the woman. "That road from the base travels low ground. I just hope Jim has sense enough to stay where he is. Look at those electric wires down outside. I guess it's good the power's off."

"My friend's on a big crab tender," said Jody. "They were waiting to unload. I'm not sure where I ought to . . ."

As Hank left, Jody called after him to be careful. He picked his way down the road, around poles, wires, cars, and shooting water. People milled and talked, laughing nervously. At a church, a priest with arms bare under a cassock shift scurried businesslike to a nearby house with a broken statuette in his hand, and Hank remembered it was Good Friday. Downtown, two men ran with arms full of bottles from one of the bars with the bartender yelling "Looters!" after them. In the stores, goods lay tumbled from shelves. Hank glanced into the beanery. Old Mike stood mesmerized, steaks and crockery strewn in a wide pool of grease around him. Hank started in to help.

A siren began to whine.

Men ran toward the boat harbor, and Hank joined them.

The tide was high enough to bring almost horizontal the ramp that connected the pier to the floats. The floats themselves shivered under everybody's tread. Geysers of water shot between the boards. Lightpoles had fallen across, and their electric wires were arcing. The *Rondelay* was tied inboard of two other boats. Jones and the others were working feverishly to exchange the moorings and maneuver out. Hank joined, grabbing lines. The siren continued in town above the shouts around them.

Steve thrust an axe at Hank and told him to stand by the bow and chop their line if the water came suddenly. "And keep your footing. Ain't nobody can fish you out."

"What are we trying to do?"

"Get beyond the breakwater in case a wave hits, ride her out in open sea." The engine puttered out, and Jones rushed to examine it with Steve in tow.

Hank held the axe nervously, wondering if he would recognize a wave in time to chop. Engines were gunned and the floats clamored with people, including women and children. In town, smoke rose from several fires. Firemen were running a hose down to the water to attach to a pump. They stood on the harbormaster's pier, where not long before he had noticed the tide receding under several feet of exposed pilings. Now the water was higher than he had ever seen it before, so close against the pier top that the fireman dropping the pump hose could wet his hands. A putrid odor drew Hank's attention near the boat. Black bubbles the size of crab pots rose around them, and the rest of the surface was streaked with motion. When he glanced again at the pier, the water covered the edge and people were backing away. He looked for the breakwaters. Their long ridges of stone were covered or gone.

"This ain't a wave like ever I've seen," said Ivan hoarsely. "She's supposed to suck out all the way, then bang in like hell. This here's spooky, the way water's coming in slow."

Everybody had left the pier, and the water had risen to the hubcaps of the dozen trucks and cars. Hank recognized Jones' pickup among them, and called down, "Want me to run move it?"

"You stay here."

Boats all around were revving engines and moving out. Some floats, as they rose with the water, flooded and disappeared. With a crack the ramp connecting the pier and floats split, tumbled apart, and washed away. One boy had just been ready to cross the ramp. He ran back toward them when it broke, jumping over fallen lightpoles and wires, but the connecting boards on the other side pulled apart. Steve was just coming from the cabin, where the engine had started again, with Jones calling instructions for testing. Hank pointed to the boy, who stood wide-eyed alone on a piece of float with water around his ankles.

Steve ran to the wheel, calling for Jones to stand by. He pointed

138

to their taut mooring lines and yelled to Hank, "Chop the fuckers!," then gunned recklessly among unmanned boats to nose against the float where the boy stood. Hank and Ivan leaned over to pull him aboard. As they gripped his arms, the boat surged up and the float anchored below cracked apart.

The boy's grip remained tight on Hank's arm. "You're okay now. Go in the cabin and lie down if you want."

"And miss all this?" But his hand, when it left Hank's arm, gripped a stanchion until the knuckles glowed white.

Boats milled crazily, those floating without crews blocking others trying to make it beyond the invisible breakwater. Some boats passed free over the line where the rock wall had stretched. Up on the now-deserted pier, the water had reached the car windows.

Jones at his wheel was calm and deliberate as he tried to make it to open water. After the others had tied fenders along the side—tires, crab buoys, anything they could find—they all joined him on the open bridge and watched together. "Funniest tidal wave I ever saw," said Jones. "Just oozed in on us. How'd the earthquake feel on the boat, before I got here?"

"Bump bump bump, up and down like we were bouncing."

"You've seen other tidal waves?" asked Hank.

"Never a killer wave, but I've seen the water come in before." Jones maneuvered and ducked around the flotsam, making little progress. "Goddam, this is the time to get out!" They all watched the water height against the vehicles on the pier. "Long as those pilings don't buckle, I own a truck that needs overhaul." He contacted someone ashore by radio to send word that the boy, Jerry, was safe, and to ask how things were in town.

"Water's crept up a couple feet in Kraft's Drygoods, and she puddled up into the main district. Stopped coming, though, I think she's peaked."

"Where was the earthquake?"

"Nobody knows. Anchorage radio's dead."

"Peaked, eh?" said Jones to the others. "That means she's only got one other direction to go." He gunned straight through a cluster of empty skiffs and logs. "We either make it over those sunken breakwaters now . . ." He changed direction to point the bow toward the short section of the submerged breakwater alongside the narrows, since the normal opening was clogged. Suddenly a force took hold of the boat and raced it along. As they watched, the buildings along the waterfront seemed to rise. The cars and the pier emerged, then the pilings, straight down to their barnacle-encrusted foundations.

"Goddam, the water's sucking out like a bathtub with a hole."

Their view of the town disappeared as the rock breakwater rose from the water beside them. They had passed over it. The *Rondelay's* engine started to miss, the propeller to whirr at a high pitch. Jones shut it down. A moment later the hull scraped, and the boat gradually listed to port so that they had to grip the mast and shrouds to stand on the slanting deck. The water of the harbor had drained, and they lay dead on the bottom surrounded by mud. The stench was immense. Fifty yards away, the long bare breakwater towered above them. At least they had crossed it and were outside the harbor. Its stone and concrete foundation at eye level was black with sea growth. The top rocks that normally stood out of water were covered with drowned rats, their bodies clinging in crevices. As gravity loosened the claws the fat corpses plopped into the mud.

Ivan became agitated. "We better climb on those rocks and run for it; that water's coming back! When I was a kid in the village, my grandfather, he always told how the water came back if the boats ever scraped mud, come in like a wall right over the boats."

"You'd sink over your head in mud getting there," said Jones. "She's a sturdy little boat. We'll weather her." But under his breath he muttered, "Wouldn't mind being further from that wall."

Other boats lay equally helpless around them. Close by was the *Linda J.* Joe Eberhardt's frowning face poked from the cabin and peered around. They could see halfway up the narrows. The three-hundred-foot-wide passage was as drained to the seafloor as their own area, with one small fishing boat heeled over in the center as if at the bottom of a canyon. A man on the boat held onto his mast and appeared to be calling up to the people on the cannery pier, where someone kept trying to throw a line far enough to reach him. The sun had long gone behind the mountains in back of town, and the land was darkening. A chilly breeze puffed around them, agitating the stench of the seamud.

In town, the siren started again.

"Anybody wants to pray," said Jones quietly, "nobody's going to laugh." Ivan fell to his knees, crossing himself and muttering silently.

The statement gave Hank his first chill of fright. He thought through the first lines of an "Our Father" with little concentration.

They heard a thundering, crashing roar, like a train on the way. People on the cannery pier ran toward shore, and the man on the little boat disappeared into his cabin. Down the narrows came a wall of water three or four times the height of the boat as it lay. A forewave lifted the boat from the bottom and started it upward, but a second later the main water roared against it. Hank's last glimpse as Steve shoved him into the cabin was of flying boards as the boat disappeared and the wall of water crashed onward.

The *Rondelay* rose as if on a racer dip, pointing upward so that they tumbled against each other while water poured through cracks in the boat that heavy seas had never reached before. Plates flew crashing from the cupboard. At one point they were nearly vertical, and then the boat spun in a circle. Objects bumped and smashed against the hull. A diesel odor permeated everything. Jones engaged the engine and leaned his full weight into the wheel, but it tore from his grip. Hank fell on deck among broken crockery. He could hear the water beating beneath the boards an inch from his head. As he scrambled to his feet away from it, ripples of water were just flowing clear of the windshield. Outside in the twilight, other boats and objects were spinning.

"She brought us through," said Jones calmly. "Good little boat. Hank, don't just stand there, pick up some of that broken shit on the deck. You're supposed to be the cook."

When they went out on deck, they saw that the *Rondelay* was swirling helplessly with other boats, back in the harbor. The water was high on the harbormaster's pier again, and those parts of the floats that remained were broken and disoriented. Jones gunned and gunned the engine, pointing the boat to sea away from the narrows. "Washed us right back over the breakwater! Better than slamming us into it, but this time while it's submerged we've got to make it over and stay." All around the deck, pieces of gear had disappeared. "Can't batter this boat forever."

Suddenly the water took control in a new way. They gained momentum in a straight line, with everything else in their vicinity traveling in the same direction as the water hissed around them. "I'm not entirely in control here," muttered Jones as he jammed the throttle and turned the wheel desperately. "We're headed for the narrows, right over the top of the breakwater." The water of the narrows rushed out with the roaring whiteness of a waterfall. Hank remembered the tree log at Whale Pass, sucked under. Nothing affected their course. Jones tossed life jackets from the chest by the wheel. "Hank! Put mine on the kid there. Listen. If the rocks are still there she might tear us apart. Grab something that floats and kick toward shore."

But nothing happened. The breakwater must have washed apart. The current drew them toward the chaotic water moving out of the narrows, as if by cables. They grabbed poles to fend off large bumping debris. The boat was turned backwards, and Jones had no control. They moved stern-first around the apron of land where the narrows began. They might have been a stick in a rapids. Faster and faster it took them. They shot past the now-smashed cannery pier as the wind of their motion whistled through the rigging. Jones struggled to bring their bow around, but the water sucking in their wake held it fast. The stern, pointed in the direction of the current, kicked and bounced from side to side. Other boats and broken objects traveled with them, including a black buoy whose light continued to flash.

"At this rate, we'll be out the other end in a couple minutes," said Jones. "Mebbe we'll make open sea after all."

The forward-moving stern hit an object, bounced, veered, settled back on course. "If the son'bitch don't break apart before we get there," said Steve. A calm had settled over them all. "We're not calling the shots," said Jones, "so we might as well relax."

They had zoomed past the airways hangar when Ivan pointed with a cry. Several hundred feet ahead, a boat was tumbling end over end. "It's moving *toward* us!" While everything around them moved inexorably northward, the objects ahead approached head-on in the opposite direction. A terrible spuming no man's land began to explode where the waters collided.

"Holy Virgin Mother, we're trapped," cried Ivan.

Their forward motion stopped with a jolt and the boat spun a full turn. A moment later they were being transported back toward the boat harbor where they had started, in company with the flashing buoy and everything else. Ivan, watching the water with wide eyes and open mouth, knelt and crossed himself, while Jones and Steve laughed crazily. "I'll collect two bucks fare apiece for that ride," Jones declared. But before they were free, the current reversed itself again. It carried them back with less speed but still firmly as far as the airways hangar, then finally returned them to the jumble of boats in the harbor. The boat that had tumbled end over end now floated on its side. As Jones and Steve discussed whether they could save it, Hank recognized the *Olaf*, Chip's and Tolly's boat that they had corked and battled with the summer before.

"Mebbe somebody trapped," said Jones.

"Go alongside, I'll hop aboard," said Steve.

"Too dangerous for you," said Ivan. "I'm going. Chip Hansen and me, we're Aleuts together."

Before they could take any action, the roiling waters had separated them again, and the *Olaf* went its way dipping under.

Daylight had left quickly. Kodiak was dark except for headlights everywhere, crisscrossing, forming lines on the road that led to the top of Pillar Mountain behind town. Jones got on the radio to see whom he could reach. Conversations sputtered and died, but it was obvious from the bits they heard that the town was evacuating, with more waves expected. The town had received no communication except through Hawaii, but somebody had heard that Anchorage, Seward, and Valdez had been destroyed. The *Rondelay* was trapped in the harbor, with logs, boats, and other debris blocking their passage to open water. Some time after dark, the light of a full moon took over, casting objects into black silhouettes, outlining the roofs ashore. Time advanced, with events as jumbled as the debris around them. Sometimes they drew close enough to other boats to shout exchanges, but the general din of water in motion and objects colliding drowned out their own voices.

A dark, shouting figure in an open dory bobbed by, and they grabbed him aboard. It was Tolly of the *Olaf*, haggard, laughing now with relief, his gold earring still in place. He had been alone on the *Olaf*. She scraped a rock and the water came in faster than the pump could carry it out, until the engine flooded. He had grabbed a dory floating by, and last saw the *Olaf* racing out the narrows.

"If I could get back to the narrows," Jones said, "mebbe I'd get through this time."

"No!" said Ivan. "That place is haunted now, from that poor fellow whose boat tore apart around him."

"Everyplace here's haunted by now, I expect."

The water drained out and stranded them on the harbor bottom again, the moon glistening on the temporary mudflats. This time they were inside the breakwater. Flashlights and bonfires flickered all the way up the mountain behind town, and the beams of massed car lights cut into the sky from the top. It was growing chilly. The water on their rigging turned to frost. The crew shared coats with Tolly and the boy, because nobody cared to weather it below.

The third wave roared in over the breakwater, picked them up, and carried them partway into town. They threw a line around a power pole to keep from banging into buildings. Close by their flashlights made out Kraft's Drygoods, and Jones declared they were at the foot of Benson Avenue, but then the big building floated away and they realized they might be anywhere. When the water receded, they found themselves on dry land. Tolly and the boy thanked them and took off uphill at a trot.

It was a ghost town of skewed buildings and piles of wreckage, with clusters of lights from other grounded boats. They climbed down and walked around the *Rondelay*, examining it with their flashlights. She was marred and scuffed, but still whole except for a loose rudder which Jones hurriedly started to fix. As Hank held the light, Jones said, "This ain't the end, and no telling what's coming. Better get yourself up the hill."

"No chance."

"Then stick close, be ready to jump back aboard."

Not far away, a big power scow the size and shape of the *Billy II* was also stranded. With deck lights ablaze, it was the brightest object anywhere. They called back and forth to the crew, and learned that she had three thousand king crabs aboard which she had just come in to deliver.

From a dark boat's shape farther into the harbor a woman's voice called, "Everybody over there all right?"

Steve walked down to the water's edge. "Sure am. How are you?"

"Can't complain, but it's a little scary. My husband's away in Seattle to get parts, but I've run things pretty good."

Steve shone his light in her direction. She had graying hair and wore yellow rain gear. Her boat was listing badly.

"We'll get you off."

"No, no, I can't abandon the boat. I'll be all right."

Steve raced back to the *Rondelay* for a coil of line. "Best pull her off," said Jones.

"She can't lose that boat. I know them people, they've had hard times. I'm going to ride it out with her."

"No. Boat's half sunk, and another wave might do it."

"Bullshit," said Steve easily. By the water's edge he called, "Now, missus, grab this line and secure it. I'm coming aboard."

"Oh!" Her voice brightened. "That's good of you, but I'm fine."

Steve paid no attention except to call "Catch!" The siren started somewhere on the hill. The woman caught the line with alacrity, and they felt it tighten. Jones kept objecting, but he joined with Ivan and Hank to pull as Steve waded out. The boat was still thirty feet away.

There came a terrible roar of crashing and splitting. The moonlight caught a rim of foam on top a black-glinting wave, higher than houses, advancing across the breakwater. Steve lunged into the water, hand over hand toward the woman's boat. Ivan and Jones grabbed him with a lock around each shoulder and raced to the *Rondelay*, with Hank trailing after. Steve cried out, then scrambled aboard with the others. They tumbled into the cabin just as the water hit.

It crashed through their windshield and engulfed them all in glass and foaming water even as it lifted them high and swept them wildly bumping into buildings. Steve cursed and wept as the woman's scream sailed past them and was lost in the general roar. Poles split around them—one barely missed the boat. Timbers broke to a sound like gunshots.

With the window broken they could watch as soon as the *Rondelay* righted itself. The boat swirled in circles, moving up into the business street, past the Mecca Restaurant which strangely remained, then down the street past the supermarket and Tony's Bar. They were headed straight into a wall of Tony's when the big building rose from its foundation and pivoted ahead of them sluggishly. Other boats also dipped around buildings, their lights blinking. It was wild, Hank thought, like hell in the Bible. He could have laughed had it not been for the woman. The big power scow with the crabs aboard sailed grandly past them with lights ablaze. Then the water pulled them back into the harbor, bouncing them against objects like a puck in a pinball machine.

Other boats swirled with them, often close enough to touch, but each boat and its men rode alone.

For more than an hour the hand of the water pushed them in one direction, then returned them. Moonlight gleamed on white-painted boards and parts of structures, while above the dead town refugee lights flickered along the mountainside. "I'm sure Adele's up there safe," said Jones. "Wonder if I've still got a house?" The objects around them sometimes traveled alongside, sometimes moved in colliding directions or disappeared. In the middle of the harbor they rode for several minutes with the Standard Oil Building, its square roof slanting and dipping, and then the waters pulled it out to sea as Jones tried unsuccessfully to follow, while they were whirlpooled back into the center of flotsam. The general roaring and cracking continued, and the smells were everywhere of diesel oil and churned bottom mud.

At length the narrows sucked them in, transported them through white water like a log in a flume past bare shoreline that had recently held the canneries and airways, and spewed them into open water. Their engine grabbed hold and at last pulled them from the grip of the currents. For the first time in hours they rode again in a boat at least partially controlled by themselves.

13

MUD

The Alaska Good Friday earthquake of 27 March 1964 originated fifty miles east of Anchorage, about 200 miles northeast of Kodiak. With a Richter reading of 8.6, it was the heaviest quake ever recorded in North America. In Anchorage, parts of Fourth Avenue dropped thirty feet in seconds. The seismic shock followed from land into the seafloor like a crack through china, and the sudden upheaval generated a chaos of water that roared out in giant sea swells called tsunamis. The swells traveled as terrible walls of water down Prince William Sound and through the Gulf of Alaska to Kodiak Island and beyond. They roared up inlets to destroy the Seward waterfront, and most of Valdez. The water obliterated one village on the mainland (Chenega) and one on Kodiak Island (Kaguyak), while wrecking others to the point where they were eventually abandoned.

The town of Kodiak has several small islands near its harbor (one of which parallels the eastward shore of town to form the narrows), and these diverted the oncoming swells into tricky patterns coming from different directions. It saved Kodiak from a single, total onslaught while subjecting the harbor to a variety of other destructive forces. Throughout the Alaska earthquake area, the total loss of fishing boats and canneries was figured at $13.6 million in 1964 dollars, of which Kodiak suffered the lion's share of $10 million. This included in Kodiak, according to one official set of statistics, 46 crab boats and 35 salmon boats lost and 86 others damaged. There were 17 known dead in the Kodiak town area plus four others in the villages. In the five blocks of downtown Kodiak, 65 structures were destroyed and 23 others damaged, with the inventories of 71 businesses wiped out. This represented 75 percent of all commercial facilities. Beyond the business area, 158 private homes were destroyed and many others severely damaged. Three-quarters of the food supply was also gone in this town of 3000 dependent on imports. The earthquake itself left a permanent mark on Kodiak: it sank the town and the harbor floor five feet.

WHEN the current finally freed them, Jones, like an animal let from its cage, sped the *Rondelay* full power in a straight line. Only the thumps of debris stopped him. The moonlight illuminated an oily swath of ripples and eddies between the black mountain shore of Kodiak and the low line of Woody Island a mile opposite. As they moved, silhouettes of boats, invisible without their lights, appeared in the moonpath. They spent the rest of the night, as did other boats under power which had escaped the current, boarding the pilotless boats, pumping them if necessary, then dropping anchors with maximum chain. Hank kept a list, to tell the owners. Further tsunami waves rolled under them at regular intervals, each lesser than the one before. In open water the waves were graduated rather than crested, so that the *Rondelay* merely rode their tops.

There were boats, or pieces of them, for which nothing could be done. One sank as they watched; others were flooded beyond any ability to pump. On one the hydraulic anchor winch was broken, and Hank followed Steve into oil-thick water up to his thighs to search out the controls and fix them.

They found the *Linda J* riding fully lighted, with coffee water boiling on the stove, a foot of water sloshing in the bilge, deserted. Hank went into a deep malaise, although he continued working. Two hours later, a boat bumped alongside and there was Joe Eberhardt yelling and stomping on the frosty deck of the *Hesperis* as he asked if anybody had seen the *Linda J*. It seems the *Linda* had beached during one of the outsurges, and as Joe, alone in the boat, scrambled underneath to caulk a split seam the next wave roared in. It washed him against a rocky cliff and he clutched and climbed, the water sucking around his waist as he struggled. "I don't ever need to kiss death any closer until the real time comes," he said easily as he gulped coffee aboard the *Rondelay*, but his hands trembled. He was covered with cuts and bruises. "Well, sir, I clung by my balls for one–two hours, because that water never went down again, until finally somebody's skiff floated by, and then later Jack on the *Hesperis* found me. Whoo! You don't know how good it feels to have a deck between you and the water until you've tried it bareass."

They found Joe's boat and Hank transferred over to help clean up and bring her in. Joe continued talking in a hyper state until past four in the morning and then, at Hank's promise to call at any hint of danger, crawled into his bunk, and with a groan fell asleep.

Hank watched the moonlight fade as the sky lightened. With daylight he could see beyond pockets of debris to the vastness of wreckage that sluggishly moved with the water. There were peaks of whole buildings, upturned boats, single splintered boards that eddied in clusters, and an upturned boat. It was like the Hindu creation, when everything first had to be destroyed to start again. Was there a town left? He wondered about the dead, heard the woman's scream again in his mind, shuddered at the never-forgotten touch of Pete's rigid hand beneath cold water, hoped no bodies would float by. It was a time for large and serious thoughts. Nothing had touched him; it seemed nothing *could* touch him as he flexed the firm muscles beneath his shoulders, yet in his mind he knew he was as vulnerable as anybody else, as fragile to fire and water as a piece of paper.

Joe Eberhardt woke with a cry of fright, then gave a deep, self-conscious laugh when he saw Hank's concerned face. They returned up the swirling currents of the narrows, now benign enough to allow passage under normal power. The twin onion domes of the little Russian church on the hill were intact. Then the sights of destruction began. The complex along the narrows had been swept away: cannery, cold storage, plane hangar, fuel dock, boatyard, stores, chandlery—everything. Only the big fuel tanks on higher ground remained, and a few shards of piling.

They entered the harbor. It, too, was swept clean except for debris, where the day before had stretched the two protective arms of the breakwater and had bobbed the long boardwalk floats with their clustered fishing craft. One segment of the breakwater remained standing on the side toward the Navy Base road, a jagged line of stone clotted with the wreckage of hulls and masts. A whole square building floated free, and the humps of broken boats dotted other parts of the water. Beyond the harbor and the low islands, the mountain snows gleamed hazily in the pink early light.

Gone was the entire dock with its cars and harbormaster's hut, and the irregular line of stores and houses in back of it that had fronted the harbor had been replaced by a mudflat through which streams of water trickled. Some boats lay beached on their sides far into town.

Joe Eberhardt began to laugh. "Oh, what a fuckin' mess. Let's find a can of beans that's not waterlogged to celebrate our survival."

They threw out the anchor and waded ashore in mud up to their knees. Water in his boots had for so many hours been part of his condition that Hank merely poured out the excess and waited for the remainder to warm to his body temperature. They slogged up to where the buildings remained. Kraft's Drygoods was only a foundation. Part of the building itself now rested a block farther uptown, where Tony's Bar had stood, and Tony's had been transported to rest straddling the road with a corner on the site of the vanished laundry. A wrecked fishing boat lay alongside. The big power scow that had sailed fully lighted past the *Rondelay* the night before now rested upright two blocks still farther up, between small caved-in stores and houses on one side and an undamaged schoolhouse on the other. Dazed people walked around, kicking at rubble and debris.

"My God," said Hank, "I wonder if Jones Henry still has a house?" He cupped his hands to scan across the harbor. The buildings against the hill appeared to be intact. To himself he admitted that part of his relief was for the safety of his dry clothing (dry shoes!) and camera. Next he wondered about Jody. He left Joe and walked up over the roads, homing toward the domes of the Russian church, to find the house where he had last seen her. All along the way he passed houses moved from their foundations, roofs caved by toppling chimneys, poles down amid tangles of wires, and cars piled against each other. People wandered everywhere, pulling at household wreckage. The corner of one house rested on a child's bike and a smashed wardrobe with clothes tumbling from it. He joined two men and a woman to lever the house with a pole and pull free the clothing. They invited him across the street to another house for coffee. Stepping across the broken pickets of a white fence, they entered a mud-tracked living room where a dozen people sat around the floor and several children of all ages milled among them. Wood blazed in a fireplace, and a coffeepot steamed on a rack near the embers. The woman who had salvaged the clothes passed a jacket and a sweater to two men in shirtsleeves near the fire.

"Thanks. What house do you live in, when I return this?"

"With all your stuff lost? Just keep it."

Hank learned that most of them had spent the night on Pillar
Mountain, but finally around two had grown so cold they decided to risk
further earthquakes and tidal waves under a roof. With its fireplace and
a chimney not tumbled, this was the only house in the neighborhood
that could offer heat and cooking. A couple came in with a carton of
half-thawed steaks. The freezer wouldn't keep things without power,
they announced, so everybody might as well dig in and be merry. Soon
the smell of sizzling meat filled the room. Hank had not realized his
hunger, after a night of candy bars and coffee, until he started eating.
Someone had a battery radio, but they could find no station.

"Up on the mountain last night," said a man, "I heard somebody's
radio pick up Honolulu through the static. It really upset us, because
we heard that Anchorage was wiped out. Then the fellow said Kodiak
and everybody here was washed away, so we figured at least part of the
rest was bullshit too."

Everybody laughed. One man guessed he was ready now to
face the sight of his store downtown and see if anything was left. As he
said, it was now eleven and way past time to open shop. Hank had
peeled his boots and socks to dry by the fire, but the process had barely
begun when he replaced them to move on. Their sogginess was at least
warmer. He decided that Jody could be anywhere (and didn't care
about him that much) while dry socks waited for him back at Jones
Henry's. With the storekeeper he walked down into town, over a ridge
that gave a view of the gutted narrows. Large debris still sloshed through
on a sluggish track.

Downtown, people were pulling mushes of litter from stores and
bars. The storekeeper opened his door, and water and goods poured over
his legs. Hank stayed to help pull some of the heaviest debris into the
street, then moved on. At the beanery he found old Mike staring helplessly at the mess. Half his kitchen equipment had disappeared; the rest
was a jumble. Somehow a telephone pole had washed through the door
and lay blocking everything. This was all he owned besides his house,
Mike declared over and over. How was he ever going to make any kind of
living now? Hank persuaded him to go home and sleep, and promised
he'd come back to help when he could.

He reached Jones Henry's house to find that a mudslide had
tumbled the house from its foundation and that his knapsack and cam-

era were part of the general debris. He owned what he wore, plus a sleeping bag full of seawater and broken glass back on the *Rondelay*.

Adele Henry, her smudged face wrapped in a bandanna and a pair of Jones' boots slapping around her legs, threw out her hands when she saw him and declared, "Will you look at this? And I just painted all the goddam rooms." Then she hugged him and cried. "Oh, I'm so tired. If I could sleep I think I could face it. *He* won't help, Jones won't help, he's already back on his damned boat repairing leaks. It's our living, I know that, but he didn't even look twice at the house. Just said he was glad to see me alive and wanted me to know he was the same. Oh! The praying and agony all night as those terrible waves crashed, and I could see you boys splintered apart in that little boat. . . ." Her fingers dug into his shoulders. He patted her and mumbled whatever he could think that was soothing, not knowing what else to do. At length she released him and wiped her face. "Thank God we're all alive."

He had meant to return to the *Rondelay*, but he stayed with her for the rest of the morning to move lamps and furniture from the living room, where the floor was smashed, to other rooms that had survived intact. The house now tilted downhill, as did all the floors. Other houses nearby were in the same fix. He looked down at the harbor, where broken boats and parts of buildings floated everywhere. The few boats intact looked small and vulnerable without the security of the breakwater. Over in town, sky reflected in the water that meandered through mud-flats where stores had been. Whole buildings lay helter-skelter hundreds of feet from their foundations, with beached boats listing alongside. Where would you start cleaning, and how could it ever be the same?

Hank had been scheduled to leave Kodiak for Baltimore the day after Easter, and by that time a partial plane service had resumed. But you don't leave a friend in need, he told himself. He compromised by signing a waiting list to make a phone call home.

Kodiak was indeed a town in need of willing backs, a muddy mess of a town. The wrecked part had to be destroyed to allow room for the remainder to function, while that which had survived needed to be set right again laboriously. For a day or two, nearly everybody was in a daze. The Navy Base, which had sustained its share of destruction, sent over guards to cordon off the business district. Only storeowners could enter.

As people pulled themselves together and felt in themselves the strength to rebuild rather than to abandon, they identified priorities. The prime ones were to patch a wharf so that supply ships could unload, to clear and burn the mountains of debris, to restore the seafood plants so that a fishing income could again be generated, and to construct a new breakwater and floats to protect the surviving boats. With disaster status, the town began to receive heavy equipment through the Navy Base and from the Army Corps of Engineers. Hank watched with relief as a crane hoisted Jones Henry's house back onto its foundation. However, it remained for humans to do all the crowbar and shovel work. The downtown was a soggy jumble of broken furniture, boards, boat pieces, crab pots, clothing, and spoiled food, which bulldozers shoved into piles for burning. Every boat needed repairs. Jones, with the *Rondelay* at least running, helped clear the harbor. Among other jobs, they lassoed and towed to safe anchorage the entire loft of a cannery building, floating intact with the stored seines of at least thirty boats inside. When they brought it close to the wrecked cannery itself, Hank saw Swede Scorden, his mackinaw torn and his yellow cap greasy, directing repairs as he put his shoulder with the rest to a piece of machinery.

The *Rondelay* also carried fishermen along the shores of the islands near the harbor to search for their missing boats. They found one boat safely transported to an island lake, another intact but two-thirds buried in mud, others broken into pieces.

The town quickly assumed a collective vitality. It never seemed to sleep except in the earliest morning hours. A new school building had been designated as the refugee center. Many worked there as volunteers while still setting their own properties to rights. The center served the Kodiak homeless and the shaken native villagers brought in by fishing boats, and also functioned as a community resource pool, since electric stoves were inoperative and most food on grocery shelves had been spoiled. In the kitchen, disheveled teenagers in sneakers joked and shouted as they washed hundreds of dishes and hustled them back for immediate reuse.

Downtown, signs appeared on storefronts with inscriptions like "Visit scenic Kodiak, and see the boats come in and the buildings go out." Said one grocer to Hank with a wink as he shoveled the gumbo from the front of his place: "Don't knock mud and Post Toasties unless you've tried it, son." One silt-floored bar passed out free beer to the labor crews and advertised for a price such new mixtures as the All Shook-Up and the Miss Sue Nami's Special. However, nipping appeared to have replaced boozing for the moment, even with Ivan, and no one occupied a barstool for long.

When Hank finally reached his parents by phone, he was unprepared for their emotion. They had feared him dead. After their voices steadied, his father asked him to be careful, but said that they both respected his desire to help evacuate women and children before the town was abandoned, as they knew was happening from newspaper stories. "Hey, Dad," shouted Hank with a sudden heady sense of pride. "My town's *alive!*"

Activity and humor did not signify an absence of misery, even despair. A modern community with houses tied to roads and electricity cannot casually revert to a life of caves and bearskins, even a community as accustomed to ruggedness as Kodiak. The sunny weather left. It began to snow and rain. Until power was slowly restored day by day in various sections, every house without a fireplace was dark, cold, and damp. Nor had the quakes stopped: new tremors shook the town daily, one of them strong enough to bounce objects from shelves and tables again. Hardly anyone, including Jones Henry, carried earthquake or flood insurance, so losses were total. There were the burials. People referred wryly to their nightmares. Hank occasionally saw men as well as women, giddy with fatigue, leaning for support against the tide-skinned wall of a building as they clenched fists or bit back tears. The wonder of it was that so few departed and that so many pulled themselves together day after day to face the work again.

Two great shadows hung over town: the tides and the winds. People grew to ignore the residual earthquakes, but they watched the water with morbid attention. It remained high and rose from a new level on each normal flood tide. A strong blow might drive the water straight back into town. As for the boats, what would protect them from a heavy northeaster until a new breakwater and floats were completed? The tsunami had also washed clean the harbor bottom, so that anchors had only rock to grip. Uptown, some of the merchants deferred any replenishment of stocks until they saw the effects of two extreme high tides predicted for April.

The first planes into town had brought a predictable wave of reporters and politicians. The federal disaster people followed soon after. By midweek, Kodiak had a population of strangers who wandered through the mud in new boots and store-fresh parkas without turning a hand, stopping busy people to ask questions and running into the paths of machinery to take pictures.

With Steve and Ivan both aboard the *Rondelay* to help Jones, Hank took off to clear the beanery for Mike. The first job was to horse out the monstrous telephone pole. Mike had meanwhile taken inventory of his equipment. The waters had made some strange tradeoffs, and he found both his safe and his long counter washed through the window into the bar across the street, while he himself had objects around his stove that he had never seen before. As Hank sweated and inched the heavy safe back from across the street, he had to give way to a tractor hauling a fishing boat back to the water. The crew was busy steadying the boat on an inadequate wheelbed.

"Hey, thought you'd be safe in school by now." It was Jody, in the driver's perch. She was as smudged and tattered as he and the rest were. Hank left the safe to walk alongside. She asked how Jones and the *Rondelay* had made out, and liked the fact that he was helping Mike put the beanery back together. "Where do you sleep?"

"Jones Henry's or the boat, whichever's closest when I'm ready. How about you?"

"Friends."

"You sure stay a mystery woman."

"It's called independence."

A photographer and reporter came over as a team, taken by the sight of Jody on the tractor. While the photographer danced in front and to the side, the reporter brushed Hank away as he said in a businesslike voice, "Now, sis, to begin with I need your name and where you're from, and then I want to interview you. Can't you stop that thing?" Jody replied with a string of obscenities that shocked even Hank after all he had heard. Taking his cue, he told them to move off. Jody looked at him and started laughing, and the two of them could barely stop. Hank felt lighthearted for the first time in days.

During the next days as Hank set the beanery to rights they crossed each other's paths often. They even had a couple of beers together. Jody was as rough as the worst of her surroundings, but she smiled only when she meant it, and her eyes, even tired, sparked easily with humor. Hank relaxed and smiled back directly, enjoying every minute of her company in a way he had not done before.

One night she walked him down in the rain and mud to the *Rondelay,* which with the other surviving boats rode at anchor in the absence of floats. Next day would mark a week since the tsunami. Heavy equipment had just arrived to start cutting rock from a mountain and move it in, but the two legs of the breakwater remained no more than a jagged line in the water. Hank shouted, and Steve brought the skiff to fetch him.

"Hi, Jody," said Steve. "You sure look tired and wet. Ivan and me, we made a good codfish chowder and there's plenty left. Stove can dry your clothes. Got a spare bunk, too." Without hesitation Jody climbed into the skiff.

On board, Ivan fidgeted to clean the mess until Jody calmly told him to stop it and go to bed. Steve had already peeled and hung his wet clothes, pulled into dry long johns, and crawled into his bunk. While Hank watched, unbelieving, and Ivan became so flustered he grabbed the toiletpaper and disappeared outside, Jody undressed, hung her clothes around the stove, asked which was Hank's sleeping bag, and then slipped down inside it, naked.

"I . . . guess I'll clear this bunk up here . . ."

She looked at him with a tired, amused raise of an eyebrow and folded over the flap of his bag. He undressed quickly and eased in beside her. Whatever his fatigue, the touch of her skin woke him at once. Within the tight cloth their arms worked slowly around each other. After the cold and wet, he had never felt anything so comfortable as their bodies together, and their sex developed as spontaneously as breathing. When Ivan bumbled back into the cabin, they were easing into a contented sleep.

Hank was aware simultaneously of a scraping bump that made the entire boat shudder, and Steve's exclamation as he snapped the light cord and scrambled into clothes. Ivan followed, muttering and cursing. Outside, the wind blew in a high-pitched wail. Hank wriggled from the sleeping bag and dressed. His clothes were only half dry.

"Sounds like the worst kind of blow," murmured Jody soberly.

Steve rushed in dripping and knelt to start the engine. "Go put out all the fenders you can find, then help Ivan with the anchor. Hold tight to the rails."

On deck in the blackness, wind and icy spray roared around his head like jetfire in a furnace, cutting through his oilskins and striating his face painfully as he struggled to put over mats and tires. Ivan was releasing the anchor chain link by link to retain control against the wind force. Without warning the wind shifted. The chain groaned and tightened in the new direction, then gave a shudder as the anchor lost its grip on the bare-rock bottom and jumped.

Steve appeared. "Wish Boss was here," he yelled over the noise. "I got the engine warmed; we maybe ought to head to sea." They turned to the spot where the town lay invisible in the dark. Somewhere a few hundred yards from the boat, Jones probably paced the beach, helpless to join them.

A while later, in the first gray of morning, smoky spray swirled from wave to wave, covering the harbor with long fingers. Jagged exposed patches of the ruined breakwater loomed close astern. Two boats had already broached against its rocks and were being beaten by the wind-kicked water. The *Rondelay*'s anchor jumped again, moving them closer. Steve's mouth was tight and his eyes troubled in a way Hank had never seen before. "Maybe ought to pull anchor and steam out. But if the engine stopped, without the anchor, we'd blow straight to the rocks, wouldn't we?" The question gave Hank sudden unease. Their glances kept wandering instinctively toward shore, where in the dim light figures moved everywhere. Steve chewed his lips. "What if we tied a line to the skiff, picked up Jones from the rocks?"

"Couldn't pull back against this wind," said Hank.

"God*dam* it, Boss would sure know what to do!"

The wind carried a man's cry. They looked to see a boat—the *Linda J*, with Joe Eberhardt on deck—drifting in their direction, toward the rocks. Joe had a coiled line that he tried to throw to them, but the wind blew it back in his face.

"Must have slipped his chain," Steve exclaimed, suddenly turning decisive. He unlashed a coil of line and heaved it. The line traveled with the wind, but just as it was about to hit Joe's deck a counter gust dropped it in the water. Steve had already freed another coil and sent it flying. Joe caught it, and scrambled falling on deck to secure it.

The *Linda J* had now blown past them. The line between them drew taut. Joe had only managed to pull in a foot or two of slack, not enough to tie, and he held the weights of the boat and wind in his own hands. Steve threw their own line off the bitt—they only had a few feet themselves—and the three of them with Jody, who had appeared, gripped the end and dug their feet into the stern rail for support. For a moment Joe had slack, but the motion of the boats pulled it from him before he could use it. Spurts of blood shot from his hands as his end of the line whipped free and fell into the water.

The *Linda J* glided into the rocks with a crash they heard above the wind. Splinters of wood shot in the air and blew away. She quickly broached. Joe had grabbed a pole and desperately tried to push from the rocks. The boat smashed, eased off, smashed again. His pole snapped and he found another. Hank watched his smallness, seen from the *Rondelay* against the horizon of spray swirls each as big as the boat, and knew the fight had a foregone conclusion. A violent broadside threw Joe from his boat onto the rocks. He clutched the gunwale and pulled himself back aboard, then groped along the tilted deck to switch futile fenders to the inboard side. Finally the boat began to sink lower as he fended off again with a pole. He threw some gear onto the rocks and, with a box under his arm that Steve said was his radar, abandoned her. As he staggered down the breakwater toward shore, leaning into the wind, the smoky spray closed around to hide him from view.

The wind gusted and the *Rondelay's* anchor scraped again, jumping them closer to the rocks.

"We better do something!" Ivan exclaimed.

"Jesus Christ," cried Steve in anguish, "what would the Boss do?"

"Look," said Hank. "Stay at anchor and kick the engine forward to take the strain off. Just keep doing it until the blow stops. Anything wrong with that?"

Steve considered it for a second, then began to pound his back. *"That's* it!" His face relaxed. Soon he stood by the wheel inside, kicking the engine.

Hank stayed on deck longer than the others, as if by watching the battered *Linda J* he might salvage her. Sometimes the wind seemed to slack, but then it would scream to a higher pitch than before. The storm around him was frightening; so was the whole fishing business. Good his life was not committed to it. He found it hard to picture the calm and green-budding world back in Maryland. A few days and he'd be there again. Except for Jody . . .

Before going inside, he struggled back to the bow against the wind to inspect the anchor. Suddenly he felt like the skipper of the *Rondelay,* removed from the others by the responsibility of decisions. Was this how Jones Henry felt? Steve's relaxed face grinned up from the window by the wheel, at the level of his legs, as he gave an extra engine spurt which made the chain droop slack with a clank. It was a gesture to prove how well the plan worked. Hank nodded his comprehension gravely, then left the miserable weather for the warmth of the cabin.

PART 3:
1970, WINTER TO FALL

14

SHRIMP
BOATS

ORMER Lieutenant Henry Crawford of the U.S. Navy, recently returned from Vietnam waters and more recently discharged with
honor, stepped from the plane at the Kodiak airport. Snow covered
the mountains more thickly than he had seen in his summer and spring
trips to the island six years before, and snow lay on the ground. It was a
sunny February day, no colder than back east. The glare hurt his eyes as
keenly as it might on a ski slope in Stowe. He waited for his bags to appear, trying to remain detached and dignified as he consumed every
detail.

Jones Henry, his hair grayer and his glasses thicker, advanced
smiling with arms open and bear-hugged him. Adele Henry, heavier,
with her hair now bleached, followed with her own big embrace. Hank
forgot his lieutenant's reserve, shouldered his new seabag exuberantly,
and followed them to the pickup truck.

He sat between them straddling the gear shift as they joggled
along the rough-paved road to town.

"So they made you an officer? I ain't surprised. Wait'll you see
my new boat. She's got plumbing."

"You've been to Vietnam," said Adele. "Hank, was it terrible over
there? Are all those college students justified in the ruckus they've
made?"

He claimed the right he had seen many take in order to avoid
admitting to the boredom, the dissatisfactions of such a war, and his own
general doubts. "Rather not talk about it. Sorry."

Adele put a hand to her mouth, completely cooperative. "I

shouldn't have asked. Tell me, were you on any of those Navy ships that picked up the astronauts when they came back from the moon?"

"Afraid not."

"And I promise you won't recognize the boat harbor. She's a regular marina. As for the town, you get a buck from me for every building you can recognize from the old days before the earthquake."

"I find it hard to remember the old town," said Adele. "We still don't have an opera house, Hank, but we've got some decent buildings. And of course Jones and I've flown down to Seattle and San Francisco a couple of times, and even to Honolulu last Christmas, so I've had a look at a few of the world's glories. But *you*—you've been all the way to the Orient."

"Remember Gibson's Cove down there? The National Marine Fishery boys, they go out with the Coast Guard now to board the Japs and Russians. Every now and then they seize one of the bastards and bring him in, since we've finally got a law or two and the foreigners can't fish closer than twelve miles. Don't have the sight of 'em from this hill any more, taking our catch from under our noses. You know, it wasn't more than three weeks after the earthquake—you'd left by then— that a whole Russian factory fleet moved in sight of the harbor and looted our king crabs. Figured our boats was too smashed to compete. Bastards even used tangle nets, the kind that tear up the throwback crabs so half don't live, the kind there's a law against Americans using." Jones' face flushed and his voice rose. "If I'd live to be three hundred I'd never forget or forgive—"

"Now, Daddy," Adele interrupted. "Does you no good, so let's change the subject. Hank, did you like the Navy?"

"Ships were so big I hardly knew I was at sea. I'm spoiling to be on a proper fish boat again."

Jones stopped the truck on top of the ridge overlooking the harbor and town and waited for his reaction.

"It hasn't changed!" Hank exclaimed. He had feared to see a metropolis of hamburger joints and skyscrapers and factories, and here it was the town of his memory, slightly enlarged. Cannery row on the shoreline below them had a longer line of the ugly steaming sheds on pilings, the boat harbor was larger and more crowded, some brighter buildings bordered a new square facing the waterfront, and the hills leading back along the narrows had more houses where trees had been —but changed? There remained even the little twin domes of the Russian church, painted a bright fresh blue. He could have kissed the ground.

"You just haven't had a chance to see," said Adele.

"Not changed?" Jones was annoyed. "Look at all them boats. Whole new shrimp fleet's been added. We've got three times the dock space! Look down there, straight below. Ever seen so many canneries in one line? And look at the new town square, you recognize a *thing* in that from the shanties on old Main Street?"

Hank laughed happily. "You're right, Jones, it sure has changed."

"I should hope so." They resumed their drive.

As they entered town, Hank saw without question that there were more homes on the hills. Jones turned at a filling station and parked in a wide square where a row of waterfront stores and houses once had stretched. Boxing the square on three sides were new buildings, none higher than two stories, all of them sheltered sensibly from the weather by a continuous roofed walkway. The fourth side opened on the harbor several hundred feet distant, guarded by a high little harbormaster's building and fronted by a sturdy wharf.

"Daddy, Hank's traveled for twenty hours, he wants to go home and clean up, not stop in town."

"What do you want, Hank, take a bath or see my *Adele H?*"

"Excuse me, Adele, I really would . . ."

"Well, I'll go shopping, and you can pick me up in the dress store when you're done looking at boats."

"You bought three new dresses in Honolulu."

"Go play with your boat."

From the wharf, the distant mountains gleamed majestic and white in the sun, the water was blue, and the assembled masts formed a community of snowcovered rigging. Birds dipped everywhere. A high, sturdy breakwater enclosed the boats as before. Hank followed Jones, creeping sideways down a ramp with treads iced smooth, and along the slushy boardwalk floats.

"There she is," said Jones grandly, and swept his arm toward a chipped white boat with ADELE H painted across the stern. The *Rondelay* had been forty-two feet long, and here was a boat of seventy feet with a fully enclosed wheelhouse above the cabin.

Hank walked up and patted the rail. Snow tumbled over him from a stay. "Hey, Jones, she's a honey." He climbed aboard, slipped and fell on deck, and rose brushing snow from his overcoat. "Just a honey."

"I figured you'd appreciate her."

Hank went astern to examine a long drum wound with heavy net. "So this is shrimp gear? Really different than the old seine. You sure you're willing to take on a green hand? I've gone pretty soft."

"Be a pleasure to have you," Jones said seriously. "But I doubt the fishing life's going to suit you any more, with all your learning and being an officer. And, like I wrote, with Steve and Ivan being my regular crew all these years on a three-man shrimper, I can't even pay a part share, just your feed. You're always welcome in my house for however long, that goes without saying."

"Every bit of that's fair enough, Jones. After college I worked for a stockbroker, then did the Navy thing when my draft board closed in. The only thing I've ever done that stays in my mind was fishing on the *Rondelay*."

"You'll find that changed too. When you go out in the winter, there ain't much fun left in fishing. You do it to meet the payments."

The cabin door flew open, and there was big Steve in boots and long underwear. The black pirate's beard had strands of gray, and the face was weathered, far older, but who could have mistaken him? Steve's huge hand engulfed Hank's as they pounded each other's backs.

The cabin of the new boat was luxurious compared to that of the *Rondelay* as he remembered it. The extra twenty-eight feet made possible a galley with table and seats, a wide counter, and a four-burner stove; bunks in a separate compartment forward; the enclosed wheelhouse above; and an engine room below.

Steve kicked one of the lower bunks. "Hey, you drunk Aleut, shake your ass and see what's come."

The low, Ivan-type groan started new memories in Hank's mind. He had seen men in the Navy made punchy by booze, so that as the feet in dirty socks began to twitch, he waited apprehensively. Ivan's swarthy, high-cheeked face looked up at him with eyes clearer than ever before, as he grunted, scratched his chest, and grinned. "Son of a bitch, the highline kid." He leaned over and slapped Hank's leg affectionately. "You going to catch some shrimp with us? Good. Bring us luck."

On the way back to Jones Henry's house they stopped to buy him boots, thermals, foul weather gear, and lined waterproof gloves. By the time they had finished a long lunch with a bottle of wine (Adele's idea), and he had talked alternately about fishing with Jones and the larger world with Adele, it was three in the afternoon but already turning dark outside. He watched the town and harbor through the picture window in the living room as a blue glow settled over the snowy masts and roofs and lights began to flicker.

So many people to ask about. Some, like Sven the *Rondelay* cook, had drifted their ways to other boats and places, while others like Steve and Ivan remained. Some of the skippers and crews had died by the sea, some had new boats, others fished as before. Tolly Smith was now his own skipper: the *Juggernaut*. Joe Eberhardt, following the destruction of the *Linda J*, took a government disaster loan and bought a boat big enough for king crabbing: the *Nordic Rose*. Somewhere along the line he had separated from Linda (or the other way around, as Adele interrupted to tell it). Swede Scorden was meaner than ever: he now ran three canneries, including the one Hank had known, for a company headquartered in Seattle.

"Then you mean there's still salmon fishing of the old *Rondelay* kind?" asked Hank. Jones' affirmative answer brought him great pleasure, especially the information that the *Rondelay* itself still pursed the salmon. When he had run through all the other names he remembered, he asked about Jody, the one foremost on his mind. "Guess she's married."

"Jody?" Adele shook her head with satisfaction. "The girl's still free as a man. Hope she stays that way and doesn't panic. I saw her in town the other day, just back from six months in San Francisco. Said she missed the shrimp fleet in the winter. She had two carts full of groceries, buying for a boat, I forget which."

"*Shalimar*," said Jones. "Mike Stimson's boat."

"Did you, uh . . . tell her I was coming back?" asked Hank.

"I mentioned it," said Adele. "She thought she remembered you, but she wasn't sure. Looks like no girl's got you on the leash." Hank shrugged. "Well, sometimes I think fishermen marry their boats, no matter what girl they take to the preacher. Maybe nobody up here should marry, just live around and not get stuck."

"Sometimes you talk like a commie," Jones growled.

"Daddy, I raised three children for you. I scraped and struggled with it all alone while you scraped and struggled out fishing to pay for it. Now all three kids live somewhere else, and we get letters from them now and then. You still fish, and it's your whole life, you've lost nothing. I'm left home holding the bag."

"With all the bills paid, and no more worries. I even added a sewing room to the house."

"Trapped in man's country, you mean. Why, even when I bullied you into trips outside, you thought of nothing but how your boat was doing." She slapped her hand on the chair arm. "I'm going to run for the Council next election."

Jones studied her for a minute, then slapped his own chair arm. "What the hell, I'll vote for you. Council couldn't be any worse than it is now, and it'll mebbe get you off my back."

By four in the afternoon it was night. Hank excused himself to walk into town, promising to return for dinner at seven, when Steve and Ivan were invited. The cold penetrated at once. He had been in the tropics too long; it would take getting used to. Lights glimmered in town and reflected on snowcovered rigging and cannery steam. Often he stepped to the roadside for cars, a problem he had not remembered from before. Downtown had indeed changed its configuration. It had to be approached as a new place instead of an old friend revisited. He looked hopefully at each face. They were the same types, but he recognized no one.

The excitement of returning to Kodiak had carried him through the pressures of disengagement back east, but now he felt his doubts with dizzying force. The town was lonely, sufficient without him, and he came to it as an adult stranger without a kid's options of washing dishes and bunking in a barracks or town jail. His parents, for what they mattered, had challenged him to define what on earth he thought he wanted, to go backward to the life of a fisherman. His answers had been a jumble of illogic within the East Coast context. To waste the precious time when young men laid the groundwork of their careers? Said his father: "Take responsibility in business or some other affair that matters, and you'll find plenty of adventure and satisfaction. Fishing's honest work, naturally, if you haven't trained for anything."

He went into Tony's, noisy with hard-beat music and shouts as ever, sat on a barstool beside two shaggy fisherman types, and gulped down a double Scotch. It had begun to take effect, and he had ordered another, when he recognized Jody. She sat on a wall bench, surrounded by burly, ruddy men, and they were all laughing. Her hair style had changed, but not the wonderously wide mouth and the lively eyes. She looked no older. How would he have appeared to her standing straight in lieutenant's uniform? Often she had returned to his mind over the years, as a gauge for other women, and no one had ever duplicated for him the night in the sleeping bag.

"Hi, Jody, remember me?"

The smile that had been there already stayed as she looked him over. Then, cheerfully, "Bring up a chair, Hank," as if she had last seen him a week before.

She introduced him to the others by first names alone, and they shook with the big, water-softened hands of fishermen. He ordered a round.

"So, where have you been all these years? Someplace where they give haircuts, I see."

Hoping to impress her, he said, "Vietnam, Navy."

"I thought you'd have had the brains to talk your way out of that one."

"Shrimp's the big thing up here now, apparently," he said to change the subject. "I don't hear a word about salmon and crab any more."

"This is shrimp *season*, Hank. Come in May for salmon talk, and start the king crab talk in August. What brings you to Kodiak—curiosity? Or does some college have you writing a book on how the fishermen take their booze?"

"I came back to fish." He hoped they would not laugh. "I'm going out with Jones Henry on the *Adele H.*"

"Jones has a full crew."

"Work without pay until I shake down, then look for a boat that needs somebody."

"What's wrong?" asked Jody, less harshly. "Get in trouble back home?"

"I want to go fishing, that's all."

"You mean for a week or two?"

"I had in mind a career."

"You mean like one of those government jobs, and then you get retired on full pay?"

His face felt hot and prickly. He looked at his watch, and rose casually. "Do it a step at a time, I guess. Hope to see you guys around again. And Jody, nice..."

She regarded him seriously. "You just order that shot for decoration? Keep us company. Maybe the boys can tell you which boats to look for."

With Jody's guidance, the tone of the conversation changed to how he was going to get along. As far as they knew, no skipper had an opening, but at this time of year out there, guys had enough accidents that it didn't hurt to go the rounds of canneries as each boat unloaded.

"You ain't the only one out looking," said Mike, and pointed to a burly kid of about twenty who sat alone on a barstool, nursing a beer. "He's been around since Christmas, looking for somebody to take him. Skippers give him trips now and then just for grub, the way you're doing. What's his name? Let's call him over."

"Seth, get over here," said Jody. The kid hurried over with a hopeful, almost puppydog expression. "Seth, shake hands with Hank here."

"Hello, sir," he said in a husky voice. "Seth O'Malley. Are you a skipper?"

"Oh, Jesus," laughed Mike. "Its so cold out there."

"Afraid I'm just looking for a shrimp boat too," said Hank gravely. The difference in their ages was painful: O'Malley resembled half a dozen enlisted kids to whom he had assigned daily shipboard jobs in Vietnam to the accompaniment of respectful salutes.

O'Malley's manner changed to caution at once. "No work around, I can tell you that." He looked warningly at Hank. "Two or three of the skippers—the *Juggernaut, Lady Eve, Columbia, Dolores R*, all of those —said they'd take me for sure if they ever get an opening."

"Okay," said Hank. "I'll steer clear of those."

The statement relaxed Seth somewhat. "Well, when I get a berth, I won't mind telling you what else I might see around." Hank learned that he slept in a deserted cannery and bummed meals off fishing boats when he could. He himself felt like an old sage as he pulled out his pipe and filled it. "I used to wash dishes in a beanery around here. It fed me all the food I could hold."

Jody threw back her head and laughed. "I remember! You squirmed in there as wet-dog as Seth here the first time he came to the boat, scared shitless I'd charge you for a coffee refill or something. And I'd been in Kodiak a whole six months, I knew all the score."

"You were a stranger too? I thought you were born here."

"Order us all a round, Mike." Jody lit a cigarette as Mike complied and said lightly, "Army brats are never born in a single place. I could tell you about Okinawa, or Texas, Germany, Georgia. . . . They all look the same after the Army clears a space and puts up barracks. So. You played soldier through the Navy, eh?"

"Hey," said Seth, relieved, "you're with the Navy Base out there in Women's Bay, aren't you? You're just kidding about a shrimp boat?"

Hank shook his head.

By the time he returned for Adele Henry's dinner at seven, he was pleasantly full of Scotch (plus a round of rum that came by mistake), and singing to himself. Things looked terrible, but things weren't so bad.

Steve and Ivan sat awkwardly in overstuffed chairs, their hands rigid on the arms. Adele seemed to tower over them. "You boys want to wash up?"

"No, ma'am, we already washed on the boat," said Steve, gazing up warily.

When a bell rang in the kitchen and Adele bustled off, all three men relaxed visibly. "What's your poison, Hank?" asked Jones. He and Steve held glasses of whiskey and ice. Ivan, clear-eyed and gloomy, drank an opaque yellow liquid.

Hank flopped loosely on the couch, on the end close to Ivan, as his thickened tongue bumbled over the words. "Just anything you got, babe, make it double and don't bother with the rocks."

Jones glanced toward the kitchen. "You take it on the rocks in this house, my friend. Mrs. Henry says it ain't refined to drink it any other way. Now, sherry, you can have that straight from the bottle."

Hank cheerfully clutched his throat.

Ivan turned a stolid, indignant face. "You stink like a barroom, you know? Either you move or I got to move. People could get drunk just smelling your breath." Hank stared, amazed. His face must have shown he was about to make a joke of it because Steve frowned and shook his head. "And I want to tell you this," Ivan continued earnestly. "Booze is no good." He gestured toward Jones Henry approaching with a filled glass. "Hank, just say: No thanks, Boss, I know you mean okay but I'm through. Pour that devil's shit—" He glanced with apprehension toward the kitchen. "I mean, say to him—Boss, pour that evil stuff down the crapper where it belongs." He looked up at Jones and appealed, "Boss won't mind, will you, Boss?"

"Drink your pineapple juice," said Jones, and handed Hank the glass.

Adele Henry returned, and both Steve and Ivan leapt to their feet. "Sit down, boys. Daddy, I'll have my martini. Now, Hank. We've had President Nixon in office nearly a year. I want to know how you think he's doing."

Hank eased to a seat away from Ivan as he fumbled to make his answer sound intelligent. He disliked Nixon's face and manner, yet the new President's decisions seemed like good ones. As for Agnew, he could say with authority as a Marylander, "I didn't even like him as president of the PTA." Adele clung to every word.

"Then you tell me this," said Jones Henry. "When we can't get them Russians even to honor agreements to stop overfishing our stocks, what makes you think we'll get anything but a jumbo-sized shaft from these Strategic Arms Limit talks they started last November? I think Nixon's a fellow ought to come out here and try to pull a few shrimp or crab away from a Russian trawler before he sends people to Moscow to make bargains. They'll never make any agreement they won't cheat on, and what have they got that we need so bad?"

"I . . . think we've got to trust . . ." Hank was not that sure of it himself.

"Daddy, stop running your mouth when you don't know a thing about it. Hank's just *been* in Washington where it all happens."

The dinner, when she finally served it, was elegant. Hank had not eaten such fish since leaving Alaska. Adele insisted he open the wine and serve it properly, since Jones wouldn't know the difference between chablis and barswill. The last thing he wanted was more alcohol of a different variety, but he drank his dosage, as did Jones. Ivan was allowed a glass of ginger ale without question. Steve's lips curled beneath the beard at the taste of the wine: when Adele turned away for a moment, he got it over in a single gulp. She, however, mellowed with the wine enough to insist that Ivan and Steve take heaping seconds of the food, and then to comment that Jones was lucky to have a fine and reliable crew.

Possibly Hank slept that night. But he leapt from bed the instant Jones tapped, and with nervous hands dressed in everything warm he could pack against his body. Outside, a cold wind cut across the harbor. They bent into it, saying nothing.

After the cold, he began to sweat almost at once in the stifling heat of the boat's cabin. The air was full of the heavy bacon and coffee odors he remembered. He removed some of his clothes and went to the stove where Steve was flipping potatoes in a big iron skillet. "Better let me get started on something easy, mate."

"Hey," said Steve heartily, "he's already smelled the job that gets him out of the cold."

As they ate breakfast around the comfortable table, Ivan pointed his thick finger at Hank's face and said through a mouthful of food: "You won't be a highline kid much longer if you don't lay off that booze shit, Hank."

Steve splatted catsup over Ivan's eggs and roared, "Shut up, you reformed Aleut."

"Hey, I don't like that much catsup!"

"You've sure gone on the wagon," said Hank.

Ivan's dark, high-boned face flushed with excitement. "Thank the Lord Jesus Christ and His Mother the Holy Virgin! I saw the dawn before it was too late. Steve and Boss helped me." His eyes watered. "I'll never forget it."

"Eat your fuckin' eggs," said Steve.

Jones and Steve began to discuss the depth they would set the trawl. "I don't trust that portside door," said Jones. "She came loose last time. Check it before we go out. Hank, we'll show you some of this gear while we're in harbor water. Finish up."

173

Outside, they swept and shoveled the snow from the deck. Then Steve took Hank aft to the long drum around which the net was rolled. "You've never gone drag fishing, right? This trawl here's nothing but a big fancy bag made of web, with all kinds of gear to make it lay proper. You unwind it from the drum into the water, weight it to the bottom with its mouth open, and drag it along to catch up the shrimp."

"Ever seen a butterfly net, Hank?" called Jones from the entrance to his wheelhouse on the deck above. "She's wide at the mouth, and she gets narrower all the way to the cod end."

"Now here's how you keep the mouth open," said Steve, patting a series of floats wrapped under the webbing on the drum. "These string along with the head rope and hold up the top as she drags." He slapped some gray metal balls in a different series. "These are your bobbins. They're heavy, they go with the foot rope and weight down the bottom end of the mouth. They bump below the web on the seafloor and save web-snags on the rocks. Then the sides of your mouth, that's what the doors keep open." He pointed to a massive steel square secured against the rail on either side of the boat. They resembled slightly curved doors.

"You want to be accurate, Hank, you call the doors otter boards," said Jones. "When you lower them hooked to each wing of the net, they plane out as you move through the water. They keep the mouth apart, and they hold everything down to the bottom. They each weigh seven hundred pounds. You stay clear until you know what you're doing, because if they start slamming in seas they smash where they please."

"Boss is right," Steve added. "You let Ivan and me handle the doors, understand?"

"The whole trawl," continued Jones, "she's tuned and balanced. To begin with, the webmaker sews together a dozen separate pieces, and the way he cuts and fits them tells the way she'll ride. It ain't like a seine with just a simple long wall of web. Then, as we shoot the trawl, I control where I place it by the length of cable I let out and by my speed. It's a whole new set of tricks from seining. For instance, the salmon swim near the beach and close to the surface, but these little shrimp buggers live in the mud forty–sixty fathom deep except when they come up to feed. Sometimes my new sonar helps me see what's down there, but don't count on it."

"Then you have to push the bottom mouth of the trawl through the mud?" asked Hank.

"No, she rides up a few inches above the bobbins, or she'd scoop crab and all kinds of trash. I adjust my dandy line on the head rope to keep her raised, and right forward of the mouth you drag your tickler chain, and this stirs the shrimp a foot or two up in the water so that they pass right into the trawl mouth. Trawl gear has all kinds of little tricks."

"Looks complicated," said Hank seriously as they unmoored.

"You're *fuckin'* A it's complicated," Steve declared.

After stowing lines, Hank put his hand on Steve's shoulder and asked in a low voice, "When did old Ivan go on the wagon?"

"About three years ago, after he near died from the DTs and the judge dried him out a month in jail." Steve looked at Hank sharply. "It wasn't funny." Hank nodded. "Well, Jones and me, we got the priest at the Russian church, and we all worked him over together. It was a bitch. The day they let him out of jail we dragged him straight across town to the church, and there we was, Jones and me choked on the incense, those gold and silver statues with holes for eyes staring at us, the priest talking in both Aleut and Russian, and Ivan running around on his knees yelling and praying. That's a day I won't forget. Then Jones and me, we had to give up booze for a while to keep him straight. Then he got over feeling sorry for himself, and now he's glad when he can smell booze on somebody and give a lecture." Steve grinned. "They got an AA in town. Ivan goes whenever he can, and I hear he jumps up all the time to give witness."

As soon as they left the breakwater they entered high, rolling seas. The first streaks of day shone in the sky as the *Adele H* pitched into it. Hank rejoiced at being aboard a real boat in seas he could feel, and when he became as seasick—as he feared might happen—he took it in stride and they all joked about it together. After the second hour, as the glow left and the misery sank in, he huddled in a corner of the deck away from the wind. Snow sliced across the sky and seas gurgled over the deck to swish around his feet.

By noon they had reached their grounds, a bay north of Kodiak Island. Steve told him to stand by and watch the first shooting of gear. "And stay clear of lines." Indeed, the setting of a trawl made the other fishing he had done with purse seine and crab pots seem simple. While he followed easily the sequence of the net off the drum, there were a great variety of line and cable attachments at different points which he failed to grasp the first time around. In the few seconds between releasing the big steel doors and lowering them into the water they swung out, then thudded back with a force that made the boat shudder. Steve and Ivan stood by the windlass against the housing and payed out the thick cables attached to the doors, calling to Jones each twenty-five-fathom mark. Jones shouted for them to set at a hundred fathoms.

Hank had psyched himself to work, had anticipated for a month the time when he would pitch in again on a fishing deck, and what he saw was a closed-loop operation for two men. "That's it?" he asked when they secured and headed back to the cabin.

"Rest while you can, dumbhead," said Steve cheerfully. He and Ivan settled into a game of cribbage.

Jones dragged the trawl for an hour and a half, then called them back on deck. Steve and Ivan spooled in the cables, and when the doors rose, hurried to secure them against the side. Next they rolled in the net over the drum astern, making all the adjustments of lines and cables in reverse. The rolling deck had acquired a film of ice. Steve and Ivan raced surefooted as cats along the surface, their knees bent and their bodies low. Hank imitated them, but as soon as he gained confidence and forgot what he was doing, he would slip.

Despite the snow, wind, and seas, hundreds of squawking seagulls suddenly gathered astern to dive at the water. The red-meshed cod end of the net floated up with the fatness of a submarine. The seagulls perched on top and plunged their beaks through the webbing.

Although they could return the bulk of the net to the big drum astern, the cod end with the catch had to be maneuvered to the side and lifted to deck by boom. Steve and Ivan grabbed lines and fastened blocks with quick precision. The net became a taut column that stretched high and dripping above them. It could be lifted from the water only in increments. Ivan leaned over the side to double-wrap a rope around the column, and then the boom raised the strapped portion. At last a bulbous, pear-shaped bag rose from the sea, oozing pink shrimp fragments and green mud through the mesh. The weight made all the lines rigid and started them groaning in the blocks. Jones leaped to deck and began to work with Steve and Ivan as part of the team. The bag—it was at least five feet across—cleared the rail and swung free over the deck with the force of a wrecking ball.

"Near five–six thousand pounds, fair start," said Jones in good humor. "Here, Hank, you pull the clip." He pointed to a short line attached underneath to the pin of a brass coupling that held shut the pursed opening of the bag. Hank hurried gladly from the sidelines, and jerked the line with all his might. The bag merely swung and carried him with it.

"Better let me do it," said Ivan.

"Let him be," said Steve, laughing. "Snap your guts, Hank."

Hank gave an angry yell as he pulled again. Out popped the pin. The bag opened, and twitching shrimp poured around his feet like concrete from a hopper. "Look at all that, my God!" he shouted.

Jones returned to the wheelhouse. After they had set the trawl again, Ivan rigged a heavy pressure hose and began to cut trenches into the mound of shrimp with a water jet, while Steve and Hank walked through culling out what Steve called "the trash." There were crabs, and large flapping fish, and hundreds of white candlefish no bigger than the shrimp that Steve told him to ignore. As each layer washed from the main pile, new fins and claws emerged like artifacts from a dig. Hank looked anxiously as he threw them back in the sea to see if they swam. Some did, and others floated dead. "You call this trash?" he asked, holding up a twenty-pound halibut.

Steve took it from his hands and flung it overboard. "Everything but shrimp's trash when you're shrimping. Nobody pays for the rest. And you needn't moon over the dead ones, they'll feed something else down there."

Hank still examined some of the creatures, grotesque fish colored throbbing pinks and reds, others so spiny they stuck through his gloves, the shrimp themselves which were exquisitely detailed. Even the seaweed was marvelous in its variety—fronds of kelp as thick as industrial belts, slimy stalks the shape of insects' eyes, lacy fan-shaped twigs, brown clusters of balls. He had surely known it before, but it gave him fresh pause, the vastness of unknown things in heaven and earth, the forces that gave them life.

"Grab your shovel," said Steve. "You ain't a biologist has to study each fin and asshole, you're a fisherman, remember?"

Under Ivan's hosing, the high mound of shrimp was leveled to an even layer over the entire deck, and the mud (which Steve said was green from all the shrimp eggs) had been washed through the scuppers. Steve shoveled through the mass to open a space around a hatch cover. He opened it, slid down through the opening, and beckoned Hank to follow.

Hank eased through the hole just as a sea broke over the side to wash his face with shrimp and to trickle a volley of cold water down his neck. As his feet landed in ice chips and his head disappeared, Ivan above clanged down the hatch cover and bolted it tight. Hank felt entombed in the sudden dark. The boat continued to roll, and the stuffy air smelled of old seafood and ammonia. He crouched on the ice, unsure where to go as his seasickness returned.

"Bulb must be broke," muttered Steve from a distance.

"Okay to puke on the ice?"

"You ain't over that yet? Help yourself. Here, I got her." A dim light flicked on to show a series of boarded stalls like a horse barn. Steve removed his oilskin jacket and draped it on one of the boards, then pounded overhead with the handle of his shovel. Ivan opened another hatch, which appeared to be close enough against the housing to avoid seawash. "This here's the good job," said Steve. "Gets you in from the cold and wet." The ice was piled high in the center stalls. Steve dug into it to spread some under the hatch. With the scrape of Ivan's shovel, shrimp started pouring down. Steve layered the ice on top of them steadily. After Hank had vomited he jumped down and helped. Step by step the work appeared easy, but as the shrimp pile mounted it was necessary to hold full shovel loads of ice at head height and throw the contents so that it scattered to the far corners of the bin. When they finished he was panting, his arms ached, and he was ready to rest. But by the time they crawled topside, the next load was ready to be brought aboard.

When the new shrimp were ready to be hosed, Hank stationed himself to grab the pressure hose when Ivan left to turn it on. The thick tube suddenly stiffened with a hundred-pound weight of seawater and began to beat like an angry creature. As Hank wrapped his arms around it to keep control the boat rolled, and he slid helplessly through ice and slippery shrimp from port to starboard and back again. Jones and Steve stopped to laugh, but Ivan declared gravely, "You got to stay sober to handle the hose." He himself maneuvered the heavy water flow as if it came from a garden hose.

There was now no letup in the work, while the weather grew worse. Hank began to regard with apprehension the thickness of each cod end as it came aboard and to wonder when they would stop. Most of it was bull work, with none of the exhilaration that he remembered from seining on the *Rondelay*. Yet the four-day trip wore its course quickly. Jones and Steve did not ignore his needs as it first appeared they might, but gradually worked him in on the gear until he took Steve's place for entire sets while Steve stood aside and coached. Even the possessive Ivan volunteered his hose and showed him how to handle its inflexible weight to distribute the shrimp with successive volleys of water. After the seasickness wore off, Jones kept him in the wheelhouse for entire sets to show him how to handle the boat. By the time they docked in Kodiak he had his sealegs, and shrimping was less of a mystery.

15

NORWEGIAN STEAM

B
Y THE third trip, Hank had toughed in. His muscles stopped jumping and agonizing at night, the cold penetrated less deeply, and he he could skitter across deck without losing his balance.

Mistakes were the sobering problem. It came to a head toward the end of a rough and icy day, when he lost track of the order of gear and snapped a hook onto the wrong line. But for Ivan's indignant shout and lunge to grab them back, the bobbins would have dropped overboard and been lost. Soon after, Hank placed himself in front rather than behind the cables he was attaching between the net and the door. Steve saw the error seconds before the cable would have swept him into the water. Finally, he failed during the rush of hauling the bag aboard to secure a swinging chain. It slapped across his face, knocking him dizzy, and left a line of welts from forehead to chin. Jones summoned him to the wheelhouse.

"Hank, there's enough happens out there that you can't predict. Luck don't leave room for stupid things."

Hank forced a laugh. "Won't happen again. Be my own ass if it does. I'd better get back out there."

"Fishing's teamwork, and wintertime most of all. If you lose an arm you'll go run a business. Steve and Ivan's arms are all those fellows have."

Hank stared at the rolling water until he could find his voice. "I'll shovel for the rest of the trip. Then I'll go my way."

"No, Steve and me, we're going to teach you, if that's what you want."

"I couldn't live with it, to injure one of you."

"Then keep your wits about you." A silence. "Think her through. Don't everybody need to be a fisherman. No disgrace in doing something else, you know."

Suddenly Jones started to curse. Ahead loomed the huge dark shapes of fishing ships, their sterns truncated to serve as trawl ramps. The two other Kodiak shrimpers within view bobbed like toys, a tenth the size of the steady ships. "Fuckin' Russians back again, six weeks earlier than last year!" He grabbed the radiophone and started talking angrily with the other skippers, and then trying to reach the Coast Guard or the National Fisheries Service. "Bastards take the whole of our trip in one haul. After a few days there's nothing left but mop-up. What the *fuck* do we pay a government for if it don't protect us?" The voices of the other skippers sputtered over the radio with equal fury and frustration.

Next day, as Hank worked his share of gear with scrupulous care, the others wasted themselves in cursing the Russian ships. By coincidence, or by cause and effect, the volume of haul indeed dropped. A grim mood settled over the *Adele H* and over the fleet in general.

Hank was hosing down at the end of the day while Ivan and Steve each secured an individual door and Jones operated the hydraulics. Suddenly there was a cracking bang, an object shot past, and Ivan's door clanged loose against the side. The double block raising the seven-hundred-pound door to its gallows had snagged under pressure and shattered without warning, sending shards of wood in all directions. Ivan fell to deck clutching his head.

Jones throttled full bore for town, several hours away, while he radioed for help or medical advice. Steve and Hank carried the unconscious Ivan to his bunk, then secured the dangerously swinging door as best they could as the boat beat through the water. A wave over the side quickly washed the deck of Ivan's blood.

The Coast Guard Rescue Center sent a helicopter. As the basket with Ivan tied in swung up under the chopping blades, Steve said in a choked voice, "We ain't going to fish any more this trip, are we, Boss?"

"Hell, no, we're following Ivan."

They arrived back in harbor past one in the morning and tied at the cannery. Adele waited for them with the pickup, her hair lumpy with curlers beneath a scarf. Hank had never seen her so upset, even when the earthquake had ruined her house. She clutched Jones, and lay her head on his shoulder. "Oh, Daddy. I knew one of you boys would get hurt some day, and every night I pray it won't be . . ." She reached out a free hand to pat Steve's arm.

"What about Ivan?" asked Jones gruffly.

"They won't tell me. When the Coast Guard phoned I went straight to the hospital. They said he's alive, but they wouldn't . . ." Her voice broke.

They raced to the hospital. A nurse told them to come back at ten in the morning. She made the mistake of giving them the room number, and the four of them stormed along the single corridor until they found Ivan. He was asleep, tucked under white sheets, his hairy chest strangely naked without the layers of worn fishing clothes over the gray long johns. Hank marveled at the awful limpness of his muscular arms. A bandage covered half his face, but the other half looked exactly like Ivan, and the snore was certainly Ivan's.

"He'll make it," Jones declared.

Both Steve and Adele accepted his word, and relaxed visibly. But: "I'm staying with him," Steve declared.

By this time the two other occupants of the room had begun to stir. The nurse turned off the light again and ordered them out.

"I ain't going," said Steve. "What if he wakes up and wants to tear the place apart? Somebody might hurt him." Jones used his authority and Steve followed, protesting with outstretched hands: "Boss, them doctors would just as soon cut off his leg."

They all drove to the house. Adele brought out a bottle of Scotch, said that at three in the morning it didn't matter about ice, then took the first swig herself and handed the bottle to Steve. Their talk was a continuation of the shared experience of danger, with Adele a participant. Hank had thought little until that night of the waiting role played by a fisherman's wife. It was still dark at seven in the morning when Steve and Hank returned to the boat. The cannery crew had begun automatically to unload their catch.

"I see you lucked out," said one of the men in shrimp-splattered rain suits who was climbing from the hold. It was the burly kid he had met in the bar with Jody.

182

"Not sure what kind of luck at this point," said Hank, and explained the circumstances.

"Anything's luck after you've been on the beach since Christmas."

"Still in that sleeping bag at the empty cannery?"

The kid nodded. "You don't have to tell any fishermen you saw me here. They might think I've given up on the boats."

Steve fixed coffee and declared it wasn't worth sleeping when they could see Ivan at ten. "You think he'll be all right, Hank?"

"Sure he will." Hank dozed to the clamor of the cannery crew. If such an accident could happen to Ivan, then he, in his turn, sooner or later . . .

Ivan was too sturdy to be killed by a splintered block, although the doctor said he had a dent in his skull that would have done in most men.

"Yeah," said Ivan, scratching where the bandages permitted, "Now gimme my pants. Those Russian bastards going to take all the shrimp if we don't get back out fast." The doctor said he had to stay in bed for a week. When Ivan started to roar his objections, the doctor had his clothes removed from the room and said he'd tell the orderlies to tie him if he didn't calm down.

The threat visibly frightened Ivan. He gave a pleading look to Jones and Steve.

"You hear that," said Steve, advancing to take his place by Ivan. "They'd as lief cut his leg. I told you."

Adele assured them both that she would visit every day, and that she would have the Coast Guard radio them at sea if anything went wrong.

"You're going fishing *without* me?"

"Hank'll just take it until you get your rest," said Jones.

They left him wide-eyed and miserable. Steve was no happier. "Goodbye, buddy. We'll be back soon, don't worry."

"It's dangerous out there," said Ivan. "Steve, you be careful without me. Watch you don't get in the way of them doors."

At least for Hank it was a trip in his own right, with a crew share paid. Through the enforced responsibility he learned to handle his portion of the gear more smoothly than before. Steve, however, turned testy and unreasonable. He must have felt that his loyalty to Ivan demanded it. At the end of the trip, Ivan was waiting on the dock: the doctor had given up trying to keep him in bed. The bandage on his head was smaller, with the cleanness of fresh application. Adele had laundered all his clothes. Otherwise, it was Ivan as before. Steve and Jones made much of greeting him. He returned aboard with dignity, his eyes darting to find any signs of change. Hank had left his watch cap on the foot of Ivan's bunk. Ivan threw it to the deck. "You taking over my goddam bunk? You scratch your name yet in my deck hose?" Steve reassured him like a mother hen.

Later, Hank told Jones lightly that he guessed it was time to stick it out on the beach and find his own berth. Jones' apparent relief hurt him, as had Steve's attitude during the week. He even remembered that when Adele had met them the night of Ivan's injury she had embraced Jones and patted Steve's arm, fretting for their safety, but had paid no attention to him. He was an outsider, after all.

Jones escorted him around the floats and introduced him to other skippers with: "This here's a good man. You'll find he pulls his weight." Hank tried to recall the names of the boats he had promised the kid in the bar to leave alone. However, being realistic after several weeks, he followed where Jones led. Most of the skippers told Hank to drop by for mug-up whenever he saw them in port, but none had openings.

It was snowing as the *Adele H* passed the breakwater, and a northeaster kicked forty or fifty knots. A hard trip ahead, but he felt desolate to see Jones Henry's boat leave without him. When he had cast off their lines, both Jones and Steve wished him luck, but then neither looked back. The snow finally blurred Steve's and Ivan's glistening rain gear as they stowed the lines and fenders, and a few minutes later the boat itself blended into the wall of whiteness.

He could find no graceful way to leave the Henrys' house. Jones had insisted he stay, and Adele made it plain her feelings would be hurt if he left. He wished for the scruffy freedom of the old days again. It was difficult to be casual about meals with Adele so that he might be free to accept spontaneous hospitality aboard the boats. With someone appreciative to cook for, she wanted to prepare gourmet lunches, and dinners with wine. And, even though she was bright and intelligent, she talked incessantly of politics and art. His mind was turned to the boats.

If he could not be at sea, he thirsted at least to spend his time in galleys with other fishermen.

Others on the beach also visited the boats—not only Seth O'Malley, whose name he soon remembered. He was, after all, only part of a small, hungry coterie. Most crews tolerated them to draw coffee and sit at the galley table, and sometimes they were offered food. Collectively they stuck together, nursing beers at night around a table in one of the taverns and conversing in monosyllables. But each had a gaze that wandered individually for the appearance of some skipper back in port, and each tried to elude the others in visiting the boats first.

After a week, Hank found work in a shrimp cannery. His twelve-hour days were spent standing beside a conveyor belt, picking the hundreds of candlefish from the thousands of shrimp that passed. Once at coffee break he said lightly to the foreman, a man no older than himself: "Hey, I'm going nuts on that belt. How about letting me unload boats?"

"You've got a very important job. Keep at it."

At coffee and lunch breaks he raced the docks to maintain his contacts with boats and skippers. The foreman warned him twice about returning to the line late, and the third time fired him. Hank phoned Adele that he had to work late, and spent the rest of the day and evening hunched in the dark corner of a bar.

Maybe, indeed, he had passed in education and experience beyond the life he thought he wanted. Maybe, in fact, he didn't want to spend his life in a wet, cold, unsophisticated town, courting certain discomfort and probable injury.

Yet, whenever he saw one of the boats pass through the breakwater and start bucking the seas, he felt sick with longing to be aboard.

Then one night at a bar he met Nels Hanson. His shrimper *Delta* was tied in Port Bailey with a minor breakdown, and one of his crewmen had quit. Hank listened with growing excitement, his gaze darting to make sure none of the others on the beach might see and try to horn in.

Nels was squat and muscular, about fifty, a man with a steady look, no smile, and little talk beyond the facts. His hands on the bar were big and scarred, with black in the creases and under the nails.

"Matter of fact," said Hank, "I'm looking for a boat myself."

"Let's see your hands." Fortunately the shrimp picking had not yet softened the callouses. Nels thumped Hank's chest and arms, then drank the shot in front of him and ordered another. After a while: "If you want to come, I give a ten percent crew share. You foot a third of the grub and fuel."

Jones Henry paid nineteen percent and had absorbed the fuel costs into the boat share. Hank debated bargaining for more, but thought of Seth and the others. "Okay."

Nels' hand sealed it with a shake that slowly squeezed Hank's hand to the crushing point. "Bring your gear to the plane ramp tomorrow at first light."

Hank was waiting next morning when Nels appeared, a cigar in his mouth, just as the gray daylight had begun to delineate the colors of buoys and plane wings. Nels seemed even heavier and more squat than the night before in the bulky wool jacket he wore, and his thick wool cap smoothed his head into the size and shape of a basketball.

"Morning, boss," said Hank tentatively.

Nels regarded him through a swirl of cigar smoke. His eyes reached the level of Hank's chin, but he stood far enough distant that he did not appear to be looking up. "You got a buddy? I need two crewmen this morning."

Hank raced across the harbor and along the gravel cannery road. His first guess was correct: Seth was down in a shrimp hold, unloading. He listened to what Hank said, jammed his shovel into the ice, climbed to the wharf, peeled his cannery skins, and told the foreman, "I quit." At the closed-down cannery where he slept, his knapsack and sleeping bag were hidden behind a stack of cartons, packed. He scribbled a note to the watchman, and off they went.

"You didn't give me a chance to explain," said Hank. "This skipper only pays a ten percent crew share, and I think most two-man shrimp crews get nineteen."

"And one guy I know gets five, and all I've gotten so far is grub for the three trips I've made." Seth stopped and held out his hand. "I appreciate this, man." In shaking, he locked thumbs with Hank instead of pressing his palm.

Nels questioned Seth about his experience, felt his muscles, and examined his hands. "Three trips for grub since Christmas, that's all, uh? Give you eight percent crew share, you pay a third of expenses."

Seth accepted.

The pilot wore hip boots as he walked the pontoon plane into the water while the others eased it from the land, then jumped aboard. The flight over bays and mountains to the sheltered water of the cannery cove took no more than twenty minutes.

"Wait," said Nels to the pilot. He told Hank and Seth to unload their gear but not to follow him, then walked along the wharf and climbed down to a boat as sturdy as himself. He entered the cabin. Shortly after, there were some shouts. Another few minutes and a man emerged with sleeping roll and duffle bag. He dumped the gear on deck, tied a line to it, climbed the ladder, and pulled the gear up after him. Nels appeared on deck in rolled-down hip boots, puffing a cigar. He motioned Hank and Seth to come aboard.

"That's what I figured," said the pilot. "Nels has a time finding guys to satisfy him."

They passed the crewman on the ramp. His face was tight with anger. "Shee-it" was all he said.

"Sorry," murmured Hank. "We didn't . . ."

"See you back in Kodiak, suckers."

The shrimp trawler *Delta* was a trim, clean boat. The only thing out of order was the engine room, reached by ladder below the bunks and storage, which was a mess of oil and dismembered parts. For four days neither Hank nor Seth saw much else, except to climb topside for a few hours sleep or to eat a sandwich protected in a paper towel against the grease on their hands. Nels Hanson said little, and it became obvious he disliked others to talk around him when he worked. He knew his way through his engine. The job of his crew was to stand by at all times, to hand him wrenches, hold flashlights, or strain free a bind. He ignored their questions about the way the engine functioned or what he was doing. His own capacity for remaining with the job was prodigious: they arrived from Kodiak at nine in the morning, and at four the next morning he grudgingly guessed they all could sleep a while, but at eight-thirty he shook their bunks to get moving again. As he said, "You know a boat not by her galley and engines, but by her crew's sack time."

At last they went fishing. Hank was not surprised to find Nels Hanson a driver. He smoked a cigar constantly, and he never swore. His favorite expression, shouted from the wheelhouse as he monitored the shooting and drawing of the net, was "Hop to it!" His voice carried easily over the engine noise, although he never became excited. When it came time to maneuver the full bag over the side, he placed the boat on automatic steering and jumped down on deck to take charge, as Jones did. But it was the engine room again all over, with Nels racing to set the tackle himself while muttering and pointing instructions. On the first set he held out his hand toward Seth and said, "Double block." Seth looked around, uncertain. "Double block, stupid, hop to it." Hank hurried to free it and hand it over, leaving the bag to swing free momentarily. "Why'd you drop your lazy line, stupid? Get back there." When it came time to wash the shrimp Hank grabbed the pressure hose and cut the layers expertly. He had become proud of the way he could handle the operation. Nels grabbed the hose from him and, with his fist poked into the opening, intensified the volley of water so that the shrimp were cleaned and stacked in a fraction of Hank's time. A few minutes later he was shouting to make them shovel faster. Nels seemed to enjoy running the net. Unlike Jones, who let it soak for one to two hours, Nels Hanson hauled it in again the minute his crew had finished the icing. Under his goad, this occurred every thirty to fifty minutes. No matter how hard they worked to catch up, there was never a moment for rest.

Fortunately for Hank, the tackles and machinery were rigged exactly as they had been on the *Adele H.* It turned out that Seth, on his three grub trips, had been employed at shoveling and taught little else. Hank coached him, sometimes almost desperately under the shouts from Nels, warning him about mistakes and dangers that Steve had monitored for him only two weeks before, explaining as they went and alerting him to adjustments as they were about to occur. The weather was brutally rough and icy. Seth remained perpetually bent with sickness. Under the running pace that Nels dictated, he slipped often to gather cuts and bruises. Hank showed him how to keep his knees loose to lower his balance. In Seth's sudden deference and gratitude he saw himself under Steve, and marveled at how quickly his role had reversed.

Day after day Nels maintained the pace. He fished them beyond exhaustion and doled short periods for food and sleep as if he were being cheated personally. With their skipper the common enemy, Hank and Seth became a team, exchanging wry jokes, pushing themselves to maintain Nels' pace until they felt pride at being able to hack it.

They talked enough for Hank to learn that Seth had spent a year at Berkeley before deciding that campus life was "Unreal, so fuck it."

"This real enough world for you?" asked Hank one night as they groped aching into their bunks.

"Jesus."

The deck loads they pulled were not as full as most on the *Adele H*, but Nels trawled closer to the rocky shore, and he found bigger shrimp. "When they buy from my boat," he once declared in a rare moment of explanation, "they're paying for the best, and they know it. You fish around the rocks, you never soak your nets long each set, then you don't cut up your nets so bad."

At last the four days of almost steady shrimping ended. (Nels could push an extra day over the usual limit of three because his shrimp, being bigger, stayed fresh longer.) As the boat bucked toward Kodiak through the dark, Hank and Seth had the leisure to sit around the galley table. Their bones hurt and their hands grasped objects stiffly, but they had survived it. They debated whether to stay with the boat or leave. The low crew share rankled, especially for Hank, who had known better under Jones Henry. Maybe, in the calm of harbor, it could be discussed.

"This guy's a prick's prick," Seth declared. "But thanks to you, buddy, I've learned ten times what I knew a week ago. I hope *you'll* stay."

They tied to the cannery around nine in the morning, having fished until three and then run the rest of the night. Nels had stayed awake by his wheel all the time—he never seemed to need sleep—and had roused them a few minutes before docking. He then turned them to scrubbing the boat, topside and cabins, as the cannery gang unloaded. They knew the guys from the cannery, and joked with them from the superior level of boat's crew. Hank also found it gratifying to glance up and see the *Shalimar* headed out, to wave, and to have Jody recognize him and call back a greeting while Mike tooted their whistle. Nels stomped from boat to cannery and back again, monitoring both his crew and the scales. When the loading was finished, Nels sent them into the hold with hose and brushes. "Take up all the deck boards, scrub everything twice with disinfectant. Hop to it." It was dark outside when they had finished. They climbed to deck, talking about a beer uptown and then some sleep. There had been no time to think of visiting other boats. But they had discussed it all day, and had decided they'd paid for their berths on the *Delta* with their hides and might as well stick it. Even eight- and ten-percent shares should bring them three to four hundred apiece with the catch they delivered. And at least they'd be known on the floats as crew for a highline skipper.

Nels inspected the hold minutely, then handed them each a check. "Okay, boys." He held out his enormous hand, and squeezed each of theirs slowly to crushing. "I only work with green crew when I can't find nothing else. So pack your gear and go home. Hop to it."

"You mean we're fired?"

"I got a couple *fishermen* coming aboard, and as soon as they get here I take off."

Their checks were each for seventy-five dollars. Hank contested it. "We even worked four days on your engine."

"I took out for plane fare, fuel, all the food you ate—never stopped eating, either of you—and then for the parts of my tackle and net you messed up. I ain't paying for stupid crew, they pay their own mistakes."

"I'd like a written accounting," said Hank quietly.

The eyes remained dispassionate. "I got bad enough things to say to other skippers about your kind of weakling crew without putting stuff on paper. If I was to do it again I'd take off more. Now pack your gear and hop to it." Nels scraped his palms one against the other. His body in front of them had the bulk of a boiler.

Hank did not want to face Adele and her ministrations. He followed Seth to the shut-down crab cannery. Seth introduced him to the watchman, and they rolled their sleeping bags over flattened cartons on the concrete floor. When they had changed in the unheated warehouse into their only clothes not wet with perspiration—stinking, but dry—and started drag-footed toward town to vent their anger, they saw the *Delta* leave the cannery for the ice and fuel piers. On deck, the two new crewmen hustled under Nels' direction.

Hank spat. "Goddam it, if I can ever do that bastard a bad turn, I will."

Seth spat and seconded the vow in stronger terms.

190

16

THE COCKEYED HALIBUT AND THE TURN-SEX SHRIMP

ALASKA's fishing fame rests with the salmon and the crabs, but this by no means completes the story of commercially valuable species. The waters also teem with shrimp, halibut, herring, pollock, cod, sablefish ("black cod"), perch, rockfish, turbot, hake, and with other sea creatures such as clams. This chapter considers both the smallest and the largest of the species around which major fisheries exist, with a sideways glance at two others.

To Hank and the rest of us, involved at whatever level of trawl, pick line, or grocery shelf, the shrimp may be worthy of no greater respect than that due a cucumber. Nevertheless, varieties of shrimp feed millions of people along such diverse world coasts as those of India, China, Japan, Malaya, Australia, Ghana, Brazil, Ecuador, Spain, and Norway. Fishermen in the United States have earned more money from shrimp in recent years than from any other single species of seafood. (Pacific salmon has been second, tuna third.) Alaska since 1971 has led all other states in volume of shrimp landed.

The little shrimp fished in Alaska are vastly different from the fat whites and brownies of the Gulf fishery. They fetch only a fraction of the price per pound, but an Alaskan boat haul is reckoned in thousands of pounds compared to hundreds on the Gulf. The two types of shrimp come from different families within the hierarchy of Crustacea. Gulf Coast shrimp are section Eucarida, family Penaeus, while Alaska shrimp are section Caridea, family Pandalus, and therein lies all the difference required here between the jumbo and the cocktail shrimps.

Pandalid shrimp—the ones in Alaska—have an interesting distinction not shared by the southern varieties. They change sex in midlife. After maturing as males, they fertilize their quota of eggs for two or three seasons, then are transformed into egg-bearing females.

Most Pandalid shrimp follow the same cycle, but the following life history is geared to *Pandalus Borealis,* the little "pinks" which furnish the most abundant shrimp harvests around Kodiak and other parts of Alaska (as they do in that other land of northern water, Norway). To begin with eggs, the female carries them for six months attached to her underside as a greenish mass. Her egg capacity can be as high as three thousand, depending on her size—which depends on her age. Hatching time is generally March or April. The larvae emerge as specks three-sixteenths of an inch long. They swim free, traveling as part of the plankton mass while feeding on smaller plankton.

By midsummer they have molted six separate exoskeletons to reach a length of three-quarters of an inch. Their molts have brought them to the form of little adult shrimp, and they assume adult behavior by settling to the bottom. By now their numbers are considerably less since they have helped nourish all manner of passing fish.

The young shrimps, all males but for the sort of exceptions that nature provides, reach maturity in the fall of their second or third year (one and a half or two and a half years from hatching). The fertilization process occurs in September or October. The male and female grasp each other, and the male deposits his sperm on the female's underside. The female, whose body has molted into a special spawning shell with hairlike structures in the abdomen for carrying eggs, extrudes eggs from her oviducts. They pass through the sperm mass and lodge in her abdominal hairs, which will hold them fast for the next six months.

The transformation from male to female takes about six months, and is completed by age four and a half. Dad of one season has become Mom by the next. Males are necessarily smaller than females, since adult shrimp continue to grow throughout their lives. They grow, as do all crustaceans including crabs, through molting one shell, then occupying a larger by absorbing water into their tissues until actual growth takes place to fill out the shell. Mature male pinks average two to three inches in length, females three to four inches and more. A Kodiak pink shrimp that eludes the trawl lives six years, and during that time has participated in either one or two matings as a male, then in two as a female.

Alaskan waters provide four other varieties of Pandalid shrimp: humpie, which is smaller than a pink (neither to be confused with the pink or humpie salmon of the same waters); sidestripe, coonstripe, and spot, which are all larger. All but the latter seek smooth bottom mud. The spot shrimp, as large and fat as any brownie from the Gulf of Mexico, sticks to rocky areas that would tear apart an otter trawl and are fished only to a limited degree in Alaska, using baited pots.

The mud-dwelling Pandalids remain on bottom during daylight, then rise to feed in the night hours. Because of this, most but not all Alaskan shrimping is done during the day with trawls dragged along the bottom. (On the other hand, Gulf Coast Penaeid shrimp follow a pattern that enables them to be fished best by night.) Most Alaska shrimp are harvested at depths between thirty and a hundred fathoms, compared to seven- and ten-fathom depths for those on the Gulf Coast.

Pandalid shrimps feed on crab larvae, smaller shrimps, and other living planktonic organisms as well as on dead plant and animal material called detritus. Reciprocally the shrimps, both as larvae and adults, furnish food for salmon, halibut, rockfish, cod, sablefish, sole— whatever large fish comes their way.

The harvesting of the little northern pink shrimp is a major Alaskan fishery of only the past decade. It centers in Kodiak and in Sand Point, 250 miles southwest down the Peninsula. Until the 1960s, the cocktail-sized *Pandalus Borealis* were known as Petersburg shrimp, for the town in southeastern Alaska where since 1916 a small fleet has caught them to be processed by hand picking. Such individual attention made for a luxury product delivered at too great a price to be practical for a large commercial venture.

A fishery starts with the natural abundance of a stock, but only becomes significant with a means to preserve the stock in commercial quantity. Many credit Ivar Wendt, Swedish-born founder of Pacific Pearl Seafoods, with pioneering the Alaska shrimp-canning industry. The key to successful processing of the small Pandalids was easy shell removal.

Wendt imported and modified the first peelers from the Gulf of Mexico. He subsequently proved that the tiny pink shrimp could be marketed successfully.

The importation of Gulf technology also figured in the boats and gear to catch the shrimp, even though Kodiak fishermen soon started to figure their own local modifications. The Alaskan shrimp boats of the late 1960s were stern trawlers like the *Adele H,* rigged to fish with a single otter trawl. In 1971, larger and more efficient double-rigged boats began to come from the Gulf. The double-rigger carries a separate smaller otter trawl on each side, hung from extended booms. This increases the area of seafloor that can be dragged in a single pass and can enlarge the catch considerably. Also becoming available at the time were scanning sonars and more sophisticated depth recorders, which enabled fishermen to rely less on broad open gulleys in the seafloor that they could locate with simple fathometers and to seek the more productive contour edges while keeping an eye on the shrimp mass itself. The newest shrimp boat modification in Alaska is one the Russians and Japanese on their big trawlers knew all the time: a ramp up the stern, so that the bag of catch need never be suspended dangerously to be lifted to deck over the side rail.

A new fishery for Alaskans has just begun since the passage of the 200-mile law in 1976 made possible an American allotment: bottom-fish. This is a ubiquitous term that includes a variety of commercial species, from the pollock (heretofore dragged in quantities by Japanese and Russian factory fleets) to the cod (which have not been harvested commercially by Americans in Alaska since the days of salting). The trawl gear and the processing machinery are again a new show—or an intelligent modification of an old one—and the fishery has not yet unfolded beyond the experimental stage.

Another Alaskan fishery is based on herring, the little strong-flavored oily fish which, as Joe Spitz knew, has caused wars. While Europeans eat herring as daily food, Americans use them most for bait and fertilizer. A herring is seined much as a salmon but with web of a finer mesh. It was once harvested in Alaska for reduction to meal and oil, before South American fish meal outpriced it. Now it is chiefly used as commercial bait for bigger creatures—king crab and halibut—and for the roe, which is a Japanese delicacy. The frenzied springtime roe herring harvest in a few places like Prince William Sound, northeast of Kodiak, is a strange little fishing saga of its own: boats that lay over a month waiting for the imprecise arrival of the fish and for the opportunity to make a single set (which usually, given the number of boats on hand, accounts for the entire quota), and of nets full in such quantity that every year a boat or two is dragged under with its seine when a million captured herring decide to make a run for it. Herring is a small fishery in Alaska, but as wild as any.

The halibut has little in common with the shrimp, pollock, and herring, harvested *en masse* by net, except that they all contribute to its food supply. Halibut is one of the giants of the fish world, caught as an individual on hook and line.

A commercial halibut fishery has operated in Alaskan waters since 1888, when sailing ships began to voyage north seasonally from Seattle and Vancouver. Fishermen worked from two-man dories which the ship lowered each day, drawing in their long baited lines by hand or through a hand-cranked roller. The work was excruciatingly hard, and so dangerous in the capricious northern seas that many men and dories were lost each year. Halibut fishing has changed completely only once since that time: sixty-odd years ago, improvements in diesel engines and machinery made it feasible to haul a vastly extended string of hooks directly to the deck of a moderate-sized boat. The dory ships gave way to sturdy wooden schooners of fifty- to eighty-foot lengths. Some of these same schooners, built from 1913 through the 1920s, with modernizations still comprise the nucleus of the present fleet. The fleet now also includes smaller and multi-purpose vessels that fish halibut between other seasons. With the declining stocks of recent years, the halibut season lasts for only intermittent periods between April and October.

In the halibut fishing process, called longlining, hooks are baited and set in three-hundred-fathom units called "skates." The roller mechanism that brings in the fish-weighted line is still called the gurdy after the hand-cranked version aboard the dories, which worked like the hurdy-gurdies of the time. Now that the gurdy is mechanically driven, ten or more skates are usually tied together into a multimile string.

All northern fisheries are tough, but halibut is conceded to be the toughest: a classic fisherman's fishery, one that requires a high level of strength and individual skill within a team framework. Halibut banks are located in the turbulent open seas of the continental shelves, and the huge belligerent fish must be directly manhandled. Not surprisingly, the schooners have always been sailed principally by Norwegians, those traditional fishermen of the heaviest northern waters. Many of the remaining schooners have been handed down through families to a third generation of Larsens and Hansens, and many of the fishermen themselves are in their fifties and even sixties.

A captured halibut can thrash angrily for hours. The biggest of them can bang a hole in the boat or break a fisherman's leg if not watched, and, like Rasputin, can be murdered by all reasonable means yet still refuse to die. But as one longtime halibut skipper with a Norwegian name once told me, "It's a satisfying way of life because you go right to your very limits. The halibut's a mighty animal. You get an inborn respect for him, and it gets to be a form of combat."

Most Pacific halibut are found and caught in Alaska, with the greatest volume fished from waters around Kodiak. There are also grounds off British Columbia. American and Canadian boats have traditionally shared the fishery. Prince Rupert (Canada) and Kodiak are the principal halibut-landing ports, with Seward and Petersburg next. Until the 1960s, when bulk frozen shipments from Alaska became practical, Seattle held Kodiak's place as the principal American halibut port.

In 1923, the U.S. and Canada formed what is now called the International Pacific Halibut Commission to conserve the stocks and to avoid gear conflicts. At this time the halibut had begun to dwindle alarmingly through overfishing. The joint effort regulated the stocks back to heavy commercial strength and maintained an equilibrium that was shattered only by the advent of the foreign factory fleets.

No question that the halibut stocks have diminished again. In the 1950s the combined catch of U.S. and Canadian boats fluctuated each year in the vicinity of fifty and sixty millions of pounds dressed, and the catch in 1962 exceeded seventy million. By 1974 the catch had plummeted into the twenty-million-pound levels, where it remains. There are reasons and reasons, but the major one is the incidental catches of immature halibut taken by Japanese and Soviet trawlers dragging through halibut-rearing grounds for other bottom-dwelling species. The mortality of young halibut in these trawls has been nearly total, since the pressure within the huge bags crushes them to death. The foreign ships have actually taken more halibut in some seasons than have the licensed halibut boats. (It might be said that American shrimp trawlers and crabbers have also taken their share of incidental halibut. However, an estimated 50 percent of fish in these smaller trawls survives when thrown back, as do many halibut taken in crab pots if they are not butchered illegally for bait.) The extent of all this incidental catch was not immediately realized by authorities of the Halibut Commission, who continued to allow high quotas to U.S. and Canadian fishermen without taking into account the new drain on the resource. Although with the 1976 Fishery Conservation & Management Act the young halibut are now better protected, halibut take years to mature. The damage will be felt for decades to come.

The Pacific halibut, a flatfish with the grand and appropriate biological name *Hippoglossus stenolepis,* is one of the largest fishes in the world. The females of the species grow fastest and biggest, with a few attaining 500 pounds and one hitting 680, according to the literature. The average-sized halibut caught on Alaskan longlines these days weighs thirty to forty pounds, but some still come up which weigh 200 pounds and more. The male takes eight years to mature and the female about four years longer. The oldest age recorded for a male is twenty-seven years and for a female forty-two years. They start as minute eggs, released after spawning in late fall or early winter. The eggs, and the larvae which hatch from them in about two weeks, are buoyant enough to float suspended in midwater, and therefore are transported by currents. As the larvae pass through several development stages over seven to ten months, they rise closer to the surface and are carried into more shallow coastal waters, where they eventually settle to the ground. In these nearshore waters, a biological metamorphosis occurs—the left eye gradually migrates over the snout to the right side of the head. When the eye has completed the move, the halibut have become juveniles. They remain inshore for one to three years, then start moving out onto the continental shelves. Since larvae may be transported hundreds of miles, and juveniles also migrate, the halibut-spawning grounds may be far removed from the main fishing banks. Adults inhabit continental shelf waters thirty to two hundred fathoms deep. They feed voraciously on a variety of midwater fish, including herring, and on such bottom creatures as crab, shrimp, pollock, and even smaller halibut. Happily for fishermen, this appetite extends to dead herring and octopus chunks speared onto hooks.

The extraordinary movement of the left eye to the right side of the head is common to all flatfishes, including also flounder, turbot, and sole. These fish, of the species *Heterosomata,* are assymetrical both in their eye placement and in the color difference of their two sides. The bottom side is white, while the top side—the one with the eyes—is dark with a pigmentation that can change with the type of seafloor. At rest they lie dark-side-up, with the eyes, which protrude, moving freely. Camouflaged, they can watch for their passing food, then pounce to grab it.

Nature has accustomed the halibut to having its way within the kingdom of sea creatures as it grows older and bigger. Perhaps this is why it thrashes so murderously when brought to deck. The little shrimps and smaller fish, on which it feeds, merely twitch and die.

17
SWEDE SCORDEN

THE experience with Nels Hanson appeared more unique to Hank than to others. Jones Henry listened sympathetically the next time he was in port, but the closest he came to echoing Hank's indignation was a wry chuckle. "Nels might be second generation, but he's still a Squarehead clear to his frozen balls. Them fellows have a special pact with God and the sea, and there's no use stepping between."

And Jody, with her deep-throated laugh: "We laid odds on how long you two would last under Nels. You'd have needed a Norwegian accent and an iron rod up your ass. Remember his old crew, Mike? Made of leather, didn't sleep once in a four-day opening."

"What happened to them?"

Jody turned to the others at the bar table. "Anybody know?" She shrugged. "Died, went home to old country, broke their backs . . . every year, faces you take for part of the scene just disappear. Fishermen don't have a secretary to keep records."

"Only God," said Hank.

She studied him. Finally she said, not harshly, "That's what Kodiak needs, a poet."

Hank made excuses to Jones and Adele and moved with Seth into the deserted cannery. They brought a reading light, heat lamp, and hotplate. The dreary Spartan life suited his glum mood for independence better than the luxuries Adele provided. At twenty-five, he had graduated from college and had served as a naval officer, and here he was little better than a bum without work. Seth, five years younger, might have some justification. It bothered him most when the contrast between expectation and reality rubbed him in the face, as when, wearing slept-in clothes and looking for a boat, he slogged past some self-confident young Navy officer from the base. Or, when he wrote his parents.

He landed a single trip when a man injured his hand. At least, Nels had tuned him to the point where no one questioned his ability to keep up with the work or endure the weather.

But the money slipped away. He and Seth resisted as long as they could, then found work at Seaflower Seafood, one of several shrimp canneries in town. The manager of Seaflower turned out to be Swede Scorden, and his supervisor was Joe Cutch. Hank noted it without alarm when the two passed while he was filling an employment form. Neither would ever recognize him from a month of work so long before. Right back where he'd started.

They reported to Joe Cutch on the cannery floor, after choosing rain gear from a rack of odd sizes. Cutch had not changed from the quick-motion foreman of the old salmon cannery. He glanced at their time cards, then looked them over with his small darting eyes. "Henry, is it? Seen you around before, haven't I, Henry?"

Hank grinned. "Everybody up here's been around before. Name's Hank, if you don't mind."

"Fine, fine, Hank." Cutch studied the banks of machinery around the wet concrete floor, then grabbed Seth's arm and scurried over to deposit him in the candlefish-picking line with several women. Seth looked back as if he were being led to his execution. Hank remained in place, hoping that Cutch would not signal him to follow.

"I'm good with a fork," he ventured when Cutch returned. "Experienced unloading holds."

"No, that's not where we . . . Oh!" Cutch propelled him by the arm, up a metal stairway around the cook tanks, to a platform of troughs close to the ceiling. Steam gathered like fog around the other workmen. Cutch clapped a Filipino on the shoulder, and shouted above the noise, "Here's Hank, your new man."

He had drawn the peeler machines. After the masses of shrimp were hoisted in buckets from the boat holds and had traveled on belts past the pickers who removed candlefish, seaweed, and other trash, a conveyor carried them into big cookers and then out through troughs of water to these machines that peeled their shells. The essential part of the peeler machines were banks of long rollers that rotated in opposite directions against each other. The little shrimp washed down the crevices between the rollers, and their shells were gently ripped free of the meat. The mission of the peeler crew was to adjust baffles in the troughs so that the bunches of cooked shrimp would wash evenly down the dozen sets of rollers. The long rubber gloves Hank wore were always wet inside, but they kept the shrimp feelers from spiking his hands. Would his callouses turn to mush?

They worked a shift of eight to twelve hours, depending on the availability of boats. The loaders reported at five each morning, followed at half-hour intervals by pickers and peelers, then canners, to accommodate the passage of the product. Washdown followed the last of the shrimp through each line. It took his own peeler crew more than two hours to hose their machines free of shrimp lint and fragments, then to scrub all parts with disinfectant. He had never seen such a constant need for fresh water.

Below on the main cannery floor Hank sometimes saw Swede Sorden passing back and forth. He still wore his yellow tractor cap, and, despite graying hair, he still carried himself with the thrust and assurance of the man in charge of everything.

Hank and Seth ate with the others in a smoky little room off the cannery floor, where the management maintained a coffeepot. The dreary odors of steamed seafood and ammonia penetrated even here. Their lunch bags contained never-ending cheese and baloney, which they could keep unrefrigerated beside their sleeping bags so long as they sealed it in a can against the rats.

"*This* is the real world," muttered Seth one day. "This is the world where people get trapped, that makes them booze too much and beat their kids. I'm going nuts."

Hank rubbed his softening palms against the bench to try to restore some callous. "I'm beginning to think you can have a hundred real worlds."

Swede Scorden and Joe Cutch strode in and drew themselves coffee. There being no other bench vacant, they sat opposite Hank and Seth. Swede cocked back his head and looked Hank over. "Seen you before. You were younger."

Hank grinned. "Most people were, six years ago." He identified himself as having quit once to work on the *Rondelay* and recalled the *Billy II* disaster. Under the pressure of Swede's surprising interest, he even admitted that he had completed college and had served as a naval officer.

Later that afternoon, Cutch without comment moved Hank to another line. In his new job Hank stacked freshly filled cans into racks and wheeled them to the retort, then removed them for cooling when the final sterilization was finished. At least it required some motion and a bit of muscle to pull the heavy carts. Any cans damaged in the process were his for disposal, so at night he and Seth ate quantities of warm fresh-canned shrimp.

Every day or so thereafter, Cutch appeared, grabbed him by the arm, and propelled him to a new job. By the time he went to the loading gang he had worked on part of every line, even the one picking fragments of shell from the cooked and mechanically peeled shrimp. The shifts in jobs separated his starting and eating times from those of Seth. After work they discussed it while walking the floats in the never-ending search for a berth.

"You're either no good at anything," said Seth, "or that guy Swede's sizing you up."

"Goddam, I want to find a boat!" Hank exclaimed, sensing the latter. Nevertheless, he worked hard at each new job, enjoying at least the variety.

Sure enough, one morning at five when he reported to shovel shrimp from a boat hold, Cutch motioned him over, gave him a pep talk about the responsibility, and made him loading foreman.

It paid him more to stand around tabulating weights and making sure others did the work. He missed bending into the heavy forkloads of shrimp. But, when decisions were required, he enjoyed the scrap of authority as admittedly he had in the Navy. He rescued Seth at once from the pick line to work in his gang.

The job as foreman eased Hank into a different world. He was summoned by Cutch to councils with other foremen. As he voiced opinions, he began to move through the office area as if he belonged there. Swede's secretary, Sandy, smiled whenever he passed. Seth sensed the change. They continued to bunk together in the deserted cannery, but

there was more and more cause for disagreement between them. Seth
soon recovered from his gratitude at leaving the candlefish to call him
"Mr. Foreman," and Hank regretted having placed himself in the position of bossing a friend.

The problem with Seth, which had never become more than an
irritation, resolved itself quickly one day. The *Dolores R*, en route to
the grounds, backtracked and returned to dock. One of the crewmen had
learned by radio of a family death and needed to hurry back to Oregon.
Suddenly a pierhead jump became available to the first taker. Hank
knew of it before anyone else. He debated, biting his lip as he weighed
his new obligations and future, then called Seth up from a boat hold
and gave him the berth. Soon after, he watched Seth's busy, bouncing
form on deck as the boat left the breakwater. He himself had been a
month ashore. "Oh shit," he repeated to himself sickly. Seth had not
even thanked him.

Without a companion, a sleeping bag in a cold and deserted cannery seemed intolerable. To return to Adele's house, where he longed
for the hot shower and tiled bathroom, would be backtracking and
hypocrisy. His own cannery had dormitories, but the thought of advancing one step more toward being a cannery creature depressed him
further. He ended by checking into a new lodge in town, at a price that
made him angry. He ate a steak at Solly's, and then spent three hours
soaked deep in the tub with successive renewals of hot water, as he
drank a Heineken's six-pack and watched TV. Next day he found himself a small apartment.

It did not help his restlessness when, two days later as Nels
Hanson's *Delta* came to unload, Cutch eased from his hands the clipboard where he tabulated each hopperweight, saying, "You want to
learn something new here, now." When the first bucketload of shrimp
came up from the hold and Hank at the controls paused it in midair
to read the scales, Cutch wrote a figure on the sheet thirty pounds greater
than the actual register of the dial. "You see how she goes?" said Cutch
quietly. "We call the *Delta* a thirty-plus. Only two other thirty-plus
boats, but we've got a couple twenty-plussers. And," he winked, "one
forty-plus. I handled her the other day while Swede had you off to a
meeting."

Hank was both shocked and interested. He had wondered at the frequency with which Cutch relieved him when certain boats came in. "What number does the *Adele H* get?" he asked casually.

"Jones Henry? No number, regular weight, like all the others. He's nothing special. Swede decided you were ready to break in with the *Delta*. You got it now?"

"Any boats get minus weight?"

Cutch's small eyes looked at him blankly. "You kidding? That would be illegal."

The next hopperload came up. Cutch handed him the clipboard. Nels, who had been watching from below, called harshly, "You ain't leaving *him* to write my weights?"

"This is bullshit," declared Hank. "I don't like it."

Cutch was honestly surprised. He took back the clipboard. "You'd better go talk to Swede."

Swede's office looked over the loading dock, so that Hank could watch through the window, as Swede had, the action below. Without him, the buckets of shrimp rose from the *Delta* as routinely as ever, and with Cutch writing the weights, nothing appeared in the least bit amiss. Swede sat at his desk, the ubiquitous yellow tractor cap low on his forehead. "You have a gripe? Close the door and sit down."

"Look, I'm just a fisherman on the beach. If you want to juggle weights, do it with somebody else."

"Don't you think a highliner I can count on for volume and quality is worth more than a fellow who delivers when he pleases?" He gave a smile that creased his face without changing the sharpness of his eyes. "You don't pretend that all fishermen are equal?"

"I sure as fuck know that Jones Henry's as good as that ass-driving Hanson prick."

Swede reached in a drawer, pulled out a bottle of whiskey, and shoved it over with a shot glass. Hank shook his head. "Jones Henry gets his share of that when he calls. Nothing special about it," said Swede without haste. "I've got a better brand for the Nels Hansons. Nels brings in bigger shrimp. He also delivers to me exclusively. Now, Jones is a good fisherman. But he delivers his loads between here and other canneries, so he's not my man. And, whether you like it or not, and Jones would admit it, he ain't the fisherman Nels is. He's not an ass-driving prick, and that's what makes the real highliner." Swede poured two shots, and drank one himself. "When I fished, I once had a skipper like Nels, and it's probably what drove me inside."

"I'd have sworn you were born on a cannery line, with a dead fish up your ass." When Swede accepted the comment without throwing him out, Hank took the shot.

"Most old-timers up here have fished. And most young ones think they're the first to go out on a boat. Now, Crawford, what's your gripe? That the favors of the world are distributed unequally? For myself, I'd say that only the brave deserve the fair, only the ass-drivers deserve the bonus." He poured another round, and drank his part of it. "I can take somebody like you or leave you. With your education, I'd as soon give you a try."

"Don't waste the effort. I'm marking time until I can find a boat."

"The boats can be satisfying for a while. But they can be deep slavery when you've lost the ability to do anything else."

Hank remained silent.

"Going to blab about this?"

"No. I figure you were trusting me."

Swede moved him inside to supervise the picking lines, which employed four times as many people as the loading dock, and gave him a raise.

In his new capacity, Hank spent whole days without seeing the water except from the prodigious flow from hoses and pipes. His crew consisted of women, except for two teenaged boys who hauled and cleaned the heavy bins. His responsibilities were threefold: keep the women productive, keep everything sanitary, and make sure all foreign matter from candlefish and seaweed to shell were picked from the endless belts of little shrimp. Within this closed circle, he found himself the custodian of authority and decisions. If a hose snapped, production halted until he improvised or sent someone running for maintenance. He held the keys to the cache of cookies the cannery supplied, and at coffee break he listened judiciously as his charges maneuvered to receive larger allotments than he had been told were allowed. If the bucketfuls of shrimp raised from the boats became clogged in the hopper, the women stood in place and called to him from their stations beside the empty belts, and he would leap to the platform to jiggle doors and start the flow again. At washdown time, it was his inspection that closed the shift, after determining that every particle of shrimp and antenna had been expelled from the machinery. At the end of the week he sat with the other foremen and Cutch to verify and tabulate the time cards. Since he supervised the largest crew, this job took him longer than anybody else's. On some Saturdays he, Cutch, and Sandy the secretary would lock the doors close to midnight.

He had rented a room with kitchen and bath in an old house overlooking the harbor and had acquired a bed, rug, and some chairs from someone on the Navy Base who was being transferred. Adele Henry insisted on supplying the kitchen utensils. As she declared more than once, it wasn't often any more that she had the chance to furnish a young man's apartment.

At about the same time, casually in the way some things finally occur after too long, Sandra Dennis from Swede's office drifted into his scene. She was quiet and deliberate—the anthesis of Jody in most ways. Hank could hardly picture her on a fishing boat or using hefty language. One night after a payroll session they went to Solly's for drinks and a late meal. During the course of it, she said she came from Portland and that she liked photography, hiking, asparagus, king crab and salmon, but not shrimp, French poetry (translated), and Bob Dylan. Hank offered equal snippets of biography. Her face was plain—no highlights such as Jody's wide gamin mouth, and no particular beauty—but he liked her expressions, and they joked easily together. She had a brother who was an accountant in town, and that was how she had found her way to Kodiak. However, she lived independently, sharing a place with three other girls, two of them teachers and one the assistant manager of a small store. When she first came to town eight months before, in July, she had hung around her brother's neck and counted on him to do everything for her. One day she caught a look passing between him and his wife. "Well, I got the message all at once. People in a place like this don't cling to each other. They live on their own." To prove the point, she ordered another round—bourbon for Hank and gin collins for herself—and insisted on paying for it.

Hank had begun to wonder if, after a date or two, he might corner here a girlfriend who would come home with him at times. But in losing the polite battle to pay for the round, he decided that was still a long way off. They discussed the frequent rain and agreed it was depressing, and he told her his goals lay in fishing, not in managing a cannery.

"That's interesting," she said. "I've looked at those boats from up at the office window, but I've never paid much attention to the fishermen. Not a very clean life, is it?"

"Well, I like a bath now and then, but that's beside the point. It's a satisfying life."

"Is it? For a man who's been to college and been an officer in the Navy?" She was genuinely curious. "So many people up here do things you wouldn't expect them to do. I notice my brother's stopped wearing a suit and tie to work. I thought I was doing a strange enough thing just coming to Kodiak, but people all around me . . ." She laughed, and her face had an honest bewilderment he found attractive, possibly because there was no helplessness or coyness about it. "I'm probably ready to do something unusual myself."

He didn't consider it, he just said, "Come home with me tonight, that's different." It was light enough to be passed off as a joke.

"I wondered if you were going to ask me something like that."

"Men are all dogs. You might as well know it."

"At least they enjoy talking like dogs, don't they?" She rose, and helped herself into her coat before he could hold it. Then she turned to him, her mouth smiling, but her eyes troubled. "All right. I'll go home with you tonight. Like to lead the way?"

It was all unexpected, not the least of it that she went into the bathroom and wept when it was over, and that she then returned to bed and curled against him contentedly for the rest of the night.

In the morning she dressed, without a trace of shyness, made coffee and brought it to him in bed, and then as he lay with naked arms behind his head watching and marveling at the way events had turned, she proceeded to fix him breakfast. They ate at leisure, since the cannery was closed that Sunday. The single window, by the table, looked over the harbor.

He had seldom sat with anyone and felt less self-conscious, less pressed to make talk. At one point he held out his hand, but she slipped hers away.

"Isn't holding hands for puppydogs?" She brushed her hair back from her face. "You know what might be pleasant though? Taking a bath in that tub of yours."

"Sure. Help yourself."

"I mean together."

He found it indeed pleasant. And they followed it by returning to bed at her suggestion. He had never had intercourse with daylight streaming through the window, and it was he who became self-conscious before losing himself.

Later, she dressed again, looked around the room, and said, "Well, I cooked breakfast, so you can clean up. I think I'll go back to the apartment."

"Must be crowded with all those roommates. You'd have more room over here."

She nodded slowly. "Come on, get dressed and walk me over. I'll introduce you to the other girls and see if you give them the same line you've given me."

"What do you take me for?"

"A large dog at the very least."

He laughed, liking the image.

The town was quiet as they strolled through. Some people were evidently in church and others were sleeping late. Even the boats seemed shut down. She stopped in the square and glanced around. "Not a particularly pretty town, is it?"

"No, but I like it."

"I like it better, this morning," she said simply.

As they walked she accepted no interim physical contacts, no holding of hands, but he felt bound and identified with her nevertheless. Which of them had taken the initiative after all?

Her roommates made no attempt to remove the clothesline of slips and brassières strung across the living room (a nicety he would have preferred), but on the other hand they offered him a drink at once and settled around giving him their full attention. The doorbell rang, and one of the three left with a man whom she did not bother to introduce. Sandra suddenly excused herself.

"Some people have all the luck," said Midge.

Sally became animated. "Hank, let me fill your glass. Say, you don't have any friends, any roistering fishermen who at least stay sober half the time?"

Sandra appeared, carrying a suitcase and a knapsack. Midge and Sally gasped. "I'm moving in with Hank for a while, but I'll keep my bed here."

Hank felt trapped, annoyed, and pleased. At any rate, there was nothing to be done at the moment but follow the course he himself had suggested. Did he want to give up his freedom like this? As they passed near the harbor he looked hungrily at the masts. And what if she strung her stockings and underwear on a line across the room so he couldn't walk without stooping? She had capitulated too easily. Why hadn't he played it cooler? Then he thought of the bath they had taken together, and the way she snuggled against him. He looked at her for the first time since they had been walking. Her expression was serious, almost frightened, and she looked vulnerable. Hadn't she cried the night before? "Hey." He smiled. She studied his face, then smiled back.

The first hurdle might have been Adele Henry, since he was invited to dinner that afternoon. But when he phoned and said he had a friend he'd like to bring, her reaction was "It's about time. We'll expect you both at two."

Within a few days, Sandra had become an easy part of his life. He spoke out against stringing laundry the first time it happened. "How do you do yours?" she asked.

"Well, laundromat every couple of weeks."

"I guess a man by himself can go around up here smelling like fish. I'll buy some extra changes, and we can do it all together every Sunday."

The cannery itself was still a world he merely tolerated—he knew he was passing through, waiting for the right boat to come along—but Sandra made it easier. Made it desirable, for the time. He still looked for the boats, but not with the same intensity.

Then, just as he had mellowed, a boat he cared about would arrive to unload. There standing by the scales would be Jones Henry in his fishing clothes. Or Seth, strutting with the shaggy look of the deck about him as he talked ostentatiously of nets and gear. It took little to make Hank restless and miserable again. Worst of all, relationships were being modified by his association with cannery management. He could no longer saunter as easily into a bar and count himself a fisherman.

Once, with Sandra alongside (she a representative of the actual cannery office), they joined the crew of the *Shalimar* at a table in Solly's. Suddenly he found himself defending the cannery's right to charge fishermen a penalty for excessive trash fish in the deliveries of shrimp. "Hell, it's the boat's job to cull. If we didn't weigh out the trash and deduct it, you'd soon be delivering us a halfweight of candlefish. Nobody recognizes it, but canneries have a narrow profit margin." Their quiet attention failed to warn him, and he continued with other things Swede Scorden had told him. "Fishermen don't know the market down in Seattle, and that's what controls the canneries up here. If the Seattle market falls and the cannery tries to drop its price to the boats in order to survive, you think you're screwed by the dirty capitalists."

Jody turned to Mike and the rest of the *Shalimar* crew. "Meet Hank Scorden, Swede's boy."

"Well, Hank *is* right, you know," said Sandra, and started to explain some of the problems of cannery bookkeeping. Hank quietly silenced her. He felt humiliated and sick. For God's sake help me get back to the boats, he wanted to beg of them. Instead, he made a clumsy joke of his allegiances. After another round which he insisted on buying, they made a glum departure. Sandra never did understand. As soon as they left the bar, she said, "They might as well be told the truth. Fishermen are so unrealistic."

"I don't want to talk about it. Let's walk by the harbor."

Into the breach, in midspring, came the halibut schooners from Seattle and Prince Rupert. While Swede's cannery did not buy halibut, Hank could watch the boats moor at another pier close by. In cruised names he recognized from his earliest days in Kodiak seven years before—*Grant, Republic, Northern, Chelsea, Thor*—sturdy white-hulled wooden vessels, their bows straight with a simple grace. Nothing had changed on them, as it had in even his short experience on other fishing boats. He remembered the businesslike coils of line, the high marker poles topped with red pennants, and the covered work areas astern. Each of the schooners had a deep-grained air of serious fishing, a solidity with the sea characterized by thick planks and scarred cutting tables. He began to desert his cannery duties, to slip over and haunt the dockside where they were taking ice and bait.

It was not easy to strike a conversation with the men aboard. They seemed a separate, taciturn tribe from other fishermen, uniformly older, and men of little banter even among themselves. Their faces were set and weathered. Most had Norwegian accents. In contrast to the local fishermen of his own generation, many were more wiry than muscular, and few wore beards. Instead of the spring-footed energy he had come to associate with men on the Kodiak boats, their feet hugged the deck as they moved from job to job. They were different; yet, like the appearance of their wooden boats, they seemed the archetypal fishermen.

One day Hank stood watching a crewman on deck. The man's blond hair stuck out from a soiled white cap and the frayed sleeves of his long johns protruded from a wool shirt sliced at the elbows. As he passed line from one scrupulously neat coil to another, he filed and straightened the large steel hooks attached every few feet. The coils were beautifully even, and the leaders to which the hooks connected were set in a regular subpattern within the coil.

"Howdy," Hank ventured. The man glanced up and nodded slightly without breaking his rhythm.

As Hank watched, he realized that he called himself a fisherman without ever having fished by the oldest method of them all. Hook and line must have been invented centuries before nets and pots.

"You sure coil that neatly."

"It's how I vas taught to do it." But the man smiled at the compliment. His large red hands kept working as he said mildly, "What are you, a tourist?"

"Hell no. I fish salmon and crab and shrimp." A silence continued until Hank asked how long a halibut trip lasted.

"Oh . . . Three weeks you mostly stay out now. A few years ago ve fill the boat in ten–twelve days, but now with the Japs and the Russians, there ain't that much halibut." He pronounced the final word carefully—hahl–ee–boot—lingering over each syllable.

"I once worked on the halibut lines, slimed them after they came from the holds, then stacked them in the freezers." The story made no impression. "Some weighed over two hundred pounds, really tough to handle."

"Sure, you get some soakers. At least they wasn't flapping."

"Do they fight much?"

"Halibut? They're mean son of bitches, flap so hard on deck they sometimes knock you over."

Hank glanced toward the metal building where his duties lay, where haggling women and heaps of shrimp awaited his return. "Guess you have a full crew aboard? Don't need another man?"

"Full crew, ja." The man said it as if he were answering a strange question, but he glanced at Hank for the first time as his hands continued to work. "Ve always make the crew up in Seattle."

"You know any other halibut boat that might be short a man?"

"No . . . The captains don't like to take any fellow yust from the docks. You start as inbreaker in halibut, you know that? First year you make only maybe quarter share. Takes a fellow about three years to be a good halibut fisherman, if he works hard."

Hank laughed uncertainly, impressed still further. "Come on. Three years?" He watched the easy skill of the line being coiled and longed to try it, privately.

When he returned to the cannery, his picking line had clogged and everyone was searching for him. Joe Cutch stood on the platform setting things right with his own hands, and Swede himself was wiping shrimp mess from his clothes as Hank walked up.

"What the hell, Crawford?"

"Sorry, Swede."

"Where were you?"

Hank considered saying he had been sick, but: "I went to look over the halibut boats. You can dock me."

"Dock, shit. I either count on you or I don't."

"Look, Swede, I'm not a cannery man. I was looking for a boat."

"You're a cannery man when you're on my clock."

Hank felt the heat rise in his face from Swede's glare. He braced himself to be fired. But he only had a few bucks after furnishing the apartment, and there was rent next week, and Sandra. "Swede, I won't duck out like that again, in the middle of a shift. But I'll still look for boats at lunch break and at nights, and when I find one—"

"I need foremen I can trust to stick. You belong back behind a fork, and you'd be out on your ass if I wasn't shorthanded. Tell Cutch to reassign you to loading gang if you want to stay."

"Suits me fine." Hank looked at his picker lines, where the women were all watching surreptitiously as they worked. He had not considered the embarrassment of such a plummet. Sandra might not . . . "You mean this minute? Who's going to take my place here?"

"Me, until I find somebody. I can rely on me."

Hank grinned. It didn't matter after all. He sauntered to find Cutch. Indeed, it didn't matter. In another hour he was sweating under oilskins in a hold full of shrimp and ice, shoveling heavier forkfuls than the others, and it felt good.

That night his muscles hurt in the old way, so much so that he couldn't sleep. "This is awful," said Sandra as she rubbed him down. "And you're not even upset. Swede hardly ever changes his mind, but in a couple of days, I'll—"

"Leave it as it is. Doesn't have to change anything with us, unless you only bunk with foremen."

"Stop that kind of talk." She bit his neck and started to rouse him. But she murmured "Soap doesn't do much for that fish smell."

He managed to intercept many of the halibut skippers to ask for a berth, but the man on deck was right: none were interested in a green hand. One by one the wooden schooners left their moorings and disappeared beyond the breakwater.

On the whole, Hank found it not a bad experience to tumble to a laboring job again. The entire air of Kodiak was one of fluid relationships both of people and position. Skippers of the smaller salmon boats crewed on larger ones during shrimp and crab seasons. He had seen a man's woman of one season turn up the next with somebody else, and he had heard of men in the cannery game who went broke and started again from the bottom. Maybe the storekeepers and professional people of Kodiak maintained straight career lines like those back east—no way he had of knowing for sure—but how could men do this who worked on frail boats which the sea might sink with barely a warning? All in all, he told himself when the shoveling of shrimp someone else had caught became wearisome, or when he had to swallow directions from kids who once worked under him, it was good to be flexible and to stay loose.

After Sandra's initial shock at his demotion, their life together continued as before. He still made the most money (some weeks more than as a foreman) and contributed the larger share to expenses. However, as a member of the loading crew he had to report by five in the morning, while her day began regularly at eight. And, while she was through at five, his quitting time varied between three and midnight. Soon she had assumed all the chores of housekeeping. If he chose to wander restlessly among the boats, or to seek out fishing friends in the bars, she usually stayed behind. But she was always waiting for him back in bed. It was a good arrangement. He wondered if his father wouldn't be envious, after all the standard disapprovals had been voiced.

One by one he faced up in his lowered status to the crews he knew, as they came in to unload. Seth's potential derision bothered him: if it turned abusive he'd probably poke him. The crew of the *Dolores R* was still asleep in the dark predawn when Hank and the rest of the unloading gang opened their hatch and crawled into the ice and shrimp. They had shoveled out half the hold when touseled figures holding coffee cups began to appear. Hank met it head-on. He tossed a shrimpy snowball that hit Seth on the back of the neck, then stood looking up with a grin.

Seth's burly, boyish face peered around on the docks, then settled below as he recognized Hank. "Oh shit, man," he said reproachfully. "I was counting on you to find me another boat. The guy I replaced is coming back."

Nels Hanson of the *Delta* watched him with curious satisfaction and declared himself not surprised to see that a fellow who bad-mouthed skippers, and never hopped to it, couldn't hold a foreman's job.

"Hell," said Steve on the *Adele H* when they came in, "I'd rather be down there too than bossing a bunch of hens on that picker line."

And the *Shalimar*. Jody gave a hoot when she saw him in their hold, and summoned Mike and the others to have a look. "Hiding microphones down there?" she called. "One thing sure, that's the slowest pitchfork I've ever seen."

"Doing the best I can, what with ice laid by amateurs and the shrimp no bigger than worms," said Hank, suddenly happy.

"Swede giving you a bad time, Hank? Catch you not defending the poor hungry canneries?"

"It's too hard to leave this place from the top, so I'm trying to crawl out the asshole. Help me find a boat."

"What's Sandra say to this?"

"She's stuck with it. I'm serious, I need a boat."

"We hear you," said Mike. "I'll keep watch. Meanwhile, put your back into that shrimp of ours. Liable to turn sour just waiting for you to move."

"I'm smart as hell, but don't ask me to reverse the clock. Ever consider delivering fresh?"

"We'll be at Solly's or Tony's or the Ship's," called Jody as they left. "Join us when you can."

The trouble was, even though his old friends might recognize him again, the shrimping was good and the weather not bad. Boat's crews simply stayed intact. Salmon season would start in mid-June, but that was still long away. And king crab season, which had lasted year round during the mid-sixties, now closed in January and did not start again until August.

One day as Hank emerged from a hold for lunch break, he saw one of the halibut schooners glide through the breakwater and head for the adjacent cannery. The fleet had just left a few days before for a three-week trip. Hank raced across piers to receive the schooner's lines, his oilskins still dripping shrimp and ice. It was the boat where the man had talked to him while coiling. A hospital squad removed a crewman in a wire stretcher. Hank helped, then jumped aboard to quiz the man he knew. Seth arrived also and started nosing around.

"Ja, poor Sverre, a big sea threw him into the checkers against something sharp, maybe broke his back." Too tricky in the rough weather for the Coast Guard to raise him by helicopter, so they had left their gear in the water on Albatross Bank to rush him in. Going back right away.

"I can take his place," Hank declared.

"Oh? Got to talk to captain."

Seth had already reached the captain, a heavy, middle-aged Norwegian who was shaking his head. "Ve probably fish with the men we got." But he wavered enough to narrow his eyes and ask, "You pretty husky?"

Hank had spoken to this captain before. He edged in and began to talk, using a few of the halibut words he had picked up around the schooners. He nearly pleaded.

The captain looked over both Hank and Seth dispassionately until the man Hank knew spoke up slowly in Norwegian. They hired Hank as an inbreaker on a quarter crew share.

Within an hour, Hank had squared it as best he could with a stunned Sandra in the office, grabbed his gear from the apartment, bought hip boots and wristers at his new shipmate's direction, and leaped with full arms onto the deck of the schooner *Lincoln*.

Seth, his bushy young face tight with resentment, threw off their lines. The cannery sheds of Kodiak receded.

18

INBREAKER

H ANK knew enough to act less excited than he felt. His five crewmates seemed friendly enough, but they were very reserved.
From the apparent age of their weathered faces, all but one might
have been fishermen since before he was born. He missed some of their
names. The captain was Igvar Rasmussen, and his friend from the dockside conversation was Trygve Jensen (who pronounced it Treeg'–va
Yen'–sen). A rough-looking man his own age with ice blue eyes was
named Sven. Of the two who mumbled their names, one had a long
hound-dog face that ended in a round open mouth, and the other had
a face that was full and rosy. They spoke among themselves in Norwegian. Only the captain and Trygve seemed willing to attempt English
with him.

Igvar, from an enclosed pilothouse only a few feet above main
deck, called an order, then translated for Hank as the others started
moving. 'Trygve will show you below. Den you help cut the bait. Pay
careful attention to how Trygve shows you." His voice had an agreeable
rise and fall that Hank had heard in other Norwegians.

Unlike most other fishing boats Hank had known, with the galley
located just off the work deck, the living quarters of the *Lincoln* were
reached by descending from deck through a hatch. The overheated
room below was both cozy and cramped. Curtained bunks occupied the
forepeak in close double tiers, and seats that doubled as storage lockers
lined both sides. The stove was fitted tight against the bulkhead nearest
the hatch, with its exhaust pipe paralleling the ladder close enough to
scorch a shoulder. A table filled the center of the room. It was now raised

to the ceiling to make an open space where Trygve explained they had laid the injured man.

"Ja, poor Sverre, leave his bunk yust like it is, you take this." Trygve patted a top one that practically clamped against the overhead. For locker space, rather than move the injured man's belongings, Trygve consolidated his own gear to make room for Hank's.

The boat pitched, then snapped into a roll. Hank finished quickly below and hurried topside before the motion should begin to make him sick. On deck, water was already breaking over the sides. Amidships stood an arrangement of bins and tables. The pilothouse rose aft like a miniature conning tower, with an adjoining covered work area behind on the stern. Igvar's calm face, pipe in mouth, peered from the window as he steered. Trygve first told Hank to put on the oilskin half-sleeve wristers he had bought. "Keeps the fish off your sleeves, then every day you Lysol them. Okay, Hank, you want to cut the octopus like this." The frozen chunks of tentacles and head were sliced with a knife, and the resultant pieces had to be about three inches long and half as wide. It seemed easy enough, and Hank soon worked at fair speed even though Trygve was much faster. After the stagnation of shore, the cold slap of seawater against his legs and the salty wind around his face were exhilarating. After a while he tried matching Trygve's speed. His knife glanced off a frozen chunk.

"No use you lose a finger, Hank. Go slow till you got it," said Trygve mildly. He examined Hank's pieces, shook his head, brushed the remaining octopus to his side, and lifted a basket of semifrozen herring in its place. "Chop the herrings in two, like this. Takes time to learn octopus."

Whenever they filled a basket, Trygve sent Hank aft with it to replenish the supply of the others, who stood around narrow tables on the covered fantail putting the bait on hooks. They all worked intently, faces relaxed but hands moving as rapidly as pistons. With enough pieces cut, Trygve took him back to join the baiting.

Each coiled unit of lines and attached hooks was called a skate. Trygve lifted one to a table and began to re-coil it from the top onto a square of canvas he called the skate bottom. As he explained, the hooks were attached to the line at twenty-one-foot intervals by leaders called gangions. He speared a bait on each hook, then laid it in the center on the skate bottom as he coiled the line around it. The operation was trickier than it appeared. Several times Trygve interrupted patiently to make Hank do his part again. "If she ain't coiled right it makes a snarl, and if you don't put on the baits right they fly off."

They prepared twenty-four skates, which Trygve said would be tied together into separate strings of twelve each when the time came. At a length of three hundred fathoms or eighteen hundred feet for each skate, Hank figured it roughly at more than eight miles of line. He had counted more than eighty hooks on one skate, making about two thousand hooks they had baited altogether. His part in it had been negligible, yet his wrists and hands ached.

They all went below for mug-up. The others lowered the table from the ceiling and settled around it to play pinochle as they pulled out pipes and cigars. Hank, not invited into the game, sat watching as he tried to appear interested. He thought he had heard the sounds of a boat in seas before, but steel boats made no sound at all compared to the groans and creaks of the *Lincoln*'s caulked timbers. He joined Igvar in the pilothouse and offered to take the watch.

"Nei, better get your rest, going to vork like hell soon."

Igvar did not appear talkative, but in the easy solitude, as they watched the bow pitch and dip among the gray swells, he told something of himself. He had started in the boats with his father out of "Norgay, Stavinger," by the time he was eleven. "Cabin boy by thirteen, full fisherman in dory by fifteen." During the war he escaped the Germans and operated boats from England for the Resistance. Afterward, "I vas still young feller, maybe twenty-five, no sweetheart. I had a cousin in Ballard, so I come to Seattle and vas soon on boat, fishing the halibut." (He pronounced it as did Trygve, with the same lingering respect over each syllable: hahl–ee–boot.) "I vork hard and save money. Now I got a boat, a vife, two kids, and three apartment houses."

But as for turning over the wheel . . . Igvar suggested again he get some rest.

Below in the galley the pinochle game had stopped. Trygve was preparing to relieve the watch and the other three snored in their bunks. Hank disliked being idle when he had just begun on board. "Can I start something to cook?"

Trygve wagged his finger warningly: "That are Olaf's stove."

The sleepers lay on their backs with hands over their chests like corpses. When Hank crawled into his own bunk he found little room for any other position. He could not sleep. The noise of the planking sounded like small explosions as the bow—no more than three feet from his head—veered up and down in the water.

It was dark when they returned to deck under floodlights. Olaf, the one with the long horse face, had risen to prepare a meal beforehand, and they shoveled huge quantities of meat, noodles, bread, and creamed corn in silence. After the hot cabin, the air was cold and slicing. They all trooped astern and went about their preparations as if Hank had not existed. Trygve pointed to a place beside a bait bench for him to stand. "Yust vatch first time." Olaf and Sven removed the canvas tops from some of the skates and tied them together in sequence, bottom end of one to top of next. They positioned them by a high metal chute that was attached to the stern. Trygve and the rosy-faced man, whom Hank now knew as Ralph, readied several marker poles. Each pole had a red pennant on top as well as a battery-operated flashing light. Attached to the pole was a plastic buoy, and leading from this was an anchor. Close to the anchor, Trygve tied the end of the first skate.

When Igvar shouted they sprang into motion, anticipating each other's movements so closely that their work interlocked. They threw over a marker pole and buoy, then an anchor, and the first skate began to zip over the chute with its hooks clacking against the metal. It was very fast and neat. After one string of twelve end-connected skates was laid, followed by another anchor and marker, they laid the second string.

Within minutes Igvar called and they returned to the main deck, where in the dark a small flashing light approached. One of their red pennant poles drifted into the pool of deck lights. Sven hauled it aboard and bent the attached line over a power block they called the gurdy. Ralph began coiling the anchor line as it payed in. Trygve called Hank to set up the boards of several bins both on deck and adjacent to the table area in the center. "This is the checkers, they call it. Fellow who dresses the halibut keeps the checks on how many we got." Trygve slipped his arms into wristers as he nodded toward Sven at the gurdy. "Whatever you do, stay clear of the roller man, ja? Unless he calls and we run with gaff hooks, but you yust watch that too, stay clear."

"What regular job can I be doing?"

"Cut more octopus like I showed you. No, not octopus, you don't know enough yet. Cut herrings. Yust stay clear of everybody." When the anchor came to the side Hank forgot the directive and went to help. Trygve barked him back.

Suddenly, to the sound of a collective "Hah," Hank looked up to see a halibut fly over the rail on Sven's gaff hook. The big flatfish landed in one of the checkers, and immediately started to thrash so hard that the boards shook. Trygve beat it on the head with a club until it lay still, then plunged his gaff into the head and lifted it onto the table. "Faster you kill him before he gets bruised, better he keeps," he explained to Hank. "Maybe seventy pound, eh?" The halibut was still alive, a monstrous and beautiful creature glistening under the deck lights. Its flat, thick body was olive-brown on one side and white on the other, about three feet long from tail to head. Hank stopped work to stare. He had handled dead halibut on the sliming line, but the impact of this huge breathing fish that spread over most of the table was vastly different. Both eyes were crowded grotesquely onto the brown side of the head. Their hooded stare was angry. The mouth gasped open to show teeth. Trygve without ceremony sliced a half-moon cut into its side where the throat might have been and scooped out a mess of entrails—a minuscule gutting for a creature of such size. The halibut flapped with its whole body even as the angry eyes glazed.

"You call this hole the poke when the guts come out. Iceman in the hold stuffs it with ice; that makes the whole fish keep."

By now Sven had gaffed another. He swung it over the rail, then flicked it free of the gaff hook, meanwhile continuing to run the line and to knock the hooks clean of untouched bait. Hank remained staring in admiration as he tried to impress the job on his mind.

"Goddam it, inbreaker, cut de baits faster," roared Igvar from the wheelhouse. Hank started chopping vigorously.

"Skate!" yelled Ralph, who had already coiled a skate, detached it from the string, and tied on the canvas bottom.

"You, Hank," said Trygve, "hurry back to fantail the skates as soon as Ralph makes."

Hank lifted the heavy bundle of coiled line and hooks and staggered with it over the rolling, slippery deck. He had been too engrossed to notice the force of the seas around their legs, and now he righted himself just as a wave surged over the rail and slapped him in the chest. Icy seawater sloshed down his neck and saturated the top of his long johns.

The others clicked as a team, never rushed, yet unbelievably fast and adept. Olaf lowered himself into the hold, and after the sound of his shovel loosening ice, he called up. Hank at Trygve's direction slid down the first halibut they had caught, which had been lying gutted for at least half an hour. Suddenly the creature thrashed its tail against his arm with the force of a two-by-four.

From being too idle, he soon had more work than he could perform. Just when he would begin to catch up chopping bait, Ralph and then others in their turn would yell "Skate!" and he staggered another coil aft where one man baited. The halibut piled in the checkers while the icer kept calling Hank for more fish. In the middle of it, Trygve set him to scrubbing slime off the deck. When he finished, he tried to grab a moment to rush below for a drink of water to ease the salt in his mouth. Olaf practically screamed and Trygve said gruffly, "You don't wear dirty oilskins in the cook's galley. And, hey, you call that scrubbed? Wait till you slip some day. Scrub him harder."

About three in the morning Olaf poked his head from below— Hank had not noticed his descent—and declared solemnly "Comen." The deck work continued at a slower pace as they took turns below after hosing the slime from their oilskins and hanging them by the hatch door. The table below was set with a roast the size of a halibut, with stacks of bread and butter, and big tureens of oatmeal, noodles, potatoes, and thick gravy. Hank ate with Sven, the blue-eyed man his own age, who silently dumped everything together with gravy on his plate, then bent close and pushed it into his mouth with bread as fast as he could chew and swallow. He downed it with six cups of coffee. In fifteen minutes he was climbing to deck again.

So it went, day after day. Somewhere each day, Igvar called time for three to five hours' rest, depending on the soaks. They would all descend the ladder, lay cross-armed in their bunks, and drop off on the instant. When Igvar called them awake again, Hank rose stiffly with the rest, already longing for the next time he could lie down. More than once he was in such a misery of pain and fatigue that he vowed to quit when they reached the blessed shore.

At least after a few days he hit a rhythm, and learned to block sleep from his mind for hours at a time. Under Trygve's tutelage he was first entrusted with cutting octopus, then with baiting the hooks unsupervised, then actually with slicing the poke. He bent all his effort to doing each job to their standards. As for dressing the halibut as they thumped under his hand, he had cut heads from hundreds of living salmon without a thought to the life he was snuffing and had probably crushed underfoot a few thousand shrimp, but never had he extinguished such large lives as these. In his sleep the first nights aboard he had chopped endless herring to the sound of Igvar's shouts, and now it was the thrashing halibut that he was helpless to clear from his dreams.

The first time the man at the roller yelled for help and the others grabbed gaff hooks from the rack, Hank did as Trygve had told him and watched from the side. They all bent over the water, plunged hooks into the creature's head, and heaved up together. Igvar judged the weight at one hundred and fifty pounds. The men relaxed enough to joke about it in Norwegian before returning again to silent work. "Dot's a baby soaker," Trygve told him. He hammered its head repeatedly, but it still thrashed its tail so hard against the bin that the boards bowed outward. "Vait till you see a real-size soaker."

When it came, Hank grabbed a gaff hook with the rest. Leaning over the water into the huge thumping fish, with the spray of the combat churned up into his face, he felt as if he faced cannon smoke. He drove his hook into the flesh with a blood cry and felt through his arms and back the fantastic weight in motion as they lifted the halibut aboard. It was too large to throw into a checker. For a moment it lay still, seemingly defeated, its bulging double eyes staring with the desperate malevolence of the cornered.

"Goddam, who gaff him in de side?" roared Igvar. All the punctures were in the head except Hank's, which had torn into the body and exposed a slice of bleeding meat. The others turned to him in solemn disgust, as Trygve explained quietly that he had ruined the fish for the highest price, because the flesh around the wound would spoil before it had reached the unloading dock. "And that's a halibut maybe two hundred fifty pound, a hundred-dollar fish at forty cents a pound if it was in good shape."

In his fatigue Hank's voice broke as he apologized. It seemed, in the isolation of the roiling gray seas, like a capital and unforgivable crime rather than a blunder from ignorance.

"Yaaw," said Igvar mildly, signaling the end of the incident. "You don't do it again. Roll the gurdy, no money comes in otherwise."

Suddenly the boated fish rose double, straightened with a snap, and broke two boards. They clubbed it several times but did not dare to lift it to the dressing table. Three hours later, after lying quiescent, it exploded into one final action.

Next time a soaker came to the rail, Hank approached with trepidation. He drove his gaff squarely into the head with the others, and watched panting with relief when it was over without new disgrace.

There were no Sundays on the halibut grounds. They passed other of the wooden schooners laying and hauling. One day they stood guard as a Russian trawler worked the water close by, and Igvar remained on the gear they had just set, to protect it.

The creak of the wooden timbers, the galley stuffiness from the smoke, the rolling of the sea itself, and the weight and smell of halibut all became so concentratedly a single world that after two weeks none other existed for Hank. His tired body tuned more and more to what he was doing. One day his crewmates, after considerable discussion among themselves in Norwegian, allowed him to accompany Trygve into the hold to ice the halibut. As Trygve explained, none of them in the old country had entered the hold for half a year.

Icing was heavy, close work, all of it predicated on the need to preserve the halibut without freezing for up to three weeks from the time of catch. The icer first stuffed ice into the raw poke where the viscera had been removed. Then he stacked the heavy carcasses like shingles and sealed ice around their edges. All this with the continuous, sometimes violent motion of the boat. The most important thing of all, said Trygve gravely, was to lay the halibut white-side-up, since otherwise blood would settle into the meat and discolor it so nobody would buy.

On the day the trip ended, Hank felt himself a man returned from a year in the far deserts even though Albatross Bank was only a few hours' run from Kodiak.

The houses among the misty hills and the square buildings of the waterfront, even the low corrugated sheds of the canneries, had a beauty beyond their appearance. He hoped Sandra might be waiting on the pier, but she was not. Still hours of work ahead. He followed the others behind Igvar to a room in the cannery. There, with a blackboard on the wall and a bottle of whiskey, Igvar sat at a table with the managers of rival plants and bargained the price per pound for his catch. The crew stood behind him, watching silently. The ceremony took more than two hours. On the boards were squares for the size categories of halibut and a column for each of the bidders. Igvar held out firmly for the price he wanted while drinking shots of the whiskey, bantering, slouching back in his chair for long periods without a word. Once he declared they would go on to Seward or Pelican for a better price. At length, he came down half a cent on mediums and one cent on large (which fetched a higher basic price), while the winner of the bidding rose two and a half cents on each. The men around the table shook hands, and the manager of the host cannery offered drinks to the crew.

They moved the *Lincoln* to the pier of the high bidder and started unloading. Hank worked in the hold with Sven and Trygve. They gaffed the huge carcasses from their ice sealent and slid them into a cargo net, which a crane raised. The catch of a few weeks took several hours to unload. Then they hosed the ice apart with hot water—the hold filled with steam like a sauna—and scrubbed all the boards with disinfectant.

As part of an agreement within the halibut fleet, the schooners laid up several days between trips. The others planned to fly home to Seattle next morning, stopping in Anchorage en route to call on their injured crewmate, who had been flown there to be hospitalized.

"Ja," said Igvar, "we go out again in eight days."

"See you then," said Hank.

"I t'ought maybe you was tired of halibut inbreaker. We probably find some Norwegian with experience down home. You know you got to join the halibut union in Seattle if we keep you?"

"I'll join," he declared, forgetting all vows never to fish halibut again.

Igvar told Hank to phone his home in five days. "You t'ink about it and I t'ink about it."

Rain poured steadily, as it had for days. Hank slogged to the apartment in the dark, utterly depressed. At least there was Sandra.

Her first comment: "Don't they have a shower on that boat?"

Hank exploded. Without a further word she put on her raincoat and left. He drank cold beer as he bathed and bathed. He fell asleep in the tub, finally climbed into the empty bed. What kind of fisherman's woman was she, to understand so little? He wondered about it a very short time before falling asleep again.

Hank and Sandra made it up next morning by common silence and no discussion of their differing viewpoints. It being Sunday, they spent most of the day together in bed. The next two days for Hank were a luxury of hot baths and sleep. On the third he ventured out. The rain still poured. He found Seth, who remained a prisoner of the beach. Seth listened with glum hostility as Hank explained how he had approached the *Lincoln* before, and knew one of the crewmen. "Captain wasn't going to hire any greenhorn until Trygve spoke up, so I wasn't cutting you from anything. And man, you can thank your luck. Halibut inbreaking makes that trip with Nels Hanson into pleasure."

"Okay, let's trade places."

"Come on, I'm buying booze and lunch."

Hank welcomed the comfort and rest, but by the time of his talk with Seth he was glancing across the floats at the halibut masts. By the morning of the fifth day, he stood wistfully in the rain in front of the *Lincoln,* yearning to remain part of her.

He finally summoned courage to phone Igvar in Seattle. The injured crewman would need months to recover, Igvar said. He needed a man for the season. Hank asked to remain. The unbelievable answer: "Ja. Okay, you doing pretty good, Hank. I put you on half share next trip, and then we see."

Back aboard the *Lincoln,* any euphoria vanished after a day's baiting and dressing in heavy weather.

The standards of his crewmates were absolute, rigid. He could only be one of them by accepting the same standards and concentrating to reach them. It meant to coil for practice in a precious few minutes of leisure, to cut the herring and octopus exactly, to measure the right placement of each bait on the hook, to bait with a constant eye toward bent hooks that needed to be set, to drive the gaff with precision when a thrashing halibut came to the rail, to leave no membrane in the poke when cleaning, to handle each heavy fish without bruising and to ice it neither too much nor too little, to scrub slime again and again until not the slightest trace remained. It meant to do each job so no one had to repeat it or so that no mishap occurred from a deficiency, and to maintain this standard at a steady speed even when groggy with fatigue. He came to appreciate the long old-country apprenticeship as he watched the quality of his crewmates' work. They, finding that he tried as hard as he could and that he was improving, began to address him by name and quietly offer pointers. They even dealt him into the pinochle.

On a calm day—it was still raining steadily—they had a conference over his head in Norwegian, and then solemnly Trygve beckoned him to the roller. Trygve showed him how to stand and pointed to a lever. "You see a halibut coming up, stop the gurdy when the halibut is this far from rail, ja? Then you gaff him over the rail onto deck. You got to gaff him right the first time, or you maybe see him swim away and everybody sorry as hell." The roller man was also expected to knock loose the remaining baits just before the hooks passed through the gurdy. "The hooks, now, Hank, watch out for those bastards. A hook fly loose over the gurdy, cuts you like a sharp knife. You got to watch it all the time."

Behind Hank's back at the rail, the steady rhythm of the boat's work had slowed. The gurdy moved by someone's adjustment at a fraction of its usual speed as he fidgeted to watch the water and knock loose the bait simultaneously. He broke into a sweat as he was forced to halt the motion altogether to clear some of the baits, using the hook awkwardly.

"Jaw, Hank," drawled Olaf as he stood behind Hank and coiled. "Iss okay."

Trygve nudged him. "Look at de vater and keep steady."

Hank tensed and almost cried out. A huge white shape rose with increasing clarity through the layers of green water, flapping slowly. The sheaves of the gurdy creaked with the weight of it and the taut line snapped off flecks of water. He had never seen one so big. His legs locked as he grasped the gaff hook and leaned over. "My God, she's a soaker, everybody better—"

Trygve beside him shooshed the others back.

Up came the halibut. No soaker, but the hugeness of it! It began to twist.

"Use de gaff hook," said Trygve sharply.

Hank reacted. He stopped the gurdy, and with a single sweep accompanied by a yell gaffed it in the head and swung it over the side.

They all cheered as Hank stood panting and excited. Trygve knelt, swiped his hand across the halibut's body, and smeared it on Hank's face to their approving laughter. Blood pounding, he started the gurdy again.

He lost the next one, and the gaff hook besides, as the outraged fish twisted straight from his grasp.

"You want to take it back?" he asked Trygve, scared.

"No.

Hank licked his lips, flicked a bait, and braced for the next twisting white shape as it rose. He landed it correctly, even though it flapped and wrenched his arm. Sweat streamed from under his wool cap to blur his eyes. A snapping hook sliced through the sleeve of his rain jacket.

After one skate, which yielded eight halibut and two stray black cod, plus the halibut lost, Trygve said, "Ja, Hank, that's good for the first time, you go rest a minute now."

Hank relinquished the gaff hook, but to show he was okay he went straight to the baiting table and started to cut. His legs and hands were shaking. Olaf, who had gone below, handed him up a mug of coffee. "Tak," Hank said, using a word of the basic Norwegian he had set himself to learn. The others went about their jobs as in gruff but amused Norwegian they discussed his performance.

When he was allowed at the roller again the following day, he did a smoother job. The day after was so rough that they passed him by. As seas rose and swept over the rail, Sven at the roller sometimes had to scramble up and cling to the shrouds to keep from being washed away. Everybody worked grimly, but they did not stop.

Finally the blow became so severe that the line snapped. They went to the marker at the other end and worked in the remaining skates —no one considered abandoning the gear despite the weather—and then Igvar declared work suspended. They stowed and lashed down everything they had been using. Then, since land was forty miles away with a headwind, they hove to and endured the weather. The salt-bearing wind howled and rattled around them. Except for the man on watch they slept. Hank took his tricks at the wheel, then lay braced in his cubicle of a bunk with hands on his chest like the others. The smell of their smoke and the cadence of their Norwegian contented him, as did the loud groaning conversation of the wooden boat itself with the sea. This was fishing: ultimate, basic, classic.

Hank's honeymoon with the schooners halted abruptly one day at the roller. He yelled "Soaker!" for good reason, and collectively they all gaffed aboard a two-hundred-pound fish. He leaned down just as the creature gave a terrible thrash of its tail. A wrecking ball could not have smashed him more effectively. It broke his left arm in several places, and at the least dislocated his shoulder. Two hours later, biting a wad of cloth against the pain, he rose in a basket to a Coast Guard helicopter and somewhat later lay weighted by a cast between the drearily clean sheets of a bed in the Kodiak hospital.

Igvar carried insurance that covered injuries, so Hank continued on boat's pay. They all visited him at least once, and Trygve was very kind. But Igvar brought up a cousin from Seattle to replace him, and the *Lincoln* soon left on its next trip. Hank walked the town glumly under the weight of a shoulder cast, a man of enforced leisure and temporary income. Sandra possessed him again, along with the compromising forces of civilization.

"It's a shame you had to burn your bridges like that with Swede," she said. "Why don't you see if one of the other canneries would consider hiring you as a foreman?"

The suggestion depressed him further, but it was certainly practical, since he was stuck with a cast until beyond the start of salmon season. He delayed looking, however. The steamy shrimp lines again, after the halibut schooner, was too sudden a comedown.

At the Ship's Bar one afternoon, Swede Scorden settled beside him and nodded at the cast. "That the new way of clubbing halibut?"

"Beats reasoning with them."

After a relaxed pause, Swede asked if he had ever worked in a salmon cannery. Hank reminded him of the time in sixty-three before he ran off on the *Rondelay*. "Hell, I made boxes for you, pewed, gutted, headed, retorted, canned—did everything but handle the money."

"Yes, now you mention it. Never were reliable."

"Not in canneries. Just to change the subject, you told me once you had fished. Get tired of it?"

"Smart enough to go before it killed me." Swede ordered cigars and a new round. "Before I went in the Quartermasters during the war, I'd purse-seined up and down Puget Sound."

"Great, wasn't it?" Hank was feeling mellow. "I could seine salmon for the rest of my life and be happy."

Swede gave his dry laugh. "This was before power blocks, when you broke your back each set. Canneries treated you like shit, sold you meat with maggots, paid a couple cents a fish, dropped the price if they pleased."

Hank was unimpressed. "I'd still have gone seining."

"Well, with the Depression, if you found a berth maybe you would. Being romantic is a luxury for the well-off."

"So you went into the Army, came home, got a job in a cannery, and worked your way to the top."

Swede slowly prepared his cigar. His lean face, even in the dark barroom light, had a controlled lack of expression. "No, I took my GI Bill and went to college in Seattle. Business Administration. Did it through the summers, and had my degree in two and a half years. I figured that would deliver me from the fish boats. *Then* I was romantic enough to go fishing again, just to get the cobwebs out of my system."

Hank declared that such a decision called for a new round, and ordered it.

"I'll tell you what interested me. Ever hear of Lowell Wakefield? A couple of years after the war, he outfitted a special ship to see if he could make a fishery of king crab up in the Bering Sea. Lowell planned to catch the crabs and process them on board. What the hell, I said, here's something new, so I signed aboard. We built that crab fishery from scratch. It wasn't pots back then; we dragged weighted nets down in the mud. Started to experiment with the pots later. You kid fishermen pull your square pots with a hydraulic block and never think that all the gear was developed for you by men still living, half of whom went broke in the process. You've probably never fished king crab."

"Only in the year before the earthquake. I helped Jones Henry put over those old circular pots."

"*Well*. You've fished pots that don't exist any more; you're already part of the history. That's how fast it's changing. It gets to me sometimes, the changes I've seen." He raised the fresh shot glass. "Here's to may I never have to work on another fish boat again."

"Suits me. Here's to fuck the canneries."

Swede ordered another round. "Crawford, I could tell you things. I remember the first time we figured how to home on radar buoys to find our pots. And how we worked out by trial and error the best way to separate crab legs from their shells, and then to run them through the line without spoiling their flavor. We were pioneers, and as a matter of fact, it was exciting."

Hank watched Swede with new respect. "When I first met you back in sixty-three, it seemed to me you'd run that salmon cannery for a hundred years, the way you had everybody hopping."

"Well, I'd been there about ten years, and manager nine of them. The company that owned it then stole me away from Wakefield with a promise that I'd be boss pretty quick, and gave a bonus that a man with a young family wasn't going to refuse. You know I left a year or so after the earthquake and started my own cannery?" Hank registered appropriate surprise and interest. "Up through nineteen sixty-six there was so much king crab around here it filled the pots wherever they dumped them. The boats were lined up to sell their crab. I decided I was ready to be my own pioneer, since I'd been a part of figuring out the processes myself. But I came in at the tag end, just as the bottom dropped out in sixty-eight. The big canneries barely stayed on top. Most were diversified with salmon and shrimp so they toughed it. To get any boats to deliver me enough crab to stay in business, I paid more than I was able to recover. For a while after it fell apart, my wife and I were both back working on one of Wakefield's picking lines to pay the rent, alongside some of the people I'd hired, while the bankruptcy people assessed my building and machinery. That was only two years ago."

Hank lifted his glass unsteadily. "Here's to your balls."

Swede rose and clapped Hank heavily on the shoulder. "Walk me back to the cannery."

Sandra, in Swede's outer office, looked up with surprise and a smile on seeing them together. "Seattle's been trying to get you," she told Swede, and he disappeared into his office with instructions for Hank to wait. The disadvantage of having his girlfriend working close by was apparent at once. There he was, when he wanted to be privately with his thoughts, standing mildly boozed under her scrutiny.

"Well, what does he want?"

Hank grinned, trying to make it enigmatic. "Jus' old friends bull-shitting."

"Yes, I see. Get some coffee. Swede drinks people under the table and you'd never know he's had any. He's good at keeping control."

Hank nodded wisely and went to the coffee room. Swede's door stood open when he returned. If Swede wanted to reinstate him as picker foreman, why not? Nothing better to do until the cast came off.

Swede was a different man behind his desk. His lean face was tense and irritable. "Goddam Seattle office dictates my prices, then holds my ass responsible. Yes, Crawford, what is it you want?"

"Not a damn thing." Hank started to leave.

"Okay, sit down and pay attention. You know I manage three plants for Seaflower Seafoods, the big one here in town, and then two salmon canneries in summer, the old one west of here and one down at the far south of the island. My south manager isn't coming back this year, he told me last week. Joe Cutch runs this one. If I could find another Cutch I'd take him. Second choice is somebody with enough education to read, who's not afraid to work, whom I can trust. The question in my mind is, can I trust you?"

"Run the whole *cannery?*"

"The day-to-day part of it. I'll be back and forth."

Hank whistled, impressed. But, as he thought about it: "You know me, Swede. I want to fish. You'd train me, then figure I'd screwed you when a berth came along." He patted his cast. "I'd guarantee to stay for this whole season."

"That's all I had in mind trusting you for. Assuming you hacked it, you'd get a one- to two-thousand bonus, depending on the season's pack, and salary of three hundred a week. Long days, and bullshit from everybody. Don't think being in charge is anything but that. You'll have your own house. Now, I know you and my clerk out there are shacking up—no, let me finish—and since I need a clerk down there I don't mind sending her.

Hank gazed over Swede's shoulder, through the window that looked over the loading dock. Should he take Swede's first offer, or would Sandy tell him too late that he should have bargained for more? The thought of all the responsibility appealed, cannery or not. "Okay, boss, no fish boats again until September."

"You're on the payroll. Supplies get delivered soon. We'll fly down tomorrow." They shook hands.

19

TRIAL BY CANNERY

THE names of south Kodiak Island—Olga Bay, Akhiok Village, Cape Alitak, Deadman Bay—have the same origins in Russian-Aleut and early disaster as those in the north and west of the island—Whale Pass, Kupreanof Straight, Terror Bay, Uganik Bay—where Hank had once canned salmon for Swede Scorden and fished for Jones Henry. But there the similarity ended. The eighty air miles south from Kodiak town took him from a country of mountains forested in near-tropical density, which often ended at the water in bluffs, to a country of bare smooth mountains, scrub marshland, and spits of gray gravel. Beyond the shore, the low bald islands of the Trinities rose glumly on the horizon. The same mists that played over the high northern trees hovered here like witches' breath. Thick spruce landscapes had molded Hank's concept of the wilderness, places restless and challenging. This by comparison was land's end, a place to dampen the spirit, a far extension of the earth.

Not that Hank was depressed. The plane circled to land by the piers built over the water. "Hey," he shouted from his seat by the pilot, "I'd forgotten how big these canneries are." The complex of long white buildings stretched nearly a quarter mile, bordered by gravel shoreline. It was laid out in a T formation. The living areas formed the crosspiece in a band paralleling the beach and the work areas made up the stem with massive sheds built on pilings into the water. The chowhall, machine shop, and other service facilities were clustered where the two sections joined. Off to one corner lay about twenty seine boats on trestles, painted identical colors. "We own them," Swede said. "Skippers lease them and agree to deliver to us. That's how you assure a steady flow of fish."

The plane landed in a bay and cruised in on its pontoons. With low tide, the pier rose fifteen feet. Above them a dog yapped. The watchman called to warn of a loose ladder and to tell Swede that Kodiak wanted to talk to him. His face was weathered and unwashed, and his whiskers were stained with snuff juice. Hank expected him to say colorful things, but he was shy and gave only monosyllabic answers. They all walked together down the wide boardwalk from the pier, past the cannery sheds to the office at the juncture of buildings.

The radio room was part of the office, located within a hive of small rooms. Swede showed Hank how to use the equipment as he called Kodiak; Joe Cutch's voice announced that a cargo ship with their season's supplies would be delivering next afternoon. Also, the Seattle office wanted Swede to fly down on tomorrow's plane from Anchorage for an emergency conference of area managers.

Swede cursed the arbitrariness of Seattle. "Hank doesn't have the experience with bills of lading and storage. Fly down yourself tomorrow with a crew of four."

"Right, Swede, but the number two retort just busted. Whole line's backed up, with *Shalimar* half unloaded, *Delta* waiting, and *Miss Lucy* due at three in the morning."

"Yeah, you stay there, Joe. I'll be back tonight. Have Sandy make my Seattle reservations. Then set up that gang to fly down. Send Sandy along with the forms; she understands them." He glanced at Hank with half a smile.

When he had finished on the radio, Swede swung absently in his swivel chair. "Before regular planes, a canneryman could forget the fucking home office."

"Tell Seattle you're too busy to come."

"No, with rumors of a shakeup, I'd best be there."

They inspected the length of the cannery complex, rain stinging their faces. The dog first challenged every step, then accompanied them with contented sniffings. The long chain of white buildings that provided the living quarters started at one end of a spit with the individual house that would be Hank's. It was raised on blocks, with steps and a porch, and three rooms inside. From there, boardwalks traversed a series of two-story dormitories with covered porches. Each room slept two or four. They contained chairs stacked in a corner, metal beds with mattesses, a table or two, and a curtained rack for clothes. Toward the center of the complex, the boardwalk widened to connect all the central facilities— a fire-engine house, big equipment sheds, the store and offices, a messhall with tables and benches, and a galley with oversized pots and stoves. The final long bunkhouse ran beside the row of beached seiners, and the end of its porch looked out over the misty rocks of the harbor.

"Every bit of the place needs paint," said Swede. "When the maintenance crew comes, make sure that's what they do whenever it stops raining."

"Right." Hank carried a notebook, grown soggy from the rain, which he opened to make a notation.

The shedlike cannery buildings were cavernous. They seemed vaster without people, with the untended machinery gleaming dully in the dark. There was fish odor everywhere, neither spoiled nor fresh but deeply residual, steeped into the boards and concrete. Hank recognized the basic layout from the other salmon cannery long ago, but the fact that he would be responsible gave this one a different dimension. Swede took him through it station by station as he explained the progression of processes.

"Know the names of all these machines before you talk to the mechanics, especially old Pete, or they'll ignore you."

There was the fish elevator to bring the salmon from the tenders, the bins to store them, the sorting belts and sluice troughs to convey them by species to the indexers for heading, and then the Iron Chinks. Swede pointed out some of the major blades, brushes, and water hoses of the high, complicated machines. "In the old days before my time, they shipped up Chinamen to do the butcher work, and now the Iron Chink takes no more than a second for all the guts, scales, fins. Sometimes the Chinks break down, and the foreman has to set up a hand line. Then you'll see what those machines are worth, you'll kiss the ass of the man who keeps them running. It's Pete Erikson in this cannery, be coming up in a week or so. He's an old fart now, and he snits easy. Not your worry to choose the people to feed the indexer and Chink, but whoever they are he'll take offense. Change the crew whenever he bitches. Kids on starting pay come and go all the time, but we hold on to Pete.

Larry Petrovich is foreman there, part Aleut, good man. He handles it every year. These foremen work together season after season, so you stay clear unless they come to you."

They followed the roller belts to the sliming tables, where people with brushes, knives, and hoses cleaned the fish carcasses coming from the Chink. Next came the filler machines, with chutes feeding into them from the ceiling. The chutes brought down flattened cans that were opened automatically, while parallel blades sliced the fish and put the pieces into the cans. "You have your two sizes of cans, one-pound talls and half-pound flats, and you decide ahead what you plan to pack that day. Everything, everything's got to be planned ahead. Last January I made out my final supply order for the whole summer. That includes I don't know what-all: nails, lumber, salt, cans, all the spares we might need, food for 140 people for two months, all the diesel for our twenty seiners and the others that fish for us . . . You run short, it takes a month to get anything up here from Seattle."

"Just of empty cans you must need thousands."

"Thousands? That ship's bringing seventeen *million* cans."

"Come on."

"We'll process about a hundred thirty thousand pinks a day—that's five thousand fish an hour for each of two lines, or about twenty-five thousand one-pound tails an hour, more than three hundred thousand cans in a twelve-hour day. Figure it yourself for an eight-week season." He waved toward the filler machines. "One of those opens and fills a hundred twenty-five cans a minute. Ever seen one can get jammed the wrong way and the whole line back up? You've got to have mechanics nearby all the time. Another thing you need to keep moving is water, fresh water, everywhere. Those salmon need as much water to travel through the line in pieces as they ever did swimming live. That means tubes and lines, stuff that breaks. When you locate a seafood cannery in the first place, no use thinking further on a site if it lacks a heavy water flow. Except for a piece of shore to build on, water's everything. You need deep enough harbor for the boats and tenders, and you want tides strong enough to take off a million fishheads plus a hundred forty people's daily shit. Well, we have sewage treatment now by law, and inspectors who can shut down your plant. That'll be one of your jobs. Inspectors fly in when they please, and you've got to take time from whatever you're doing."

"Do we have anything to hide?"

"*Hide?* No, but they'll treat you like you do. If something breaks while they're watching they'll likely cite you for it. Okay, the open cans full of fish pass through the weighing machine here, and any that are underweight divert automatically to the patching table. You'll find the older women have the best patience to be patchers. It takes some judgment, so they can't just daydream and move their hands like they might do on other jobs. A one-pound tall has to contain fifteen and a half ounces of salmon, as it promises on the label. The patchers stick in another piece of fish to round out the weight, and they're supposed to make sure no bones or skin shows up top. But you've got to impress on them they're to put in just enough extra, no more."

"What difference if the customer got another ounce?"

Swede took Hank's pad and figured for him that three-tenths of an ounce overweight on each can amounted to a thousand pounds of salmon a day. "And that's dressed meat. Remember the cannery buys whole fish, and pays for the heads and guts."

They continued down the line to the clinchers that put a code number on the can and a lid that remained slightly loose. The cans then passed through the exhaust box or vacuum sealer, which pulled vacuum and made the final seal. In the final operation, the cans were stacked on big mobile trays called coolers and rolled into the cooking machines, called retorts. "They cook by steam, under pressure, about eighty minutes at two hundred forty degrees. That kills all the bacteria. In the old days, you had to boil the cans in water for six to seven hours, and that meant you couldn't turn out but a quarter of the present volume. Without the Iron Chinks and the retorts to speed things you'd have no industry on a modern scale. Those two machines were developed over forty years ago, and nothing's changed much in salmon canning since then." Swede pointed to a separate area of tables and hoses. "That's a change, in a way. Remember how salmon eggs used to be for the seagulls? Well, the Japs love them in brine so heavy it burns your mouth. The supervisor for the egg line's a Jap from the company that buys the stuff. He runs it by himself. They put it in boxes with Jap lettering, and a Jap cargo ship collects it."

"Better watch it, the Japs'll soon own your cannery."

"Not likely. Look, up there, water through the ceiling. Make a note and we'll trace it when we get upstairs. I'll spend the rest of the day showing you where the stores go. Remember, what they bring tomorrow sees us through the summer. Check it down to the last bag of cement."

The next days made Hank feel that he had never left the Navy. His authority fell into place at once. Although the laborers sent from Kodiak were all guys he had shoveled with, even taken orders from, he saw to it that they did what he told them. He himself pitched in as best he could with an arm in a cast, then withdrew easily back to the level of boss. Even Sandra accepted his new role. She stood checking inventory, ready at once to appear at a new location if he called.

Before they finished storing supplies the weather closed in. Wind smoked across the bay, and no plane could land. There was general glee among the crew because they expected to lie in at company expense. Hank firmly set them to work on repairs, driving them for ten and twelve hours a day as he did himself. However, he had discovered the liquor cache with his office keys. Each night he produced a bottle. They partied together and had a fine time. Two of the guys asked if they could return under him for the summer. It gave him a new sense of power to tell Swede he wanted them and to have them arrive with their gear a few days later as part of the regular maintenance crew.

He kept track of the days only because he was working on deadlines. There was the day when the machinists would arrive, then the day for the foremen to assemble and hold briefings, finally the day when all the workers descended. Each event presupposed a body of other work completed—roofs repaired, galley in partial and then full operation, the flow of water restored to machines and lavatories, the rooms clean and the mattresses aired. He worked eighteen-hour days, then lay awake fretting over things not done.

However, Swede commuted from Kodiak, and Hank came to realize how little of the show he ran himself. It had been Swede's planning months before that determined what supplies were shipped, and he had merely checked them off. When the mechanics came, they suffered his presence while proceeding their own way with the job. Likewise the cooks and the foremen, unless he carried Swede's direct orders. When skippers came to talk agreements with Swede, he witnessed a process of barter so encoded that he remained a stranger to it. When he asked for an explanation, Swede found a way to change the subject.

Sandra arrived with her luggage, smiling. She settled for form's sake in a dormitory single set aside for the bookkeeper, put up curtains at the window, left some token clothing, then moved into Hank's cabin. Suddenly the bachelor trailings were stowed and the place assumed a cheerful order. But they had little time together except at meals in the chowhall, and these were shared in the executive room with the foremen. At night Hank worked late. He often climbed exhausted beside her into bed, murmured "Have a good day?," and fell asleep.

Within a space of two days the bulk of the cannery workers arrived, transported from town both by plane and by the cannery's tenders. Most had flown from Seattle to Anchorage to Kodiak, and many of the younger ones had spent at least one night rolled in a sleeping bag on some floor. About half were Filipinos, men and women, older by decades on the average than the Americans. Their faces were stern, and they spoke sharply even to each other. Many of the Americans were green kids, recruited in Seattle with some vague notion of Alaskan adventure. Except for their guitars and motley knapsacks, they reminded Hank of fresh arrivals at boot camp, and he found himself playing the role of boatswain as he oversaw their issuance of blankets and beds. Sometimes he shouted at them to keep order. Two galley crews—one American and one Filipino—had arrived early. They worked at separate ranges in different parts of the same big kitchen and laid out their food alongside each other at adjacent steam tables.

Hank's first major gaffe came when he assigned bunks to the two nationalities together. No one had bothered to tell him that the Americans lived in the buildings to the east of the office and the Filipinos to the west. He thought his only task was to keep the sexes separated and to accommodate people by age. Some of the older Filipinos returned to complain angrily, just as shouts announced trouble. Hank ran to intervene. A young Filipino held his switchblade level while one of the American kids, confident from smoking marijuana to judge by odor, held a chair ready to throw it. At issue was the cot by the window in the room they had been assigned together.

"Stop that!" yelled Hank. The boy with the knife only snarled as he crouched and weaved, while the other continued a string of obscenities as he tried the chair in different positions like a matador with a cape. It was one of the older Filipino men who broke it up. He snapped a command to the boy of his own nationality and gestured him outside. The boy lowered his blade, argued with the man in a normal voice, then left.

"Put that chair down," commanded Hank at the tail of the action. The American shrugged and obeyed.

"I'm going to reassign you," Hank continued, trying to sound stern as he wondered how far his authority extended. Swede appeared and fired both fighters on the spot. "Got a tender going back to Kodiak in an hour. Get your bags down there or charter your own plane."

The Filipino boy cried out and threw his knife to the floor to show his contrition. Swede shook his head, and the older Filipino declared, "He no good for this place, Mr. Scorden, you get him home."

"I didn't pull the fuckin' blade," said the American. "He attacked me."

"Get packed," said Swede. "If you can't hold grass, don't smoke it."

Outside, Swede set Hank straight about the bunking arrangements and gave him hell for not having figured it for himself. "And why didn't you fire them? You've read the rules."

"How was I to know you'd back me up? That's three hundred bucks airfare lost. We'd never talked about it."

"Okay, maybe. Put this in your head. You find a handgun on a man, or a knife in his hand he's not using to cut fish, and you push his ass on the next plane or tender. Dock his wages against the fare if he has any. Fitsfights, now, look the other way, good steam valve. Offer Merthiolate when it's over. Mostly the Filipinos and the others only fight among themselves. That's why we bunk them separate. I don't care about screwing, so long as they keep it off the boardwalks and the women stay with their own. The Filipinos police themselves if they can live in their own community, and they're the hard, steady workers who stay the whole season without giving you bullshit. Now, hard drugs, fire anybody on the spot. As for booze and pot, I forbid those on paper, and that's to keep it down. Cannery work's wet and dull, it sometimes needs help. Unless they can't hold it and might fall into the machinery. Or if you get some white kid like that one who takes on the spics after a few puffs."

"I don't think he started that. If I hadn't bunked them—"

"I make it a rule to can both sides when it's interracial. Saves

241

other problems, and puts everybody on notice. Remember, there's no doctor here, just a first-aid kit. Go on, now, unfuck those room assignments before something else happens."

The season opened. It was like waiting for a battle to begin. The cannery crews were restless, their jobs assigned but nothing to do until the tenders arrived to unload. Hank watched the clock; he knew when the second arrived on the grounds that set off the guns, when pelican hooks clanked open all along the waters to free the skiffs for the first set. That set, in crowded bays, would be the crazy one. Crews would be corking each other and tangling web with furious insults, with fights if boats scraped close enough for leaping aboard. Plungers would pop as the nets closed. Men would peer and peer for the turbulence that betrayed a big jag of fish. Oh, shit, he thought, to be out there straining up a moneybag of salmon, to have a hundred reds or humpies empty over your legs slapping and gleaming. He stared from the window of the radio room at the bare, low mountains that hid it all from view. The radios were silent except for empty crackles. Skippers were too busy with the fish.

Next morning at three the first tender docked. Hank was on hand to grab a line and inspect the haul. By five the salmon had been transferred to the cannery bins, and the processing began.

He began the first day as roving troubleshooter, with no duty and all duties. It took little time for something to blow. A hose that had probably been tested five times broke loose like a frenzied snake, spewing water over everyone. Most of the people wore rain gear. But Pete Erikson, who maintained the Iron Chink, wore only coveralls with wrenches weighting the pockets, and the hose soaked him down. One of the kids feeding fish started to laugh. Pete declared he was quitting rather than take filthy cracks from some punk. Hank quickly shunted the kid to another line. The foreman, busy with the loose hose, came back to give Hank hell for moving one of his men without consulting him. It was all shouted above the clanks and hisses of machinery. Then, while Pete stormed to his locker to find dry clothes, the Iron Chink clogged and had to be stopped while Hank ran to coax Pete back.

On the sliming line, one of the inexperienced girls cut off her fingertip. After the hysteria had run its course and she was carried in shock to the little infirmary where one of the foremen with first-aid training treated her, there was the job of finding the fingertip to make sure it was not included in a can of salmon. One new boy, slightly effeminate, came to Hank with tears in his eyes to declare that he couldn't stand the sight of fish guts, that no one told him it was going to be that organic. Hank worked a transfer with a girl stapling boxes. At the far end of the line they were shorthanded loading cans for the retorts, and he pitched in to catch them up. At another point he had just donned an apron to help the slimers (to show that he himself looked down on no job), and was joking with some of the pleased women, when a din of screeching metal erupted among the filler machines. Somebody loading cans from the loft had dropped a carton the wrong way, and a hundred collapsed cans had poured through the ceiling to jam into the moving parts. They shut the line for thirty minutes while the mechanics, cursing loudly and implying it was Hank's fault for not watching the loft, yanked crumpled aluminum from the fish-coated fillers.

At coffee break he joined the workers rather than the foremen. He glanced critically at the dingy little room and made a note to himself that it should be kept cleaner. Suddenly a native woman who worked at the patching table accused the woman who worked alongside of blowing her nose near the open cans. She turned to Hank: "You better stop her snotting right into the salmon, Mister Manager." The accused knocked off the other's plastic sterile cap, and they started pulling each other's hair. When no one else intervened (the men watched laughing while the women goaded), Hank broke them apart. They both turned on him and told him to mind his own business. By lunchtime he was glad for the privacy of the executive room.

The summer continued in a hectic pattern. Occasionally he cut loose to run along the beach or climb in the low mountains to let off steam, but usually the grind kept him nailed in place. While he managed to rise above the status of whipping boy, everyone considered his time their own. Skippers with engine emergencies banged on his door at two in the morning, and it was up to him to find a mechanic willing to help so they could rush back to the grounds. From his days as a shipboard officer, Hank was no stranger to the wheedling grip that subordinates could exert on anyone above them who betrayed a sympathetic tendency, yet he allowed himself to be conned. Late at night, and during his breaks, he found himself listening wearily, ostensibly to advise, to tales of woe concerning restless girlfriends back home, estranged husbands behind on alimony, aching backs and mysterious stomach cramps, and incompatible roommates. The women told on each other like children. If one left the monotony of the lines even to hose the floor or push a bin, he was sure to hear of it.

"I'm the chaplain," he complained to Sandra.

She stopped kneading his shoulders long enough to bite his ear.

Swede caught him one day ducked behind a wall. Hank explained he was avoiding a guy who was sure to pin him down with misery talk.

"You're crazy. Growl and they'll leave you alone."

"Some have real problems."

"They'll have them with or without you."

"You have a black heart, Swede."

"Don't forget it."

While the cannery routine often extended late into night when the salmon were coming heavy, a whistle blast always started the lines again at eight. By then the tenders had arrived from the grounds with the catch of the day before, or Hank had talked to them by radio. He had also talked to Swede in Kodiak. At seven-fifteen breakfast he joined the foremen to plan for the day, telling them the distribution and nature of the day's pack—the size can to be used, the amount of fish to be diverted for freezing—and relaying any other instructions from Swede. They discussed any breakdowns, potential shortages, or personnel problems. Most of the longterm foremen kept a distance, but as Hank settled in he managed to stay on top of the job, juggling the sometimes delicate line between his own authority and their little empires. He learned to refuse good-naturedly some of their own drudgery tasks if they tried to shunt them his way (tabulation of time cards, for example), while accepting others philosophically.

Swede commuted between the three canneries of his authority. He maintained in each of the radio rooms a chart of the Island stuck with pins for his boats and lettered pennants for the fourteen tenders under his command. (Two of his tenders flew the Jolly-Roger pennant of cash buyer to lure fish at higher prices from other canneries, and Hank was never permitted to talk to these himself.) Swede coordinated the tenders as if he were conducting a naval engagement, and he also kept in touch with the hundred-odd seiners and forty setnet sites that delivered to him, working in a fine steam as he leapt from the swivel chair by the radio to juggle pins on the chart. The game was to help the fleets follow the fish and then to keep the tenders in the middle of the action. He flew regularly over the grounds himself to spot salmon concentrations, then issued directions in an elaborate code.

Swede based his general code on numbers and colors in combinations he devised himself. They changed each day in a prearranged pattern that each skipper had. Favored skippers—the highliners—might have their private code for the season, based on the number sequence of a secret word or phrase. *Spiro Agnew* was a perfect one: two sets of five letters, none of them repeated. The letters of the first name would represent major locations and those of the second one graduated brackets of quality. "Yeah, Swede, doing a low G here, got a low G, figure tonight we're heading south R."

There would be mix-ups. "Chip, you've got a thirty-one in East Yellow, that's a thirty-one?" Swede would say with forced nonchalance as he leapt excitedly to search his chart for the nearest tender, muttering away from the mike, "Jesus, twenty thousand humpies and he couldn't have made more than three sets since dawn. We'll divert the whole south fleet down to Moser Bay, and they weren't fishing shit there yesterday!" And the other voice would continue: "Right, Swede, thirty-one. Oh. This Wednesday or Thursday? Change that. Fishing forty-two in East Green, that's a forty-two in East Green, okay." Swede would settle back into his swivel chair as he shrugged at Hank and bit a new cigar. "Right, Chip, okay, keep at it."

The season was a good one. When it climaxed, Swede's game of the boats, which might have guaranteed his survival in lean years, became unnecessary. By midseason they were wading in a nightmare of salmon. The lines worked fifteen and sixteen hours, and the bins were so backloaded that they often processed through the traditional Sockeye Sunday. Sometimes a load aged from waiting too long and was frozen for bait. Swede quietly discontinued his two pirate tenders. At one point he even placed a limit of 750 fish per crewman per day that his tenders would buy. The workers accumulated formidable overtime, but the grind was telling. Hank listened to more and more complaints. Except for the Filipinos, people quit arbitrarily over such matters as too few cookies at coffee break or a sour word from one of the foremen. Kodiak and Seattle scraped the dregs for people, and strange misfits arrived as replacements.

One boy, with a spooky cast to his eyes and mouth, lasted a half hour at the sorting belt and went berserk. He leaped into the bin full of fish and threw them around screaming. Hank and the foreman followed, grappling with him until they were all rolling in slime and gurry. Finally, with no other way, they tied his arms in back and dragged him kicking to the infirmary. For two days the weather was too bad for a plane to fly in from Kodiak. The kid thrashed and yelled the whole time. Hank, to whom most of the watching fell, tried to clean and change him, but gave it up. By the time the plane made it, with a nurse from the Kodiak Hospital who grogged him at once with a shot, both the kid and the infirmary stank with rank gurry. At least, Hank and the foreman were good friends thereafter. Next night they shared a bottle together after the line was secured. Two other foremen joined them.

As the machinery became overworked, it broke down with greater frequency. Likewise the boats, which began to send in so many emergency calls that Swede hired back one of his pirate tenders to ferry parts to the grounds.

Hank had little time to spend among the boats when they came in on Saturday night. He wanted to keep away from the docks, with the certain discontent they held for him, but he was unable to resist visiting when the *Shalimar* or the *Adele H* docked. Jones and Steve, relaxed in their fishing clothes, had all kinds of new anecdotes from the grounds.

"Look," said Sandra to ease his restlessness, "this isn't the only season. I just don't understand why you want to be on a boat so badly."

Hank would close his eyes against her version of logic and return to the job of running the cannery.

20

HORSE'S HEAD

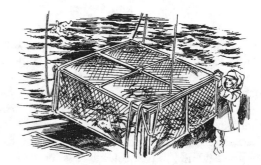

THE season tapered with the end of the humpie runs in early August, and Swede returned to his coded maneuvers. The chum salmon, though abundant and larger, failed to fill the gap. Swede had Hank close one line and ship the workers home, then finally in late August disbanded the other. He diverted the remaining fish by tender to the Kodiak cannery and left Hank to close down. Sandra, having finished the payrolls, returned to Kodiak also. All at once within a few days Hank was supervising the shutdown of a ghost village. His companions were old Pete Erikson and two other machinists, and a handful of maintenance people. They ate together in the executive dining room, final stronghold of the diminishing kingdom, and played cards to pass the lengthening evenings. There were days when the water had a cold sparkle, but the westerlies blew more and more, so that the harbor swelled gray, and all land beyond the radius of a few hundred feet disappeared.

One by one the crews returned the cannery boats to the ways, stored their seines in the loft, and flew to Kodiak. Some of the larger independent seiners began to gear for king crab. Hank watched them impatiently. As soon as a cargo ship came to collect the last vanloads of the salmon pack, his job was over, and he could search again honorably for a boat. No discussion of this with Swede, but he assumed it was understood.

His relationship with Sandra had reached a curiously comfortable level. He took for granted that they lived together since she had long ago moved from her old apartment as her roommates watched wistfully. Now the bungalow at the cannery was dreary without her.

There was one sadness to it all. Sandra came as close as any woman he had ever met to his specifications for a wife, based on the stable values of his parents, which he could modify but not ignore. But it was in the presence of Jody that his impulses turned alert. This had been so practically since the day he had met her.

The *Shalimar*, its crew weary of steady fishing for shrimp and then tendering for salmon, came into the cannery dock. Mike and the crew radioed for a plane to fly them back to Kodiak to tie one on for a long weekend. Jody decided to stay and mind the boat. Her mouth spread in that wide smile that characterized her for Hank. "Booze it with you guys? I need a rest, not a brawl."

Hank was delighted, for no other reason at first than for her company in the increasingly dull surroundings. He offered to restore the heat in one of the dormitory rooms for her use. "What, move my gear? But I will use your shower, and I won't mind if you put some hot water in it." As for eating with them: "Sure, but don't expect me to do your dishes."

At lunch, within minutes, she had breathed life across the entire table. Pete Erikson, whom no one contradicted, began to lecture the group on the combined impropriety and bad luck of letting a woman live on a fishing boat. In a few sentences he had progressed to the inferior quality of fish caught on such a boat—fish so old since nobody could keep his mind on the work that they fell apart in the cannery machines. Jody laughed derisively. Pete turned a glare on her that would have puddled any of his subordinates. "Young lady, you don't know much about the fish business, I can see."

"Your machines are a fuckin' heap of tin without the fish I know how to catch."

Hank, long forced to endure Pete by Swede's dictum, gave her a grin and wink. She regarded him with blank curiosity.

Later, he was showing her a loft where the *Shalimar* could stow gear for the winter. "Sure glad you told Pete off," he said.

"Nobody's ever paid me enough to kiss ass."

He felt stung. "A woman doesn't have to play games to get along, she can always marry if it gets too rough."

Instead of the retort he expected, she said seriously, "You believe that." She stood before him, a head shorter, her hands in leather work gloves, her hair bunched in a loose ponytail and her face smudged, wearing an open wool fishing shirt under a torn slicker jacket, completely feminine and a complete individual. "If you spout that kind of shit, I'm surprised that Sandra hasn't blasted off from you by now. Or has she?"

"No. We're fine together. She says her piece sometimes, if that makes you feel any better." He considered, then added, "We go our ways, though. We keep it independent."

"That sounds like a big relationship."

Hank felt himself blush. It had earlier crossed his mind that the loft might be a place to start again what he had never forgotten from seven years before. Sandra and he, after all, had exchanged no promises. But he didn't like to talk about her to Jody. He busied himself opening storage space for the *Shalimar* among the draped seines and piles of equipment, then glumly followed Jody back into the blowing rain, along the slick boardwalks to the boat. She lit a cigarette expertly against the weather and started down the ladder.

He stood, waiting. She glanced at him with detachment. "Come have a beer if you want."

In the galley of the *Shalimar*, she banged a beer can on the table in the way she had slung his coffee in the beanery the first time they met, and he told her so.

"Well, I haven't changed," she said curtly.

"Here's to that!" He thought he was being gallant. "If Jody changed, the world would be poorer."

"For a decent guy, Hank, you surely sometimes talk like an asshole." She wedged herself into the cramped seat opposite him at the table and opened her own beer. "The fellows say you tough it all right on the boats, and most people at the cannery here think you did fair. We've wondered a couple of times where you're headed."

"Me? You've talked about me? Well, I want to get back to a boat as soon as I can find one. That's where I'm headed."

He wanted to change the subject, since it seemed pointless. "You've probably forgotten, but I still think now and then of that week after the tidal wave. We shared a bunk out on the *Rondelay*, you know, just before the gale that broke up Joe Eberhardt's boat." Her hand rested on his arm unexpectedly, and she laughed in the deep way which over the years he had grown to use unconsciously as a measure of other women's laughter. He wanted to clap his free hand on hers, but remained still, enjoying her touch. "We saw the earthquake together up on the hill, remember? Held that woman's kids in the doorway as we watched cars bounce down the road."

"I'd *forgotten* that. Then I sent you down to help with the boats, and during the night with the tidal waves I worried that I'd sent you to be drowned."

"You worried? That sets me up."

Her hand left his arm as lightly as it had come. "A shivering green-head from back east? Anybody would have worried for you."

"Come on, I'd fished the *Rondelay* all summer before."

"So you knew how to handle a boat in a tidal wave."

"Be fair."

"Well, you *did* do all right on the *Rondelay* during the storm, when Jones was ashore and Steve was afraid to take charge. You'd probably make an okay skipper if you stuck to it."

"Tell you what," he said quietly, hoping for the best. "I'll work at it and make my way. When I'm a highliner, I'll come back and propose."

"Do that. I'll put you on the list."

"Big list, is there?"

"Sometimes I feel like a picture that everybody wants to hang on his wall."

"Mike? Is he one?"

"My skipper? No, or I wouldn't be aboard. It's hard for people to believe, but men and women can work alongside each other and then go to their own beds at night."

"Ah, Jody," he teased.

"What's that supposed to mean?"

"You're inscrutable."

"I thought I was honest." She gestured toward the remains of a six-pack as she rose. "Help yourself to beer, Hank. I'm sacking in. That's why I stayed behind. To sleep."

"May I follow?" he asked quietly.

"No."

He knew she meant it. Alone, he sipped at the beer without taste, then left in a few minutes. What Sandra back in Kodiak might have said did not bother him. No commitments, and this was the wilderness, despite a few walls protecting them against the weather.

At supper, Pete Erikson for once was silent. Apparently it took less to shut him up than anyone had imagined. Jody presided automatically. She had a quiet good humor that brought the conversation to life, and the men outdid themselves to tell anecdotes that might earn her smile. Later, at poker, she proved as tough and straightfaced as any of them.

Hank walked her to the boat in the perpetual blowing rain after unsuccessfully inviting her back for a drink in his cabin. As he plodded along the boardwalk among the black shapes of buildings which a week before had been peopled and lighted, he chuckled and wondered what he had hoped to pull. She was nobody's doxy, and he should have known.

When the crew of the *Shalimar* returned in subdued good humor, one of them sporting a bruise on his jaw, Hank cast off their lines. Jody waved and smiled from the deck, as once more she slipped away.

The cannery closedown ended with the arrival of a cargo ship to remove the last of the canned salmon from the warehouse. Hank saw to the invoices, and then he was free. Over a drink in Hank's cabin, the captain offered him a free ride to Seattle via Kodiak, and even agreed to take Sandra. The season had been good, with Swede promising him the full bonus, so he could afford her a trip. Fly to Hawaii together, return through San Francisco, and still be back in Kodiak to look for a boat in a couple of weeks. He broached the idea to Sandra on the radio. She was so thrilled that he was glad he had thought of it.

"I'll be skinned. I remember you, and I think the name was Hank."

The growling, self-confident voice came from a sunburned face that was almost rosy, dimpled, like Santa without his beard. Huge handlebar mustache, eyes in a perpetual squint, hair a sandy tangle. But it was the height of him—half a head taller—that brought the name. "Joe Eberhardt!"

They pounded each other's shoulders and ended in a bear-hug embrace. "When did I last see you, Hank?"

"When you lost the *Linda J* on the rocks after the tidal wave. I was on the *Rondelay*, and we tried to throw you a line."

"That, that, yes."

"Linda?"

"Long story, Hank. I couldn't see myself tied down to a house and brats, and I expect she got tired of living on a boat. I sometimes miss her." They both fell silent. "Lovely girl," Joe added gravely, then looked around. "I was hoping this ship had brought me some new crab pots from Seattle."

"Those yours? *Nordic Rose?* Yesterday before my guys flew back to Kodiak I had them stack your pots out behind the parts shed. Twenty seven-bys, right?"

"You talk like you run the cannery."

"I do, up to this point, but I'm looking for a boat."

"Got some frozen fishheads to sell me cheap?"

"Hell," said Hank expansively, "since I still run the place I'll do what no cannery's ever done before, I'll give you some. Tell me, you know of any boat that's short a man?"

Joe studied him and thumped his arm and chest with a ruse of playfulness as he joked about the free bait, then declared: "One of my men just quit. You want to go crabbing out by Horse's Head?"

"You're fuckin' A I do!" Hank shouted. "Where's Horse's Head?"

And that was the end of any trips to Hawaii with Sandra. When he told her by radio, he blocked out her disappointment with a vow to make it up to her sometime. Nor did Swede's cool reaction bother him. He stepped instantly and exuberantly from the role of manager telling his men to cart off a batch of heavy crab pots to a crewman straining the same pots back on dollies and returning them to the pier.

The rain blew as they geared the new pots with bridles, hooks, lines, and buoys, then winched them clanging to deck. Joe handled the controls and shouted instructions. He worked them in a straight line. By the time they had hefted one of the steel-framed pots astern and lashed it, he had another swinging down above their heads. Hank was in a fine sweat by the time they finished. Quickly he packed his fishing clothes and stored the rest with the watchman to be returned by plane. Within four hours of meeting Joe Eberhardt again, he was pulling up fenders to the deck of the *Nordic Rose* as they headed into a dark and kicking sea.

He had only met his new crewmates, Sam and Frenchy, on the run. After checking him out on basic deck equipment, they settled together at the galley table while Joe in the forward wheelhouse steered them to the grounds. The two were both approximately his age. Sam had an easy drawl and quiet eyes behind heavy brown hair and beard. John French, who went by his last name, was notably cheerful. His face was round and smooth-shaven, the rest of him hefty and square. In answer to their query, Hank said he had only been crabbing for a week several years before but that he had fished everything else. "Bear with me a couple of sets, and I'll be on top of it." The boat swooped into a trough. Hank closed his eyes and held the table.

"Our new friend needs a salty piece of fish," Frenchy declared.

"That's what I need." Hank leaned his head against the padded seat. "Put it on a string, then I can use it over."

"Go on, crawl in the sack," said Sam.

"Are we through for the night?" They both laughed. "Guess I'll stay up." He rose as casually as he could and slipped into oilskins. On deck he paid his ritual entrance fee again with the vomiting, then watched through teary eyes the buffets of spray breaking over the stern and the foaming whitecaps that glowed in the twilight.

Frenchy came out and suggested they ready the bait cans, since Hank appeared to be enjoying the outdoors. They climbed to a storage bin on the dark wheel deck and groped out cartons of half-thawed herring as well as some of the hard-frozen fishheads Hank had contributed. The herring was so mushy that Hank had to hold the carton against his chest. He aimed it for the thick wooden bait tub below, missed, and ended scooping hundreds of slippery little fish from the deck as seawater washed over his boots and hands.

"Keep at it, Hank. You'll make master-baiter yet."

"Does a medal go with that?"

"Gold cock." Frenchy chopped some of the herring in the tub with a sharp-edged iron pole and stuffed the pieces into perforated plastic cans. "Crabs like that oily herring. Then, sometimes they like the big meaty stuff. Best give 'em their choice." He banged some of the fishheads apart, impaled them on spiked hooks, then fastened a can and a hook together and held it up. "Hang bait, man. Now you know every trick of it. Make up twenty and clip them on that clothesline, then get inside and see if you can hold some chow. We'll probably make a night of it."

Two hours later, as they dozed at the table braced against the boat's motion, the engine slowed. Hank popped awake with the others and automatically pulled on his rain gear. Joe pushed past onto deck, muttering that he'd found a good fathom curve, and thumped up the ladder to the outside bridge. The others followed quickly. They pushed each of the new heavy pots to the rail ("Wait for the roll of the boat, Hank, then she shoves easier"), slammed open its gate, lifted out the buoys and heavy coils of line, clamped in the bait ("Watch that gate don't come loose and bang your head, Hank"), recorded the buoy numbers, hooked shut the gate, and with a collective grunt ("Watch fingers, Hank"), fulcrumed the pot over the rail and at Joe's shout shoved it into the water. Hank endured their instructions, glad they cared while disliking the implication that he was a greenhorn. Joe worked them at such a driving pace that the twenty new pots were soon launched and they sat again around the galley table.

Hank found a whetstone and honed his deck knife, too long unused, as Frenchy and Sam started a game of cribbage. The engine roared full gun, the cards slapped, and jars of peanut butter and pickles rattled in the rack. The clock showed 10 P.M. When Hank finished he went to the pilothouse and asked Joe if he wanted to be relieved.

"No, thanks, I usually hold the wheel and let the guys rest when we're working. Now you're here, I'll check you out on the electronics for later."

Afterward, Hank settled into a fold-down seat beside Joe and watched ahead in the dark. A single light from another boat rose and dipped, but otherwise they had the water to themselves. He and Joe updated each other on their careers. As Joe talked, Hank realized that for all his hearty poise he had changed, grown restless. He now chose to fish in the remote places when the seasons would let him, with crab around Dutch Harbor and shrimp around the Shumagin Islands. "Just spent August out in the Bering Sea for the first time. Even in summer the weather's too rough for a fifty-eight-foot boat, but I wanted to give her a try." He stood straight by his wheel, so tall his head brushed the ceiling, a strong man all around, but his deep voice was soft. "I keep this limit seiner so I can still fish salmon if I want, but these Kodiak bays are too full of the past, Hank, I'll probably never go back. Get a bigger boat soon. Shit, now, before I put over these new pots I should have pulled one or two I'd left soak, to see what we had out here. Even coming back to the far end of Kodiak throws me. Don't worry, Linda's better off without me, and I never talk about her. Seeing you brought it up. When we start to haul, fishing's all that matters."

Hank asked about the name Horse's Head, and Joe lighted the chart to show him the area they had entered southeast of Kodiak Island. The line of the fifty-fathom curve traced the shape of a horse's head. The area was all continental shelf, with nothing deeper than a hundred fathoms until it went beyond thirty-fathom Albatross Bank into the Pacific Ocean to plunge quickly to three thousand fathoms. "Those fathom curves and trenches are good places to find the crabs," said Joe. "I set those pots we're heading for, and then we ran to the cannery for my new ones, so this'll be our first look at the crab this season." He checked his radar and loran often. Around midnight, after a search among pots laid by other boats, they found their own.

Frenchy had set up more bait hangs while Hank visited in the pilothouse. He turned the rest of the job over to Hank and suggested he keep at least four baits ahead of the pots. As Hank chopped herring in the bait tub on the port side, the other two hurried around deck setting up. They turned the crab block out on its davit by the starboard rail so that it hung over the water ready to receive the pot lines. Frenchy lifted a two-foot plyboard hatch near deck center. Water welled from it over the deck as the boat rolled. "There's where we throw the crabs into the live tanks, Hank. Watch you don't go in yourself." Hank eyed the open hole dubiously. Right in the middle of where they worked? But every boat had its working conditions.

Hank remembered the grappling and coiling procedure from the *Rondelay*. When Sam had coiled most of the line, Hank took his place by the rail and received the boom hook from Frenchy. He pressed his knees into the side to brace against the roll, and hoped he remembered what to do. The thick iron hook had a good feel. He watched the surging water, whitecapped and dark green in the pool of decklight, black and endless beyond. Beautiful, beautiful, no other place he'd rather be. A two-branched strap announced the pot. He leaned over to fit in the hook, and the picking boom took over from the crab block under Frenchy's control of the levers. Up came the pot, water surging through its web and frame. Light shapes moved inside. They were all looking, including Joe, who had left the wheel to stand on the bridge rail above them. Hank gave a cheer as the pot rose stuffed full of crabs.

"Oh, shit!" cried Frenchy. "Four hundred females and jacks, and this string's all picker pots." Joe above them scowled and declared that they'd best clean out the pots on the double, stack them on deck, and move to better grounds.

Sam steadied one edge of the pot and directed Hank on the other as Frenchy raised it to the side. "Brace her tight against the side," said Sam. "Wait for a roll to port, then she'll swing without us pulling the whole weight ourselves. *Now.*" Frenchy raised the pot just over the rail, and in it swung on the roll of the boat. It was lugubriously heavy. The force took Hank off guard, and the pot dragged him with it across deck as the others yelled.

The boat rolled back to starboard. With Sam's end braced and Hank's swinging free, the pot pivoted and slammed into objects like an elephant on the loose.

"Frenchy, drop her anywhere," yelled Joe as he leaped down the ladder to help. The pot thudded to deck with such force the boat shook. All four grunted and strained to position it where the hook could raise one end back against the rail where it belonged.

"Sorry," Hank panted. "Forgot how heavy."

"Maybe three thousand pounds," said Joe seriously. "She dasn't run loose. Got to put more asshole to it." But no one seemed upset further, now that it was over.

With the big pot tilted against the rail, they opened the gate and leaned in to throw out the crabs. Not a one of the males was large enough to be kept. Like machines they grabbed two and three crabs simultaneously by the legs and sailed them over the top into the water. Joe helped, goading them to go faster. When he saw a section of ripped web he mended his needle through it with ferocious speed. They threw the coil and buoys inside the pot, pushed it to the far rail, and tied it down. Every job interlocked, and Hank soon gained the rhythm of it.

Each fresh pot that rose to the rail was a nightmare of useless abundance, with hundreds of females and nothing to keep. The work of removing the crabs was the same as if they had all been keepers and money in the bank. And the pots, which if plugged with the right kind of crab would have been rebaited and returned over the rail to the same grounds, now had to be pushed astern and tied together. Joe drove them tirelessly by his own example. Eventually pots were stacked across the entire deck. They boomed others up to a second layer, swaying with a sinister force until they landed secure. Crouched on top to receive them, his toes dug into web for support, Hank could feel the pots shift with each boat roll.

On the run—there seemed no other pace—Hank fell into the open hold. One leg went down all the way, and the other scraped painfully. The icy water rose beneath his rain pants and filled both boots. His legs were so heavy with water as he pulled them out that he wondered (no, he knew) how he would fare if he fell over the side. Everybody joked about it and he joined them. It furnished their only break.

When the thirty pots of the string were stacked, covering even the open hold and towering above the deck like superstructure, Joe trotted through the galley to the pilothouse and gunned the engine. Hank was swaying with fatigue and his throat felt coated with salt sand. As he started inside, thinking only of fresh water and bed, Frenchy said, "Hurry back and I'll help you fix the baits."

"We're not through?"

"Oh, man, Joe keeps his pots at work, not deadass on deck."

Inside, when everything was ready, Sam and Frenchy threw their rain jackets under the table and peeled rain pants over boots without removing either, then lay back on the benches. Hank quickly emptied the water from his boots and found old newspapers to stuff inside, then stretched on the metal deck under the table and fell asleep at once.

A half hour later the engine slowed. It was four-thirty and growing light outside as they dragged back on deck. Hank ached everywhere. They pushed the closest pots to the rail, pulled out the line and buoys, clamped in the bait hang, and launched them at Joe's shout. Then they boomed down the top layer. When some deck space was opened by both rails, Sam and Frenchy suddenly began to compete. They each hefted pots by themselves—about seven hundred pounds empty—and scrambled to be the first to have one ready by the call to launch. The spirit caught Hank and he scrambled with them. Within minutes the final pots had hit the water, and they all panted as they grinned. They continued in motion, stowing scattered tielines, drawing seawater from the live tank to slosh seaweed and broken crab from the deck.

The sun rose orange over the foamy swells and burned into their eyes for a few minutes until it reached the height of the cloud ceiling and disappeared for the day. The low mountains of Kodiak Island and the Trinities glowed purple in the distance. Hank watched, wonderfully content.

They slept and drifted for a few hours. By eleven they had eaten a large breakfast cooked by Frenchy and were back on deck running gear.

The next days blended into each other. Joe had more than a hundred pots, and he kept trying to work them every day. If the keepers had been abundant enough to return the pots directly to the same grounds he would have succeeded, but he had not found the crabs. They rarely collected more than fifty keepers (a modest single potful in the old days four years earlier) in an entire string, and often they pulled merely throwaways and bait fish. Joe drove them without respite until they were all bleary with fatigue, and then as the others slept he studied charts or talked on the radio to other skippers on the grounds, trying to figure the crab. Suddenly he would announce a new strategy. Once they moved all their pots from near the Trinities to the gulley off Two Headed Island without sleeping for twenty-seven hours, in winds gusting sixty. Then they moved again out on Albatross Bank, within sight of Japanese trawlers and the halibut longliners. When the westerlies blew too hard they spent a few hours with the other boats in Jap Bay or Kaguyak Bay. Joe tied alongside boats he knew, and while the crews slept the skippers would quiz each other in an elaborate, jocular ritual as they tried to determine who was on the crabs.

"I'll find the fuckers," Joe muttered often. It was virtually the only thing he said any more. If they tried to kid him back to some perspective he regarded them blankly.

Finally they had to return up the coast to Kodiak for supplies and to deliver their meager catch. Joe cruised at night after fishing all day, to save time. They were moored by eight in the morning at the cannery pier. Frenchy's wife met him and they went together to buy groceries for the boat. Hank borrowed a fork lift and loaded a new batch of frozen bait, then filled the fresh-water tank. Joe changed the engine oil and with Sam performed some hasty deck repairs, including new hydraulic hoses for the block. After unloading, they moved to the fuel pier to fill tanks, then persuaded Joe to tie in the boat harbor for a few quick beers and lunch.

"I'll do it to keep my crew happy," he growled, "but we ought to be getting back there in case the crab strike. Lines off at one-thirty."

"Come on, Skipper," said Sam, who had been with him longest. "Three."

"Bullshit!" Joe considered. "Two-fifteen."

Hank and Sandra ate in the apartment, saying nothing of the broken Hawaii trip, then went to bed despite the daylight.

"I miss you," she said softly over and over. "Nights are so lonesome without you."

"I miss you too." He tried to forget the boat and to enjoy the moment, lying on clean sheets as she rubbed his back.

"Swede would take you back. He hasn't hired anyone else, and he's not mad at you."

He gave no answer.

At two-fifteen sharp the *Nordic Rose* headed south again. Ten hours later they reached the grounds and resumed working gear.

One day, suddenly, whether Joe had found them or they him, fat keepers began to swarm into the pots. In place of spidery, three-pound adolescents the color of dead marsh grass, up came eight-pound mature males, their dark purple shells glistening. The difference to the men's spirits was like that between prison and sunshine. They cheered the first potload. After the second and third had proved a pattern, they danced around. Joe pounded each on the back in turn and roared promises of a great debauch when they sailed into town with a highline load. Work became delight and recreation; the abundance dizzied them; they could not work the pots fast enough.

Now, instead of pulling pots aboard and stacking them, they baited and returned them instantly, leapfrogging one into the place of the next they drew. Each man had always kept count of the keepers he himself threw into the open hold, and then Frenchy had tallied them in his head and shouted the total up to Joe to record. Now the numbers each declared were "sixteen" and "twenty" instead of the former "one" or "zilch." The crabs were so big that few even had to be measured.

They worked on and on, grabbing sandwiches on the run and washing them down with gallons of powdered soft drinks. It never occurred to any of them to stop. At first they shouted jokes back and forth to the wheel deck, with Joe leading the banter. When the first burst of exuberance had been dispelled, they channeled all their energies into the work. After a few hours it was no longer pleasure in the way it had started, but rather ferocious satisfaction. A hailstorm pelted them, but Hank only noticed when he slipped on ice.

Hank had gradually assumed his share of the coiling and the controls. For variety they rotated these jobs with the baiting every ten potloads. They were clicking as a team: their work dovetailed, they anticipated automatically, they watched for each other's safety. Only in competing to tally the greatest number of keepers did they act as individuals.

Dawn after the first twenty-four hours came with orange streaks over the distant mountains rather than the usual gray. The wind shifted, the sun shone, and it turned biting cold. Only the latter fact meant anything. The water that had invariably crept under Hank's heavy rubber gloves seemed to freeze. His equilibrium of wool underwear and wool shirt beneath rain gear, which absorbed and dispelled his continuous sweat and kept him warm, changed with the temperature and he had to add a bulky coat. The cold also crept through his boots from the sloshing water. He was slowing in spite of himself. When they had a few minutes' respite while Joe cruised to a new string, Sam sauntered to the rack of tielines, selected a large one, and started skipping rope. Hank laughed to see a man in boots and floppy yellow rain pants thumping the deck. The roll of the boat made it clumsier. But Frenchy took over, doing it on one foot. Hank's legs felt so heavy it seemed a foolish waste of energy. Frenchy handed him the rope. He took his turn with a shrug, and the heat started pumping through him again. They attacked the next pots with fresh vitality, as if they were starting the day after a night's sleep.

By second nightfall they had worked their entire string of pots twice, and the hold held close to fifteen thousand crabs. Frenchy had a roast going, and as they swung in the crab block they joked about whether they could stay awake long enough to eat it.

"Don't need to stow the block," said Joe as he leapt down the ladder from the wheel deck. "Be about ninety minutes."

"Hey, Skipper," said Sam. "We need to sack out a few hours."

"When we're on the *crab?*" Joe faced them. He was tallest by half a head, disheveled, red-eyed. Pieces of ice clung to his mustache and frizzled hair. The Santa dimples had become tight as a fist.

No more to be said. They ate, then lay back where they sat on the galley benches while Joe piloted them back to the beginning of a string they had set the night before.

It became a simple fight with pain. Joe Eberhardt, the easy-drinking buddy of the past and the glum driving skipper of the empty pots, became irrational in the presence of abundance. He begrudged two hours' sleep a night. If Hank made a mistake or worked too slowly, Joe roared invective and leaped from his wheel deck to do the job himself. He did it to the others also. When Hank fumbled with the coiling, Joe told him to do nothing but bait. Sometimes he screamed abuse for no reason at all. Sam and Frenchy simply took it, turned their backs, and continued working.

They all became haggard, stumbling. "Stick with it, man," said Frenchy once when he saw Hank biting back tears at the pain in his arms as he tossed the heavy crabs. "Think of each of those fuckers as a quarter in your bank account, may be more."

Hank forced a smile, ashamed to be caught.

"Don't worry, we all do things out here we'd never do on land. This is no fuckin' civilized life. Someday I'll quit it and never look back."

A few pots later, suddenly as such things happen, a coil of line snagged as they dumped over the pot, Hank reached to free it, his arm caught in the bight, and like a fish flipped on a line he was pulled overboard. Water closed over him instantly. The snagged line had the full weight of the steel pot dragging it to the bottom. The icy cold was like a blow as it rushed under his oilskins. I'm dead, he thought. Desperately with his free hand he yanked his deck knife from its sheath and sawed the line between the pot and his arm. The weight pulling him snapped free. He tried to climb hand over hand back up the slack line, his legs immobile in the heavy clothing. He clutched the line—he could feel them drawing it back above him—as the pain in his lungs exploded into his head. He gasped in seawater and blacked out.

261

The terrible cold in his bones was his awakening sensation, and then, with Joe's mouth breathing air into his chest, sickness as he choked and vomited.

They took him inside to the galley floor and stripped off the heavy, wet, clinging clothes, then wrapped him in blankets brought from the bunks below, and carried him onto Joe's bed on the same deck level. He could not stop shivering. It was like red-hot irons of ice being passed through his body. They massaged his legs and arms. Joe had some brandy, and Frenchy brought hot tea and bouillon. He felt so weak he did not want to raise his head to take it, and Joe ended cradling him. Feeling foolish, he sat up, took two sips of the brandy, and fainted.

When he came to again, an outer layer of warmth was creeping in toward the cold. He heard Joe's tight voice in the adjacent pilothouse calling on the radio for help. Frenchy's round face was wide-eyed, and Sam watched him with a grave expression. "Hey, come on," he declared weakly, "I'm okay. Worry about your lost fuckin' crab pot if you want to worry about something." The two laughed uncertainly with relief, and Sam brought Joe in. Joe frowned as he towered in the doorway, listening to Hank's firm declaration of good health.

At last, they headed straight for Kaguyak Bay, anchored, and slept.

Hank, down in his own bunk again in the dark hold with the noise of the live-tank circulators drumming close by from the engine room, began to shiver again whenever he woke. The water had closed over him like lead. Dead black water. Our Father Which art in Heaven . . .

Next day they were back on the grounds, all working together on deck. Their jokes were louder than before, and their silences longer when they came. Joe did not drive as hard as before, and they began to average five and more hours' sleep a night.

After another few days their hold was plugged, and they returned to Kodiak to unload. Hank watched the town approach around Woody Island. He wanted a break, yet he feared it. Surviving a devil's world was a simple decision if you were trapped, but coming up was a chance for escape.

He soaked and soaked in tubs of hot water as Sandra washed

his clothes and exclaimed at the stench. "Don't you people smell your-selves?"

He had learned to take the comment without reacting. "It's dif-ferent out there. It doesn't matter."

"How long does this awful king-crabbing go on?"

"Into January."

"*January?* That's four months, and it's getting colder."

Hank forced a grin. "Unless we continue to Dutch Harbor through February or March. That's where Joe usually heads if the season drops here."

She faced him, her expression troubled. "What kind of life is that? Aren't any of these men married?"

"Navy wives, doctors' wives, fishermen's wives, they all make that decision before they say yes."

"Do you *like* it out there?"

"Beside the point. It's how I've decided to make my living."

"You know, Swede had some kind of showdown in Seattle, and they ended making him a vice-president. Now he's looking for an assis-tant. I think he'd consider you. In summers you'd have complete charge of one of the salmon canneries, and I'd go too. Hank, that's a *career.*"

He closed his eyes and lay back in the tub to avoid answering. When he looked at it coldly, he was sick of crabbing, sick of the ugly creatures themselves and of the misery. With college and Navy as back-ground there were other options. Wasn't life too short to spend pushing like a desperate animal? He knew well enough what the coming winter at sea would be like, and all the others in the future. Ever since his near drowning, admit it, the black water scared him.

"Swede's got to find somebody. You won't have another chance."

Hank ran more hot water and settled into it. The warmth felt good beyond belief. "I don't know. Okay, I might stop by tomorrow and shoot the breeze with Swede."

She rushed over and kissed him. They were soon in bed together and she had never been so tender. During the worst times on the boat he had dreamed of returning to this. A man needed a wife, a home, to settle.

But, in the dark, the image persisted—it had been unleashed by stating that he would call on Swede—of the *Nordic Rose* kicking spray as it left harbor without him. He lay awake, watching distant masthead lights through the window. Been feeding Sandra words. The fishing boats had hooked him the first day he saw them in Kodiak harbor. Black water or not, he'd better see it through, or he'd spend the rest of his life making excuses to himself.

He told her next morning, passing it off as a joke.

Her face, normally less expressive than her voice, twisted strangely. "You mean, you plan to spend your *life* at this?"

"Other men do it, Sandy."

"You never consider anybody but yourself, do you?"

"What kind of talk is that!" He had never thought about it before.

"You play the big hairy fisherman, and think of your woman as chattel you can take or leave. Well, I'm sick of pretending to be that kind of woman. I want a life of being first choice, not the one after all the boats and fishermen have left."

"I guess Adele Henry makes it all right."

"I'm not so sure."

He forced a laugh. "Come on, dear. A man has to make a living, and this is my way." He could hear his own voice, coming deep and confident from his chest. "Of course you're my first choice of woman."

"Oh, a *man's* living. Body all achin' and wracked with pain? What a noble sacrifice to your living, to set us up for a trip to Hawaii, then cancel it for the first boat that came along. I know that really tore you up."

"I *am* sorry about that, and I'm going to make—"

"Make it up when there's no crab, shrimp, salmon, or halibut running? My God, you've only got a heart for one thing in this world, Hank, and it's not me!" Tears streaked her face. He went to hold her, but she brushed him away as she began to name all the times he had chosen boats instead of her.

Hank listened, subdued. He knew she was right. He did not love her, but he wanted badly to comfort her and make it up. When her tirade was finally lost in sobbing he drew her close and rocked her, wondering what he could do that would not trap him.

They had a quiet, sad meal together before he went fishing again. The next time his boat returned to town, the apartment was empty.

21

SAGA OF THE KING CRABS AND TANNERS

THREE major species of crab are fished in Alaska, and two are biological imposters. The true or ten-legged crab, genus Cancer, is the dungeness, western brother to the smaller East Coast blueclaw of the Chesapeake Bay and points south. King crab is a member of the genus Paralithodes, a fellow crustacean but one that possesses a different joint structure and one fewer set of legs. The second imposter, tanner crab (commercially often called snow crab), belongs to the genus Chionoecetes, again a creature of differently proportioned parts. All three live in shells consisting of a carapace (central body) and legs, which they molt at intervals in order to grow larger. All three provide meat that is white, chunky, and succulent. To fishermen, cannerymen, and consumers, the latter is all that really matters.

In appearance, the dungeness crab has a thick central body and relatively stubby legs, two of them claws that it uses with agility. It weighs two to three pounds, and among the crustaceans resembles a boxer, always coiled ready to fight. (The Chesapeake Bay blueclaw is less than half the size, but many times the fighter.) The king crab is three and four times as weighty—seven to eight pounds is the commercial average, but ten-plus pounders still appear in the crabpots hauled north of Kodiak. The king's carapace is a many-hued purple, rounded, and covered with thornlike protective spines. It resembles a big medallion. Many people in Alaska polish and mount them. The carapace breadth of mature male kings (six to nine or more inches) is no greater than that of the dungeness, which has a brown, smooth, oblong shell, but the bulk of the king's rounded body, along with its meat-filled legs which extend more than a foot (for a total span of three to four feet), make it a vastly larger creature. Compared to the boxer dungeness, however, a king crab has a sluggish nature. Its two pinchers, inexorably strong when they close on an object, are just as likely to wave open. Last of the three, the tanner crab, has long spidery legs which emanate from a frail brown carapace that few would think of displaying over a fireplace. Its weight may reach four pounds, but compared to the feisty dungeness or the heavyweight king, it is unimpressive, an Ichabod Crane with a watery constitution.

To say which of the three crabs is the best eating is a matter of choice. Prepared under equal conditions, each is so good that one forgets the competition. There are beer ways and wine ways to eat a crab. The great beer way is straight from the steam pot, with the crabs warm and their natural juices still flowing from the shell. The San Francisco and Chesapeake Bay method involves a leisurely ceremony with mallets and fingers, as one picks out lumps and slivers of meat throughout the shell and claws. Dungeness and blueclaw are the ideal picking crabs, the ones around which the ceremony was developed. Their compact structures concentrate the meat in chunks throughout their body and legs. The tanner is the least satisfactory picking crab because its meat clings to the shell. King crab contains the richest meat, but a single tube from one leg provides the entire meal, so it is no pick crab. With kings, try rather the wine ways: elegant cold salads or sautéed in butter. As for tanner crab, one could make a case for it having the best flavor of them all. Place a bottle of wine beside it.

Until two decades ago, dungeness was *the* West Coast crab. The Japanese had maintained a Bering Sea factory fleet to harvest and can king crab from 1930 until Pearl Harbor, but Americans had seen little of it. When I first visited Kodiak in 1952, in the Coast Guard, and then returned home to Chesapeake Bay country with a photo of myself holding a four-foot king crab across my middle, people thought I was playing a joke with papier-mâché.

Before World War II there had been tentative U.S. endeavors at a king-crab fishery, principally from aboard the *Tondelayo*. This small factory ship was first outfitted for Bering Sea king crab in 1938 by a canneryman named Kinky Alexander, and then in 1940 explored the same grounds under a one-year government grant. The true pioneer of the fishery is conceded to be Lowell Wakefield, member of a cannery family who processed herring at the time in a small plant to the north of Kodiak. Beginning in 1946, Wakefield organized a series of king-crabbing forays into the Bering Sea, principally aboard the ship *Deep Sea*, which he built especially for the purpose. In a work combination which has generally proved impractical to U.S. investors (including Wakefield), a fishing crew aboard the *Deep Sea* harvested the crabs with nets, later pots, and sent them directly belowdeck to be frozen and canned by a separate crew. The *Deep Sea* survives as a floating king-crab processor anchored in Aleutian harbors—she stopped performing her dual role in 1956—respected by Alaska crabmen, many of whom, like the fictitious Swede Scorden, learned his profession aboard her.

By the 1950s king crab was a small fishery, controlled mainly by Wakefield, which had shifted its operations to Seldovia at the mouth of Cook Inlet. This area had good king-crab grounds within commuting distance of shore-based plants, making it possible to bypass the heavy logistical problems of the remote and turbulent Bering Sea. By the 1960s the center of king crabbing and the men most active in it had moved a hundred miles south to Kodiak and a seemingly endless super-abundance of the huge crustaceans. In 1953, the total Alaska king-crab industry delivered 4.6 million pounds. By 1960 it had grown to 28.5 million pounds. Then came the Kodiak years, when in 1965 and 1966 *Kodiak alone* delivered 76.8 and 90.7 million pounds of king crab. Kodiak was a crab-crazy town, with plugged boats sometimes waiting days in line for a cannery to unload them, and the crabbing going year-round except during the spring mating season. Suddenly the Kodiak catches tumbled: 63 to 22 to 13 million pounds in the next three years. While by the mid-1970s it had risen to the 20 millions again, the superboom was obviously gone, apparently through overfishing, and the fishery shifted westward toward the Bering Sea and the Aleutians. The Alaskawide harvest of king crabs today is approximately that of the peak Kodiak year.

In most fisheries, the road of trial and error to a general technology has been lost in time, but with king crab many of the men who worked out the methods are still active (Lowell Wakefield died in 1977). These men, who experimented with new processes, grounds, boats, and gear, were individual cannerymen and fishermen, not funded GM research executives or university researchers subsidized to compare notes at annual symposia. They had a living to gain, but their shirts to lose.

For the embryo cannery operator there was first the basic problem of preserving the king-crab meat with flavor and texture—even color—that people would buy. For preparing the meat, there was a literature of general seafood knowledge, even regarding other crabs, but the modifications to king crab were far from automatic. Many variables had to be balanced. Canning and later freezing problems included discoloration in the can and mushy thawed legs, needing adjustments—e.g., in cooking times, volume of washes, degree of brine quick-freeze.

The mechanical stages to prepare the crabmeat, from butchering and cooking to extraction and packing, had to be translated both into special machinery and into cannery lines where one step would flow efficiently to the next. (Often, still, a crab canneryman sets up his lines with enough personal innovations and specially tooled equipment to bar visitors and cameras to prevent his ideas being scouted.) New terms that entered the cannery vocabulary indicate some of the jobs in the process of preparing large crabs: the breaking table, where the workers twist the cooked crab legs in two at the joints; the wringing station, where rollers press out the narrow strip of meat in the lower leg; the blowing line, where compressed-air jets shoot out the fat tube of meat from the main leg; the shake line, where with the flick of a wrist the chunks of meat closest to the body are shaken free.

On deck, the king crabs were first brought up by net, both trawls and tangle nets. The weight of the catch in a trawl crushed enough crab for Americans to abandon the method even before a law was passed against it. Tangle nets enmesh the crabs, so that many, including females and juveniles, are torn apart and killed while being picked out. The U.S. outlawed tangle nets to its own crabbers in 1954, but was powerless for the next two decades to prevent their use by the Japanese and Soviet king-crab factory fleets.

For Americans, crab pots appeared to be the solution. The existing near-shore fishery for dungeness crab used circular pots that weighed up to 150 pounds. Fishermen first enlarged the openings of these to try them for king crab. They were certainly neater than nets, but they were so light that they tumbled and drifted with the tides. The pots evolved by trial and error are square, with steel frames and nylon web. They are generally three feet wide by six and a half to eight feet square (650-pound "seven-bys" are most common these days), and they have the shape and weight to stay solidly on the bottom at fishing depths of fifty fathoms or more. Crabs, attracted by bait hung inside, enter through a web corridor that tunnels upward, then fall off into the pot itself. One of the early design problems was the tunnel. In the first versions it was horizontal, and too many crabs crawled free as easily as they had entered. Somebody had to think through the angular tunnel, while still leaving some escape route if the pot became full (king crabs jammed too tight to move soon become the prey of sea lice that eat them alive). The initial pots also had wire mesh, which disintegrated in a few months through an electrolytic interaction in salt water with the steel frames. Although nylon web is now used, pots still have a zinc bar attached to reduce this batterylike exchange within the framework itself.

Then the deck machinery had to be developed to haul these vastly heavier pots. In the early days the pots were winched strenuously and slowly with boom and deck-mounted hauler. The present hydraulic crab block self-adjusts to take up sudden slacks in heavy seas, and it moves so rapidly that a pot loaded to 3000 pounds can be drawn up from sixty fathoms in about three minutes. One of the principal developers and manufacturers of this crab block, Marco of Seattle, had also placed into production the Puretic Power Block which, as noted earlier, changed the seine fisheries of the world. Marco president Peter Schmidt had accepted Puretic's invention after several larger manufacturers had turned it down, and it furnished the bedrock of his young company. This was a time for many to gamble their substance on the future. Some—like Schmidt, Wakefield, and many individual fishermen—came out splendidly. Others, if not dead or crippled, ended up fishing on somebody else's deck for a living.

The boats had the problem of keeping crabs alive until they could be brought to the canneries. On the first small boats out of Seldovia and Kodiak, crewmen stacked the crab belly-up in holds primarily meant for salmon, and delivered them, still sluggishly waving their claws, to the nearby canneries within twelve hours. For a longer-range operation it was necessary to develop tanks with pumps that circulated fresh seawater completely at least once every thirty minutes.

And the crab boats themselves! The first ones were converted

from other fisheries, including old Monterey sardine seiners, and larger
Alaska salmon seiners (legal size limit fifty-eight feet) whose owners
wanted to fish more than the summer salmon runs. Limit seiners for the
shore-hugging salmon were not built for the steady punishment of open
sea where the king crabs schooled, and the Monterey seiners suffered
from superannuation. Both had stability problems when several layers of
pots stacked on deck raised their center of gravity. Many of these makeshift crabbers, cruising to the grounds with a deckload of pots, caught a
sea and capsized, or simply broke apart. Early king crabbing was a
death-and-disaster fishery, the wonder being that it was not more so
given the typical weather around Kodiak and the Bering Sea.

As king crab began to promise high payoffs, men afforded long-
terms debts for boats better adapted to the work. By the 1970s there
were extensive conversions of large surplus military vessels and of shrimp
trawlers bought from yards in the Gulf of Mexico. However, in the late
1960s, Seattle yards had begun building boats 90 feet and longer which
were especially designed to cope with rough seas and unwieldly crab
pots. These "Bering Sea crabbers" have become the standard king crab
vessels of western Alaska. They are big, full, heavy boats—tailored to
be stable all-weather work platforms—characterized by a large square
deck for carrying a maximum number of pots, by equally large hold
capacities to permit extended fishing without the need to return often
to unload, and by a full bow structure that keeps the boat from plunging
deeply in heavy seas. The boats have heavy-duty marine diesel engines
ranging in horsepower (figures for Marco boats) from 575 in the 90-
foot class to 1200 in the 120-foot class.

Except for the big tuna seiners, these Bering Sea crabbers are the
largest and most elegant fishing boats in the United States. In their
spacious galley and berthing areas they seem like the vessels of a different profession than the little *Rondelay*-type seiners. Yet nothing inside
can mitigate the brutality of the weather the crews must face on deck,
the maverick swinging of ton-weight pots, or the endless hours required
to work the pots. It is a hard fishery, considered by most fishermen second only to halibut longlining for the toll it takes in danger and physical strain.

The king crabs themselves, subject of this attention, are bottom-
dwelling creatures. While slow-moving and sluggish when viewed from

minute to minute, they commonly migrate more than a hundred miles during a year, walking or scuttling but never swimming as they move inshore to shallows for spring mating, then return to the deeper flats of the continental shelves.

Studies by the Alaska Department of Fish and Game indicate that, despite this movement, crabs school in tribes that do not mingle beyond their own distinct areas. There are five such areas around Kodiak Island. Kings also appear to return to the same grounds within their area after mating. They are gregarious, but tend to stay segregated by sex and size for much of the year after reaching maturity. This makes a bonanza for the skipper clever or lucky enough to set his pots on a colony of keeper-sized males—and misery for the crew that pulls a string of picking pots jammed with nothing but throwbacks.

Young king crabs of about age two (still sexually mixed and half a decade away from harvestable age) sometimes are found in an extraordinarily gregarious state, clinging together in a pod that may measure twelve feet across. The six-thousand-odd crabs thus podded all face outward from the center and circulate within the mass so that the top layers move continuously around to the bottom where the food lies. Sometimes they disband temporarily to feed, then all pile together again. Divers have observed several pods joined together into a long mound across the seafloor containing collectively up to 500,000 crabs. Presumably the podding is for protection, since small crabs furnish dinner for many large fish, including halibut. By their third year the young crabs have peeled off and gone their ways in more horizontal packs to graze the ocean floor for food. The diet of a king crab includes detritus, sea plants, clams, snails, other crustaceans, fish, sea lice, barnacles, worms, sea plants, echinoderms, sea urchins—virtually anything living on the bottom rocks and mud that fits their claws.

According to the best calculations of biologists king crabs may live as long as twenty years. Big older males have a crusty, weighty look, with barnacles covering their spiny dark purple shells. Both sexes of king crabs grow at the same rate until they reach sexual maturity at age five. Then the males become progressively larger. By age seven or eight the male has attained a carapace width of six and a half to seven inches, which makes him legally harvestable depending on the area, and he continues to grow, while a female seldom reaches this size no matter how long she lives. A male keeper weighs seven to ten pounds, depending on his age, with Bering Sea crabs smaller and basically about a pound lighter than those around Kodiak and Dutch Harbor. The largest female ever documented weighed ten pounds, while the largest male weighed twenty-four pounds six ounces and stretched out five feet from leg to leg.

The king crab, like all other crustaceans including the shrimp, grows by molting. It sloughs one exoskeleton and takes water into its tissues to swell its size, after which a new shell hardens around its body. It then grows solidly to fill the new shell. During the initial years of growth king crabs normally molt twenty-three times, but then as adults only once a year at a predictable time.

The annual molting occurs at the same time as mating, nor can the king-crab female perform her part of the reproductive function until she first molts. During late winter, both sexes start moving in from the hundred-or-more-fathom shelves to kelpy ocean banks or shorelines of forty fathoms and less. Upon arriving, the females occasionally pod together, apparently to emit a collective sexual attractant strong enough to guide the males to their location. Males follow a less regular schedule. Some "skip-molt": pass by a year. If males molt before meeting the females, they must harden for about ten days before they can take their part in the mating. The younger females are taken first. Nature gives the male the instinct to grasp the female of his choice for several days. This may serve merely to guarantee his presence when the crucial moment arrives, but it also protects her at a vulnerable time and furnishes help in sloughing her old shell. The female—doomed to be one of the most eternal egg-bearers in all the creature kingdoms—may still be carrying the fertilized eggs of the year before if she has not just released them, and may actually hatch them during the days while the male is grasping her. When her molt is completed with the male's help, the male in a few minutes deposits sperm externally around her gonopores, and releases her. He goes his way to rest a while and then to do his duty by another female. She at once extrudes her new eggs—50,000 to 400,000, depending on her size—which are fertilized immediately as they pass through her two gonopores into her abdominal pouch. She then starts the long crawl back to deep water, carrying the eggs she will shelter and care for throughout the coming year.

King crab eggs hatch to liberate larvae one-thirty-second of an inch long. For two months they live within the water column and swim weakly with the currents, a zooplanktonic meal for any larger creature with a taste for them. On the fourth molt they acquire an exoskeleton half resembling a crab. By now they are a third of an inch long. They settle to the bottom for the rest of their lives and never swim again. The next molt delivers them into crab shape, complete with jointed legs, claws, socketed eyes, and soft abdomen. About eighteen molts and four years later their carapaces have grown to four inches, they reach sexual maturity, and they separate for good into male and female groups.

Males may be mature for two seasons before they reach commercial size, and they can fertilize several females during each season. Thus the process of reproduction is not threatened by the harvesting of large males. However, all the forces affecting king crabs are not yet known. Biologists have noted that large females (the ones carrying the most eggs) primarily mate with large males.

In the early days, fishermen took king crabs when they chose, being regulated only by size. Later, while being forced to respect the molting season by conservation regulations, they would fish the crabs during the three summer months following, when the meat was still lightweight and watery before it had filled out the new shell. Since 1970, king crab has been regulated by quota. Since quotas are limited, the canneries and Alaska fishery officials have eased the Kodiak and Bering Sea seasons into a period late enough for the crabs to have filled to their heaviest. (By careful processing a cannery can recover 25 percent of a full king crab's total weight as meat, but only about 15 percent from a recently molted crab.) By the time the crabs have grown heavy again, most in Kodiak have migrated farther to sea, and the autumn storms have begun. Thus smaller boats may compete for only that portion of crabs which remains in some large deep bays, and men who want to stick with the king crabs must finance larger boats that will take them farther seaward.

Dungeness crab provides a relatively small commercial fishery in Alaska despite its abundance. Thus far it has been caught principally for live-tank sale to West Coast restaurants such as those on Fishermen's Wharf in San Francisco, during a time when the crabs fell off on California and Oregon shores. This great picking crab lacks the large sections of meat that in kings and tanners can be shaken or rolled free on a cannery line.

Dungeness crabs spend their lives much closer to shore than the other crabs discussed here, and the fishery for them is not as strenuous. As already noted, they are fished with circular pots weighing up to 150 pounds. The dungeness around Kodiak mate in late summer, after molting as do kings, with the same grasping procedure. However, the male sperm remains dormant in the female's abdomen for several months before the eggs are fertilized. The eggs then hatch in the spring, and the planktonic larvae float free before several molts send the creatures to the bottom. Dungeness are noted for eating their young. Their lifespan is about eight years if they survive themselves. As also noted, their carapace span can be as great as that of king crabs (six and a half inches is the usual legal commercial size) but they are considerably smaller, with a weight range of two to four pounds.

Tanner crabs have been around as long as any of the others. The Japanese know them well from their own coasts as well as from Alaska, and they have marketed them in the U.S. for years as snow crab. While king crabs were abundant, Americans generally ignored tanners, since they were less meaty and more difficult to process. However, now that U.S. king-crab fishermen have payments to make on their million-and-a-half-dollar Bering Sea boats, they need a crab fishery for longer each year than kings alone can provide. With better tanner-crab markets in recent years, higher prices, and improved processing technology, tanner crabs are filling the gap.

Ironically, the Japanese spurred American interest by sharing some of their tanner-crab processing technology. In the late 1970s, the allotment of Bering Sea tanner crab to the Japanese became the first test of the 1976 Fishery Management Act (the "two-hundred-mile law") as American fishermen acquired the boat capacity to fish virtually all of the eastern Bering Sea tanners and the Japanese, with the future of two factory fleets at stake, fought at the diplomatic level to remain in the fishery.

The tanner crab weighs in at half that of a king crab. The name derives from one species within genus *Chionoecetes, C. tanneri*, which is neither of the species found at commercially viable depths in Alaskan waters. The principal Alaskan species, abundant from the Gulf of Alaska to the Bering Sea, is *C. bairdi*. The *bairdi* is two and a half times larger than *C. opilio,* which frequents the northern Bering Sea shelf. As the Japanese are eased further out of the fishery, they are being allotted quotas of *opilio* or nothing.

The cycle of tanner crabs is different from that of kings, so the two can be fished in separate seasons. At present, the boats in both Kodiak and the Bering Sea follow the king crabs from September into January (until the quotas of different sizes have been taken), and then fish the tanners from mid-January to April around Kodiak and to mid-June in the Bering Sea.

The tanner reproductive process differs from that of the other two crabs in that the female does *not* molt when she mates, but rather keeps the same shell from maturity until death. She has a considerable range of egg capacity—24,000 to 300,000—which appears to have nothing to do with size. Tanners live eight to twelve years. Males, as with the other crabs, are bigger than females, with a fat *bairdi* keeper weighing from three to four pounds. Tanners inhabit shelf waters as deep as 250 fathoms, but they also school in the hundred-fathom areas of the king crabs. It appears, however, that tanner crabs and king crabs compete for the same food and normally do not coexist. Except for juveniles, king crabs would be the obvious winners of a territorial dispute. On the other hand, waters in which large king crabs have been fished out may suddenly become abundant with tanners, providing at least a compensatory crab fishery for several seasons.

The experimental early days of king crabbing only three decades ago are over. An established king–tanner fishery now employs thousands. On the boats, it makes for some of the roughest fishing in the world.

Part 4:
1972, FALL TO
1974, SPRING

22

Dutch Harbor, Aleutians, and Bering Sea

THE tandem settlements of Unalaska and Dutch Harbor on the Aleutian island of Unalaska lie six hundred miles southwest of Kodiak and about two thousand miles northwest of Seattle. They dot the shore of the only major harbor near Unimak Pass, which in turn is the first entrance to the great fishing grounds of the Bering Sea.

Unalaska is the third of the fifty-odd principal islands (there are hundreds more) that form what is called the Aleutian Islands chain. Beginning at Unimak, the chain curves westward a thousand miles to Attu, then two hundred miles farther to the Soviet Komandorskyie Islands. None of the islands are more than a few miles from water to water, yet the interiors of many have never been formally explored. It is a mountain land of fogs and gales, of shorelines peppered with shoals, of dormant volcanos that sometimes erupt, an ocean-dominated world of primal austerity.

This thin Aleutian barrier is one of the world's most famous swirling points for foul weather. It is the clash line between the equatorial warmth pumped by the Japanese Current along the Pacific side of the islands and the arctic cold that blows down across the Bering Sea. Sixty-knot winds are commonplace, hundred-knot storms to be expected, with fog and slanting rain or snow a virtually perpetual condition. However, the islands have their own beauties when the fogs allow them to be seen. The mountains rise from the sea in big lumps and cones. Snow stays atop some the year round, streaking down extinct volcanos like melted ice cream. There are no trees, excepting stunted handfuls planted by lonely Russian fur traders two centuries ago and by lonely American soldiers four decades ago. But in summer, the hillsides are covered with greenery of an intensity usually associated with Ireland. And even in crevices among the high rocks, wildflowers bloom with a profligacy not seen in the tamed portions of the earth.

Back at the time of man's first evidence on the islands 8500 years ago, the present continental shelf of the Bering Sea was exposed land. Apparently some of the Asian peoples who migrated across the land bridge far to the north traveled down this territory, where now the king crabs burrow in abundance under sixty fathoms of water, following the ledge of the exposed shelf as they sought seafood. They spread in both directions, to dead-end in the west on Attu, to move northeastward up the Alaska Peninsula and over to Kodiak Island. These were the ancestors of the present Aleuts. By the time they reached Kodiak they had evolved into the subgroup Koniag, the name from which Kodiak derives.

When the Russian fur barons "discovered" the Aleutians in 1741, the islands were inhabited by an estimated 12,000 to 25,000 natives. (The name Aleut, pronounced Al'-e-oot, derived from a Russian perversion of a native word, but scholars disagree on which word.) The natives lived in sunken sod houses, in hundreds of small groups throughout all the islands, dividing the coastline into sustaining parcels much as small farmers divide land. Their life was harsh beyond the most marginal present standards. With no trees and scarce driftwood, the Aleuts had no steady fuel supply beyond small quantities of sea-mammal oil. Their buried dwellings were rarely heated, and they ate most of their fish and seal meat raw. Nor could they fire pottery utensils. While the land supplied some roots and berries in season, the sea was their supplier—one of the roughest of the world. When they put out in their skin boats, they often had to paddle miles from shore, in waters that still regularly sink steel ships. Many never returned, and the general life expectancy was short.

When the Russians came, the meeting of civilized and primitive man followed the ugly conquistadorial pattern. Some natives were friendly, some fought, but all were subdued. Under Russian guns and whips, the skilled Aleut hunters were enslaved to provide gluttonous quantities of sea-otter pelts. The otters became practically extinct. The Aleuts themselves fared little better, dying both from mistreatment and from white man's diseases. Ninety years after the Russian arrival, the native population had been reduced to approximately a tenth of its original number, an estimated 2200, with most of their settlements wiped out entirely. The 1970 census counted 1635 Aleuts in thirteen villages, only six of which are actually located on the Aleutian Islands themselves. Ironically, the Aleut people today, from Atka to Kodiak, have only one church—the Russian Orthodox. And the overlay of their culture, especially in the Aleutians, remains predominantly Russian, however many ballots they may cast for American presidents.

Until World War II, the Aleutian Islands were considered little but an appendage to either Alaska or the United States. When military strategists began to pay attention, they saw what a dangerous bridge of air bases the islands could provide an enemy who wanted to bomb the U.S. West Coast, and conversely what a convenient platform the islands might provide for bombing Japan. By the time of Pearl Harbor, the U.S. had built a base in the wasteland of hills known as Dutch Harbor and had stationed about 5000 men there.

Japan moved quickly after its stunning Pacific victories in early 1942 that ended with the fall of Corregidor on May 6. Prime target was Midway Island, west of Hawaii, but as a tactical diversion, and also for a double victory, the Japanese decided to take the Aleutians simultaneously. The battle of Dutch Harbor took place June 3 and 4, 1942. It resulted in two bombings by Japanese Zeros and a loss of seventy-eight American lives. However, the burning fuel tanks and dense smoke along the hills were deceptive, and the long-range effect on the Dutch Harbor base was one more of harassment than of destruction. Down south, the Battle of Midway had turned into an unexpected Japanese disaster, and Japan changed its plans for taking any but the farthest western Aleutian islands. Three days later they occupied Attu and Kiska.

The Aleutian expedition yielded a small, temporary, and expensive victory for the Japanese. They remained on Attu and Kiska for less than a year. The U.S. gathered its forces and established a base on Adak, an island halfway between Dutch and Attu. (A large American naval base remains on Adak today.) The battle to regain Attu lasted from May 11 to May 30, 1943. It was a battle to the death second only to Iwo Jima in the Pacific Theater for the ratio of U.S. casualties to men deployed, with 549 dead. The cost to the Japanese was even greater, with 2351 counted dead and hundreds more presumed buried before the count.

Only twenty-eight Japanese allowed themselves to be captured, none of them officers. At the last, 500 Japanese soldiers collected for a final stand, then held grenades to their chests.

Dutch Harbor-Unalaska had survived the bombing and remained a naval base throughout the war. The 2000 military men remaining in Dutch Harbor gladly closed down when the war ended. They left behind the ghosts of their dead, along with tons of equipment, plus hundreds of empty buildings and Quonset huts. The ruins remain, and, depending on the structure of an afterlife, so do the ghosts. The approximately 200 inhabitants of Unalaska village had been evacuated. When the war ended they were returned, and the reduced human activity of the area shifted back across the strait to their collection of frame houses clustered around the domed Russian Orthodox church.

The ghosts should remain even more deeply for the Japanese. They are closer geographically to the Aleutians than are most Americans (Attu is approximately 1200 miles from Japan, 3000 miles from Seattle). They lost more men, and in despair rather than victory. A nation of traditional fish-eaters and fishermen (the United States at this point is neither), they had been harvesting king crab in the American Bering Sea since 1930, and in fact had always known the Aleutian geography and marine biology better than its owners. In 1952 the U.S. decided that the punitive aspect of the war was over and allowed the Japanese to resume fishing around the very islands where they had been defeated and committed mass suicide less than a decade before. The fact that the Japanese, and then the Russians who followed in 1959, exploited the Aleutian and Bering Sea fishing grounds with little thought for either conservation or American fishermen is another story.

As the word *Dutch* is used now by fishermen and cannerymen, it encompasses both the natural estuary called Dutch Harbor on five-mile-long Amaknak Island within Unalaska Bay and the Aleut village of Unalaska on the shore of the main island only a few hundred feet east across a narrow strip of water. Without a bridge or steady ferry, one is isolated from the other except by boat. Processor ships have located on both shores over a space of miles. Each is self-contained, with shore-based or floating bunkhouses and chowhalls. Unalaska village is the only formal community among the diverse cannery complexes. Its center consists of a white-clapboard general store, a new small post office, a pizza-type carryout set up in a trailer, a shacklike building that houses the bar, and the little Russian church. The village runs a few buildings deep along the shore, with an unpaved road connecting the other houses behind.

When the crab are running—which, with kings and tanners combined, occupies more and more of the year—the Aleuts are so outnumbered that they barely seem to exist. Fishermen accept them as part of the general melange, but give them no further thought. Some crew on the big boats, and some own smaller boats, but most are absorbed into the canneries at the picking levels. Whether the new power given the Unalaska Aleuts by the Alaska Native Claims Act will make them masters of their ancestral area, or at least larger participants in the fishing boom, remains to be seen.

Whatever happens, Dutch Harbor-Unalaska is now a place of the future, at least for outsiders, where the future is closing fast. Dutch will undoubtedly remain the major port for American boats fishing the Bering Sea; the Aleutians lack a choice of large sheltered harbors. And the American boats on the scene increase every year as the U.S. uses the provisions of the 200-mile law to loosen the hold of the Japanese and Russian fleets on the available seafood stocks. The continental shelves of the Aleutians and the Bering Sea are one of man's biggest graineries. And Dutch has become the place where he keeps the silos.

23

KISS A CRAB

HANK CRAWFORD waited packed against the bar of the Elbow Room in the village—the only bar in Unalaska and Dutch Harbor combined—until Charlie sold him two Scotches and the others passed them overhead. With Jody alongside he would have chosen to sit at one of the few booths, had there been space, but standing on the puddled planks was at least better than drinking outside in the snow. The chatter and smoke were terrific.

It was October 1972. Hank had become leaner, darker, since his final days of adolescence aboard the *Nordic Rose*. He spoke more deliberately. Few any more would have recognized him without his full beard. There were scars on his face from maverick crabpots and hooks, and the hand that held his glass had a finger missing.

Jody, her face pushed close to his chest by the crowd, looked up and smiled her smile. They locked arms and swallowed from each other's glasses.

"Nervous?"

"Wouldn't admit it if I was."

"You're ready, don't worry. Every skipper has to start with his first trip."

Rosa the barmaid elbowed her way through to them bearing a tray with six full glasses of Scotch. "Hank, one of your friends just six-packed you, honey. Where do I put it all?"

"Who?" he laughed. She nodded toward a table where Tolly and Seth sat with two cannery girls. They waved him over insistently. Instead, he and Jody toasted them, then shared a long, leisurely kiss.

Five hours later, to time with slack at Akutan Pass, Hank stood in the little wheelhouse of the *Nestor* and guided his boat out of Unalaska Bay. In the predawn light the surrounding mountains glowed blue where the snow lay thick, dark blue where wind had exposed rock. Lights shone in isolated clusters from the processor ships and reflected on the water. Below he could hear thumps of gear as the others readied for sea. No use dwelling on the strangeness of it, that this was the first time he had ever held the wheel rather than hustled on deck when leaving harbor aboard a fishing boat. The wheel itself of the *Nestor* he knew from thousands of hours behind it, a hundred at least while others worked the pots, but there had always been a skipper to call for questions. He grinned to himself. About time. They passed through the inlet, close enough to the Pan Alaska dock to hear winches creaking from a boat being unloaded of its king crab and to see bundled faces of cannery people. The village was quiet beneath its backdrop of lumpy mountains. The door opened to the shack that housed the Elbow Room, spilling light across the snow as someone staggered out. He altered course on a range with the church, pointed his bow toward the opening between the sweeps of mountains, and soon started to buck into the wind. Often he looked astern to make sure the tiers of sluggishly clanking pots rode secure, even though he had climbed among them personally: as he had checked the bait, and the engine oil, and other things that Joe Eberhardt usually trusted his crew to do by themselves. A particularly high wave rose ahead. He felt sudden hollow fear as he throttled the bow into it. The boat pitched upward in the foamy crest, and he eased off. No broach, no disaster. He had done it before, but never with only himself to answer. Good, sturdy boat. It was now light. Behind him, the jagged snow mountains of the bay were obliterated suddenly by a squall that pelted ice on the windows.

"Watch over us," he muttered in spite of himself, "our boat is so small."

The normal odor of bacon drifted through the transom that looked down on the bunkroom. He could hear their voices but not their words. Discussing him? Their right, with no reason for confidence in a man who had merely worked alongside them on deck. What if he found no crab, couldn't even pay for the trip? Worse, suppose he mishandled the boat while they worked the pots, and caused an injury? He began to sweat, in a wheelhouse not that warm, as he reviewed his scanty first-aid knowledge. Six hundred miles from the Coast Guard in Kodiak. The swells towered over his head when the boat hit a trough, then spewed water over the bow that blew back to cover the windows. The fathometer dropped from the sixties to the forties. Forgotten shoals? He rushed to the radar and the chart, but it was only the fathom curve he had crossed endless times before. What if a sea swept one of them overboard? Could he come alongside coolly enough not to broach over the man or chop him in the screw? If it happened in the dark besides, my God. How much more solid and safe the boat had seemed with Joe in command!

Joe had been a good skipper, once you settled in with him and knew the rules. In two years together, they had progressed from the fifty-eight-foot *Nordic Rose* to the seventy-eight-foot *Nestor*, which had only shrimped before, and Hank had learned much about boats as they converted to crabbing. Between personal explosions, Joe was willing to teach. "I won't place anybody above you, Hank, as long as you stay with me steady." Frenchy had been the first to be replaced, with brutal suddenness when Joe learned he had mellowed out one night at the Elbow Room and told an old buddy the *Nestor*'s best crab grounds. When Hank tried to intervene, Joe merely glared, while Sam told him abruptly that a basic boat's rule had been violated and a basic action taken. Sam, after working his turns as winter relief skipper and saving, now owned half-share of a boat on which he and his partner alternated commands of the pilothouse and deck. That left Hank senior man, relief skipper at twenty-seven, with sixteen thousand dollars saved from two years' hard fishing, plus ten percent ownership of the *Nestor*. During other winters, Joe had only gone south for a month, but this year he and Linda had decided to try again, and they were going to spend several months together renovating an old house in Oregon, leaving Hank a command through the winter and into the spring.

"Take your breakfast, Skipper," said Seth. He wore red suspenders over his bulky wool shirt cut at the elbows, with long-john sleeves hugging his thick wrists beneath. Both of them braced automatically against the violent pitch of the boat.

"Bring it up, would you? We're coming to Akutan Pass."

Seth called below gleefully, "I fuckin' told you so. Now he's skipper, he won't give up the wheel. Shall we kiss his ass, or leave him hungry?"

The burly Seth's bullshit always relaxed him. It had been his recommendation that brought Seth aboard after Frenchy left, so they had worked alongside each other for more than a year. By now they had often trusted their lives to each other. "Watch it, kid. If you bad-mouth your skipper, he'll bust you back to boat-puller where you belong."

"That'll be a long demote, from working for a greenhorn who's scared to give up his wheel."

"Only two pancakes. I'd better learn to eat less, since most of my work's going to be making you deadasses hop to instead of doing it myself."

After eating, the crew drifted up to the wheelhouse to lounge and talk: Andy, a crabman of ten years who could be deck boss on any boat, but who refused the responsibility of command; Dan, signed on as Hank's replacement just the trip before, a husky kid they had selected by vote to be their crewmate from among a dozen who were roaming hungry on the beach, some visiting each boat for months in search of a berth; and Seth. Hank sat in the padded captain's chair by the controls, Andy in the wooden portside seat. Dan stood between the chart niche and the binnacle, his legs braced and arms folded. Seth leaned against the window rail.

"Figured where you'll set our pots?" asked Andy. He was lean and wiry, as much at ease as a farmboy on a mule, but a man of only necessary words.

Hank had been hoping they would ask. "Well," he said calmly, "since we're starting a new season on new grounds, we'll prospect some. Joe Eberhardt did a great job of sticking with the rest of the boats where we all have to pull at the same crabs. I've charted out some possible new places. We'll lay pots in test patches across the fifty-fathom curves from deep to shallow the way Joe would do, but I'm going to do it farther out and also closer in than the others. Try to catch the crabs before they reach the other boats."

"That's what I like," said Seth admiringly, "fuckin' strategy."

Andy was less impressed. "Joe always did pretty good where he set."

Water broke over the bow in streaming sheets and splattered noisily against the windows. Seth glanced around, winked at Hank, and declared that the tarp on the bait box had better be more secure than it looked. "I tried it good," said Dan uneasily, and a minute later slipped below. The others laughed together as Dan's figure appeared on deck, holding tight with one hand against the boat's motion as he tugged at the tarp ropes.

"Oh, shit," Seth crowed, "I love greenhorns. He worked thirty minutes to get that tarp right; if it was more secure we'd need to cut it open. Go on, Hank, give him a bath."

With Joe on board, Hank would, without a thought, have altered course to catch a drenching sea. He considered it, then held his course tight to make sure nothing happened.

It was afternoon when he reached the first area he planned to prospect. As the others on deck climbed over the stacked pots with hooks and straps, he studied the chart, excited. Almost be an omen, to set the first pot into crab. Joe had coached him often to find the slope by passing with the fathometer, to look for the soft readout of the depth graph that showed mud rather than the hard contours of rock. Head into the sea, take her a little on the quarter. Not too fast, watch the roll, remember men on deck. He propped open the door to the afterdeck. "Let her go!" They heaved, and the first pot splashed into the water.

"N- fifty-two," called Seth, and Hank recorded the buoy number.

Pot by pot, out they went. Hank could picture the big square frames settling in fifty-fathom darkness; the currents flowing through to carry the scent of herring and live bait across the seafloor; the big purple crabs stirring sluggishly from the mud to give it a try. "*Get* in there, every one of you bastards," he muttered happily.

In his preoccupation to find the right spots and record them exactly on the chart he turned the boat wrong and broached a full sea over the men on deck. They catcalled as they clutched the tied-down pots, the water sluicing from the hoods and shoulders of their oilskins. As soon as he headed the boat correctly, he rushed back to the rail above them to apologize. Before he could speak, Seth called, "Get your fuckin' mind off Jody, up there." None of them appeared angry.

He altered his abject words. "Hey, maybe *that'll* move your

asses!" But he was trembling as he returned to the wheel. Enough of a
sea to have washed one of them overboard.

After setting the deckload of pots, they returned for their others.
He relinquished the wheel until Akutan Pass, then took it through himself. The others slept, as fishermen do when they have the chance. He had
a following sea, and the boat all to himself, with the throb of the engine
and the crackle of radio voices for company. Jody would have been
good beside him. Tolly's voice called him over the radio to ask how
he was doing, and he answered with confidence.

Good to be fishing alongside Tolly Smith, and as skippers at that.
Tolly had changed little since the days when they had first bunked together in Swede's old salmon cannery and then finished the season
aboard rival seiners. He still wore his gold earring, and the former
happy swagger remained intact. When they strolled through Unalaska
to the bar, Tolly beamed at everyone and received a like response as he
bantered with them all by name, fishermen and natives and cannery
people alike. He had fished from his own boat, the *Juggernaut,* for three
years, and he owned one side of a partitioned house in the village. But
his wife, who, it was rumored, ran his life when they were together,
lived most of the time in Anacortes.

Hank had a key to Tolly's house. Actually, the door stayed un-
locked when nobody was inside: the key rather assured privacy. Hank
and Jody found it useful.

His relationship with Jody had lasted a year and a half. She was
independent as quicksilver. "Look around you, dear," she had said with
unusual gentleness when he had first proposed. "Women who marry
fishermen either divorce or get the shaft. First they compete with the
boat, and then they get stuck minding the kids."

"But I wouldn't be like that." He named some fishermen's mar-
riages that worked well. She countered with more that had soured or
been broken. But now she adjusted her life to his. When the *Nestor*
followed king crab from Kodiak to Dutch Harbor, she rode the trip. This
season in Dutch she worked supervising the shaker and pick lines on
one of the processor ships.

Once, when she became pregnant, he was certain it would settle
the marriage question. Instead, with virtually no discussion, she had an
abortion. It upset Hank deeply. He had thoughts of denunciation and

leaving. At a time when she might have needed his concern for her health, it was she who expended the effort.

"It wasn't your choice, Hank. My freedom would have ended, not yours."

"Goddam it, I make enough to support us."

"Who wants to be supported?"

"I love you, Jody."

"I know, I know." She said it softly, and, he thought, sadly. "That doesn't mean you have to own me, dear." Her hand ran down his arm. Whenever she touched him now it was with special tenderness. "I'd marry no man but a fisherman. And no fisherman but you . . ."

"Ah, Jody, why are we wasting our lives, then?"

"Maybe we're preserving them."

Aboard the *Nestor*, Hank steered as he puffed one of the special cigars she had ordered from San Francisco to celebrate his command. He would have thought, before experiencing it, that it would matter that she had slept with others before him. She wouldn't drift again, this he trusted. For his part, even when absent from her for weeks, he no longer joined the others in looking around if they pulled into an isolated cannery or town.

Her face: every inch of it had distinction, and the few years since their first meeting had only increased its vivacity and character. When her mouth drew into that wide smile and her eyes came alive, there was no painting that had captured such a woman. Even when angry. And when tender, when her expression softened toward him alone. . . . How easy had been all those little girls along the way, little Elsies who'd roll at his glance, and those occasional women like Sandra with whom he might have made it but for the bright shadow cast by Jody.

When his parents had visited him in Kodiak, Jody's simplicity and natural warmth had moved his father, who had come to regard Hank's Kodiak life with an interest close to envy, to comment privately, "That's a rare woman. You're some guy if you can handle her. Be like owning a Rembrandt or a Picasso."

They returned next day with a new deckload of pots. Hank was tense to try his prospect pots and see the fruits of his judgment, but the wind was blowing fifty and gusting higher. He had them put out the stabilizers and assigned two-hour wheel watches to kill time in a straight slow line back and forth. But his sleep in the separate skipper's cabin adjacent to the pilothouse was not relaxed. It was almost lonely up here, without the grunts and smells of the fo'c'sle. He had long possessed the fisherman's instinct to go under fast but jolt awake on the instant with some change in the engine rhythm. Now, with every hesitation of the boat his feet hit the deck. What if any of them dozed, with other boats jogging close by? Yet he had to trust his crew. Their jobs were interdependent and he couldn't do it alone. Back in the bunks he would have laughed at a nervous skipper, then begun to lose confidence in him. But, close to midnight, he jumped awake when the boat shuddered, and bounded to the wheelhouse. The boat was on course in a snowstorm, pushed by a following sea, nothing worse.

Dan leaped from the skipper's chair when he saw Hank.

Come on, thought Hank, let me earn it first.

"Shitty night, eh, Boss?" They traded some heavily colored anecdotes of terrible weather.

Hank forced himself back to bed, but he lay awake. For a while he addressed Jody in his mind. Sure he wanted children, wanted a family with all the stability and continuity it implied. Couldn't you give up part of your life to that, like other women? He stood ready to work with all he had, to provide.

Next time he popped awake, at one-thirty, the heavy motion of the boat had subsided. Not drifted into the lee of some island, near shoals? He hurried to the wheelhouse. Seth nodded to him from the skipper's chair but did not rise. Hank checked the radar and fathometer. Plenty of depth. It was the wind that had changed. "Why didn't you tell me it had stopped blowing?"

"What's there to tell until the waves go down? Say, while you're here, one of the hydraulic hoses looks thin, and that order from Seattle's a month late with new ones."

"I'll call around in the morning and see if we can borrow one," said Hank absently. He peered out at the lights of another boat a mile away. They remained constantly visible, rather than dipping and disappearing as they would in high waves. "Go rouse the guys. We'll start pulling." He waited with some unease to see if they would challenge starting work at two in the morning, but soon he heard their groans and yawns through the transom.

It took him longer to find his first pots than he had expected. In the dark, through alternating bursts of snow and clear weather, he cruised the area he had marked on the chart. The searchlight reflected on the wings of random birds and on the white crests of diminishing waves, at last glowed on a pink buoy. He maneuvered to it scrupulously, and earned a derisive hoot from Seth on deck when it turned out to be somebody else's. He, a naval officer, unable to handle simple navigation electronics!

"Let's pick her," called Seth.

"Put it back. I'm not operating that way."

At last he found his own. The water was rougher than he had hoped, but nobody complained. He watched, trying to appear calm, as the pot rose to the rail. A dozen females, nothing else. They had no room to stack it, with the full deckload of other pots.

He went to the next trial area and they raised a pot. As he concentrated on handling the boat, they shouted for him and he rushed back to the rail. Andy tossed up a big purple crab. It pivoted in the air as Hank caught it. Without gloves, the spines cut his fingers. Its legs and claws bent slowly at the joints, as if the crab were still seeking a hold on the seafloor.

"Your first keeper," said Seth. "Got to kiss it for us."

"Right you are." And he did so, with a sense of relief.

He surveyed all his prospect sites and set his pots on the best. But, day by day, the crab kept slipping away. The weather turned bad, with the deck sometimes sheeted in ice, yet Tolly in the week delivered a load to Dutch Harbor and was now fishing a second, while the *Nestor* had not come close to a full hold. The failure rested on his shoulders. He decided the crab had migrated southeast and followed to head them off, but he must have traveled too far. When he returned to the congestion of the fleet, he could see through binoculars that other boats were taking twenty to fifty keepers in a pot, while he himself drew five to ten if any. At night, after eighteen-hour days spent virtually alone in the pilothouse, his eyes still haunted the charts as he tried to figure some strategy. On the radio, voices with Norwegian accents griped their ritual about lousy catches, but then they returned to port with enough to unload.

A quiet settled over his crew as the days dragged by in work with small reward. They ate in an atmosphere of gravity and visited less casually to the pilothouse. All fishermen learn to accept periods when they catch nothing no matter how hard they work, but not when other boats around them are pulling it in. Hank sometimes stared in desperation at the sea itself, as if the crabs might give some sign like the jumper salmon. How could any man tell what moved beneath such vast water?

Finally he dragged their pots close to those of other boats and tried to make up for lost time hit-and-miss. By dogging Tolly's tracks he managed to set on the edge of a crab mass. Two days saved him. They worked around the clock without sleep, until they were all dragged beyond simple fatigue to a robot state. Once a rotten sea object came up in one of the pots. As Hank watched enviously from the solitude of the pilothouse, sick with exhaustion and confinement, the others halted work to toss it at each other with crazy abandon. When it fell apart, Seth bounded to the upper deck, cut loose a spare buoy, and started an even more frenzied toss that ended only when the thick plastic was shredded.

Their total harvest was about seven thousand crabs. Not necessarily a disaster. But then, other boats were taking less time to deliver twenty and thirty thousand.

Hank slept five hours, then took the wheel for the rest of the trip back to Dutch Harbor. He could hear the others snoring below him. No one had bothered to fix a meal, and he chewed tastelessly on a piece of salt meat and a candy bar, while his stomach ached from drinking too much coffee. Once in port, would Andy wire Joe Eberhardt to hurry back? If Joe didn't want to come, he'd probably let Andy and Seth hire replacements for themselves through the winter. What would Jody say? A cold wind had cleared the sky, and moonlight shone on a ghostly landfall of mountains and snow. The first sight of Unalaska Bay as he rounded a corner was the blaze of lights from the closest processor ship. Steam rose from its cookers like glowing cotton, and the stink of boiling crab gusted over the water. The shapes of raw mountains towered above. Except for Jody being there, Dutch Harbor was a sinister place to approach in the dark.

He tied at his cannery's ship outboard the *Northern Queen,* one of the large Seattle crab boats half again the size of his own. The snowcovered deck was deserted except for two cannery men in the hold throwing crabs into a wide canvas bucket. Even a glance showed the crabs tight-packed as honeycomb, compared to the swimming space left in his own tank. Seth, who had jumped over to tie their lines, stopped and looked at it too. Hank debated staying in the pilothouse until his crew had gone ashore, then decided to face them if they had anything to say, and went down to the galley.

They seemed more concerned with taking showers in the bunk-house beside the processor ship and then with finding a boatride across the channel to Unalaska Village and the Elbow Room.

"If Jody brings a boat, you're welcome to ride," said Hank. "But I'll have to call around. She may be working."

"We'll launch *you* and paddle you over," said Seth lightly.

He would rather they had told him off.

In the wheelhouse he tried to rouse Jody on the sideband, but nobody responded from either the receiver at Tolly's house or at Pan Alaska where she worked. Before deciding what to do, he climbed aboard the *Northern Queen* to learn their plans. As soon as he opened the door to the big galley he was enveloped in smoke and noise. Around the table sat Arnie Larson, the skipper, and his four crewmen, as well as their wives and girlfriends and, hunched together nursing coffee, three of the jobless men who haunted the boats. Arnie was strumming a guitar and singing in Norwegian as he and the other crewmen played poker. Their women snuggled against them or held their arms. The table was a scramble of Scotch and rum bottles, butt-filled ashtrays, stacks of change no smaller than quarters and bills up to twenty dollars, and a hock of red salted lamb with a carving knife stuck in it.

"Hey, Hank!" exclaimed Arnie heartily. "Move over, you guys, make room." Arnie was as big as a Viking. He had a full beard and eyes that were simultaneously warm and calculating. "How you do out dere on your first trip, hah?"

Hank shrugged. "Ain't stolen your quota yet."

"Ha ha ha ha. Hey." Arnie pointed to Tom, the jobless kid closest to the galley. "Somebody get Hank a glass. Vant to deal in here, skipper?" He pushed the bottles and meat toward Hank.

"Thanks, but I'm looking for somebody."

"Jody was down here a few minutes ago. She went to tie the skiff, so you better wait here."

Hank accepted the place offered him. He drank a slug of Scotch and cut himself some lamb in thin slices as the Norwegians did. It was an acquired taste—the meat was salted raw and had a strong flavor. "This Squarehead food is terrible," he called over the music as Arnie raised the volume of his song.

"Ja, have some more."

"Thanks."

Jody arrived with a flourish. She kissed him and declared: "Out ten days, you must have plugged the boat!"

"Sure, sure."

"How many?"

Didn't have to quiz him in public. "Talk about it later."

She searched his face. "I saw Andy and Seth outside, and they wouldn't tell me either. That bad, eh?"

He would not have expected his crew to brag, but it bothered him afresh that they were ashamed. No use making a secret; it would be known as soon as the cannery weighed them out. "Seventy-one hundred."

Arnie stopped his guitar for a moment, there was silence, and then the noises resumed.

"You look tired," she said quietly. "Let's go across."

"We'll wait and take the guys over." He poured some Scotch in his glass and handed it to her.

At the end of the hand, Arnie threw down his cards. "Ah, bullshit, play me out a couple times, I got to stretch." He climbed from behind the table, tapped Hank in passing, and motioned discreetly for him to follow. They went up in the wheelhouse. It was twice as large as the *Nestor*'s, with electronic gear several degrees more sophisticated. Arnie spread out a chart of the area that was full of pencil notations. "Ja, Hank, you show me where you set your pots. Maybe I give you some ideas."

An hour later, Hank and Jody were headed for Tolly's house among the cannery trailers and equipment, then past weathered little homes lighted by a single bulb or by kerosene lamps. Snow blew around their legs. She sought his hand inside the flap of his parka. "Bad out there, huh?"

"Couldn't have been worse."

"Sure it could. You paid expenses, and then some."

"They all saw how the *Nordic Queen*'s hold was packed. Dan might stick it since he's been on the beach so long, but why should Andy and Seth scratch with me after a good summer in the Bering and Kodiak? The way I'm doing, they certainly won't follow me to Adak next month when the weather turns really bad."

She produced a joint and they shared it, but the sweet smoke failed to calm him. "I'll tell you another thing," he said in a burst. "Skippering's miserable. I'll never make it. Jesus! You just stand by the wheel all day. I've turned flabby already from standing around instead of working. Then when you fall into bed, there's no good tired feeling like you've earned it. Your bones don't ache, your head does. You lay awake and worry it won't go right. Then it doesn't, and the whole blame's yours."

They passed the long frame building that housed the Elbow Room. The thudding rhythm of rock emanated from inside like shock waves. "I don't feel like sharing you," she said, "but I guess you need a stiff one."

"No, they'll all ask how I did. If you can stand me, let's go home."

In Tolly's two-room house, heavy with the smell of the oil stove, she heated water and he sponged down as they exchanged alternate drinks from a can of beer and puffs from another joint. To start a more agreeable mood, he asked: "How's life at the cannery?"

"I love it there or I wouldn't go for twelve hours every day. All the crab you can eat. It's fun to settle the Filipino girls' bitches about who gives who the evil eye. And the couple of men are pissed that they have to answer to a woman, so about once a day I have to stand them down. The plant manager kept pawing my ass until I said he'd get a knee in his balls. Canneries are nice. They keep you off the lousy boats where you might have to answer to yourself."

"Oh, boy. That puts me back in place." He took her hands. How small she was beside him, despite her strength. Paying attention for once, he found her expression vulnerable, divided between humor and the deep seriousness she seemed bent on avoiding. He wanted to hold her like a child. "Hey, I love you, Jody."

"Well, Hank," she said softly, "I love you too."

Without bothering to dry his chest he bent down and lifted her in his arms.

They had just settled in the bedroom with the light turned out, when someone started pounding the door. It was Seth, with Andy and Dan behind him in the snow. Seth held a bottle by the neck. Boozed and come to tell me off, thought Hank.

"We saw your light just go out." Seth's burly face was expressionless. "But we ain't through with you tonight. Going to invite us in?"

"Come on."

They settled solemnly around the table. Seth broke the seal on the bottle. He took a long swig, then handed it to Dan, who did the same and passed it to Andy.

Andy cleared his throat and pursed his eyebrows, as if he was preparing to speak. Instead, with almost a sigh, he handed Hank the bottle. When Hank had drunk, Seth took it from his hands and started it on another round. They were all frowning, and silent.

A half hour later, when they had drained the bottle, Seth muttered thickly: "Andy! You're deck boss."

Andy rose unsteadily and raised his arm. Hank watched him with swaying vision, thinking in a person outside himself: they going to beat me up?

"Okay . . . Skipper. Next time out we'll find the fuckers. So don't worry."

Dan banged his ham of a fist on the table. "That's what we say, Boss."

Seth reached over, tousled his hair—more like tore it off—and declared: "Yeah, you asshole, don't worry. We'll find crab, even if we have to dangle you for bait."

24

MANEUVERS

HANK and his crew on the *Nestor* fished the king crab season around Dutch Harbor during October, then followed the openings westward along the Aleutians. The weather was predictably rough and cold. He could not shake his initial tension, but he learned from other skippers to keep stomach medicines in the wheelhouse to help him through. (The shelves of the single store in Unalaska were full of them.) As for fishing, he became adept or lucky enough to set their pots in a few good schools of crab and to scratch adequately in the intervals. Thus he survived the season without further disgrace. As they pitched back up the coast toward Kodiak, with Jody aboard, Dan produced a mandolin from his bunk, they all sang and joked, and he relaxed at last.

His experience as a skipper had already affected him more than service as a naval officer without a command had ever done. Granted, he found the new disciplines onerous—to push himself under the tension of being responsible for others' safety and livelihood; to skip meals that made his mouth water while still growing heavier; to watch the relieving horseplay on deck without participating; to make decisions he could not retract. But he liked being able to speak and know they would listen. He had come to expect their mild deference as his due. When the pots came up full, he felt it was more his doing than he ever had as a deckhand. Above all, he enjoyed chasing the crab and figuring their movements. There was one particular night he decided he would not forget. As hail hit the windows and he maneuvered the boat successfully to keep seas from breaking over the men below, a new string of pots came up plugged from the start with fat keepers. They were fishing untried grounds. He had calculated the location three days before during one of their sleep breaks while the others snored below. At sight of the full pots, he felt a crazy jubilation. This is my time and this is my place, he thought. It can never be better!

They reached Kodiak a few days before Christmas, in time for Andy to take his wife and two children down to Bellingham, where their families lived. "Keep in touch," said Hank. "There's the Kodiak shrimp opening in January."

"Joe never fishes shrimp this time of year."

Earlier, Hank would have felt the need to justify and defend. Now he stated: "Fish and Game predicts a super haul, and Kodiak's my territory." He had no intention of being idle after deciding to save in earnest for a boat. Andy must have sensed his firmness.

"I'll give you numbers where you can find me. Old lady's going to be pissed."

"Say I promised her a bunch of checks she hadn't counted on. Won't hurt to get our share."

When he phoned Joe Eberhardt in Oregon, the voice had a mellow growl in contrast to the uptight one of Joe the driving skipper. "Go ahead, if you want to shrimp. The more the boat fishes the more she pays. You know where our trawl gear's stored. Just get to the Bering Sea with a deckload of pots by the March opening. Yeah, the house is coming along, and Linda says howdy. You'll see us when you bring the boat to Seattle for May overhaul. Be good to take over again."

Right, thought Hank. And I'm going to grab every possible bit of experience before I hand her back.

"You've changed, *Mister* Crawford," declared Adele Henry at Christmas dinner. He had just returned from phoning his parents, to yawn over helping to draft a protest to Washington demanding immediate removal of the Japanese and Soviet fishing fleets from Alaskan waters. "Jones, remember that bright young Hank Crawford who saved you from the State Department, with ideas crackling from his fingertips?" She wriggled her fingers to demonstrate, then leaned over her plate and made a bulldog face at him. "You don't speak French any more or read Baudelaire, do you? Jody, does he ever talk to you about anything but fish?"

"If he did I'd yell rape. I'd think it was somebody else."

"Come on, Mother," said Jones. "Who ever heard of a Kodiak fisherman talking French?"

Hank felt himself blushing as he played with his wine glass. "I'm too busy now learning my trade, Adele. Who'd listen to me anyhow, until I amount to something?"

"He does pay his dues to the Marketing Association," said Jones.

"Wrong kind of dues for a fellow like Hank," said Adele. "Back in Washington—I'll let Jones give you the details—do you realize who's blocking a law that would give American fishermen control of the fish the foreigners are stealing? The State Department, that's who, the State Department! And do you know why they won't let us have a law? They're afraid we'll offend the Russians, who'd like to fish us bare and bury us besides. And because we'll upset the poor Japs who just a few years back were torturing and killing our boys. That's what we're fighting!"

"The *bad* thing," said Ivan sententiously, "it's that everybody boozes too much and they don't go to church like they ought." Only the newcomers to the table, Seth and Dan, paid any attention.

"Well," said Jones, "she's right. We've got to be strong back here to bargain with the processors for a decent price, and then we've got to be strong to face up to the government that's supposed to be looking out for us. Now, Ted and Maggie . . . that's Senator Ted Stevens and Senator Magnuson, I've met them both." He paused for effect. "They told me down in Seattle not long ago when I was part of a delegation—and Adele was there, she'll back me up—they said their Senate Commerce Committee's going to push hard next spring for a two-hundred-mile law. That would extend the fishing we control from twelve miles to two hundred, you see. But they told me they need our support in any way we can make it loud and clear."

"Then you're damned right, I'll do some letters," said Hank.

"I'll thank you when I see them," said Adele. "Jody, you make sure they're good ones. Daddy, carve more turkey; the plate's empty. Seth and Dan, you're new here, but I want you to know that anybody on Hank's boat is always welcome. I'll just say we don't stand on formality so long as we mind our manners. Isn't that right, Steve?"

"Yes, ma'am," said Steve uneasily. His face had turned wider and redder, and gray had begun to spot his hair and beard, but he appeared no more comfortable at Adele's table than he had ten years before. His big hands crawled over each other in his lap when he was not exposing them for as short a time as possible to cut or fork his food.

While Adele and Jody cleared the table and stacked the dishes (Jody had promised Hank beforehand not to make it an issue), the table talk returned to the new steel-hulled boat Jones Henry was having built in Seattle, and a monologue from Jones directed at Hank on the features and merits of work from different boatyards. "This is a fishery on the move up here," Jones declared. "In my short time I've seen boats of all kinds turn obsolete. They're experimenting now with fiberglass hulls that you'll never have to paint or maintain, but they're still too expensive. Next boat after this one, mebbe."

"Would you rather have a bank or a cannery hold the mortgage on your boat?" asked Hank.

"Bank, bank, when it's one that understands the fish business. If you owe it to the cannery you can't bargain special price deals." He winked. "Then again, cannery's more likely not to foreclose in a bad year."

"Yeah," Seth broke in, "I hear skippers get settlements at the end of a season that the crew never hears about, no matter how hard they've busted their asses."

"Watch your talk in front of a lady," said Steve anxiously. For a moment they focused on Adele, as Seth apologized and she accepted, and then the women were ignored again.

"Well," said Jones, "you'd better understand, the skipper who owns his boat takes all the risk. He's got to meet the boat payments. And insurance too, more and more of it these days. Hank! Let me get a pencil and show you how I've opened up my new boat for maximum hold and deck space—I figured out a trick here myself and it'll be the only ninety-foot combination shrimper-crabber in Kodiak to have it. You other fellows are going to be interested in this too. Steve and Ivan, they've seen it, so you can move closer."

"Gonna be some boat, Boss," said Steve. "But like I've said before, all that new gear to figure out? The old stuff *works*. Me and Ivan know it back and forth."

"If I was to allow it, you'd still be pulling web by hand," said Jones. "Me, I'm only fifty-two, and I'm ready to try the new things. Hank, I'm going crabbing to the Bering Sea with this boat—starting fresh on new grounds, just like I did with the shrimp ten years ago. If you're taking the *Nestor* up there next March we'll be greenhorn skippers together. With all that's happening out there, I want to see some of the action."

"One thing I don't like about this new boat," said Adele. "He'll be less easy to track down, fishing out there where it ought to be left to the bachelors."

Jones, his head turned from her, winked.

Hank learned the meaning of his reaction when they started fishing alongside each other on the winter shrimp grounds north of the island. Many wives, Adele among them, owned home sideband radios and monitored the fleet from their homes only a few miles away. Adele called Jones whenever she chose, as if it were a telephone. One morning, while Jones was in the sweat of a haul, with seas breaking over deck and winds blowing in the forties, she demanded to know the exact time of his arrival in harbor so that she could plan dinner. Jones answered patiently. As soon as she signed off, a chorus of anonymous clucks and hoots came in from other boats.

The designated radio frequencies and the sideband were a vast party line of communications for skippers. They complained, swapped knowledge, compared catches, sought emergency parts, often merely rambled. Out westward Hank had remained on the fringes even after taking a command, because the talk was so dominated by Norwegian words and experiences. Now, back in his own Kodiak country, and with Jones around, he became an easy talker, hedging some information on his hauls and sharing the rest. Jones and he developed their own code, and Jones sometimes steered him onto better grounds.

Hank delivered his shrimp to Swede Scorden's cannery. On the first occasion, he sauntered through the processing lines, enjoying his new role as he greeted anybody he recognized from the old days. He avoided Sandra's old desk near Swede's office, occupied now by a girl who appeared less bright and intelligent, but once inside his feet lifted easily to face Swede's on the desk. The bottle and glass were slid toward him, and he caught a cigar.

Swede had aged more than might be expected over two years, and his gestures now included a restless glance and hands that always fidgeted with some object.

"Making lots of money?" asked Hank for openers.

"Why ask that?"

"Just want to make sure my six cents a pound's fair share, buddy."

Swede took the comment seriously. "It's fair, it's fair. You know yourself there's not more than fifteen percent recovery from these little shrimp, so figure nearly forty cents a pound we pay you for the parts we can use. And I hear you fellows want to squeeze us for more. Shrimp only pay to keep the plant open. They're so expensive to process I couldn't make a real profit unless I could double the capacity while holding down the work force. We count on big runs of humpies and dogs to keep us in business. And look at the low salmon hauls for the last couple of summers. The fact is, for three years I've operated in the red, and Seattle's going to shut us down if they can't find somebody to bail us out. Don't think this cannery's alone. Incidentally, do you ever hear from my former secretary?"

"Nope."

"Sandy was a nice kid. Your loss, you dumb bastard."

You'd have to meet Jody, Hank thought.

Jones closed his season early to pick up his new boat in time for the Bering Sea crab. He delivered his final load from the *Adele H,* tied her in the harbor, and prepared her for the transfer to another owner. Hank, as he moored at another float, could see Jones' wiry frame bounding over the deck and superstructure, and the hulks of Steve and Ivan moving with moribund slowness.

He met Ivan walking toward the ramp, carrying a box on one shoulder and a spare crankshaft on the other as if he were burdened by the weight of two crosses. "What's Boss want to go sell our boat for?" he demanded of Hank. "New boat won't have our smell to it, so big it needs another man. How's Boss going to find somebody that can fish as good as me and Steve together?"

Hank shook his head sympathetically.

Steve followed behind. While not as miserable as Ivan, he was glum enough. "Hey, cheer up," said Hank. "Jones Henry's not changing, just the boat."

"Funny thing, Hank, that's the trouble. Jones ain't the same." He put down his seabag. "Son of a bitch, he can't look enough at the new gear in magazines, then he talks about it till you fall asleep. This new boat, she's got more fuckin' stuff . . ." He glanced over his shoulder toward the *Adele H*, and lowered his voice. "We've never fished but the one net on that drum, and now we've got to figure out all the tackle on a double-rig trawl. That's the big change I'm scared of. And then there's one little thing after another he's added. Needs a new man. None of it's going to be like the old fishing."

"Steve, you're one of the best fishermen I've ever known. You'll have that double rig down in three sets."

"But the new guy won't understand Ivan the way I do, won't want to put up with him. I see changing everywhere, and it was all better the old way."

Hank strolled along the boardwalk floats to where Jones stood prying the letters ADELE from the bow of his boat. He reached out to catch the A as it loosened, and they exchanged grins.

"They'll survive it," said Jones. "Wish I had my design to do over. Just thought of something last night. Finish this and I'll draw it. You'll be interested. While I've got you. We need a better price for shrimp this year. I want you to be part of the negotiating bunch. I figure we'll shock the canneries by asking for ten cents." He winked. "Settle for eight."

"Sure they can afford it, Jones?"

"Them guys? They're gold-plated; don't let your friend Swede shit you. Down in Seattle you ought to see the price of shrimp in the stores. They've never paid us our share. Plenty of fishermen around here support a strike. More than one has a new boat to pay off."

"Not the cannery's fault."

"You a fisherman or a cannery manager? Listen, a cannery needs a strong, modern fleet or it loses the product. You don't have seafood running into your nets any more, the way it was when I first started fishing up here. Oh no. A new boat with the latest gear is the only way you can do it. I'll tell you, we have to stay atop, or fishermen from other parts of the country'll move in. Adele reads a lot, she's good for something. Back on the East Coast you find the Russians have fished out everything worth taking, down off Oregon and Washington it's no better. Where's the only place a fisherman can still pull more than scratch, eh? You're coming to your own at a good time, Hank. Mebbe it ain't the old easygoing life—has Joe Eberhardt stuck you with the tax forms and

Social Security? No? Well, you're lucky, so far. Paperwork the government expects might get worse every year, and you might have to deprive the old lady of a few dresses to keep up on the latest electronics, and you might have to look harder to find the fish, but I'm glad I'm still around to take my part. It's something to see, I say. This year we're going to fight the canneries to make a real jump in prices we get. That'll give us the strength of money. Next year, we'll start on the foreigners. Nobody else is going to do it for us."

The final letter of ADELE dropped into Hank's hand, and Jones patted the clean bow. "Nice boat here. Wish I could keep her along with the other. I'd make you permanent skipper."

Hank was genuinely flattered, and he said so.

"Truth is, you'd better think fast about buying your first boat. Steel's going up, I don't know what all. Talk to your friend Swede about financing. Once you've got that first boat you've got tax shelters and capital construction to help you." Steve and Ivan returned, glum as before. Jones ignored their mood as he gave instructions for shutting down. "One more thing, Hank. You going to marry that fine girl? Adele pesters me over and over, as if I'd know. She's got no idea what men talk about on the boats."

"Tell Adele that if Jody said yes, I'd do it tomorrow."

"My old lady's a fixer. Dont say that if you don't mean it."

The shrimp season wore its course into February. Hank had struck a good pace with his crew at the start, but without Jones around he began to grow restless. One day, in the heat of bringing the bag to the rail, when he saw better than they did some mistakes they were making, he found himself yelling at them, in the manner of Joe Eberhardt. On deck the men continued as before in handling the potentially dangerous weight, until Dan jerked loose the pin and emptied the shrimp. Then, led by Seth, they started pelting him with trash fish from the haul. He started to laugh, but they did not.

"You know what's the trouble," he said at dinner to break the silence. "I'm up there jumping out of my skin because I see things you don't, and I can't do it myself. Maybe that's what bugs Joe, too."

"It's what skippers have to put up with," said Andy.

"We'll take that shit from Joe," added Seth, "but not from a relief skipper."

Hank glanced at their stern faces. Dan was in the pilothouse relieving the wheel, but it was still three to one. He had not thought of
being skipper in those terms before.

When the *Adele III* came gleaming into the harbor, Hank was on
hand to catch its lines. Adele and Jody watched also. She was a splendid
white boat, with a high bow and a wide afterdeck, so much larger than
the old *Rondelay* and *Adele H* that Jones looked dwarfed in his enclosed pilothouse. He tooted whenever they waved, until Adele exclaimed, "For heaven's sake ignore him, or he'll never bring it in." She
had packed boxes of cheese, smoked salmon, cake, and other special
food. Hank had brought bottles and jugs. An open house began on the
boat as soon as the lines were secured, announced by a final tattoo on
the whistle.

Indeed, compared to Jones' former boats, this was a palace. Even
though it was only twenty feet longer than the first *Adele H*, the en-
largement had doubled Jones' former deck and hold capacities. Soon
the boat was crowded with other fishermen who came to admire. Jones
held court by the wheel, showing off his twin radars, scanning sonar, and
fine-tuned depth recorder. On deck Steve, his wide face flushed with
pleasure, showed off the big vapor lights, the high-pressure hydraulics,
and a variety of lesser innovations. Only Ivan remained aloof. When
Jones led friends through to the engine room to inspect the new diesel
and the special circulating pumps, he pretended to be mending his
clothes. In the galley, Adele presided over food and coffee, but the
booze, by Jones' specific direction, stood unattended on the table for
help-yourself.

The inside was soon blue with smoke and shoulder to shoulder
with people. Backed against the far end of the galley table, Harry the
new crewman banged his guitar and roared songs. Others joined in or
shouted their unending exchanges on gear and engines above the noise.
It turned dark around four. Outside it had started snowing, but groups
continued to spill over the deck and onto the float. Despite stacks of
plastic glasses, bottles passed overhead and went the rounds by open
neck. At one point on deck some Norwegian crewmen burst into a boot-
stomping dance. At another, a small fistfight ended with a man in the
water and another snuffing blood into the snow. (Neither left the party,
but the man overboard came inside.) When the alcohol was gone—

Hank had brought six gallon jugs of whiskey plus several bottles of Scotch and rum—the momentum continued regardless.

By some time in the early morning—other booze had come and gone in the interim—most people had staggered home or back to their boats. Suddenly, there stood Ivan, swaying and popeyed, his face as stony as Frankenstein. A bottle dangled in his grip and the other hand was bleeding. He clumped across the room on legs like straight pieces of wood, smashed open the door that stood ajar, and continued out on deck in a straight line. Steve stumbled after him, calling for help. Jones and Hank wobbled to their feet and followed. When Ivan reached the back rail he turned and started swinging the bottle. "Fuckin' change," he roared. "Change ain't gonna—change ain't—fuckin'—" The bottle broke against the side, but he continued waving the jagged neck. It was Jody, unsteady as the rest, who coaxed him to drop the glass stump into the water and to come back inside. His hoarse, guttural diatribe continued. They could not sit him down. He smashed whatever he encountered.

Steve planted himself face to face with Ivan, sighed, and knocked him unconscious.

By dawn they were all asleep, flopped across the table and over the galley deck. It had been a good bash, one discussed appreciatively among the boats for the rest of the season.

Fridays, as Jones said everybody knew, were only days to start a fishing trip if you wanted disaster. He wanted everything right. When Adele bustled aboard with a potted plant for his cabin, he wasted no time in explanation. It left the quickest way possible, into the water. "Jesus, woman, don't you know you never bring dirt and green things aboard a fishing boat?" His upset was so genuine she did not become offended.

On the deck below, Ivan, wallowing in shame, recovered briefly to mutter to Hank, "Shouldn't even a woman come aboard the last day. Next thing she'll bring some umbrella or black suitcase, and then we've had it."

"Shouldn't even be saying the words, you drunk Aleut," said Steve heartily. When he had become satisfied that Ivan's lapse with the booze was temporary, he lost no chance to rub it in.

"Don't call me that."

Up above them, Jones grumped: "Don't do to take chances, especially with a new boat that's just breaking in."

"Of course not," Adele said soothingly.

Jones lowered his voice. "You never bring green on boats, never even paint 'em green. You don't see that color in the fleet, do you? They say it makes the boat want to seek the green on land. Same way with dirt. Shouldn't even talk about it."

"You're jumpy as a colt."

"Best not to mention animals. Come on, let's get you off the boat, woman. I'll buy you lunch in town."

Hank, an auditor to both conversations, motioned the new crewman to the float. He explained quietly that umbrellas meant rain, and that a black suitcase resembled a doctor's bag. "That's the best I can figure those two." He grinned. "Here's one I can't figure, but pay attention. Don't talk about horses, don't say the word if they're on a superstition kick. I guess you've been around long enough never to whistle up a storm in the pilothouse, or to replace a hatch cover upside down to make the boat think she can go that way herself. Even an enlightened guy like me worries about these, from habit. Oh . . . with Ivan and Steve, you don't want to whistle on deck either. They once threw me overboard for doing that."

Harry, a big, bright kid with glasses that were always fogged, said, "It's bullshit, but thanks for telling me." He had come from a small boat with a young skipper and crew.

On Saturday under a bright sun, the *Nestor* and the *Adele III* started the four-day trip in company to Dutch Harbor, and thence to the Bering Sea. They each carried a deckload of Jones' pots—Hank's were stored at Dutch. Jones' new boat held nearly ninety seven-bys, twice that of the *Nestor*. The wind being westerly and moderate, they took the more sheltered route down Shelikof Strait around the northern and western sides of the island.

As they cruised through Whale Pass, Hank experienced his usual remembrance of the *Billy II* disaster, of Spitz and the red-haired Pete. Even at slack current the tide rips boiled and kicked his bow. "Guess we've experienced something here together," he said to Jones over the sideband. "Remember?"

"Why do you think I jumped from *Adele One* to *Three* in naming my new boat? Watch your helm." Jones refused to converse again until they had passed into the wide Kupreanof Strait.

Jody came from below. Her auburn hair hung fluffy and loose in a ponytail, her denim shirt was crisp beneath a bunchy checked wool jacket, and her eyes were lively. "Hey, Skipper, you going to eat up here or have lunch with the fellows?"

"I don't know. You able to take the wheel?"

"That's what the cook's supposed to do at chowtime."

The Shelikof seldom allowed easy winter passage. Before they had run its eighty miles the wind shifted, and a cold, clear northwesterly began pushing their stern. It blew spray that coated the superstructure with a film of ice. Not a buildup—on Jones' boat nearby he saw no one on deck chipping, so he was not concerned. However, he followed Jones closer to the mainland for a lee. The snow peaks towered above the *Adele III*. They were higher and more jagged than those of Kodiak Island thirty miles across the strait, their lonely tops swirling with ice smoke against a blue sky. While the others steered and slept, Hank studied his charts and Coast Pilot to make sure he knew every inlet of the area. There were several, but the Pilot described none without cautions. As the mountains turned pastel reds under the last of the sun, he was glad not to be alone.

Darkness released the light of a full moon. It gleamed on the white mountains to make them appear even higher and more impersonal than during the day and glistened on the thin ice along his anchor and rigging. A moon path outlined Jones Henry's boat, shining on the bars of the clumsy square crab pots stacked astern. Her little green starboard light and plain masthead light seemed incredibly precious amid the sinister dazzle of the wilderness.

Around midnight the wind rose. Suddenly ice started to build on the anchor and chain that Hank was watching, from a shiny skin to a thick padding with a whiteness of its own. Hank could feel the change in handling the boat. Her quick roll turned sluggish. "All hands on deck to chop ice," he yelled down the transom. "Jody, get up here and take the wheel so I can go too."

"*Nestor*, do you read me?" barked Jones on the radio.

"*Adele Three*, what do you make of it?"

"Run for shelter and chip like hell."

309

"Puale Bay, right?"

"Western end's all shoal. I'll guide, been there before, but study your chart in case anything . . ."

"Jody's at the wheel, I'm going on deck."

"No, you're skipper, *she* can't handle, *stay put.*"

During their brief exchange, the shrouds had expanded their diameters by an inch.

"*Nestor,* this is *Adele,* turning now, hang on, turning into it, might be rough."

Hank shouted a warning to the others as he took the wheel to move from a southwest to a north heading. The difference brought leaps of spray, first across their beam, then over the starboard quarter so high that it shot diagonal arcs of water across the entire deck. Some of the water turned to ice in midair, and clattered like pebbles. The boat became a bull to handle—it barely responded, and the wheel kept kicking from his hands.

Jody dressed for deck against his protestations. "Promise you'll tie yourself to something. *Please* stay clear of the rail." He reached to hug her but she slipped away, grave-faced, blowing a kiss. Went as casually as he would have gone. Is that how wives felt with their men at sea? he wondered in fear.

The wind began pushing the weighted boat so that it paused at each portside roll before recovering. He strained to watch the shoreline on radar, watch the plunging lights of Jones' boat ahead, watch the hunched figures under the deck lights, coordinating it all in his mind as he muttered prayers for Jody's safety. How could he reverse course if she fell over? He remembered the way the water closed like lead.

On deck, Andy quickly took charge. Thank God he assigned Jody the sheltered winches to pound. Her quick-moving figure was so small compared to the others. Spray kept arcing. It froze on their rain gear and crackled off like fine glass. When Dan beat the shrouds, tubes of ice splintered over his head and shoulders.

On the radio, Jones was calling the Coast Guard to report their position and danger. Hank wondered if Adele back in Kodiak could hear any of it.

Seth climbed the rope ladder, so coated with ice he had to kick footholds with his feet, and straddled the boom to hammer his way along

310

it. His progress was marked by crashing chunks. Each time he paused, spray froze to weld his legs to the metal tube.

The crab pots astern stacked three high gathered ice throughout their honeycombs of web, beyond the reach of hammers. As Hank watched, their mass solidified into a wall that reflected back the deck lights on its lumpy surface. With each portside roll their weight dipped the deck into the water.

He grabbed the mike. "Jones, your pots, I'm dumping them."

A pause, then: "Okay on that, Hank. Be careful. I'm chancing it with mine, only a half mile before we get the lee."

He called instructions to Andy. They tried to reach the top pots for a hookhold and nearly slid into the water on the roll. Like climbing a glass mountain. Then Jody, the lightest of them, slid along the deck to the wall and started up. Hank shouted for them to stop and gunned desperately for shore.

At last, abeam of Cape Aklek, land began to shelter them from the spray-bearing wind and the ice they chipped did not re-form.

Hank, having read his Coast Pilot, could observe to Jones: "Not supposed to be good anchorage in here. Do you know any spots?"

"Negative on that, Hank. We're safe from the icing, but not from the woolies. Not firm enough bottom for us to tie together and pass the time. Might drag. We'll move closer to the western side and anchor with five hundred feet swing space between us. Suit you?"

"Roger. We'll drop our hook and sack out. See you in the morning."

"Strongly suggest, Captain, you keep an anchor watch."

Hank learned the truth of it quickly. The wind, blowing through low passes, gained momentum as through a tunnel. Twice it struck in williwaws of more than hundred-mile velocity, and the anchor bounced on its groaning chain.

"This is fishing vessel *Delta*," declared a stolid voice over the radio. Hank recognized at once his old enemy, Nels Hanson. "All boats and Coast Guard, please read, please relay, possible Mayday."

Hank leaped up and turned it loud.

"This is *Delta, Delta,* icing heavy and fast. Possible Mayday. I'm located ten mile due north of Marmot Island, Sealion Rocks to port quarter, running for shelter Tonki Bay. Heading into wind, icing heavy and fast. Bad bow list to starboard. Possible Mayday. Request Coast Guard assistance. Fishing vessel *Delta*. Mayday." The distress call was delivered in a voice that showed no more emotion than his old orders to Hank and Seth to hop to, when they had been slaves on the deck of his shrimper three years before.

The radio bands became tensely busy with relays. The others aboard the *Nestor* had gone to bed, but one by one they appeared in the pilothouse to listen. The event was taking place to the north of Kodiak, miles away, but it shared with them the same wind.

"He can't buck into that," said Jones on the sideband. "Nels should know better. He's too far from land to make a run for it; he'd better put his stern to the wind and ride it."

"This is *Delta*. I've reversed course to slow icing. Boat has little control. Got a strong set toward Sealion Rocks. Icing has slowed, but sixty-knot wind still piling it on. Inflatable raft standing by. Request assistance. Mayday."

The Coast Guard station near Kodiak started talking. A helicopter had just taken to the air, and the cutter *Storis* was steaming from Womens Bay en route.

"That Coast Guard chopper," said Jones Henry, "he's committing suicide to fly night rescue in this weather."

"At least he's got the moonlight," said Hank.

Nels' emotionless voice spoke again. "We're hammering the ice, but she's pulled us below the starboard rail, flooded part of the engine room. Men not holding out good, not my best crew. I'm signing off to go hammer, make 'em hop to it. Not going to abandon."

"Can't even stop now shitting on his guys," muttered Seth in a husky voice.

"What's he got the life raft for?" said Hank.

Andy cleared his throat. His voice was husky also. "Ever been on a raft with icing in that kind of blow?"

An hour later the Coast Guard said that the helicopter had begun icing at search altitude and was forced to abandon the search until morning. ETA of the cutter *Storis* was another two hours.

No further communication from the *Delta*. Outside in their own bay the wind howled and moaned, and the moonlight continued to burn on the snow mountains.

"I reckon," said Jones, "he was chasing that one last deckload before the season closed. Poor Nels was a fisherman through and through, he pushed to the limit."

"Poor fuckin' crew," said Seth.

Both their voices were hushed.

At 4:00 A.M. the Coast Guard announced that the cutter *Storis* had taken aboard two survivors of the fishing vessel *Delta* and that their search continued for the third. No names, pending notification of next of kin.

Jody started to cry. Hank was choked himself as he held her. His feeling against Nels had long ceased to matter, whether as a survivor or the missing. He didn't know the others. Collectively they were his own blood and body.

His arms held Jody tightly as he stared at the terrible glistening ice that made a monolith sculpture of his pots and rigging, that weighted his stern to sluggish incapacity. "Marry me," he murmured. "We might have died tonight. Life's as tricky as that."

"Hank, darling," she said quietly, "we've got it all without the preacher bullshit. What difference?"

"To me, if not to you. I want it declared and known."

"Then you'll want kids."

He knew she was right, that some day he might try to force it, but: "Only when you do."

"What if I don't, ever, want to be tied like that?"

"Your choice, Jody." In the years ahead, something would happen to make it work out.

The wind exploded in a williwaw that shook the boat. He kicked the bow into it to ease the anchor strain, then returned to the subject.

"You know I have a past, Hank. From time to time you'll come up against talk."

"But your present and future's with me."

"Yes. Yes . . ."

Their watch continued in the pilothouse to sunrise. Hank sat in the upholstered skipper's chair with Jody on his lap. The radio sputtered intermittently with voices but no news. At eight, with the snowtops glowing pink and the wind continuing to blow, the announcement came:

313

Nels and a crewman rescued, one crewman presumed dead but the search for the body continuing.

"The dead are dead," said Hank. "We're alive. Marry me today." She studied his face, then nodded.

When Hank approached Jones Henry by radio: "Adele ain't going to like missing this."

"We'll get her to stand by on somebody's boat radio."

"That's right, and you can get a preacher the same way."

"No, Jones, we like the idea of you doing it. Somebody from Kodiak can dictate you the words. You're a commanding officer, aren't you?" Despite the shadow of the *Delta* he started to laugh, he was so happy. "You're official as any captain on the *Queen Mary*."

Jody, now that she had consented, thoroughly entered into the spirit. She took the microphone. "Do it for both of us, Jones." She said it in a voice so persuasive that it settled everything but the time.

They were married that afternoon in the wilderness bay, as the northwester roared through the mountain clefts and the snow steamed around the tops. The *Nestor* and the *Adele III* tugged at their frail anchors. Seth stood as best man, Andy and Dan as bemused witnesses. They could hear the conventional emotion in Adele's voice as she spoke for matron of honor a hundred air miles away from a Kodiak radio. Within sight, Jones aboard the *Adele III* read the ceremony and waved to them from his pilothouse window. Ivan and Steve stood stiffly in the cold wind, grinning toward Hank's boat. When Jones made the final pronouncement and gunned his whistle, they fired their hunting rifles over and over. Then they pounded each other on the back as they danced and slipped around the icy deck. All it lacked was booze.

The honeymoon in Puale Bay lasted two days. Finally the wind changed direction, allowing them to hammer free and proceed safely to Dutch Harbor.

25

THE BERING
SEA

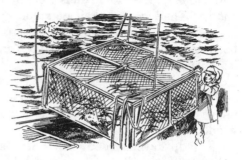

ARCH in the Bering Sea was a miserable business of northerlies
and of floating ice that blew down from the arctic packs. Life
ashore in Dutch Harbor and Unalaska was little better. Foggy
wind howled through the mountains without pause, and snow clung with
wet heaviness to everything. The climate and time of year separated the
natives from the outside cannery workers even more than usual, even
though they worked shoulder to shoulder on the lines. When a boatload
of crab came in and a cannery turned on its revolving light to summon
employees, the natives appeared from their little frame houses, donned
slickers and aprons with the rest, did the tedious work for the long hours
required, and then returned home with barely a word. Most of the outside people had come to Dutch Harbor to save money away from it all,
before realizing how far they had come. They spent their spare time
mumbling to each other about being trapped. Drinking was endemic in
both the native houses and the dormitories. The Elbow Room, the only
common meeting ground, remained principally the province of fishermen
in from a trip. The jukebox pumped the same old rock, but it had become a din for grim boozers whose winter had lasted too long rather
than an accompaniment for spontaneous dancing and an occasional
recreational fight. A disagreement at this time of year was more likely
to end in drawn knives than in a few fist thumps followed by drinks all
around.

Life on the boats was a simple case of endurance at sea—a package bought in advance by any but novice fishermen—of pitching decks,
freezing water, the crunching danger of small icebergs, and bull work

made more exhausting by the cold. Only the Norwegians seemed content, although the radio bands were filled with their complaints to one another. They worked their pots during gales that sent other boats to harbor and spoke of it with gloomy satisfaction. "Well, shit, no Squarehead's completely happy," said Tolly, "unless he's got a wind blowing at least sixty and ice up to his ass."

Hank and Jones Henry fished with the rest of the fleet off Cape Sarichef. One night they anchored close ashore to catch a complete night's rest, then consumed three hours in the morning breaking the windlass free of ice to raise the hook.

Jody stayed aboard the *Nestor,* against Jones' advice about all women on fishing boats. She cooked, baited, and stood wheel watches, all of which made life easier. Moreover, her acid realism, delivered in language as free as theirs, kept them in good humor even during hard periods.

Hank was happy. He loved Jody and she returned it. When they stood side by side in his skipper's cabin, which she shared, or in Tolly's house ashore, he saw in the mirror the woman he knew of gay mischief and energy, her hair tied back for action, but her eyes were now alive with a warmth even greater than before whenever she looked at him.

His own reflection in the mirror was that of a dark-bearded barbarian, teeth white against wind-swarthy skin. He felt more and more self-confident. When he declared a course of action, both his boat and his crew responded. He began to plot the movements of the crab like a hunter stalking prey. When the pots emerged with keepers, he no longer needed a cheer from deck. He glanced toward Jody, and she sent back approval by a wink or a flicker of smile.

Now that he had a wife, he began to think even more of owning a boat. He dreamed with Jody over brochures, plotting what he could afford with the thirty-five thousand he had saved for a down payment, and how much he could risk in debts and mortgage. "Look—this design has jumped since 1971 from three hundred fifty to four hundred thousand. I can't even put down ten percent any more. Got to save more and commit myself before it gets worse."

"I've saved eight thousand we can put toward it."

"You?" It was a dimension of being together that had never occurred to him. "Better hold your money, dear."

"What the hell for?"

He laughed. "Think what a bigger pain Jones would have if Adele thought she owned his damned boat."

Seth, Andy, and Dan disappeared fast, leaving him alone to take what he had brought on himself. The force of her assault pinned him to the seat. The lively eyes turned flashing cold, and the wide, smiling mouth that he had romanced became a trapdoor for curt words. Not that she raised her voice: she merely used it with the thudding efficiency of a marlinspike. At first he tried to counter angrily, but each time he spoke she sliced him further. When it was over, she had made it clear that she expected equality in all his enterprises. He sat at the table, absently fingering his beard. Not much barbarian left. The funny part was, as he thought about it, she was probably right. Have to be damned strong to stay atop this woman he'd landed.

When they first arrived on Bering Sea grounds and began exploring for crab in the known places, they encountered some Russian trawlers. Whenever Jones Henry spied one of their dark shapes he growled into the sideband: "Set out pots here and they're as good as gone. This is why we need a two-hundred-mile limit."

Hank, perhaps reflecting his general contentment, eyed the big vessels with more interest than hostility. It had been a decade since the incident outside Kodiak harbor when the Russian ship had tried to run down the *Rondelay*. Since then a twelve-mile U.S. fisheries zone had been declared, and the Coast Guard every year had seized some foreign ships caught in violation, so he judged the situation to be at least under limited control. He studied the Russian ships with their high H-beams and lopped sterns through binoculars. One day he maneuvered the *Nestor* close to one as it pulled its trawl, and they all gathered in the pilothouse to watch. The best view came from directly astern, since they could see up the ramp. The filled net moved slowly from the water. It resembled a fat snake oozing mud, attended by hundreds of screaming gulls. But only when they saw it on deck, an oval tube as high as the crewmen and long enough for a dozen men to flank it shoulder to shoulder, could they comprehend the quantity that had been brought from the ocean in a single haul. The catch overflowed into bins—millions of fish that men waded through up to their hips.

The Russians themselves were faceless from a distance, dark figures in bulky coats and fur hats with long earflaps.

"Bunch of thieves," Seth declared. "Those fish belong to us."

Hank knew he would be unpopular, but: "We'd never fish that pollock with salmon and halibut around. Wouldn't bring a cent a pound. Americans wouldn't eat it. Why be dogs in the manger?"

"I might not be a skipper," said Seth, "but I read *National Fisherman*. You know what American fish sticks are made of? Fuckin' foreign-caught pollock that they sell back to us."

"Look, look!" Jody grabbed Hank's binoculars. "What they're piling on deck along with that fish nobody else wants. The objects were king crabs, by the hundreds. And the Russians were tossing them into containers, not returning them to the sea.

Hank continued to spend part of his boat's energies on prospecting new grounds, often leaving Jones behind with the main fleet on the usual fathom curves. One night Andy challenged him. "I don't mind no amount of work so long as it makes sense. But what's anybody going to get from a pot here and a pot there where everybody else knows not to bother? You follow behind the highline skippers. They know where the crab is."

"This is still a new fishery," said Hank. "Nobody knows it all."

"New for you, maybe. I've crabbed here ten years."

"Don't they fish grounds now that they didn't then?"

"But they found 'em all long ago."

"Hell," declared Seth, "you've never heard of research, man? Out here you need the balls to try new things." With Seth's support, Hank prevailed. He already had three charts stored above his bed, which only Jody saw, covered with the marks and notes of his explorations.

And then it paid off. The first of three pots laid in an uncharted trench came up bulging to the web with fat keepers. The pot was so heavy the line groaned, and they attached an extra double block from the main boom to bring it all over the rail. Hank set his iron mike and leaped down to deck. They stared at the pot in near awe.

"She's plugged like in the old days," said Andy reverently.

Jody caressed Hank's arm and Seth pounded him on the back.

They all took turns posing in front of it for Hank's and Seth's cameras, while Hank calculated out loud how long it would take to run to their closest string, clear the pots, and hustle them over. The picking was exuberant but silent as everyone counted his own. Every crab was a large male, wonderfully heavy for the Bering Sea. There were nearly four hundred crabs in the pot, compared to their normal haul of twenty to sixty.

"We've set on the fuckin' wrestler's convention!" yelled Seth.

They raised the other two pots to find catches of equal size. When the first two pots had been baited and returned and the third lay bulging on deck ready to be unloaded, Hank grabbed Jody and broke into a crazy dance. The others clapped time. Then Seth and Dan started together, and Jody went to Andy as the dance continued to the thump of their boots.

Suddenly Hank glanced at the water and exclaimed, "*Juggernaut's* coming. Unload that son of a bitch!" He raced up to the wheel and steered so that his bow blocked Tolly's view of the deck, while the others silently hustled the crab into the hold.

Tolly maneuvered his boat into voice range and called through cupped hands, "Doing all right, are you?"

It might have been Hank's chance to show gratitude for past favors, but with the time come he'd no more have told Tolly the truth than would the others.

"Having a little grab-ass to warm up."

Tolly grinned. He wasn't fooled, and he had ten empty pots on deck. "Guess since you're only working three here you won't mind if I set a few."

"Help yourself," said Hank, trying to be casual. "Maybe you'll have better luck." They watched helplessly as Tolly's crew set their string. Hank paced and churned inside. At least better for Tolly to share it than a stranger.

Then he felt guilty. He'd have hidden that trench even from Jones Henry, his fishing partner to whom he owed the most. To make up for bad intentions (or was it, he was honest enough to wonder, because the trench was no longer a secret?) he radioed Jones, who was working pots thirty miles away. After some standard exchanges, he said, "Not so impressive out here today. Only a Molly seventy-six."

319

A pause as Jones evidently checked the words, which were their code (never yet used) for the ultimate catch. Then a curt "Read you. Too bad. Out."

In a few hours they had both pulled and stacked a deckload of pots and had steamed back to lay them in the trench alongside Tolly's.

Next day at dawn the three boats converged to work their pots simultaneously. They maneuvered close enough to each other to shout back and forth, since it was one of those Bering Sea days of rare calm. Tolly joked a long time about all the new buoys in the water.

"Well, buddy," called Hank, "prepare to pop your eyes." He was reconciled to sharing the trench, glad to have it with these two. After all, he'd discover others. "Go on," he urged Tolly. "Pull yours first."

The pot came up with six keepers. The next had only three, and another was flat empty. Jones' pots, and his own, were no fuller.

Hank made light of it as best he could. To Tolly he called: "Crew does a rain dance and people think you've found crab."

"Ah, buddy, does Jody do that to you? You owe me a six-pack of Scotches at the Elbow Room."

"My pleasure."

"That's the fish business," said Jones, also without rancor.

When the two had stacked their pots and left for better grounds, Hank remained. He cruised a grid over the spot, covering the chart with marks to correlate fathometer depths with loran and dead-reckoning fixes. The attempt to envision a seafloor through fifty fathoms of water made him feel like the blind man fingering an elephant. Finally he announced to Jody and the others in the wheelhouse, "It's no trench, it's only a hole. About ten fathoms deep, and not much more than a hundred fifty feet wide. How many could we set in there, Andy—half-dozen?"

"Even then, might snag your lines. Have to do it careful."

"Maybe we shouldn't bother," said Hank tentatively. "We're a good distance from our other gear, and the crabs might not fill the hole any more."

It was Andy, the conservative, who had been affected most by the sight of the plugged pots. He gave the answer Hank hoped for. "I say it's worth a little gamble to see that sight again." The others agreed. They had all sniffed the chase.

They placed six pots in the hole with the precision of bomber pilots on a mission. Encouraged by their attitude, Hank next moved northward into new territory with the remaining pots, following his hunch of how the crabs might have migrated. They set clusters of two and three over a space of fifty miles, up close to the floating ice. Then they cruised back full speed to join the *Adele* and worked twenty hours straight to service all the pots they had left soaking.

They returned to the hole, spelling each other for one-hour tricks at the wheel through the night. The six pots came up plugged as full as the first time—more than two thousand heavyweight crab. Although they had taken no more than a few hours' sleep in two days, they raced in a party mood to the other experimental pots. The first cluster was empty except for a large halibut and some codfish and pollock, which they cut for bait. (Hank regretted the halibut and insisted they slice a steak from it for dinner, but with their bait running short, a sixty-pound fish, illegal or not . . . They all did it.) The next cluster yielded a few keepers, and the next had been dragged away by an ice floe. The final two strings produced about two hundred keepers in each pot. He had found a new ground, fifty miles from the ones generally accepted. They couldn't stop shouting, twirling Jody, slapping each other on the back.

The next days were spent moving gear from the old grounds, then racing to Dutch Harbor to unload and start with empty tanks.

Tolly's boat was in also. During the hours it took the cannery crew to toss crab from Hank's hold, he found Tolly and gleefully six-packed him with Scotch at the Elbow Room, making sure he drank it all. Then, with Tolly grinning and glassy-eyed, and with Jody watching in disbelief, Hank told him about the new grounds. Tolly heard it through absently. The jukebox was pounding and Hank had lowered his voice. Tolly tapped a fist affectionately against Hank's chin and staggered off to find his latest cannery girfriend.

"Stupid!"

"I owe him favors, Jody. We even bunk in his house."

"The hell with that. He brings in full loads without you. Help him if he's in trouble, but otherwise keep your mouth shut."

"Now wait. I figured those grounds, they're mine to—"

"They belong to your *boat!* Think your crew worked those extra hours for fun?"

He had drunk too much with Tolly, and her intensity made him feel cornered. His chair clattered back as he rose and declared roughly "I'm skipper. Remember?"

She was up beside him, her chin no higher than his chest, but her eyes fierce enough to make him back away. "Then stick to finding the crab. The other decisions are my department if you can't do better than this."

They stormed back to the boat in a furious mood, not speaking. The fact that she was right did nothing for his anger. What had he married, what had he bought for himself? Couldn't even leave her ashore. Should have listened to Jones Henry.

The next days were busy and sleepless as they transferred deckloads of pots and committed themselves to the new grounds. Tolly apparently had not comprehended the message in the bar, to Hank's relief. They heard his banter from another area altogether. As for Hank and Jody, anger was difficult to sustain in the interdependent world of a boat, especially when they shared a narrow bed.

All at once the Bering waters north of Unimak Pass exploded with Japanese ships. The smallest of the foreign vessels was larger than any American boat on the grounds, while the factory motherships to which they delivered their catches were at least a dozen times as large. Coast Guard planes flew overhead, and a Coast Guard cutter sailed among them, evidently monitoring. The count of Japanese vessels, according to a conversation Hank overheard between the cutter and a plane: seven factory ships and their satellite fleets—five factories to process pollock, attended by ninety-four trawlers, and two factories for king crab, with thirty catcher boats. There were also twenty additional independent trawler-processors.

The crab factory fleets spread through the area where Jones and most of the other American skippers were crabbing. "Sons of bitches!" Jones' voice exclaimed over the sideband. "Jap ships have dumped little pots all around me. My pot average has dropped from the forties to the twenties since they came. And the State Department lets them do it! I fought at Iwo, and now I pay taxes to kiss Jap ass."

"Don't forget de fuckin' Russian asses," added a deep Norwegian voice.

Hank's own grounds were located north of the concentration, where only a single Russian trawler was working, and it kept him detached. He wove the *Nestor* through the ships, watching curiously the busy little Japanese in hard hats and smelling with renewed amazement the processing stenches that evolved from fish that had just come so fresh from the sea. The number of foreign ships seemed excessive, but the Americans' level of resentment troubled him also. He saw open water on every point of the horizon. Beneath it all, on levels through sixty fathoms and more, swam millions of sea creatures that constantly regenerated. Subsistence Asians relied on fish for protein, and here was the abundance. What of that concept of free enterprise that he had been taught to admire—didn't it apply to other nations? What American fishermen needed to do was explore beyond their established grounds, as he was doing.

They set the last of their empty pots from the old area, then worked the ones that had been left to soak. Each pot continued to yield between a hundred and two hundred keepers. It was a satisfaction beyond imagining.

The others recognized it. Even Andy began to ask his opinion on matters he normally would have handled himself. Jody acknowledged his new status in less obvious ways, but he felt her approbation.

The weather ran the variety of the Bering Sea, from frigid blows that carried ice and kicked twenty-foot waves to gray flat calm. Hank let Seth relieve him at the wheel occasionally so that he could stretch his muscles on deck, when seas were safe under the control of a novice, but, increasingly, the stimulus of the chase held him close to the charts and depth sounder. When pots produced no more than a hundred, he plotted new locations within the area to increase their yield. He began to hope he might become one of the season's highliners, equal to some of the Norwegians. Then they delivered a load to Dutch Harbor in less time than any other boat. Suddenly he became obsessed: the *Nestor* under his command could become *the* highline boat. He stopped talking by radio for fear of interesting other skippers in his position. He drove himself and the rest, regardless of the weather, for as long as they could endure and then beyond.

"Even the devil stops sometimes, you know," said Jody. "Your guys are dead. They're getting careless." They had just run gear without a break through a day and a half of rough seas, and he was preparing to race down to their hole to pull the six special pots, then to return and work another string through the night.

He blinked through sandpaper eyes and snapped in a voice flat with fatigue, "I'll judge when we get to the accident point."

"That's now, Hank."

"No. There's more in all of us. The guys aren't complaining. Don't you think I've worked on deck? You keep on the crab when they're running. It's what makes a highliner. They know it as well as I do. Go down and sleep. Nothing's keeping *you* up."

Her eyes filled. It was the first time he had seen her even close to tears except after the *Delta* had foundered. He put his arm around her and said gently, "Come on, darling, get some sleep. We're okay." He walked her to their cabin, pulled off her boots and rain pants and covered her with a blanket. By the time he had kissed her and turned out the light she was asleep.

A few hours later, with hail splattering white sheets across the water, the surge became so heavy that three lines snapped in succession. Hank blew several short blasts of the whistle. Within a minute the men had turned the crab block inboard, secured all gear, and gone inside. Through the transom came wordless grunts as they flopped into their bunks, hardly with time to remove their clothes. He checked the radar on all scales. Only the pip of the Russian trawler five miles away. The boat could drift safely. In bed, he eased Jody over to make room, set the alarm for four hours, and fell asleep on the instant.

Next afternoon, in clear weather, they had finished a huge meal and had run most of a string when he noticed the deck lights and mast of another crab boat on the horizon. If Jones Henry had come to share, okay, maybe even Tolly, but others . . . He called several times on the sideband before rousing her. Trying to sneak up. It was the *Nordic Queen*, Arnie Larson's big Seattle boat. Through binoculars he saw that Arnie carried a deckload of pots.

"Start stacking," he called down.

"You crazy?" said Andy. "We're on top these buggers."

"*Nordic Queen* coming this way. I might owe Arnie a favor, but nothing like this."

No further explanation necessary. He kept the *Nestor* turned so that they emptied and stacked a few pots with the bow blocking the

Queen's view. Then he circled back to the start of the string. By the time he permitted Arnie a clear sight of his deck they were raising empty pots—those they had picked and returned to the water only two hours before.

When the *Nordic Queen* eased alongside there were nine pots stacked on the *Nestor*'s deck. As many more remained in the water that were reliably empty, except that the crab on the seafloor were so abundant that most pots had already accumulated a few.

"Hey there, Hank." called Arnie. "Way up here by yourself, I figure shit, dot fellow must be on the crabs."

Hank shook his head ruefully. "Yesterday maybe so. Fuckers seem to have moved away."

"Too bad." Arnie's eyes narrowed in his weathered face. "How many keepers vas you getting?"

"Oh . . ." He hated to be forced into a direct lie. "Of course it picked up for a while or I wouldn't still be here. But looks like she's fallen apart."

Arnie nodded slowly, glancing everywhere on the *Nestor*'s deck. His crewmen along the rail did the same. Hank cursed the good weather to himself. A blow would have kept them farther off. Only a few more pots left before those plugged with crab, and then he'd have to think of an excuse not to pull more.

"I hear you deliver in Dutch Harbor pretty frequent."

As Hank shrugged and figured what to reply, Seth called from deck. "Talk to him for us, Arnie. He won't stay put. Last time I ship with a skipper on honeymoon. First he's into port so they can be alone, then he's got to be out where other boats don't crowd him. You got an extra berth over there for me?"

Arnie pulled at his beard for a while, then gave up the subject. "Ja, Hank, I see already you got the old lady working baits. Dot's gude training." His big "Har har har" sounded like the Norwegian version of Santa Claus. "Hey, Jody, how you like being married to this guy? Should I say congratulations, or you vant us to give you a ride back to Dutch Harbor, eh? Har har har."

It started them all joking back and forth. Being as far from other boats as they were, and on a calm day at that, Hank should have invited Arnie to tie alongside for mug-up. But then the Norwegians would see the mass of crab in their tank. He continued to hold out for time, as the *Nordic Queen* circled and circled.

Two pots remained of the ones he could count on when Arnie called, "You coming back to the main grounds? I vait and we go together."

"I'm not through experimenting." Hank grinned. "Still on my honeymoon."

"Ja, ja." Arnie tooted and left. Hank held to the game of empty pots until the *Nordic Queen* had left binocular range. Then he harvested the remainder of the string, with two hundred keepers and more in each. The game both shamed and exhilarated him. Alone as he was except for the Russian trawler, there might come a time when he needed help, and he knew Arnie would give it freely. Well, as would he himself. The rest was the fish business. If Jones Henry had come, that would have been different. No doubts on the part of the others. Seth was the hero of the day for his quick tongue. They relived the scene over and over as they worked the pots.

Yet the mast and deck lights of Arnie's boat did not disappear over the horizon. Hank checked often on radar to make sure. The boat was hovering nine miles away, or laying its own pots.

The Russian trawler, which had at first traveled a long path as far away as the *Nordic Queen*, moved closer daily. Hank decided to bide time by paying a visit. Besides, "Better let him know we're here so he looks out for our pots."

The ship had its trawl in the water, as evidenced by two taut cables slanting from the stern. As Hank brought the *Nestor* close, the rusty white hull of the Russian grew proportionately higher until it rose triple the height of their own wheelhouse. Hank adjusted his boat to the snailish trawling speed and tooted his whistle.

Heads appeared from all parts of the rail and housing above them—at least forty. Some men on the bridge wore gold-braided uniforms, while one wore a suit. The men on deck wore varieties of fur caps with earflaps and grimy quilted jackets. A few women stood on a deck below the bridge. One held a broom. "Looks like the janitors and kitchen help," said Jody from the pilothouse.

"Don't forget the processing lines."

Some of the men above pointed cameras. Hank waved and

326

grinned. The expressions he received in return were reserved but not hostile.

"Hello," he shouted, and added the only appropriate Russian word he knew, "Tovarich." As Seth and Dan laid fenders over the side, he indicated with his hands a desire to come aboard.

A young man his own age, with a trimmed beard and a black visored cap, leaned over the rail. "You ... have ... difficulties?"

"No, no trouble. Wish to come visit, see fishing."

It was a tricky communication, with the sea lapping against both hulls and surging between them. Hank had to rephrase his message, calling it word by word, before the interpreter understood and relayed it to the authorities on the bridge. The man in the suit said a few words without changing expression. The interpreter leaned far out and moved his hand back and forth in a negative gesture. But, with a self-conscious smile: "You ... have ... girlie magazine?"

"Hey, you speak American! Seth and Dan, give up some old skin stuff, okay?"

"Right, Boss."

While they waited, Hank tried other questions, to learn that there were ninety in the crew and that they had been aboard fishing in the Bering Sea for six months. He learned also that the ship was eighty-four meters long and that it was called a "Class Mayakovsky." A cargo ship came every few weeks to receive their fish meal and frozen fish and take it to Vladivostok. Before answering each of Hank's questions, the interpreter spoke to the men on the bridge, and the one in the suit returned monosyllabic answers. When Hank asked how much fish they caught each day the interpreter's English, which had grown steadily better, suddenly deserted him, and no amount of rephrasing could induce him to comprehend.

"Hey," said Hank finally in an easy tone. "You're damned if you'll answer that one, right?"

"No understand." But a smile twitched on his face.

When Seth appeared with a handful of magazines, a basket was lowered quickly on a line. Hank tossed in a carton of his own cigarettes besides and indicated they were for the captain. On the bridge, the man with the most braid on his sleeve bowed slightly when the interpreter relayed the message, and left. As for the basket, several hands groped out to help it aboard, and the crew of the *Nestor* was rewarded with some grins and waves.

"Thank you. Wait. Please." The interpreter disappeared.

"Gone to get you some Russian pinups, Seth," said Hank.

"That's what I need by my bunk, a big Katrinka."

Jody laughed. "Those sisters up there could probably judo you thirty feet across the deck." She stepped into full view for the first time, to wave to the women. They looked at each other, started exclaiming, then returned the wave enthusiastically.

When the basket came down again it contained two bottles of vodka—present of the captain, according to the interpreter—and several booklets and magazines with titles in English including, *USSR Decades of People's Progress, Space Exploits of the Soviet Union,* and *Inspirational Encounters with N. Lenin.*

"Thank you," called Hank. "May we come aboard and visit you?"

The interpreter made his negative gesture again, and said it was necessary to bring in the net so would they kindly move clear of the ship?

On the *Nestor* they had started a laughing jag over the booklets, and they transferred their good humor to waving and calling goodbye. The Russians reciprocated with less reserve than before, some calling messages that sounded like their equivalent of "Good luck" while cameras clicked again. When Hank nodded toward the bridge, the captain and the man in the suit inclined their heads gravely.

"They seem like pretty good Joes," Hank declared.

"Yeah," said Andy, "but I didn't see them lower no Jacob's ladder."

It was nearly dark, and the *Nordic Queen* had left. They were alone with their grounds to themselves again.

The next day, as if the bright pink marker buoys of the *Nestor* had not existed, the Soviet trawler dragged through Hank's grounds. The ship severed the lines of twenty-eight pots even while Hank roared alongside, blowing his whistle and shouting. No faces appeared this time at the rail or on the bridge. Several dark figures on deck continued working as if he did not exist.

Hank turned wild. He blasted away at the ship with his hunting rifle. It had the deterrent effect of a mouse spitting at a cat.

Twenty-eight pots, each producing seven or eight hundred crabs a week! He radioed the Coast Guard. A few hours later a cutter on nearby patrol arrived on the scene. "We'll stand by," the captain told him by radio, "while you load your pots and move south with the rest of the American fleet."

"This is my fishing ground," Hank declared. "It's sixty miles from U.S. land, and I'll call that fuckin' U.S. waters!"

"*Nestor*, I read your message, but that's negative under current law. You're crabbing outside the pot sanctuary areas where the Soviets agreed this year not to fish. We have no jurisdiction." The Coast Guard voice had the formality and detachment that he himself had used as a naval officer.

The incident darkened Hank. The only physical expression he could give to his fury was to smash the bottles of vodka.

They entered the main grounds with the rest of the fleet, sharing the area with hundreds of Japanese pots. If they pulled thirty keepers to a pot of their own, they were lucky. Yet he drove himself and the others even harder than before. He justified again in the name of high-lining: when the crab ran scarce, you worked twice as hard to make a decent load. The crew turned quiet in his wake. He fantasized a breakdown of the Russian trawler that would force it to dock in Dutch Harbor, and in fact monitored the radio bands constantly in case it happened. To catch the bastard off his boat for ten minutes! His hatred spread to all foreign fishing ships. When Jones Henry tied alongside to visit and inquire about the Russian experience, they watched the Japanese crabbers pull their multitude of pots.

"I'd like to sink every one of them," said Hank.

"You understand me now."

"Yes."

His restless maneuvers took him to the edge of the main American grounds, but he could not escape the ubiquitous Japanese ships. Unlike the single Russian trawler, which processed its own hauls, these were smaller ships working in bunches around the nucleus of a huge factory mothership to which they delivered. They cluttered the water in every direction.

At last the crew of the *Nestor* had been driven enough. They gathered in the wheelhouse, Jody included, and told him they were going to rest for a ten-hour night.

"But the goddam weather's calm. Why didn't you pull this on me during a storm?"

"Because," said Seth quietly, "we need a complete, easy uninterrupted fucking sleep."

"We'll take turns on watch," Andy added. "Too crowded with Japs to drift. We want you to sleep too."

Hank started to explode, then checked himself. "Okay, take your rest." He eyed a monstrous factory ship riding a few miles away and started toward it full throttle. "I'll use the time to visit a Jap."

"Oh, Hank, for Christ's sake!" cried Jody.

Andy's eyes narrowed as if he might at last be readying a challenge. Hank had forgotten that this was not his own boat, and that when Joe Eberhardt returned he would be back on deck. "I'll sack out later," he said reasonably. "But we need evidence of what these foreigners are doing to us."

Andy and Dan went to their bunks, but Seth and Jody were interested despite themselves. They passed one of the satellite trawlers. It was pulling in a full bag of fish. "Watch this," said Hank, calm again, as he circled. "I've seen it through binoculars." Instead of the catch being brought aboard—the stuffed bag appeared to be as long as the vessel itself—the crew of a red motor skiff detached the bag from the main net and started towing it toward the mothership. The men on the trawler deck attached a new bag and set their net again at once. "See that?" said Hank. "They don't lose a minute of fishing. And I've watched enough in the last week to know they have enough crew to fish day and night without stopping. That's what we've got against us."

The dark factory mothership rose like a small city. It blocked more and more of the horizon the closer they came. The side was a black rusty wall forty feet high. Hank's whistle echoed back at him with the sound of a toy toot. He tried the radio bands, and found one that brought him a careful, singsong Japanese voice.

After several minutes of palaver, the voice excused himself. An interval, and then the announcement: "*Nessor* boat, yes, captain of *Tono Maru* invite captain of *Nessor* boat for visit. We send kawasaki boat. *Nessor* boat please remain five hundred meter away. Kawasaki boat pick up captain." The phrasing and cadence of the Japanese's English echoed all the Jap villains of World War II movies they had seen on television. They started joking about it, and forgot they were tired.

One of the little red tugboat skiffs was unloading a full cod end of fish alongside the mothership. A crane from above raised the dripping bag secured in thick straps as gulls dove into it wildly. The bag, a bulging sausage of fish, was larger than the tug, nearly as big as the *Nestor* itself. When the tug was finished, it headed toward the *Nestor*.

"Oaw," said Seth with nasal mockery, "that must be kawasaki boat, come to get captain of 'Melican fish boat *Nessor*, give him Hokkaido snow job."

Over the radio sideband Jones Henry's voice said: "Hank, we heard all that. You be careful. Remember what them Japs did to us not so many years ago."

"Hear you, *Adele Three*, hear you all the way."

The kawasaki boat maneuvered alongside. Hank turned the controls over to Seth and started aboard. Suddenly he turned back to Jody and took her arm. "Hey. Come along?"

"It's been such a one-man show," she said dryly, "that I didn't dare ask."

"Forgive me. Come on." She became the conventional woman, worrying about her appearance. "Just a Jap fishing boat, honey. And you'll have to climb a Jacob's ladder." But she disappeared into their cabin, emerging briefly with clean shirt and pants, brushing her hair.

The two Japanese who ran the kawasaki boat were polite, curious, and uncomfortable. The boat itself was essentially a deep bin, powered from a small wheelhouse. The decks were covered with slime and mashed pieces of fish.

When they arrived alongside the factory ship, a crane lowered a basket with floorboards. The men helped them inside, and up they were lifted high over the water. They barely had a chance to enjoy the novelty before the basket reached the top, and the crane swung them inboard above the decks of the factory ship.

Hank grabbed the sides and stared. Below spread two vast areas of pollock, each the size of a full football field. Dozens of men worked in the mass up to their knees and waists, leveling it and pushing it toward conveyor belts. Their paddles might have been working grain, there was such abundance.

"I knew they were raping our seafloor," Hank gasped, "but, Jesus! I never dreamed it was half of this!"

"You're right, but shut up while you're here. They didn't have to let us aboard."

They landed on a platform above one of the two fields. With it close to dusk, floodlights spread a dead glaze over thousands and thousands of the foot-long white fish. Hank gazed, mesmerized. A grave, polite Japanese in khaki coveralls and hardhat bowed slightly, shook their hands, and asked them to go with him, but Hank held back, burning the sight into his memory.

"Please come on," said Jody. "They're already worried by the way you're acting."

When they entered the housing and started descending ladders, the decks were so stable and the areas so large that they could well have been in a building ashore. Their guide gave them white cotton gloves and walked them quickly through a warehouse-sized complex of processing machinery. It had the familiar dins and smells of any seafood plant, although the equipment was different than any he knew. In one section, a continuous belt of fish serviced a bank of heading-gutting machines. At each machine—he counted twenty of them, but more blended together at the end of the line—stood a man feeding fish rapidly into the blades. Their gloved hands moved like pistons, pushing more than a hundred fish a minute. He tried to see differences from Americans. Their black rain pants were belted at the waist with rubber thongs, for example. But they wore colored shirts and baseball caps, and their faces had the blank concentrated stare of any assembly-line worker. It was the quantity that was different, the obscene quantity!

Some pollock fillets went in one direction for cleaning and freezing, some in another for a series of renderings into a white mush that the guide called "Fish paste, surimi, high protein, eat much in Japan." The heads, bones, and tails went into cookers on the engine deck, utilizing the heat of the engines, for rendering into fish meal. The banks of machines and the men operating them stretched on and on, as did the areas for bagging the meal, packing the frozen fish blocks and filling color-coded containers with paste. They peered into vast holds white with frost, where figures stacked boxes by the hundreds to await transfer to a cargo ship.

At the end of the tour Hank declared, "Very efficient."

The guide was inordinately pleased. Hank smiled at his pleasure and forgot for a moment that he faced a threat to his own livelihood, not merely a fellow human.

As they followed the guide up through more decks and passageways, Hank peeled off to walk through a boot-lined corridor and glance into living quarters. He saw bunk areas sleeping eight or ten, all characterized by a cramped and steamy atmosphere, walls with voluptuous pin-up girls (both Oriental and Western), and small cookstoves on which simmered pots of food. Off other parts of the corridor, rain gear hung in heated drying rooms. Toilets were holes in the deck with treads for the feet. One room contained adjacent deep tubs of hot and cold bathing water. The men he encountered watched him curiously but with no hostility. One group sitting crosslegged in front of curtained bunks looked up from a card game, cigarettes in their mouths, and offered him a drink from a bottle of clear liquid. Raw, gin-type stuff, probably saki. He grinned and thanked them, and they all nodded and grinned in return.

The guide was trying to take Hank's inquisitiveness in stride, but obviously it made him uneasy. And Jody—she chided him like a conventional wife rather than a fellow adventurer.

Outside the door to a carpeted room, the guide in his groping English asked them to remove their boots, and handed them each a new pair of sandals sealed in a plastic bag. As they put them on, a mild worried-looking man in an open shirt came from the room to greet them. The guide introduced him as the captain. He shook hands brusquely, bowed, and held out a business card printed in both Japanese and English. Hank nodded, and tucked it in his pocket.

"Captain say, you have card, please?"

"Sorry, I don't carry one."

A stony-faced discussion ensued between the Japanese. It was as if he had arrived at the all-star game without a ticket. Finally: "You will come in, please."

The four sat stiffly at the end of a large table while a white-coated waiter served them each a plate of hors d'oeuvre and a bottle of Japanese beer. The food consisted principally of crackers garnished with sardinelike fish in a sweet yellow paste, set atop squares of spiced meat. At the captain's bidding, the waiter turned on a television set. The first picture it showed was of grossly fat wrestlers. The waiter hurried away, and soon afterward the screen blanked, then resumed with a song program delivered by Japanese girls in traditional costume.

As Hank watched his wife slough her fishboat toughness and become quietly gracious, even charming, he realized that he had not been playing the game. He made up by complimenting the captain on the efficiency (magic word!) of his ship. His interest was rewarded by being told that everyone on the ship worked very hard and that everyone was proud to be loyal employees of the company. It was a large, important company, one that owned not only this small fishing fleet but many others all over the world, a company that was a father to all who worked for it. Everyone stayed with the company from the time he was young until the time he retired, and the company cared for him when he was old just as it did when he was young. Within this fleet, there were 450 men aboard the factory ship, and another 300 on the twenty catcher-trawlers and the support boats. Because they were all efficient, they could process forty tons of fish an hour around the clock, every day. Sometimes more. The information was both delivered and translated with pleased satisfaction.

"And captain say, no waste, fish used every bit. Crab, other big fish, no waste either, freeze especially. Everything efficient."

Jody kicked Hank under the table, anticipating his reply regarding crab. A game, why not? He accepted another beer and was persuaded to give the catch statistics of his own boat. The comparison was so absurd that they all shared a laugh. After this the conversation traveled a relaxed route of pleasantries, led by Jody. It culminated with their admiring photos of the captain's wife and children in Japan.

At parting, the captain made a formal little speech which translated: "American and Japanese are friend, fishing together. There is much fish, and all are happy."

Jody gave her smile and made an acceptable reply for both of them. As for Hank, one further look at the masses of fish, as the basket lowered them back to the kawasaki boat, and any tenuous feeling of fraternity was erased from his mind.

26

INTERNATIONAL
FISH

OR several centuries, nations have felt entitled to control the waters three miles around their coasts, that area considered practical to defend with shore-based cannon and gunboats. The sea beyond was any-man's land. However, this was a military prerogative. Fish were considered the property of the fisherman able to take them, even within three miles. Thus the concept of legislating the fishing waters around a national coast is new to the world, an expedient precipitated by the protein needs of overpopulated peoples and by the resultant overharvesting of seafood to feed them that has been made possible by new technologies.

Sea creatures lack national loyalty. As one fisherman put it: "A fish has a head and a tail and he goes where he damn well pleases." In practical terms, goes where the feed is. The U.S. is blessed with enormous feed-generating continental shelves. As a result, it possesses within 200 miles of its coasts a full 20 percent of the world's seafood.

With the technological advances spawned on both sides by World War II, it was inevitable that nations that fished seriously as a national effort (to date the U.S. does not) should apply their technologies to fishing, and then should send their ships to rich grounds like those off the United States. The Japanese came in force first, to Alaskan waters in 1952. Within a few years they had massive factory-ship operations that processed on the spot the catch of hundreds of fishing ships. Trawlers from the Soviet Union began arriving in 1959, off both Alaska and the Atlantic coast. Fishing ships of other nations followed. In many instances they simply edged aside U.S. fishermen and ran over their gear

335

if it got in the way. During a typical year, 1973, Japanese and Soviet ships averaged annual seafood hauls from waters within 200 miles of U.S. coasts of 4.6 and 2.2 billion pounds respectively, while U.S. fishermen landed only 1.4 billion pounds from the same fishing areas.

Much of the seafood was not being harvested by anyone and hence was legitimately available to any taker. However, there was also heavy and careless exploitation. For example, the Japanese effort included a large portion of the U.S. Bristol Bay sockeye salmon and as incidental catch the closely regulated U.S.–Canadian halibut, seriously depleting both these domestic fisheries. The Soviet fleets proved particularly voracious with single stocks. By 1970 they had overfished U.S. Pacific Ocean perch and hake into commercial extinction, and were fast doing the same to Atlantic haddock.

The tenuous control which the U.S. was able to exercise over any sea creatures in its waters came belatedly with three laws: Public Law 88-308, the "Bartlett Act" of 1964, which closed the U.S. three-mile territorial sea to foreign fishing; PL 89-658 of 1966, establishing U.S. fishery control over a twelve-mile Contiguous Fishery Zone; and PL 93-242 of 1974, which declared crabs and lobsters to be "creatures of the continental shelf" and therefore under U.S. control on U.S. continental shelves. Backed by these laws and little else besides diplomatic persuasion, the U.S. through the State Department negotiated fishing quotas with individual flag nations. Some quotas reflected more political trade-off than biological soundness. The only way of enforcing the U.S. laws and checking on the U.S. agreements was through the tireless air and sea patrols conducted by the Coast Guard in company with agents of the National Marine Fisheries Service. When some of the operations were closely monitored, it was proved that both the Japanese and Soviet fleets often harvested far more seafood (sometimes two and three times more) than they reported.

For years U.S. fishermen—a disorganized lot of intense individuals who were slow to form coalitions as did other types of workmen—had dunned their congressmen for legislation that would give them a better chance against the foreign fleets at catching the seafood stocks in their own national waters. Three congressmen especially began to carry the ball: Democratic Senator Warren Magnuson of Washington, Republican Senator Ted Stevens of Alaska, and Democratic Representative

Gerry Studds of Massachusetts. Through the Senate Commerce Committee and the House Merchant Marine Committee they and other members organized hearings and drafted bills. The bill that was finally passed in 1976 had evolved from a simple quick-action measure introduced by Stevens in 1972 to legislation that regulated both foreign and domestic fishermen.

The U.S. State Department had been especially apprehensive about the international precedent that would be set by extending U.S. fishery jurisdiction, and their reasoning carried both Presidents Nixon and Ford as well as many congressmen. (Incidentally, State resisted a twelve-mile fisheries zone in 1966, when two hundred miles was so unthinkable that nobody even voiced it.) Diplomats warned that if the U.S. claimed its biological resources out to two hundred miles, other nations would justify restrictions on all shipping—research, merchant, military—through their coastal waters; that in fact the entire concept of freedom on the high seas would be jeopardized to the detriment of other U.S. interests.

The bill, aptly numbered HR 200 during its stormy passage through Congress, was signed reluctantly by President Ford on April 13, 1976, into Public Law 94-265, The Fishery Conservation and Management Act of 1976. It established, within the year, U.S. jurisdiction over the fishery resources within two hundred miles of the U.S. coasts and set up a management structure for controlling them.

The cornerstone of the management section is a group of eight regional councils. The main product of each council is a Fishery Management Plan "with respect to each fishery within its geographical area." Included is a determination of "optimum yield" of each species that can be harvested for the year, and after subtracting that portion that U.S. vessels are able to harvest, assignment of the remaining "total allowable level of foreign fishing" within the council's jurisdiction. The management plans are forwarded by the councils via the National Marine Fisheries Service to its parent the Commerce Department, which is the final authority. Commerce checks the plans with the State Department for diplomatic implications and with the Coast Guard (Transportation Department) for enforceability. Ideally, according to its congressional authors, the law provides an innovative form of government guided by a regional concept of lawmaking, with a healthy interaction

337

between central and regional authorities. Inherent in it all is the potential clash between politics and the varying loyalties of experts. Indeed, opponents feared that regional fishing interests would subvert any mandate in the rest of the bill that the U.S. manage its seafood resources for the overall benefit of mankind. However, since such clashes are a basic strength and pitfall of a democracy, the regional council concept should be an appropriate format for the fishery maneuvers of the United States.

As for the foreign fleets, the bill does not provide a sweepout, contrary to popular belief. It controls the size of catches to a much greater degree than before and, in direct proportion to the growing capability of the U.S. fishing fleets, may gradually ease them from most fisheries. The bill provides that within each annual quota of fish biologists determine can be safely harvested without harming the stocks, U.S. fishermen are entitled to all they can prove able to catch, with the foreign fleets eligible for the "surplus" if they abide by the rules. The eligibility requirements for a foreign vessel are: a Governing International Fisheries Agreement between the ship's flag country and the United States; a specific allocation to the ship's flag country; a permit aboard the vessel which is issued upon payment of fees; and reciprocal fishery privileges in the flag country for U.S. fishermen. The size of the allocation within the surplus available is based in large part on the fishing "tradition" a nation has established in the waters. The latter provision makes Russia the clear winner off the East Coast and Japan the winner off Alaska.

True to warnings from opponents of the Fishery Act, other nations quickly declared two-hundred-mile jurisdiction of their fisheries—Canada rapidly enough to take effect before the U.S. law, Russia soon after, and then the deluge. However, the predicted confusion of fishery rights with other traditional rights of sea passage has not taken place. Not that all is sweetness. The councils, while still finding their way, are accused of being too dependent on the Commerce Department for the information on which they must base their recommendations back to the Commerce Department. The internationalists accuse the councils of adjusting optimum yield figures to suit the needs of regional fishermen in ways that leave fewer fish than necessary for the foreign fleets. As for U.S. fishermen, many are regulated by their regional councils more than they expected (or as much as they feared). For example, during the first year after PL 94-265 became effective, New England fishermen found to their outrage that the very stocks the foreign ships had taken from them were determined to be so depleted that several grounds were closed to them also. In Washington, Oregon, and southeastern Alaska, the small salmon trollers were suddenly regulated with a heavy hand. But, conversely, the North Pacific Council began at once to transfer most of the tanner crab and some of the pollock quotas in western Alaska from Japanese to U.S. fishermen, in the process stimulating two new big-money fisheries in the Kodiak–Dutch Harbor area.

What of the foreign fleets? They now fish less each year in U.S. waters, and they behave more carefully than ever before since their quotas are set annually. Foreign capital has begun to float through U.S. fishing circles like characters in search of authors, as it seeks to buy what it can no longer take. For example, foreign companies are proposing joint ventures that would enable their processing ships to buy U.S. quotas caught by U.S. fishermen.

For good or bad—probably both—the 200-mile Fishery Conservation and Management Act has stimulated many U.S. fishermen to take the investment trail that leads to incorporation. It may even have launched an American fishing industry. What it does to the individual who has no greater aspiration than to go out in his boat to fish for a living remains to be seen.

27

HOT
PURSUIT

Hank might have faced a crisis when Joe Eberhardt returned to claim the pilothouse of the *Nestor*, forced after seven months of command to go back on deck and take orders with the crew he had bossed. It was a routine adjustment for young fishing skippers without their own boats, but with it he would have relinquished the bloodtaste for the chase he had acquired. However, he had indeed proved to be one of the spring highliners, and his performance bailed him out.

"Ja, Hank, you ain't much Squarehead," said Arnie Larson, who needed a skipper for a second boat he had bought to finish the season. "But when I look you over out by that damn Russian trawler, I see a hard-driving bastard and a pretty good liar. Har har har." They passed a bottle of Scotch to seal the agreement. But, as for Jody aboard: "Shit, no voman belongs on de fishing boats, even a good one like your old lady. Bad luck, bound to catch up." He slapped Hank's shoulder. "You got to knock her up, then she'll leave you alone." Jody stayed ashore and worked again in one of the canneries.

The crew Hank inherited consisted of two Norwegians and two Americans. The young Norwegian was a relaxed and singing type. The older one chafed at having an American skipper, and insisted on observing the old superstitions. Hank adapted, and they all worked together to make a good account of the season. However, he dreamed more and more of possessing his own boat.

By summer, the Bering Sea crab were running in abundance, as were apparently the bottomfish for the foreign fleets. The hundred-odd boats from Seattle and Kodiak were matched by approximately three hundred Japanese fishing ships of all sizes, plus a lesser number from the Soviet Union and—newcomers—South Korea. Coast Guard cutters from Kodiak and all the West Coast took turns cruising the waters, and Coast Guard planes from Kodiak flew regular foreign fishery patrols, often accompanied by agents of the National Marine Fisheries Service. Not that they ever caught any foreigner in a violation, the fishermen observed wryly while remaining glad to have the Coast Guard nearby for rescue and medical emergencies. American crews would sight foreign ships fishing within the twelve-mile zone and radio the Coast Guard, but by the time a plane or cutter arrived the foreigner would be long gone.

"Them Japs are sly, don't kid yourself," said Jones Henry. "They monitor our radios, and they talk better English than I do."

Dutch Harbor-Unalaska had become a noisy and vital place. With heavier catches, the American boats delivered more frequently. The number of canneries had increased as other companies sent in floating processors. With every plant working full capacity, some in double shifts, hundreds of new workers spilled in—both the professionals, including the Filipinos and the drifters, and the hippies and straight college kids seeking adventure. Dense fogs continued to roll, but the bitterness of winter had abated. Above the cannery enclaves the treeless mountains turned green, while thousands of delicate wildflowers bloomed among the rocks and scrub. In Unalaska Village, the Elbow Room stayed open around the clock, and the assortment of skiffs crossing to it from Dutch Harbor made the narrows as busy as a canal in Venice. All day the single muddy road by the bar and post office was crowded with people, motor scooters, and pickups. At night in most weather, couples grappled on the debris-strewn strip of beach in front of the Russian church and the first line of native houses. It was a place in use, and being used.

"You can ram it, this dump," declared one of the Kodiak highline skippers to Hank. He had been among the first to build a large boat especially designed for Bering Sea crabbing and to set the driving pace that now characterized the fishery. "Out here I've learned to hate boats and water. I treat king crabbing like a business. Where else can you make this kind of money by pure gut work? It ain't skill beyond simple seamanship, it's how hard you hit with the hammer, how far you're willing to push yourself and your crew. When I've made my pile I'll move south and never look back."

341

Hank found such talk depressing, sobering. Yet, while still retaining his freshman satisfaction at being a skipper and delivering the crab, he understood the attitude more and more. Could he push them harder? Your share was what you could bring aboard.

A Coast Guard cutter came in from patrol. For a while after docking, sailors roamed the village looking for something to do. Except for the serious drinkers, they soon gave up and returned to the ship. Hank saw a man he recognized, a chief. He had a bushy handlebar mustache and a shock of sandy hair, face turning heavy, and the swagger of a boatswain.

"Yeah, I recognize you too. I served a tour out of Kodiak back in the early sixties, and since then I've been to Oregon, 'Nam, and California. Back here on patrol to keep an eye on the foreigners."

It turned out he was Mack—Joe McNeil—the boatswain's mate aboard the Coast Guard cutter Hank had ridden during the search for pieces of the *Billy II*. The reunion called for several drinks.

Hank gave him a proud tour of the fishing boat he commanded, but Mack's comment as he chewed a cigar: "They make 'em a little bigger now. I see you got a head, and don't have to stick your ass over the rail no more. We still get calls in the middle of the night to tow you guys when you don't change the oil and your engine breaks down. Come on over and I'll show you a *ship*."

"If the Coast Guard's such hot shit," said Hank, "why don't you nab some foreigners instead of just running around?"

They kept it on a bantering level, but Mack growled, "Without us, I'd like to hear you birds scream. Think those Japs and Russians wouldn't fish clean into shore if we wasn't around like cops?" He pointed a finger, and his sleeve drew back to show the snout of a tattooed dragon. "Like to take you out with us, knock through the ice water with us in an open surfboat, then hope you didn't cream your leg jumping to a Jacob's ladder. Want your fill of fish? You need to smell some of the holes we stick our heads to inspect a Jap or Korean been fishing six months.

Hank grinned. "Then you go back to your ship, take a hot shower, eat a steak, and see a movie."

"*Steak?*" Mack chewed his cigar. "Blue Jesus, you ungrateful fishermen get rich, and we do your dirty work."

342

"Want to trade? Give up twenty-year retirement for boom or scratch?"

Mack's turn for a beefy grin. "I'd sooner grow corn in Kansas. *Come* on, I'll show you what a high-endurance cutter looks like."

It was a white and handsome ship, with a bow as graceful as a clipper, double the size of the stub-ended buoy tenders Hank had learned to respect as the Coast Guard workhorses. On board, Mack strode through the fresh-painted passageways as if he owned them. The ship had an air of orderliness that no fishing boat could duplicate, but every sight that was remotely military made Hank glad to have left behind the world of uniforms. Mack toured him grandly around the deck equipment and small boats. He described every detail and sophistication with loving care, although when Hank asked to see the bridge and engine areas he shrugged them off as not his territory.

A civilian passed, and Mack introduced him as Ed Langhorn, the National Fisheries agent who helped inspect the foreigners. He was a cool-eyed, vigorous man of middle age.

Hank told of his experiences with the trawler and the mothership. "I still hope to catch that Russian bastard in here some day."

"Be an international incident," said Langhorn. "Hope I'm there to cheer you on."

Mack led him to the smoke-filled chief's mess and introduced him to other chiefs who were dozing over magazines. They settled into leatherette lounge chairs facing a TV perpetually dead in the Aleutians. Mack brought coffee and cold cuts. "Steak, hah. But you don't get this kind of comfort on a fish boat, eh?" After a discussion of baseball standings in the Leagues, Mack announced generally, "Crawford here says he wants to see the bridge and the engine room. If you find out why, tell me." The Quartermaster and then the Engineman chiefs gave him enthusiastic tours of their special areas, reeling off information until he was groggy with it.

As Mack escorted him to the gangway they encountered Ed Langhorn again. Hank ventured some questions about the foreign fleets and found him as generous with information as the chiefs. When he observed that he had seen few Russian ships compared to Japanese, he learned that major Soviet concentrations came in the winter, between February and April. However, even at this period the Japanese fished more heavily. The patrols had counted 575 different Japanese ships in Alaska during the previous month, July.

He started questioning Langhorn on specific international agreements. Chief Mack became more and more restless, frowning as he shifted from one foot to the other. Finally he said, "Look, uh, Crawford, I've got things to do. See you later at the Elbow Room." It freed Hank to follow Langhorn to his cabin in officer's country for maps and documents, and then to the wardroom to spread them on the table. A young ensign named Sollers sat in. His principal duty was foreign-ship inspection, and he had the same zest for the subject as the Fisheries agent. They showed Hank profiles of various Japanese and Soviet fishing ships with their specifications and produced copies of the international agreements. The material was more complicated than Hank had imagined, with rules and quotas for specific areas bargained separately with each fishing nation, Canada included, that changed with each annual or biennial renegotiation.

Sollers said earnestly, "And we know they're cheating out there, don't we, Mr. Langhorn?" He turned to Hank. "You know, half the violations we see can't be enforced? We find incidental salmon and halibut aboard a Jap boat and it's only a violation of the INPFC agreement, we can only turn them over to their own government. We find a Soviet trawling through a pot sanctuary, we can report him, nothing but *report* him! Our only chance is to catch him in the CFZ, somewhere between shore and twelve miles. Even then, we have to surprise him in the act of fishing, have to prove his gear was in the water. Their radars are as good as ours—better. If they see us coming they pull their nets before we can get close enough." He screwed his face with a kid's impatience. "I want to nab me one of those pirates so bad ..."

Langhorn glanced at Hank, amused. "This one never leaves the bridge when we're on patrol. The Exec or the Old Man's going to court-martial him for pestering to play hide-and-seek in the fog."

Back with Jody, Hank became more and more preoccupied with buying his own boat. He decided to talk to Swede Scorden about credit as soon as they returned to Kodiak, and meanwhile he asked the advice of Jones Henry and any other skipper willing to listen. His equity for a down payment had risen nearly seven thousand since the start of the spring season, with the price of king crab having grown through cannery competition from thirty-five to sixty-five cents a pound. Fifty thousand dollars (Hank's thirty-five previously saved and Jody's disputed eight thousand plus the new money) could make a ten percent down payment on a new ninety-foot Bering Sea crab boat like Jones Henry's that could take on anything. At the other end of the line, it could buy outright a decent little purse seiner, most of a fifty-eight-foot limit seiner, or a sizable portion of a seventy-five-foot shrimper-crabber that would handle anything the Kodiak waters had to offer. What kind of fishermen did he want to be? That was the question.

"Nothing beats fishing salmon," he began tentatively with Jody and Jones Henry. "Those bays around Kodiak Island with all the mountains, why would anybody ask for more?"

"That takes care of mid-June to mid-August, and mebbe stretch it a few more weeks for silvers if you like to scratch," said Jones. "I first started fishing nothing but the salmon, but that was a different life. You can't live in Kodiak any more and count on salmon for it all, except in some shack in a cove and cut your own wood. By the way—all that money you say you've got for a down payment—you putting anything aside for a house, or . . . ?"

"We'd live on the boat," said Hank. Jody shrugged.

"Well, *I* had to raise three kids. And Adele was a game girl, but I always planned to keep her and the boat separated. With fishing, you know, some years you hit it big enough to pay your old debts. Then some years they don't run, or you break down at the height of the season, and you haven't made expenses, so back in debt you go. That's why Kodiak fishing's become better than most. If the salmon run poor, there's the shrimp, then the crab." Jones tilted back the visor of his cap to include both Hank and Jody in his wink. "Anyhow, now that Kodiak has things to fish at other times of the year, who wants to be the only boat tied up for nine months? I'd set Adele crazy. That's the polite way to put it."

"If I had a fifty-eight-foot limit seiner I could still convert to crab and shrimp, but never on any scale. Have to stay close around Kodiak."

"Tell you one thing," Jones said, choosing his words as if they might be used against him. "I've built slow all my life, each boat about ten foot longer than the one before. Now look at my new ninety-footer, a real beauty. I've got to earn the kind of payments every quarter that used to cover a whole year's rent. Now that it's all done, I don't know. Steve and Ivan and me, we like to fish hard. But out here it's a different kind of push, a wild man's game. Fishing's no fun any more, not the way it used to be on the old *Rondelay,* or even on the *Adele H.* Remember how we'd lay over a couple days and go hunting if we felt like it? Out here, you can't even show me a safe little cove, even if there was something to hunt besides eagles."

"End of the earth," said Hank absently. "Bering Sea's no kind of life. Pulling a crab pot every ten minutes, over and over, it's dull compared to all the steps in setting a purse or a trawl. And if you make a pile, taxes take it."

Jody had let them talk, but now she said to Hank, "Don't fool yourself. I've never seen you happier than trying to outwit the crab and playing rough-weather Norwegian. And you'd get tax breaks on money you plowed into boat payments."

"Are you telling me to put us both in hock for half a million bucks with a big Bering Sea crabber?"

"I'm not sure, Hank, not sure."

"What makes you think," asked Jones, "that a first-year skipper's going to find that kind of credit? Just because you made money one year don't guarantee you'll make it other years. Banks and canneries both know it."

In mid-September, Hank was finishing his final Bering Sea trip, with a layover ahead until November before the Dutch Harbor season began. He and Jody planned to return to Kodiak for a few days of nothing but sleep, then fly to Hawaii for a delayed honeymoon. He was stacking pots for storage when word flashed along the radio bands: the Coast Guard cutter had surprised a Japanese trawler with its gear in the water nine miles from land, and the trawler was fleeing with the cutter in chase. News bulletins said the Coast Guard termed it a "hot pursuit." The chase started at noon. By late afternoon it still continued strong.

"Damn Coast Guard ships ain't fast enough," declared Jones Henry over the sideband. "Think they'd have caught 'em by now."

"Hear you on that," said Hank. "This Coast Guard ship cruises nineteen knots and has auxiliary engines for more. I just visited her. But you think one ship's going to ram another just to make it stop?"

"Don't the Coast Guard carry guns?"

"They entered international waters as soon as they left the twelve-mile zone."

"Ha!" Tolley announced. "We're steaming to give an assist. If we intercept the cocksucker don't think *we* won't shoot."

Given his own boat, however illogically, Hank would have followed. He listened to the news with the itchy excitement of a hunter left behind.

One bulletin gave some details. The Coast Guard had a hot pursuit procedure. It started as the cutter cruised alongside the fleeing trawler, sending stop signals by radio, bullhorn, and flag hoist. An hour later, when a Coast Guard C-130 plane joined the chase, it flew low over the trawler, first dropping smoke pots ahead, then dropping a message block on deck with written orders in Japanese to stop. The plane crew saw a Japanese take the message block to the bridge. But the ship continued full speed.

The American fishermen commented to each other with growing interest and exuberance, as if the entire foreign problem was being brought to a showdown. Other boats besides Tolly's had abandoned gear to head for an intercept. Hank kept the radio at blast level so that his crew could hear as they continued to work. The whole convoy was steaming northwest. There was gray cloud cover, but no worse than a light choppy sea; given the Bering, it was perfect weather for a chase.

"If the bastard keeps in that direction he'll hit Bristol Bay. Too bad their salmon fleet's done for the season. Japs have ruined their sockeye runs, and plenty fellows up there would like to get them a Jap."

"Roger that, but you have Jap factory fleets working that area. Jap probably figures he'll lose himself in the dark with all the other boats, or maybe luck out if the weather kicks up."

At twilight, around eight, the pursuit continued. At ten, and then at midnight, the news was the same. Judging from the sideband commentary, even the crews that had stopped fishing for the night stayed awake. Then, a bulletin at two in the morning announced that the Japanese ship had stopped and turned on its decklights. The Coast Guard with a Fisheries agent would board in the morning.

"Yahoo!"

"Those Coast Guard better carry handguns tomorrow," Jones announced. "Don't underestimate Japs for treachery."

But at noon the next day, after a long radio silence, the anti-climactic news came that the Japanese trawler had been seized without incident and that the Coast Guard cutter was escorting it to Kodiak.

"Hey, think the Kodiak jail's big enough to hold forty-fifty Japs? Course they're used to crowding like pigs."

"Jail? More likely the State Department flies up from D.C. and tells the Coast Guard it's violated some big treaty, and Uncle Sam pays the *Japs* a fuckin' fine. Probably donates the Coast Guard captain's head to hang in the Japs' chowhall."

But, a week later in Kodiak when Hank arrived, a forlorn Japanese crew watched from the deck of their rusty ship moored under guard at the Coast Guard Base, as "Blue Jesus, yes, that's them!" roared Chief Mack from the rail of the victorious cutter. His wide face kept breaking into a grin and his voice continued full volume as he invited Hank aboard and regaled him with details of the chase.

"There was a rumor when I left Dutch," said Hank, "that the Japs were let off. That's why I came here direct from the plane."

"From Anchorage? Keep your eyes open. You flew with our people just come back from the trial. Let 'em off? Ha!" Mack pounded him on the back and dragged him to the chief's mess. Along the way they passed sailors who were affected with a similar exuberance. Inside, the Quartermaster was describing to a half dozen other chiefs the trial from which he had just returned as a witness. The story had long before covered the main incidents, and now explored details such as the meek nature of the Japanese captain ever since he stopped running. Hank interrupted politely to ask if there had been a fine or other penalty.

The chiefs turned collectively to look him over as if he were the ultimate Jap. "Fine? You're fuckin' A there was a fine. Biggest one yet for a Jap ship, two hundred thousand, and another thirty thousand against the captain. Who are you? Oh, that fisherman from Dutch. You still think the Coast Guard sits on its ass?"

It was too much a family affair for Hank to join. In a few minutes even Mack had forgotten him, but no one threw him out. After they discussed the slippery behavior of the Japanese at the trial as well as the cool displayed by all the Americans—including the U.S. Attorney, who took no crap from foreigners—the talk shifted to old events. The stories were fragmented enough—punch lines without preamble—to be on their hundredth repeat.

The Engineman chief who had once shown Hank around had been one of the six in the custody crew that occupied the trawler for the three-day trip to Kodiak. They had brought aboard their own supplies—sleeping bags, food, water, and first-aid kit—and had lived in the pilothouse. Only four could sleep on the deck at one time, but they were alternating watches anyhow. The Japs ran their own ship, but the Americans kept a check on the navigation gear and relayed the course changes as they trailed behind the cutter. "Nobody gave us trouble, but it was cramped as hell, and stuffy."

"Full of fuckin' Jap smells, you mean?"

"Oh, the smells wasn't so bad. The Japs neither, real quiet and polite, to tell the truth. But the Jap captain . . . wish I had that note he gave Lieutenant Smith."

"*Tell* us about that note again."

"Scratched in big blocky letters like a kid. How did it go? 'Dear United States. Please excuse me from breaking the law.' I tell you that was comical, after all the chase they put us through." Hank laughed with the rest.

As he left the cutter, Hank encountered Ensign Sollers. He had seldom seen such pure cloud-floating. "We did it," Sollers exclaimed, pumping his hand. "Just wish our patrol wasn't over. I'm applying for transfer to the *Confidence* or *Storis* out of Kodiak here, since they sail patrols all year long. Like a hunt for big game out there, you know?"

When Adele Henry had welcomed Hank and Jody at the airport with hugs and exclamations, she declared: "Tell me this if you can: How many matrons of honor have to wait six months after the ceremony to see the bride and groom? I think we should have a proper wedding up at St. James the Fisherman. Meanwhile, the guest room's all fixed for you at home, a bottle of champagne's in the refrigerator, and we'll have a special dinner tonight. Then we'll celebrate again when Jones gets back to town. Why couldn't he leave his boat at Dutch Harbor and fly back the way you did?"

"Not sure Jones plans to fish out of Dutch any more."

"But he bought that big boat. Not that I don't miss him—it's awful to be alone so long. But the whole world was going to pass him by if he didn't get out there in the Bering Sea. Now I can't wait to question him."

"Adele, we're too tired to think until we've rested, both Jones and me. Bering crab's the longest pull of them all. I plan to sleep for a week before we go south. Jones will too. He won't make any decision that counts until after that."

Rest or not, Hank called on Swede Scorden at the cannery next afternoon. They started with the usual ceremony of cigar, bottle, and feet on the desk before starting to talk, but it lacked the atmosphere of ease. Swede was tense. Through the big window Hank watched a shrimp boat unloading and others tied around it. Nothing physical seemed to have altered.

"Good shrimp season out there?"

"Best in my time, these last two months. Fantastic. We're not even buying from boats that don't deliver to us regular, and we work two cannery shifts around the clock."

"Well then," he joked for openers, "I guess you're going to make me an offer to return to the cannery business."

"These days, I wouldn't wish it on that Agnew crook."

Hank came to the point. "I've skippered two boats now for a total of a year, both for winter shrimp in Kodiak and every one of the king crab seasons to westward—Bering, Dutch, Aleutians. I've saved fifty thousand, and I'm ready to get my own boat."

Swede questioned him on the kind he wanted and the fishery he hoped to enter. "New Bering Sea crabber on ten percent and a year's experience? Never. To begin with, banks expect nearly a third down."

"Don't they see the kind of money being made out there? Crab prices have doubled, and that's not the end."

"No need to tell me about prices. It's changed my life."

"You know it. Doubled. Can't a bank compare catch records to see if a skipper has the balls to make it? At new prices it'll only take a few years to pay off a boat, maybe just one super season."

"The basic help a cannery usually offers is to supply the gear— the pots or the nets—for ten percent of the catch and a delivery guarantee until the debt's paid. Not a bad deal, since we don't charge you interest as long as the product keeps coming. Next thing a cannery might do is co-sign, if they think you're good. You take the risk, and we get the boat if you fail. But now, you're talking a ninety-foot Marco-type crabber like Jones Henry's. That's five hundred thousand before gear. You don't have the reputation yet to float something like that."

The door flew open without a knock, and a Japanese wearing a dark suit and hornrimmed glasses entered as if he owned the place. "Yes, Scorden, excuse me please. The efficiency report," he said in good English, handing Swede a file. "We'll have conference in one hour, at four-ten sharp, and decide where to cut. Please, you will make sure to read it so we don't waste time."

Swede removed his feet slowly from the desk as he introduced Hank as a highline Bering Sea skipper. Hank towered over the Japanese by a head. Mr. Ato offered a hand to shake that had no grip as he studied Hank and smiled slightly. "Yes, highline? Very good. You fish for our plant in Dutch Harbor? Give me your card, please. Here is mine."

Hank's stock sank visably when he failed to produce a card, although the politeness continued. He said that he had visited a Japanese factory ship, and had been impressed with its efficiency.

It roused a spark. "Ah, yes, of course, they must be efficient. This is one of the fleets of our conglomerate. I know the fishing master. He brings in very good quantity."

Alone again, Hank stared at Swede. "*Our* plant?"

"I warned that something would give, Hank. We've been paying overprice for the raw product just to keep from shutting the plants. Had to find new capital or quit. You think there was American money for such a shaky seasonal industry? Our Seattle man spent weeks in New York. The only money ready to invest in fish was yen, my friend. Favorable exchange, historic interest. This Japanese fishing conglomerate made a decent offer. It saved us, at the price of controlling interest. Don't think we're the only ones. Whitney-Fidalgo, with plants in Kodiak and all over Alaska, went ninety-eight percent Jap this year."

"Oh, Jesus, they're everywhere."

"You might as well be realistic. You wouldn't have a plant left here to buy your fish if the Japs hadn't bailed us out."

"Hey." Hank frowned. "Now they can band together and control prices, can't they? They could dry up our fisheries by refusing to buy.

We'll never get into pollock or any other bottomfish. We've been sold out."

"Hank, I've got to read this report. They've had some experts from Japan studying the plant. I'd better make sure they haven't eliminated me. Free for lunch tomorrow? Meet me noon. We'll talk the realities of buying a boat. Don't worry, I can still help, but forget a new Bering Sea crabber. Think two alternatives: partnership with somebody or buying an older and smaller boat." He appeared tired as he nodded out the window at a shrimper moored below. "She might be for sale in your range. Remember Nels Hanson last winter?"

"The *Delta*, sure. I recognize her now. Looks like she survived the ice after all, assuming her engine runs after all that salt."

"New engine."

"What's wrong with Nels? He chisel enough insurance to get a new boat, or did he run out of crew to exploit?"

"Never heard you talk like that before."

"Nels Hanson never used you as a deck swab for two clockaround weeks, then paid you off with seventy-five bucks and a kick in the ass. Long as the old prick survived, he's back on my shit list."

"When his boat iced and capsized, he clung all night to the hull before the Coast Guard found him. One of his guys gave up and floated away. The other guy claims if Nels hadn't ridden him every time he started off, he'd have gone the same way. Nels' kind is tough on himself too, you know. Immersed in that water for hours. Lost one leg to freezing, and circulation never returned to the other or to his hands. Inside two months he was back aboard on crutches. But he hasn't been able to keep any kind of crew, and he can't do the work himself. I think he wants ninety-three thousand for her with gear, but he might have to settle for less. Sixty-five-foot Gulf shrimper, built eight years ago. All the fishing boat most young skippers ever dream about."

Hank jumped aboard the *Delta* with a curious sense of the past suspended. He entered the cabin when the familiar hard voice said "Come." Nels Hanson sat at the galley table, his squat, heavy face unchanged. No sign of disablement showed, except for a pair of crutches against the bulkhead.

"Nels, remember me?"

"Yeah, one of the crybabies. You ever learn how to fish?" The eyes stared him down. "Well, I'd consider hiring you back if I could trust you to hop to it. Mug-up and sit over there."

The unreality made Hank smile. "Pour you some coffee too?"

"I can pour my own if I want it." His hands remained motionless on the table, huge, white, and puffy, like two beached jellyfish. Hank remembered how they always showed workgrease under the nails, how he had used them to thump the arms and chest of a prospective crewman, how his handshake crushed sadistically.

"We were listening that night. Sorry you had such a rough time." He considered, then added: "Glad you survived."

"Well, if you're on the beach, don't beat around the bush. I happen to be between crews, so I might take care of you. Go on, find your buddy. Get the grub at Kodiak Market on my account. We'll go over for fuel and ice, and be out shooting net by nightfall. You afraid to work through the night to make up for lost time?"

"I'm my own skipper now," said Hank quietly. "Swede tells me your boat's for sale."

"He told you wrong! I'm looking for a goddam crew, not a sale. Listen." Nels leaned forward, rocking his thick body, his face suddenly intense. "Never a month since I first fished the shrimp in Kodiak, not a single goddam month, have those shrimp been running like the last two months. In August they landed twelve and a half million pounds. Hear that? And the run's still going. If you're a skipper why ain't you out there?"

"I'm on king crab, just back from the Bering."

"*Crab* pots? *That's* tricky gear—raise 'em, dump 'em. That all the skipper you are?" He hobbled purposefully to the stove, and by a series of maneuvers using teeth and the crook of his arm poured himself coffee, then returned with a full mug. He sugared and creamed it rapidly, with the same dexterity. "Then you're available, because king crabs are scratch around here. What kind of fisherman sits idle when the water's plugged? Huh? You know that boats what usually can't fill half a hold in three days are coming back in two days with deckloads? Crab pots! Trawl gear, *that's* fishing. You ever hauled a cod end that spilled twenty-five, thirty ton of shrimp on deck? I reckon not."

Their eyes met and held. Hank started laughing. This ugly bastard whom he'd hated ...

353

"Your boat's geared for crab, you say." The helpless hands started thumping the table. "Well, now you don't have to waste time converting." Nels' voice rose to a roar and his face turned red with frantic energy. "Well, bring your whole goddam crew aboard, there's room, I'll sleep here on the bench. Only let's get where they're running and take our share!"

Seth had arrived back that day, dirty and tired. "You're fuckin' nuts," he shouted. "You forgotten how that prick treated us?"

"You said yourself you learned on the *Delta*."

"Learned from *you*, Hank, while we near died keeping up under his shit. Listen, stupid, I've been dreaming of sack time for two months. You think Joe Eberhardt ever let us sleep?"

"I'd thought some of sleep too, but . . . You ought to see how he's worked a system of hooks and catches in his wheelhouse. He can still handle the controls himself. We'll set our own pace, and fuck him if he rides us."

"Thought you were a skipper now, not deck ape for a cripple."

Hank touseled his hair. "Man, I've confirmed it from other boats, the water's plugged with shrimp. You ever brought in trawls with thirty ton?"

"Oh shit . . ."

To Jody he explained: "Be more money toward a boat, honey. Just a few trips. Maybe then he'll sell the *Delta*, and I might want to buy. *We* might want to buy, you and me. Hawaii's there any old time."

"Don't let him do it to you, Jody," called Adele Henry in dead earnest from the kitchen. "They never know when to stop unless you make it clear."

Jody smiled her smile, but her voice was wistful. "He smells the fish. That's probably why I married him."

354

28

THE
KODIAK
SEA

WITH Swede's help, Hank found the level a bank would risk and began the search for an older boat. The status of Bering Sea skipper-owner would have to be accomplished in increments.

Nels Hanson did not sell the *Delta*. The few shrimp hauls that Hank and Seth landed him, before they returned to their boats in Dutch Harbor, provided him with enough money to wait, dead hands on the galley table, until other crews fell his way. This would remain the pattern of his life until the sea claimed him, as he intended she would.

Jones Henry knew after one season that he had overextended himself to take on the Bering Sea. The steady hardships of Kodiak fishing were lodged in his blood, but not the fanatic drive of the Westward fleet. "But now I've got the tiger's tail. Only one way to meet payments every quarter, because no bank's going to foreclose on *me*." So he followed Hank back to fish the November opening in Dutch Harbor.

The solution, figured one storming night in the Elbow Room after a gloomy assessment of the traps of ownership, had beautiful logic. Hank and Jones decided to go partners. It gave them credit beyond their individual resources, enough to order construction on a new fifty-eight-foot salmon limit seiner that could be adapted to crab and shrimp in season. Hank would take over the ninety-foot crabber and gradually buy controlling interest, while Jones would fish the smaller boat where he belonged. The tax benefits of incorporation offered ways to keep more of their income for boat payments, but the paper work! Hank learned from Jones that skippering somebody else's boat might be responsibility enough, but that as owner he needed to keep all kinds of records, for

crew payments, Social Security, insurance, deliveries, amortization . . .
Finally they hired an accountant (in small-town Kodiak, it was the
brother of Sandra, Hank's former girlfriend) so that only days, rather
than weeks, needed to be stolen from their fishing and rest to keep the
government satisfied.

Hank's equity increased a few thousand in a manner he treasured.
During Christmas, after a rugged November out of Dutch Harbor that
marked his final commitment to Arnie Larson's boat, he and Jody flew
Below to visit his parents in Maryland and hers in Colorado. Hank's
father and mother were great. He could regard them now as equal adults
rather than the arbiters of his conduct. It made him regret that fishing
had placed so many miles between them, since the years that were developing him had aged them. His mother lavished warmth on Jody, and
his father was openly proud of them both. When Hank enthused over
his plans for a boat, his father suddenly said: "Are you too independent
to take a wedding present of five thousand toward that boat, and another
five for a share as my personal investment in the industry?" Hank gave
a yell and pumped his hand.

As they were parting at the airport, with talk of a reunion in
Kodiak, Hank's mother took Jody's arm and said lightly, "One visit you
can put down for me, dear, if your own mother doesn't . . . You know
there's always more to do than you think, when a baby comes." Hank's
father was saying to him simultaneously, "Hope I'm not too old to enjoy
my grandchildren if they ever come."

The call on Jody's parents had cordiality but tighter overtones.
At Hank's house they had guarded the expletives, with an occasional slip
that brought from his mother a wince and a wry joke about the use of
soap. Jody's mother left the room when Jody dropped an "asshole," and
her father began a lecture on bad influences to his future grandchildren.
Colonel Sedwick had retired from the Army, and was writing his mem-
oirs. "You can count on it, Crawford," he told Hank with the aloofness
due a one-hitch Navy man. "Thirty years' service to my country, in the
Army where it counts, gave me worthwhile experiences. People can
benefit by reading about them."

"I'm sure of it, sir."

"Jody, now, we won't make a secret of it, she'd have married into
the Army if I'd called the shots. Still, I've always liked angling for fish

on a free afternoon, and if you can find somebody to pay you for doing it, I suppose that's pretty clever."

Mrs. Sedwick had a trim figure, with a leathery face that appeared permanently suntanned. She sipped vodka drinks after eleven in the morning and chain-smoked with hands that trembled slightly. "Jody as a kid?" she said in response to a question. "Oh, Hank, not very obedient." She smiled, revealing a vestige of Jody's wide mouth and lively eyes. "You know, she played with boys rather than girls. And with the way we changed posts every two or four years, you could say she ran wild. Of course her father thought that was fine, all the fights. But where was he when her clothes got ripped, or I had to stop in the middle of a bridge tournament to run her to a doctor for stitches?"

"Not to change the subject," said Colonel Sedwick, "but when am I going to see a couple of grandsons by you two?"

Back in Kodiak, Jones had begun to fish his pots for tanner crabs while he waited for the delivery of his new limit seiner. He only received seventeen cents a pound for them, compared to the sixty-five he had just drawn for king crabs. Yet with the king-crab seasons over, Jones and a hundred-odd other Kodiak skippers had discovered that fishing tanners through the winter met the payments better than the old idleness of less pressured days. With no room for two skippers, Hank scratched a thin living, and a hard one, back aboard Nels Hanson's shrimper. The tanner crabs at least ran close to the sheltered bays. The fabulous fall runs of shrimp had gone their way into open water. Only those trawl men who would not let go, or who needed the money, were willing to dare the storms of Shelikof Strait to follow the few remaining pockets.*

Seth went with Hank, still chafing. When it became clear that Hank would have his own boat, he offered Seth first berth with opportunities as relief skipper, and Seth was now his man. For Hank, the turns on deck under Nels seemed his farewell to youth, to the unburdened

---

* In mid-January of 1974, in fact, the new eighty-six-foot Kodiak shrimper *John and Olaf* was trapped in the Shelikof during a storm of freezing seventy-to-one-hundred-knot winds and forty-foot seas. They iced so desperately that the skipper and three-man crew beached the boat on offshore rocks in Portage Bay—the bay adjacent to the one where Hank and Jody had been married the year before while riding ice—and they apparently attempted to make land in their life raft. Their bodies were never found, only the raft. Ironically, the *John and Olaf* remained afloat, mugs of coffee still on the galley table, a horrifying specter of ice.

bull work of a crewman. It made him savor the hardship of handling ice-coated nets, even bending to the orders of a driver made doubly acerbic by his handicaps, in a way that would have made Seth crow with mockery had he realized.

In early March, Jones finally turned the boat over to Hank and took Adele south for a while. The extra position on deck had changed hands several times since the boat was new—nobody could endure the closed compact of Steve and Ivan for long—so that it was easy enough for Hank to clear a berth for Seth. To be skipper to Steve and Ivan was another problem altogether. They had served under Jones for a dozen years, and they still regarded Hank as the kid they had taught to fish. Clashes erupted often. Hank wanted to highline, to push to the brink for all the tanners he could get. One night in bad weather when he decided to continue working pots, Steve shouted him down with such vehemence that Hank half expected to be slammed with a huge fist, or to be thrown overboard by the leg as in the old days. He held his ground, but lost the argument. Seth, who was tuned to Hank's pace, was regarded by the others as an interloper. Fishing with Steve and Ivan was at best an armed compromise.

In late March the Senate Commerce Committee in Washington sent word through the Alaskan Republican Senator, Ted Stevens, that it would convene a day-long session in Kodiak to hear fishermen's views on the foreign fleets. The committee at last was considering a bill to establish U.S. two-hundred-mile fishery jurisdiction.

Despite short notice, Jones cut his vacation and flew home to testify. He had barely arrived before Steve and Ivan fell over him like children to report how Hank ran the boat. Hank himself was weary and disgusted. He argued his case in the galley before them all, with Steve and Ivan watching in hostile silence. "I've never known men who fish harder than you guys, when you feel like it." He turned to Jones. "But when they've had enough they quit. I might as well tell the waves to stop as get them back on deck. Jones, we could have delivered ten or twelve thousand more crabs, with that much more money toward the boat."

"Steve and Ivan ain't buying a boat," Jones said reluctantly.

"But they'd each have a thousand bucks more apiece."

"For who, the government? They both make all they need."

"What about their damn pride? We could be highliners instead of just another bunch of apes in the fleet."

"Well, Hank, you know—Steve, Ivan, and me . . ."

"Tell him, Boss."

Hank exploded, to keep face in front of Seth. "You guys don't have the balls any more to fish a deckload. You getting old?" The words brought Steve slowly to his feet, fists clenched. "Look," Hank continued reasonably, "just go out with me once and work it my way. Jones come too and watch. Let Jones be the judge."

They agreed, grudgingly.

First they attended the Senate hearing at the Elks' Hall. Senator Stevens arrived in the morning from Anchorage with his staff. A busy, impatient man under effort to be cordial—there were hearings in Sitka and Juneau on the following days—he listened to witnesses for two hours, then flew back to Anchorage for an afternoon session. Hank, among those who testified, told of his bitter experience with the Russian trawler and of the masses of pollock on the Japanese factory ship, while Jones and the other fishermen who spoke reiterated the same anger. But it was over practically before it began, and they were seeing the Senator off at the airport where they had greeted him only three hours before.

"Well, Ted, we'd had a banquet prepared for you tonight. But the main thing is, we're counting on you to rid us of the foreigners."

"We'll do our best, Jones."

After the plane had left: "Well, Daddy," said Adele, taking Jones' arm. "I *am* impressed. He recognized you and called you by name, just like that."

"Ted's a good man," said Jones expansively. "Come on, I'll take everybody to lunch."

Next morning it was snowing, with a thirty-knot westerly. But it was Hank's show as agreed.

"Don't corner yourself, darling," murmured Jody as they lay in bed after the alarm rang. "Remember they're not your permanent crew."

"Thank God."

He and Jones walked glumly to the harbor in the dark. The snow swirled in white halos around the street and dock lamps and covered the boats from deck to crosstree. The others were awake. Seth had bacon frying. Hank took the controls firmly, and Jones settled without a word in the seat at the other end of the pilothouse. It was four when they passed through the breakwater. Behind them the snow had already blotted the few lights of town. The sea took them over with a jolting pitch.

Throughout the day, Hank took care to be cool. He saw to it that they had time to eat—a nicety he sometimes forgot in the heat of working the pots—but he kept the pressure steady. The tanner crabs were running well. With pots yielding forty to seventy each, the main tank was layered with them by nightfall. As the wind shifted to the north, the air became colder and the sea rougher. He kept them going, through the night. Jones watched it all, a nonparticipant except once when Hank asked him to take the wheel so that he could spell them on deck one by one.

"We don't need relief," said Steve for them all. "Just you worry about the wheel, where you belong."

They fished through the entire next day. Hank had planned to stop at the thirty-six-hour mark, but when the time arrived he kept going. They were maintaining their pace. Let them speak up when they'd had enough. The longer they stuck it, the less it appeared that anyone would take the initiative to stop. The second night passed, at full work push. During breakfast the third morning, Hank broke the silence to say, "Guess we could knock off for a few hours."

"You had it already?" asked Steve.

They continued.

During it all, Jones remained in the pilothouse, but any conversation he had with Hank was monosyllabic. Hank found himself dozing and turning sick from all the coffee he drank to keep awake. He took his bellyache tablets surreptitiously so Jones would not see, as well as pills for headache. At least it would have to end when the tanks were full. But that could be another three days. His headache grew worse, until nothing reached it.

On deck they moved slower and slower, their actions the jerk of automatons. He knew they hurt worse than he did. What if any one of them got careless? If only Jones would intervene.

"The guys are ready to drop," he ventured.

"Steve and Ivan, they're tough as bricks. I don't know about your man Seth, but he seems to be keeping up."

Finally, at dinner, as the third night without sleep approached, he declared: "Okay, we've worked more than sixty hours and you've shown me up for an asshole. You're better men than I'll ever be. Let's sleep."

Seth sighed, lay back at once, and sank into a doze. He was haggard and he had begun holding his mug with both hands to get it to his mouth.

Steve picked his teeth and considered. Except for the soggy filth of his clothes and the raw salt blisters on his hands and lips, he seemed little affected. "I don't see no sense in stopping this close to full tanks. You want to stop, Ivan?"

"Shit, no."

"Seth here's okay, he's held his end. Let him sack out a while and Ivan and me can handle deck." He nodded offhand at Hank. "You can let Jones take his wheel back. We'll wake you when we get to port in a couple days."

Hank rose, dizzy. "Let's get fishing."

Steve and Ivan started pulling on their rain gear, and Seth with a quiet groan reached for his.

Hank stopped and looked them over. Was he to risk a boat so they could all act like children? "No," he said firmly. "It's over. You've won. I'm taking her in, and I'll drop the hook myself if I have to. If you want to sleep or not is your own damn business."

They steamed to the closest bay and anchored. Hank pushed aside the life jackets in a vacant crew berth, leaving Jones the cabin. Nothing was said. Ivan and Seth fell asleep at once, in their clothes. Hank numbly peeled his pants as he shut his eyes against the headache. All that mattered was the bunk. Steve, standing alongside, tapped Hank's shoulder and offered a puff of his cigarette. They smoked it together without talk. Afterward Hank lay sleepless, he thought forever, listening to Ivan's long-forgotten snore. But by the clock he drifted under in three minutes.

When he awoke next afternoon, his first sensation was the odor of Ivan's feet. Steve, scratching his chest comfortably as he dressed, met Hank's glance and winked. Hank grinned. What had he done to himself, to leave the warmth of the fo'c'sle for the loneliness of the cabin? His legs felt too heavy to lift to deck. Neither Seth nor Ivan had stirred. He started to roll over and return to blessed sleep, then thought better of it and forced himself to stand and pull on his clothes.

In the galley Jones had made coffee. Hank drew his mug and settled beside Steve. The constraint was gone. All three talked cheerfully as they made themselves sandwiches from a pack of baloney.

Jones yawned. "Anchor's holding. I figure tomorrow morning's time enough to pull the next string. I'm going to sleep the whole day through."

"Me too, Boss," said Steve.

"Sounds good," said Hank.

Sunrise next day was at five, but nobody bothered to untangle until about eight. It was gray and foggy, with the temperature around thirty-five degrees and, according to the weather report, a thirty-knot westerly in open water that might build while shifting to north. They loitered over breakfast. Hank insisted on doing the dishes. Nobody mentioned the angry push of two nights before; it already seemed that a month had passed since then.

"Anybody got a corn plaster?" asked Ivan.

"No little thing like that's going to help your feet none, you Aleut," said Steve.

Seth offered a Band-Aid, and Ivan, who could refuse anything from someone he disliked, took it and thanked him.

They had slept through the fishery news the day before, and only learned that morning that the area where their pots were laid had just been closed for the season by the Department of Fish & Game. It meant that they could pull their pots and harvest the tanners inside, but then would have to move to one of the areas that remained open. "Them Fish and Game biologists," said Jones with irritation, "they sit in their office uptown and play games with arithmetic. Anybody out here could tell them the pots are still coming up full."

"Too full," said Hank. "They count the crabs delivered, and the quota's probably been reached sooner than expected."

"Then they ought to raise the quota, since anybody can see there's more crab than they figured."

"Tricky business. You've talked yourself often enough of how they disappeared in sixty-seven."

"That was different."

362

The other boats fishing the area had already left. They pulled a deckload of pots and headed for the new grounds about three hours away. Everyone was relaxed. It was a different boat than a few days before. They all lounged in the pilothouse and took turns at the wheel. Only Seth, who had just came from deck rounds, wore anything but T-shirts and deck slippers.

Three Saints Bay, where they planned to anchor after setting their pots, was surrounded enough by close mountains to have poor radio reception, so Jones made his daily call to Adele as they cruised.

Hank talked to Jody at the same time. "Pushing hard out there?" she asked. "Ought to see you back soon, at the rate you go."

He shrugged at the others around him, taking his lumps cheerfully. "Don't look for us until you see us."

When they had signed off, Jones said, "Why not go hunting? We've earned a vacation."

Everybody agreed, even Hank, although he couldn't resist saying, "Vacation? You just got back from Hawaii."

"That was with Adele."

There was a muffled explosion within the wall of the pilothouse. Before they knew what had happened, flame and smoke poured inside. The odor caught in their throats with a brass taste. Steve grabbed a fire extinguisher and sprayed wildly. Jones headed the boat full gun in the direction of shore, shouting orders, as Ivan and Seth beat the flames with a cushion and Seth's jacket. Hank raced outside and leaped to the main deck to scoop a bucket of water. By the time he threw it against the outside of the pilothouse the others were tumbling out, gagging. Flames licked from crevices all over the structure. They burned from beneath the outer sheeting—the insulation?—and roiled against the windows inside. With the boat pitching into the wind, the acrid smoke blew back over them.

Steve and Jones raced to the afterdeck and started unbolting the lazerette hatch to get the portable pump. The others formed a bucket chain, with Ivan scooping water in the deck bucket and bait tubs, Seth raising it to the wheeldeck, and Hank throwing it into the fire. The flames divided like amoebas wherever he doused, then grew, fanned by the wind.

Hank glanced with fright across the gray water. The waves rolled in crests and black troughs, and he saw no other boat. The first line of mountains was at least five miles away. He bit his lips as he remembered the feel of it when the water once closed over him like lead.

At last the fire abated under the slosh of his buckets. The burned surface of the pilothouse still sizzled, but it was under control. On deck Jones and Steve were just clamping the hoses to the pump. He was about to call down a joke about their pace. Then he felt heat through the soles of his slippers. The fire had sucked down into the bunkroom and galley. It burned straight beneath him with an empty roar.

Instinctively he wrenched free the big mounted canister that held the life raft. He checked that the halyard was secured, then struggled the canister through rigging and shrouds and threw it overboard. The motion pulled the CO_2 pin automatically. With a bang and hiss a wide surface popped into shape.

"It's upside down," cried Jones. "What'd you do?"

Ivan grabbed the halyard and struggled to steady the raft against the side.

"Nothing, no directions," Hank sputtered. "Took care of itself, supposed to."

The boat's forward motion beat the raft. Jone's voice rose. "She'll foul the screw, why'd you throw too soon?"

Hank looked around irrationally, clenching his fists. "Why'd you speed in the wind and fan the fire?" He held his breath and rushed inside the hot pilothouse, slowing the engine control in passing. The radio mike burned his hand. He pressed the switch and called, "Mayday, Mayday, *Adele Three* on fire, five miles east of—" The blackened cord fell loose.

Steve's deck pump sputtered water into the galley below. It pushed the fire like a live creature back up the stairs to the pilothouse. Flame scorched Hank's bare arms and started his T-shirt smoking. He rushed outside, doused his shoulders from a bucket of water, then doubled over, choking and retching helplessly.

"The *bilge* pumps." Jones had been adjusting the deck pump while Steve hosed. He rushed to the switch on the deck housing, listened for the sound, leaned over the rail to check the scupper, flicked the switch again and again. Steve's water continued to pour inside. "Ain't working. We'll flood the engine." Jones disappeared through the galley door toward the control box, into the smoke, ducking Steve's spray. A minute later he staggered out, popeyed and gasping. Unable to speak, he gestured for Steve to stop the hose.

Fire immediately billowed again through the living spaces. The pilothouse had become a huge candle. Beneath Hank's feet on the wheeldeck the paint bubbled and steamed. Still retching, he jumped to the main deck with the others.

With the boat slowed, the wind brought it broadside to the waves. They were no longer pointed toward shore. The boat rolled with increasing sluggishness, lingering to far port and far starboard as if it were icing. Their freeboard had lowered a foot.

"Sinking, oh, Jesus Christ," groaned Seth. "My life jacket's in my bunk."

Jones flicked and flicked the bilge-pump switch.

Seth cupped his hands and bellowed "Help! Help!" in all directions of empty ocean.

The engine stopped. The sea was no rougher than they had lived with a thousand times, but the boat without way rolled in it helplessly. As the deck righted from each slow tilt the icy seawater washed over their legs—only Seth wore boots rather than slippers, since they had been lounging—and sloshed into the galley to continue down to the engine room.

Ivan had knelt on deck to pray, the water gurgling as it swept around him.

"What'll we do now, Boss?" said Steve in a hushed voice. Jones brushed him aside as he pried off the plate of the bilge-pump switch and pulled at the wires.

Hank staggered to the raft and started tugging at the halyard to right it. Steve was quickly beside him, then the others. They grasped the slippery edges and lifted with all their strength. When a wave trough brought air to release the suction, the bulbous side bounced up in their faces. The orange canopy to the life raft, which would have been free in the air if the raft had opened right side up, formed a heavy bucket. They had to maneuver the raft by the edge to release the water.

When it was righted, there was still two feet of water trapped inside. Hank, shivering in his T-shirt, looked at it in dismay, then found a bucket, slipped into the raft under the dripping canopy, and started to bail as he squatted in the frigid water.

Jones continued with the pump switch as he called over in an even voice, "Don't slice that raft bottom, don't use no metal that might cut."

Hank stopped and looked up at Steve on deck. Steve took the metal bucket from him, returned with two perforated plastic bait cans, and climbed in alongside.

Everyone had quieted. The fire roared softly throughout the boat. With their weights concentrated on the port side the boat had settled in a permanent list.

"Will we be all right?" asked Seth.

"Of course," said Hank calmly. "Just stand by."

Jones chuckled. "This bilge pump, she'll work in a minute, but keep bailing." He had braced himself on the tilting deck. "You know what I think happened? I've heard that damned eurythane insulation was flammable if it got too close to heat, and mebbe the exhaust pipe got tilted over too far, thing can scorch your hand sometimes."

"Anybody got coats?" asked Hank. "Any coats or rain gear on deck? Any boots? Seth, look around."

"What do you mean?" asked Seth, his eyes wide with sudden terror. "What do we plan to do?" He himself wore the scorched jacket with which he had beaten on the fire. "We're not going to abandon?"

Steve, as he bailed with one hand, dislodged two folded aluminum oars with the other and opened them.

"Just do it, Seth. Ivan, you look too." Hank felt calm, in control. The worst had happened. No longer any suspense about it. If they managed not to panic but huddled in, a boat or plane was bound to find them, or they'd make it to shore.

The wind gusted. It fanned the flames so that they bellowed like a furnace inside the housing and jetted sideways in the air through burnt-out openings. Heat covered the men, as did choking fumes. The boat listed slowly further to port. Jones lost his balance and slid toward them. The slight additional weight dipped the portside rail into the water.

"Everybody into the raft fast," said Hank. "Jump." Jones, Steve, and Ivan complied.

Seth remained on deck, wide-eyed and trembling. "Don't want to leave the boat. Come back."

366

Hank gazed at him firmly. "It's your choice. But it may be final if we cut loose."

"Don't cut loose. Please."

The two friends stared at each other desperately.

A new gust roared the fire and started the deck steadily into the water. Jones pulled his knife and sliced the line.

"Jump!" pleaded Hank. Seth leaped. Hank grabbed him aboard and held him tightly, hugged him, before letting go.

The boat kept heeling. A wave surged between and moved the raft forward. "Row," said Jones, "row fast, away." Steve already had his paddles in the water. Slowly the burning superstructure turned toward them. Burning fragments fell into the water alongside. "*ROW!*" They moved only inches as the pilothouse headed down on top of them. Because of the canopy of waterproofed canvas over their heads, they could see little. A cinder burned through and fell on Ivan's knee. "Don't let it hit bottom!" Ivan took it in his hand and tossed it out. "*ROW!*"

They crested on a wave. It carried them free of the boat. Before their eyes the *Adele III* rolled sideways and the superstructure dipped hissing into the water. The hull floated at a crippled tilt, ready to sink any minute.

"Maybe we ought to stay tied alongside," Hank ventured.

"What, and have her drag us under?" said Jones. "Besides, we don't want to spend the night out here."

They watched in awed silence as distance separated them. Hank forced a chuckle. "All those tanner crabs we busted ourselves to get." Nobody answered.

Hank looked at his watch. Two hours at most before dark.

Steve continued to row. With the canopy, it was difficult to see direction. They peered under it, watching the shore, where mountainsides sloped up to disappear in the low gray clouds.

"Must be only three–four mile," said Jones. "We'll make it easy. Steve, say when you're tired."

"I'm fine, Boss. Somebody keep me pointed. I'll do better if somebody holds my legs steady."

They were cramped. The space for the five of them was five feet wide and seven feet long, with the canopy about three feet above their heads. Their legs and shoulders twisted against each other however they moved. They could only sit or lie flat. None could move without affecting the others. Their motion in the seas was also unstable, so that when they tilted on a wave crest they pressed against each other. However much they bailed, pockets of water remained. They were all soaked.

The rubberized fabric of the raft was only a thin layer between their buttocks and the sea. With action stopped, the cold beneath them began quickly to sap their body warmth wherever it touched.

"Everybody okay?" asked Hank.

"Real good," said Seth. "Somebody want to borrow my coat?"

Each wanted it, but none spoke.

"A long time ago," said Jones, "I saw one of these life-raft buggers demonstrated. I thought enough to pay fifteen hundred dollars for it, but not enough to pay attention. There should be a false bottom. Look for a valve. She's made so we can blow air between the layers like a mattress." They found the valve, and took turns inflating as the others raised on their arms to allow the air to flow. It made a difference immediately. "What I call comfort," said Jones. "Just need a little booze to help it along."

"Funny thing," said Hank. "I've read you shouldn't drink booze in a situation like this. It might make you feel warm for a while, but it drains the circulation from your legs and arms in the long run. The one thing we've got to watch is what happened to Nels." The statement had been meant to keep up conversation, but it ended quieting them all.

Jones and Hank, pressed together, opened the raft's survival kit and laid out the contents. Each piece was in a separate package: flashlight, tablets, and bandages, one parachute flare and several hand-held flares, a knife blunted to prevent puncturing, cord, and other small accessories. Hank's arm was red from the burn in the wheelhouse, and any wind that caught it through the canvas made him wince. He found ointment and applied it. Once the seal of the package was broken, there was no easy way to store the remainder. The same applied to the other equipment. They returned it all together into the bag. Hank glanced at Jones and shrugged. No water in the kit, no food.

Steve was a strong man, and he rowed the absurdly frail oars with an unstinting back. But by nightfall they seemed no closer to shore than before. Even though the wind had slacked, it came steadily from shore, holding them at bay. The waves were eight to ten feet high, waves negligible from a boat deck that now rose above their heads each time the raft slid into a trough. As Hank watched them he thought of his Navy destroyer. From its bridge he might have termed such a low sea glassy calm.

Daylight fell away. With the cloud cover there was no sunset. The water turned from gray to black until it merged with the mist and the sky. They each stared from under the canopy at the last of the light.

Table Island Light shone clearly from its high bluff. They saw it as they rode each crest, and guided their oars by it. Hank's burned arm hurt more and more. When his turn came, he found it impossible to row without brushing the spot against Seth beside him on each stroke. In the dark, he allowed his face to remain screwed in pain. Rowing kept him warm, but it also made him thirsty. He thought of a juicy apple or an orange. He tried to discipline himself to think of Jody instead.

The canopy was a nuisance for sight and movement, but it preserved their body heat. It was sewed to the sides and raised on flexible struts, with the only openings being at the long ends of the raft. The lookout released a securing clamp and pressed his face to one of the openings. They alternated this job along with rowing and holding the rower's legs.

A small light on top of the canopy automatically activated itself, but Jones noticed it quickly grew dim, so he found a way to turn it off to save it.

"Wait until a boat comes along. Keep that lookout good."

By two in the morning their backs and legs ached, and they were neither warm nor dry. Hank's feet bothered him especially. The thin leather and elastic deck slippers had become simply boxes to contain the soggy mess of socks around his feet, so he removed them, wrung his socks, and massaged. Above all, avoid what happened to Nels. Seth shared his coat—it became the property of whoever stood lookout—but his boots stayed on his feet. Hank pictured the boots in the dark, and the dry warmth of boots inside, dismissing any thought of boots full of water as Seth's surely were.

"Boat!"

They all started moving together, like snakes in a pit. Hank held the flashlight while Jones turned on the canopy light and rummaged for the flares. No one knew how to assemble and activate the parachute flare. The directions were on the package, but it took a while to read them. The others opened both sides of the canopy and tied up the flaps so they could stand. Hank felt the cold wind at once. They could see the lights—a crab boat like their own. Coming close.

"Hot mug-up," chattered Seth. "Just a hot mug-up, no booze." He started to laugh.

"God heard my call," said Ivan.

"Hey, you Aleut, for once I'm glad to have you along. Jones, she's coming abeam fast, about a quarter mile away. Looks like Dan Kenney's *Sea Spray*. I'll buy that fucker the biggest— Got that flare ready?"

"Start one of them little ones. I've about got this figured."

They lit a hand flare. It cast a sputtering pink light that reflected on the surfaces of black water. The boat kept its steady course.

Jones activated the parachute flare. It shot into the sky and descended slowly, illuminating everything like a star come to earth. They could see the clean white of the boat's superstructure, practically read its name.

They cheered together, then fell silent as the light died. The *Sea Spray* moved on, away from them.

"That cocksucker asleep?" cried Jones.

They waved another hand flare as they shouted and screamed. The *Sea Spray*'s engine chugged steadily. The boat came close enough to show the spill of the galley light on the afterdeck. But it passed them by as if they did not exist.

"All the times I've stood watch," said Steve in a husky voice as the lights receded. "Gone down a minute for a piss or a sandwich when she was on course and everybody sleeping, Jesus!"

"Another parachute," said Seth desperately. "He's got to be back from his piss."

"Only one in the survival kit." Hank motioned Seth down with a hand on his shoulder, and replaced the canopy flaps. "Start rowing again, whoever's got it."

Despite the opposing wind, which slacked steadily, they began to make headway toward shore. Table Island Light grew brighter. By daylight, around five, they could see the small white structure itself, and the rockslide slopes of Cape Barnabas alongside. No one had slept, although they spoke nothing beyond the rudiments necessary to change watch. The closer they came, the greater their lee from the land so that each hour was easier.

"If I'd known we was going to abandon ship," said Jones, breaking the silence, "I'd have paid better attention to my tides. When we get past the rocks we're into Sitkalidak Strait, and that leads straight around the corner a few miles to Old Harbor."

"I got cousins in Old Harbor," said Ivan. "My mother's people. That's a good sign. They'll take care of us." He turned to Steve. "You'll see Aleut hospitality and stop making jokes."

"If we've hit the right current," Jones continued, "she'll ride us right into the village, but with the wrong one we'll never get inside the rocks."

"That's right," said Ivan. "That tide's a bitch."

"Ivan," said Hank, "could we walk around Sitkalidak Island if we beached?"

"That's twenty miles. How you going to get across the lagoon? And the rocks! Now, in the strait, you're likely to see some kind of boat in or out. Might even be one of my cousins."

The progress of a flat raft rowed by small oars left them hours to discuss the matter.

Around noon, a boat came out of the straits, two miles from them. They threw back the canopy to wave and shout. It kept a course toward Dangerous Cape, never stopping.

"I *know* that fellow from the village," said Ivan. "He's going to get hell from me tonight for not keeping his eyes open. Everybody knows we're in trouble, everybody should be looking."

"Why?" asked Hank. "We told the girls we'd be in Three Saints Bay and probably couldn't get them by radio."

"But somebody called a Mayday, you or Boss?"

Neither Jones nor Hank bothered to answer.

Seth, on the oars, grunted as he rowed harder. The aluminum sticks merely bent and slipped in the water from the extra effort.

A northerly wind started, icy and strong. It hit them broadside, and in a half hour had carried them past all of Sitkalidak Island, back into open water. The wind shifted to the west and the sky cleared. Rowing was useless. They tied the canopy and huddled. By second nightfall, land had slipped away.

"We'll mebbe pass some halibut boats on Albatross Bank," said Jones.

They did, in the dark, but none saw their sputtering little flares as the raft dipped into the troughs of building waves.

Time lost its meaning. There was long night, and then long day. Hank might have kept a journal with the pad and pen in the survival kit, but first his hands were too numb, then his will. His burnt arm hurt beyond description, a circle of fire exacerbated by the cold. It kept telling him, at least, that he was alive. He remembered that the temperature, the last time he noticed aboard the *Adele III*, had been thirty-five, so the seawater would be a degree or two above until they hit the Japanese current. His feet were tortured with cold. He had long ago removed his deck slippers altogether. By wringing his wool socks and massaging his feet he restored momentary circulation, and he pestered the others to do the same.

Their wretched little masthead light had long since died, and the batteries of their flashlight fell apart in the salt water.

Without incentive to row, they gradually ceased all watches. Every few hours they needed to reinflate the floor of the raft, but even this took such collective effort that the cold seawater on the other side of the fabric penetrated their bodies for long before they roused themselves. They lay atop each other for warmth, with Seth's jacket spread over the shoulders of the two on top. No one slept.

The collar of the jacket. He was not getting his share, and tugged it over. With a snarl Seth pulled it back.

The waves grew steadily larger, until waves became their total preoccupation. When they rode in the troughs, they were in a soundless valley between mountains twenty-five feet above them. Halfway up to the crest, the wind began to scream against the canopy and to shake it with a terrible "blah-blah-blah-blah-blah." When it first happened, Hank thought the canopy was going to fly apart, and by their terrified expressions so did the others. But it held, hour after hour.

Hank gradually accepted that they all might die, and by their dullness he assumed that the others did too. Yet, after the waves built to nightmarish size, they still automatically reacted for survival. As the raft rose on each crest they all leaned together to shift weight to keep from overturning. Sometimes, even so, the little deck slid nearly vertical and they had to clutch the sides. Each wave was a new struggle, a new bargain, to clutch life a minute longer. They breathed throughout the calm of the trough, then tensed together as they rose and the wind started ripping. If they heard the gurgle of water outside they relaxed and rode the high crest, balancing against the kick of wind, anticipating the blessed pause of the next trough. Like men under formal torture, they strained for the little signals that would tell them what was coming next, grabbing for reassurance that the next moment would not be the most terrible, living moment to moment. If they failed to hear the water after the wind started ripping them, they braced for their agony—the smash of the crested wave over them. Each wave that broke over them tore loose one end of the canopy, sluiced seawater through the raft, and tore out the other end. There was nothing they could do to stop it. They lived in the icy water, sat in it continuously no matter how much they bailed.

As close as they could remember, the waves started during the second night and continued throughout the third day and night.

The raft came equipped with two canvas sea anchors. As they put out the first, two of its shrouds ripped. The line was too short, and it seemed as if the tug of the anchor might rip the fabric of the raft where it was attached. Soon the sea anchor itself tore apart. They used the other to press over them for clothing, although the small irregular canvas did no more than shelter a patch of skin from the initial shock of a fresh wave.

Jones Henry, the oldest, weakened faster than the rest. His will ebbed more and more. After the third night, as Hank watched dully, Jones started to climb over the side. Wish I could do the same, Hank thought. But at the last moment, he wrapped his arms around Jones and held him in. It all happened in slow motion, without words.

Once, during the waves, he glanced out when the canopy had been torn loose by seawater to see a Japanese trawler nearby. It was drawing in its net, and seagulls swarmed around. They had no way to signal. The waves were too high to row. Their struggle to survive wave by wave was too great, impossible even to lift the canopy and stand. He prayed that the Japs would see the orange top of the canopy, but said nothing, to keep the others from getting excited. The next time he looked, they had passed the ship, which continued in the opposite direction.

Perhaps because of the constant seawater over their bodies, thirst remained a misery rather than the agony he might have expected. Cold was the agony. Only with a will could he even massage his feet, yet cold was all he could think of, whatever he forced his body to do. He tried to think of Jody, pictured her face for minutes at a time. But then his mind slipped back to the white cold.

During the fourth day, the wind slacked, and with it the terrible waves. It began to rain heavily, sending a trickle of water through the circular burn in the canopy. They bailed the raft and lay on top each other again for warmth. Hank dozed for the first time since the fire. He woke to the motion of the water, assuming he was aboard the *Adele*, and could not understand what was weighting his legs and arms. The sleep had lasted only a few minutes. He lay with his chin pressed into the fabric of the raft floor beside Seth and Jones, with Ivan and Steve on top, trying to resume the sleep, but it would not return. He hoped, at least, that it was long before his turn to change positions.

They saw distant, dark shapes of other foreign fishing ships for an hour or two. Then they were alone again in the empty water. The fourth night was approaching. Jones had not spoken for nearly a day. His eyes remained half closed and his mouth dropped open. Jones was going to go first. Seth would be next, Hank figured without emotion. Seth had become totally passive, acting only to shift his body if someone else pointed or shoved. Should they ease them overboard when the time came? More space to stretch. Take Seth's boots first. Or would dead bodies retain some warmth to crawl under? After Jones and Seth died . . . he screwed his face, but the thought came regardless . . . blood was liquid, flesh was survival. He bit into his knuckles to keep from crying out. No one paid attention. Soon his thoughts slipped back to the cold. Hank removed Jones' shoes, wrung his socks, and massaged his feet, but Jones did not appear to notice. He did the same for Seth, using all his energy to remove the boots and all his will not to put them on his own feet.

Steve and Ivan stayed together. During the shuffle of bodies, the only energy either showed was if one of the others pushed between them.

They would survive longest, Hank decided. Their faces were haggard but peaceful.

That made him third in line to go. He both saw it as a fact and did not believe it. By now their absence must have been noted. An hour before nightfall a Coast Guard helicopter passed nearby. They heard the chop of the blades. He, Steve and Ivan threw up the canopy and waved and shouted, then gasped from the effort. The helicopter disappeared, then returned on the other side of them. By the second pass, Seth and Jones watched with feverish attention.

"They fly a grid," Hank said, surprised at the difficulty of speaking. He had not noticed that his tongue was thick and that his lips cracked open when he moved them. "Looking for us."

The fourth night fell. They had no more flares or lights. At one point the helicopter flew directly over them. Ivan prayed aloud in a voice as cracked as his own. Hank mumbled "Our Father" to himself. But the helicopter passed farther and farther away, until its lights and noise disappeared for good and they were alone again.

Hank, Steve, and Ivan replaced the canopy. Seth and Jones had returned to their different catatonic states. Steve and Ivan accepted the top layer, and they huddled in for the night. Hank dozed and hallucinated again, but he did not sleep. He thought of death, of the warmth of death.

Ivan, on top of him, starting beating his back. "God heard, ha ha, God heard."

They had drifted to within a half mile of a ship without noticing, and the ship pivoted slowly toward them. Foreign trawler, that much Hank could see as it turned, showing the open stern ramp and the lighted deck with hard-hatted figures moving around a net.

"God led them to us."

God bless expensive Jap radar, Hank added reverently to himself.

The ship approached slowly, bearing all its blessed stenches of fish under steam. They untied one end of the canopy, leaving shelter for Jones from the rain, and stood in the other end of the raft waiting to be received. Steadily it came, the black hull defined in the dark by the glow of decklights behind. They could hear the splash of water from the bow. It bore down, cutting the water, towering above them.

"Fucker ain't stopping," cried Steve. He grabbed one of the aluminum oars to fight it off, like a harpooner against a whale.

Their frenzied voices filled their own ears without halting the freight-train motion. Hank's last sight upward was a wall so high he could not see the top. Goodbye, he thought. The wall brushed them aside. Steve thrust his oar into it and catapulted into the air. Hank in a second, without thinking, saw the ship's anchor pass over his head and leaped to catch it. It scraped over his arms and hands, and he fell into the water. Goodbye!

A wash of sea, the gunning shock and throb of the propeller and the turbulence, beyond his control, and he remained alive and sputtering with the deckful of men receding. By the light, he saw the overturned raft a few feet away with Ivan clinging to it. Die with Ivan at least, not alone. He found the energy to swim, to clutch the fabric.

"Steve, Steve!" cried Ivan in panic. He shook Hank with one hand. "Where's Steve?"

Steve's oar floated a distance away, glinting in the final light of the ship.

"Steve!"

"Jones! Seth! You around?"

"*Steve!*"

A fist thumped weakly from inside the overturned raft. "Who's down there," Hank shouted. He repeated it before Seth's voice said faintly, "Us. Did they stop?"

"*STEVE!*"

"Is Jones okay? Come out. We've got to right the raft."

"Did they stop? If they didn't . . . forget it."

"Yes, they stopped," yelled Hank with the energy of survival. "Get out here and help." He ducked under, caught his breath in the air pocket, found Jones, who was struggling, and pulled him out.

"*STEVE! STEVE! STEVE!*"

Hank pounded his fist into Ivan's face to stop him, then commanded him in Steve's name to help right the raft. Without Ivan's strength they could not have done it.

When it was over, the four lay exhausted in the upturned raft, covered by water. Hank found one of the little plastic cans, perforated for bait so that it barely transported water, and found strength to bail three or four canfuls at a time between rests.

Ivan leaped overboard and swam in the direction of the oar. Goodbye, thought Hank. Doesn't matter. But every few seconds, when he thought of it, he called in the raining dark, "Here, we're here."

Ivan returned. Hank helped him aboard. Ivan sat motionless throughout the rest of the night, clutching the oar he had retrieved.

Slowly Hank bailed the water down. He was alone. He felt quiet, unafraid. "Jody, I love you," he murmured occasionally. Goodbye. Warm and easy. Yet he kept bailing. There was a rustle beside him. Jones had found the other can, and was dipping water so slowly that most of it escaped through the holes before it passed over the side.

"Hello, Jones," Hank murmured.

"Hello, Hank."

Seth stirred on the other side of him and started scooping water with his hands.

When Hank slept for a while, he dreamed of juicy oranges.

The wind had returned by morning. No way to tell which direction. Nothing on the horizon. Ivan responded slowly to Hank's command. Together they battened the canopy and prepared to endure the waves again. Jones had returned to a degree of function and helped where he could, but Hank felt that he could slip away again at any time. He no longer tolerated Seth's passivity. He commanded him to lend his boots around, first to Jones, and he commanded him to blow up the floor of the raft, then to keep lookout through one end of the canopy.

The terrible waves built again. The troughs engulfed them in silence, the wind tore at the canopy as they rose, and the breaking crests foamed across their bodies.

"Let me die," begged Seth when Hank goaded him to shift his weight with the others and to bail.

"We all die together. *Move.*"

Jones motioned Hank and whispered in his ear, "I ain't doing no good. Help me over the side. Make sure Adele gets the boat insurance."

"Shut up. We stay together."

The waves beat them into stupefaction. Each time the sea crashed over top, Hank hoped it would tear off the canopy and end it. His feet no longer had feeling, even when he massaged them, and his fingers felt dead as cotton tubes. If he survived he'd be as helpless as Nels Hanson. So would they all. Why didn't he let them die if they were to survive like Nels?

Once he fainted, and woke to the small warmth of Ivan rubbing his arms and legs. None had killed themselves in his absence.

Ivan remained physically the strongest. Hank had become too weak to move except in a crisis. When they had a few hours' respite from the waves, Ivan covered the three of them with his body as best he could.

The fifth night was approaching. The wind had built to what felt like fifty knots, blowing streaks of white across the crests, and the temperature had dropped so that ice crackled on the canopy. The horizon kicked with mountains of water. They had seen no vessels since the night before when Steve was lost. Jones' eyes remained closed most of the time, and Seth barely responded. Hank felt his own spark freezing finally, whatever his will. Only Ivan had the strength to bail with effect, and to fasten shut the canopy again and again. "Tell Jody . . ." he whispered to Ivan, but lacked the strength to finish whatever he had to say.

"*Down there, is anybody alive?*" came an amplified voice from the sky.

It was a Coast Guard helicopter.

They lifted half the canopy—Ivan helped by Hank and Seth. The helicopter lowered a basket. The downblow of its rotors leveled the sea slightly, but the wind kept pushing the helicopter like a chess piece. The basket first banged in the sea, then nearly capsized the raft. At a stable moment in the trough, Ivan lifted Jones into the basket and Hank waved wildly for them to lift. The sea crashed over the basket and swept it away from the raft as it swayed up in the air. The canopy, half open, finally tore loose. They held to each other and the sides of the raft.

Up went the basket and disappeared into the hatch of the helicopter, then wobbled down again. The wind blew it into the water. The helicopter maneuvered it toward them.

"Seth next, get ready," said Hank.

They helped shove him in, with water boiling around. Ice coated the basket. It rose, fell with a sudden dip of the helicopter, then rose with Seth clutching the sides in wide-eyed terror.

Without the canopy the water crashed over them like an orgy of whips. There was barely light left in the sky, and in a trough black walls surrounded them.

The basket came again. Hank looked desperately at the lifeline and at the leadlike water, but said, "You, Ivan."

Ivan hugged him, and threw him into the basket.

The ride up was a wild bounce of water, wind, and ice. Hands pulled him free, then banged the basket free of ice and shoved it out again. The motion of the helicopter was nearly as turbulent as the raft, but at last, now, heat surrounded him.

"Jesus, he jumped!" exclaimed one of the crewmen.

Hank cried out and looked down through the opening. The orange raft below was empty. He thought he saw Ivan's shaggy head, but the water was a cataclysm of black shapes and forms. He lay his face against the deck, sobbed, and fell asleep.

EPILOGUE

People discussed the rescue for months. By the time the Coast Guard had found the raft, it had drifted from Kodiak 180 miles into the Pacific Ocean. The search before this had continued for three days, ever since a Japanese trawler spotted the burnt-out *Adele III* forty miles out, overturned, but still floating. The judgment of panic may be faulty, but no judgment concerning vessels at sea is absolute. If the *Adele*'s crew had stayed with their boat, the fire would have been a mere incident in their lives. Then again, in the middle of the night, the crippled boat might have sunk before they could cut the line, taking them with it.

As for the problems of finding a seven-foot raft in several thousand miles of storming open sea: perhaps the sincerity of Ivan's prayers conveyed his words to their destination after all. The Coast Guard ship and aircraft crews had put in the kind of hours usually credited to halibut and crab fishermen. The pilot who sighted the dull chip of orange that held four men—it disappeared into a trough just as his eye caught it and did not show again for a quarter of a minute—was living on coffee, having not slept for a day and a half of searching. When the helicopter found the raft, with darkness close, there was nothing to do but radio position, then risk everything on an immediate rescue without waiting for ship's support. Flying low in such winds the helicopter might have joined the raft, so that the Coast Guard flight crew, all with families on the base, were staking their own lives as well as those of the *Adele*'s men on the outcome.

As they recovered, Hank, Jones, and Seth shared a hospital room.

They endured together the agony of thawing from frostbite; later they slept, gazed at each other, sometimes spoke, though seldom of the experience they had shared. The doctor said that without the foot massages it would have been worse, that Jones especially might have required amputation. Their situation differed from the one that had crippled Nels Hanson the year before. Nels' hands and legs had been immersed directly in the cold seawater, without the fragile warmth of other bodies and of the canopied life raft as buffers.

Although Seth, the youngest, recovered most quickly, the weakness he had shown haunted him. Hank and Jones never mentioned it. They barely remembered or cared, but Seth asked for a bed in another room. Hank roused himself enough to forbid it. Seth left the hospital first and disappeared from Kodiak. He left only a note to thank Hank for saving his life.

Throughout the weeks of recovery, Hank and Jody stayed in the Henrys' guest room rather than at the rented place of their own. Since Jody worked, Adele could look after both men. If Seth had stayed, Hank would have insisted on accommodating him under the same roof.

As he healed, Hank felt no desire to dress or leave bed. He lay gazing through the window. Each dusk as black shadows engulfed the houses, mountains, boats, a malaise crept over him despite Jody's presence. If he slept, he woke hallucinating that he was back aboard the raft, always at the point where the canopy ripped with "blah-blah-blah" and the frigid seawater clawed across his body. Jody, in the night, soothed his groans without questioning.

During the day, Adele bustled in almost hourly with some new concoction, but he usually pretended to be asleep. All the food he really desired was oranges. He wanted a long train to his thoughts, needed time to worry about Seth, to ponder his own panic and irrationality, to weep for Steve and Ivan.

Could he return to the boats? Never without fear. What then? Cannery? Business back east? He no longer felt pushed. He was tired. Except during the nightmares, the calm that had settled on him when he knew he was to die remained. To be alive was enough. He found himself chuckling without cause. Only once did he show any vigor, when a reporter from Anchorage tried to cross-examine him and asked: "Now, how did you feel when you saw your buddy Steve—" Hank shouted him off, and no amount of persuasion roused him from a steady stare through the window until the man had left. Yet he felt great love for the people of the world. Having been placed apart had drawn him back. He wanted to see all those he cared for, to smile at them and listen to their voices. His parents flew in from Baltimore. Swede Scorden came several times, with wry jokes about life under a Japanese boss. Joe Eberhardt and Tolly Smith stopped over in Kodiak on their way from Seattle to Dutch Harbor. They joked with the heavy knowledge that the experience might have been theirs. Many others in town visited. He received them all, pleased. But after a few minutes of searching their faces his eyes focused beyond, at the mountains, and their conversations slipped away. He spent hours with Jody, merely holding her hand. His mind, most of the time, rode a train that had yet to reach its destination.

From his window he watched the signs of Kodiak springtime. The snow melted, leaving only brown on the slopes. In cruised the sturdy wooden halibut schooners with their first loads of the season. Boat by boat, the tanner-crab fleet laid up, many to convert to seine gear for the forthcoming salmon. He watched men he knew leap between the decks and piers as they boom-hoisted their pots to the backs of pickup trucks. Why did they use so much of their energy over a pile of steel cages? he wondered with detachment.

As the days grew longer, he forgot gradually to fear the approach of night. One day he watched some friends scrambling over the crabpots and envied them slightly.

The small seiners whose doors had been padlocked since the last of the September silvers now had busy men aboard again. Among the boats was the dear old *Rondelay*, directly within his view. That had been the best fishing time of them all, the time Steve threw him overboard for whistling, that Ivan had finally allowed him in the skiff, that they had corked the *Olaf* and fought it out, had toughed it together during the great dog-salmon bonanza. If ever he had the money . . . Seiner crewmen in grease-caked coveralls walked purposefully from boats to shops with machine parts on their shoulders, and others mended cork and web along the wharves. When the sun shone, he watched them climb among the masts as they scraped and painted. In the bars, he knew, the cozy winter pace would have changed as men hurried in for a quick one.

Their talk would now be stacatto exchanges on engines and gear rather than long anecdotes of seasons past. It would be alive down there.

Jody was gazing from the window also. She had come in as always in her free time to sit with him, sometimes hours without speaking, since she sensed his pace and adjusted to it. He watched her profile, the strands of auburn hair that caught the light, the face in repose that was capable of such animation. Her recent weeks must have been dreary.

"Hey," he said quietly. She turned. "Want to drive down by the boats? Maybe it's time I tried these feet."

Her eyes came alive. "Sounds good." At her look he felt a stir of energy. The wool shirt she brought from the closet, one he had worn a hundred times, seemed like an artifact from a distant world as he touched it and studied the red checks. She did not push, except that once he sighed at the effort and lay back again. "Uh-uh," she said firmly.

At last he had to do it. When he put weight on his feet, the pain made him gasp. Her grip tightened around his waist. He stood still, not wanting to make it worse, then forced himself to take steps. The difference in their heights made it easy for him to lean on her shoulder. "Long as you keep me propped," he muttered when the pain settled enough to let him speak, "I can get a job pulling nets."

"Yeah, but don't spill fish down my neck, buster, or you'll get a knock in the gut."

"I'd better use that cane and spare myself the backtalk."

Adele exclaimed and exclaimed as he hobbled into the living room, forcing himself to stand straight. Jones glanced up with disinterest. Though he dressed every day, in clothes that now sagged on every part of him, and moved a single round trip on crutches from the bedroom to the overstuffed chair by the television, he had lost all vitality.

"I'm taking Jody to lunch by the harbor. Come on, bring Adele."

Jones shook his head. "Have to go up steps."

From the window of the pickup Hank watched the boats hungrily and breathed their odors, as Jody drove onto each of the cannery piers. Friends dropped their work and climbed from decks to cluster around. When Swede saw them through the high window of his office, he appeared with flask and cigars.

"Not turned slanty-eyed yet," Hank observed.

Two of the cannery workers were gawking. Swede fixed his cold eye on them and quickly they returned to work. "Had it out with the head Jap. They might have control, but finally they were smart enough to go home to their rice and fishheads and leave me in charge. Jody, now that you've got his lazy butt in motion again, call Mary for a time you can come to dinner."

On the way back to the center of town, Jody parked so that he could enjoy the panorama of boats. Instead, he drew her over, and they necked, oblivious of people passing on either side.

"Good to have the old man back on his feet again," she murmured.

"Be a long road yet, Jody."

"That's what you think. I'd been debating for a week whether it was time to kick you out of bed. Don't think you're going back except to sleep."

"Jody, maybe I shouldn't fish again." Her hand picked at a button of his shirt. "It's tough on you, and maybe I . . ."

"Yes it's tough, but the rest of what you're saying is bullshit, dear."

Lunch in the big dark room beside the bar at Solly's became a roaring affair, the table spilling with free drinks, and friends gathered like bees to honey. Hank, though stimulated, tired quickly, and Jody, her wits and tongue gaily sharp, carried much of the conversation. He sat back, listening to the talk of boats and gear, involved in it one moment and detached the next. He watched their ruddy, scarred, bearded faces and their big water-puffed hands, and he felt the rhythms of their self-confidence. What other society in the world would he ever have chosen to join, once he had seen this one? Jody was part of it. He sought her hand under the table and she squeezed his in return.

Back at the house, next day, he rose whistling and kept to himself the initial pain of weight on his feet. In the living room, he stopped beside Jones' chair. Jones shook his head.

"Hey!" roared Hank suddenly. "The seiners are gearing, and the bars are hopping with guys from the boats. We'd better hear what they have to say. So get off your ass."

Adele leaned over the back of the chair and placed her hands protectively on Jones' shoulders. "Oh, no, Hank dear, Daddy couldn't . . ." She winked anxiously at Hank and Jody. "After all, Daddy's nearly fifty-five, and you're not yet thirty, he needs time to . . ."

Jones reached for his crutches and struggled from his chair.

Hank's recovery, once he had decided on it, came fast. His feet soon consented to bear his weight again unaided, although it took a year for the numbness to leave, and his first morning steps were routinely painful thereafter. But as he knew, what physically active man ever escapes all reckoning? Jones required longer and always afterward walked tenderly. He became fond of declaring: "What a fisherman needs is his arms, so long as his legs hold him in some kind of way."

Insurance replaced the burnt-out *Adele III*. The partners ordered a new ninety-foot crabber-trawler that Hank would skipper. Meanwhile, the new fifty-eight-foot seiner Jones had ordered for himself arrived in time for the salmon season. "We'll fish slow," said Hank when Jones expressed doubts. "Install a skipper's chair on the bridge, and you just sit while you concentrate on the jumpers. I've always wanted to be skiff man."

"That was poor Ivan's job. Won't be the same without Steve and Ivan."

"Never will be. But the two of us didn't survive to sit for the rest of our days."

"I only survived because you made me. I'd be crippled, or dead."

"Then you owe me something, don't you? Let's fish. Our big problem is to find a couple of young apes to pull web."

Often he worried about Seth. Then, during the heat of their preparations, Seth phoned from Kansas City to ask if he and Jones were okay.

"What are you doing, don't hang up, what's your address, what's a fisherman doing in Kansas?"

"I'm no fisherman. There's supermarket jobs everywhere."

"Get up here where you belong. We need a good man."

"You'd take me back?"

"You're fuckin' A!" shouted Hank joyfully. "Need airfare?"

Seth returned deeply quiet. He worked so hard that Hank had to slow him down. His presence doomed the other two crewmen to the status of outsiders. They were both kids fresh to the Kodiak docks. Seth, as senior deck man, broke them in with grave forbearance. Jones and Hank gleefully rode them at every opportunity, teaching them with the roughness of bears to cubs and growing back to health on the experience.

When Seth finally relaxed and ventured to joke again, they all became a crack team.

After that? Much of it is another story, or a continuing one.

Jones remained with the salmon. After the final run of silvers, as October gales moved in, he turned the *Adele IV* over to a relief skipper and took Adele south, where the warmth helped his circulation. He went partners in a welding and machine shop for the tuna boats out of San Pedro. After one good season he actually took Adele to Europe for a month. Each spring found him back in Kodiak to bring out the corks and web.

Neither Hank nor Jody wanted to separate. When the new crabber-trawler that bore her name was ready, she rode it with him from Seattle, then stayed aboard to cook and stand watches throughout the winter shrimp and crab seasons. Hank was soon too lost in the challenges of his boat to brood over the open waters to which he was returning. And Seth, who followed as his lieutenant, had so determined himself against weakness that he appeared to welcome the frigid waves that had nearly destroyed him a half year before. They all fished hard.

Hank brought his same zest for fishing to bear on work to assure adequate provisions for Alaskan fishermen in the 200-Mile Fishery Management Bill that was cooking in Washington. In the spring after the life-raft event he traveled with Jody to the capital to testify before the House Merchant Marine Committee. He became a goad to congressmen through letters and phone calls, working as part of the local fishermen's association.

And then? Jody never left the boats altogether. But she was already pregnant when they went to Washington, and after delivering Hank a son, she bore him a daughter in the year following. Hank delighted in them both. For the short run, Hank's mother flew in to help on both occasions, and of course so did Adele. In the longer run, Jody's loss of independence was not as devastating as she had feared. But it was bad enough that Hank sometimes dragged in from days of hard fishing to find an angry wife who yelled that she'd had it with baby shit and baby jabber. He grew wise enough to take over so that she could storm from the house and then could return to find the dishes washed, the diapers changed, and the kids either nestled on his lap listening to a book (whether they understood it or not) or tucked away. Except during

Adele's winter periods in the south, she cared for the children more en-
thusiastically than probably she had her own. For the initial summers,
Jody gladly left with her the first child, then both, and shipped with
Hank for trips. But she began to return from a week or more at sea to
find Henny, the oldest, a squalling stranger when she received him back.
Worse, to find Adele full of instructions as to what was best for them.
And what if something happened to both parents together at sea? Fi-
nally she announced to Hank: "I belong ashore for a while."

"I'll miss you," he said sincerely.

"You know where the door is." The would-be highliner began to
find reasons to return to port that he once would have mocked.

Jody on the beach became increasingly a part of the community.
Kodiak was, after all, a small town. Previously, she and Hank had run a
narrower track—the bars and eateries, cannery row, the hospital, the
laundromat, the supermarket near the harbor—which was crowded as
much with bearded men stacking boat grub as with housewives—and
the waterfront supply and service shops. Now she found that there was
also a library, that schools had a purpose for more than refugee accom-
modation after a tidal wave, that there were car dealers and filling stations, lawyers, dentists, real estate agents, cops and firemen, gift stores,
churches, a movie house. She acted in an annual summer outdoor pag-
eant about the early Russian settlers. When some storekeepers proposed
an ordinance to tax the fishing boats, she led other fishermen's wives to
become a tough antagonist at city council meetings. Her speech about
where the storekeepers or the town itself would be without the fishing
boats was quoted for long after.

No bits of civilization on a strip of northern land between mountains and sea can ever dispel the howling wilderness close by, as the tidal
wave had proved, and as ninety-knot winds kicking waves over the breakwater reminded often. Every time Hank leaves for a fishing trip, his and
Jody's eyes hold each other's for a moment, both putting from mind that
something could always happen out there.

At Easter, Hank always remembers to light a candle for Steve in
the appropriate church, and at Russian Easter for Ivan. Or, if he's at
sea, Jody does it for him.

AFTERWORD

More than a dozen years have passed since last I pecked out "Hank Crawford," "Jody," "Jones Henry," and "Swede Scorden" on the typewriter. But these characters all seem to maintain a life of their own. They declared themselves often enough while I was writing. Occasionally I needed to pull rank, although usually I followed where they led.

Letters still arrive from strangers asking how to get a berth on a boat like Jones Henry's, letters that end with a variant of, "Say hi to my girlfriend Jody." Four Alaskan cannery managers, each with a nail-driving reputation, have confided that friends assume they were the model for Swede, although I'd met only two of them before writing the book.

Once I arrived aboard the seiner Desperado out of Chignik to be handed a crew mug with "Hank Crawford" taped across the middle. During the days that followed as we fished the big Chignik sockeyes, we'd hit a snag and my crewmates would demand: "OK, what would Hank do now?"

More than once a dogeared copy of *Highliners* has appeared spontaneously from a fishing wheelhouse. This has happened in Alaska, New England, Labrador, Chile, New Zealand, and Norway. And once (not on a boat) in Kathmandu.

Highliners covers the years between 1963 and 1974 in Kodiak and Dutch Harbor. Many of the fishing industries there have changed since then, as well as the lay of the communities themselves. And they're changing all the time.

Among the changes: Hank and his friends no longer need curse the foreign ships for sweeping aside their gear. In 1977, with the Fisheries

Conservation and Management Act, the United States assumed jurisdiction over fishing waters within 200 miles of its coasts. An American fleet now works the grounds cleared of Russian and Japanese trawlers, catching masses of the bottomfish—mainly pollock—once targeted by the foreigners and scorned by Alaskan fishermen. While boats still deliver in season holdsful of salmon, halibut, and crab to the Kodiak seafood plants and crab to Dutch Harbor, now plants that freeze and render bottomfish alone line the waterfronts of both communities. The deliveries come in none but American-owned hulls. The creation of these processing lines and fleets is a saga in itself.

Other changes come and go. The shrimp had disappeared around Kodiak by the early 1980s, perhaps from overfishing but not necessarily. Most of the surviving shrimpers geared to bottomfish—among which are cod, a species deemed rare off Kodiak during the mid-1970s, which have now become abundant possibly in part by feeding on shrimp. King crabs also fell off disasterously in the early 1980s, and a fishery for smaller crabs using the same kind of heavy gear in the same brutal waters has taken up some of the slack. Crab boats now use their pots to catch cod as well. The salmon continue to run strong, with the runs of some species in some years very good or very bad, as always. The halibut fishery has altered immeasurably: traditional schoonermen now share the grounds with any other line-pullers ready to hang tough during desperate free-for-all seasons that last hours rather than weeks.

I first visited both Kodiak and Dutch in 1952 as an ensign stationed aboard the Coast Guard Cutter Sweetbrier. In Kodiak I remember those unbelievably large king crabs on the wharf of a small fish plant, the twin-domed Russian Orthodox Church, and the basic boardfront boots-and-canned-milk stores characteristic of towns in remote harsh places. Our ship also stopped routinely at Dutch Harbor and adjacent Unalaska for fuel and water when we serviced remote Coast Guard stations on the Aleutian Islands. For a seafarer in from rough weather, Dutch was no great liberty port—rusting quonset huts left from World War II and a single, small dark bar (albeit the only one within hundreds of miles)—and, apart from the ship itself, there wasn't any place to bunk. The rain sometimes blew horizontal—it still does—and wind howled throughout the dark nights.

During the time of *Highliners*, I passed in and out of both Kodiak and Dutch again, but these times aboard fishing boats. The Kodiak water-

Afterword

front had been altered beyond recognition by the tsunami of 1964 that Hank and Jones Henry survived aboard the Rondelay. The only remaining landmark was the Russian Orthodox Church's friendly twin onion domes.

In Unalaska, man had made the changes rather than nature. Instead of dense, dark nights, the rainclouded sky now bounced back a daylight luminescence from crab plants running clockaround. The throbs of industry blocked out the wind's whine, but not its sting. There were accommodations for hundreds of workers, but all on the level of bunkhouses and chowhalls.

And it all continues to evolve as both communities expand under the fortunes of fishing. Kodiak has more houses, amenities, and civic events. In Dutch/Unalaska the present crop of visitors—many on business who never slough their suits and ties—now have a choice of accomodations complete with restaurants with tablecloths and pseudo rustic bars. The place is now an occasional port of call for tourist ships.

Thus the years of Hank's maturing may have become history, at least in the details of structures and institutions. Yet, if I've told in part of a time on Alaskan coasts that was, I've also told of times that are permanent. Wilderness still howls just beyond the last building in both Kodiak and Dutch, and storms still sweep the sea to capsize boats and drown the men aboard. Some of my own former crewmates have drowned.

Unchanged are the men and women, and the waters themselves. Alaskan seas have lost none of their primal kick and it still takes special grit to work them. This turf remains a cold, wet, dangerous place to earn a living—and, between breaths now and then, a place to feel alive like no other.

—Bill McCloskey
Baltimore 1995